Nate carried Morgan into the solarium…

…stopping abruptly when he stared through the glass structure. The backyard was a riot of flowers and beyond that Haven Creek, the meandering body of water that had given the town its name.

"This is nice," he drawled.

"It's my sanctuary."

He put her down to the daybed, then walked over to the wall. Nate recognized the glass. They could see out, but no one could see in. It was the perfect place to make love.

Turning, he saw Morgan staring back at him. He smiled. "You could run around here naked as a jaybird and no one would be able to see you," he said.

She returned his smile with a dimpled one of her own. "I wouldn't know, because I've never done it."

"Why not?"

"I'm not that uninhibited."

"You're an artist. I thought most artists were."

She folded her hands in her lap. "Not this one."

Striding across the room, Nate reached down and gently pulled her to her feet. "We're going to have to do something about that."

ACCLAIM FOR THE CAVANAUGH ISLAND NOVELS

Angels Landing

"4½ stars! It's always a pleasure to discover little-known facts about racial history in America. Even better, the slow build to the love affair between the leads is believable and satisfying, on all levels. Sit back and enjoy!"
—RT Book Reviews

"Appealing, mature protagonists, a colorful cast of islanders, and a rewarding romance that realistically unfolds add to this fascinating, gently paced story that gradually reveals its secrets as it draws readers back to idyllic Cavanaugh Island."
—Library Journal

"An excellent love story...Huge messages throughout this book made for a very loving and interesting summer read."
—Blogs.PublishersWeekly.com

"These are strong character-driven books that always contain interesting twists, and a strong sense of place."
—RomRevToday.com

"I was completely blown away by the time I finished reading this book...I could not stop reading...You will not be disappointed."
—NightOwlReviews.com

"Heartwarming...I thoroughly enjoyed [it] and recommend it to all romantics."
—**FreshFiction.com**

Sanctuary Cove

"4½ stars! With this introduction to the Cavanaugh Island series, Alers returns to the Lowcountry of South Carolina. Readers will enjoy the ambiance, the delicious-sounding food, and the richly described characters falling in love after tragedy. This is an excellent series starter."
—*RT Book Reviews*

"Soaked in an old-fashioned feel, Alers's hyperrealistic style...will appeal to readers looking for gentle, inexplicit romance."
—*Publishers Weekly*

"I truly and thoroughly enjoyed the book. I found it a wonderful, warm, intriguing romance and was happy to find a new author to read."
—**Jill Shalvis, *New York Times* bestselling author of *Simply Irresistible***

"Carolina Lowcountry comfort food, a community of people who care, and a wonderfully emotional love story. Who could ask for more? *Sanctuary Cove* is the kind of place you visit and never want to leave."
—**Hope Ramsay, bestselling author of *Welcome to Last Chance***

"The author writes in such a fluid way that it captures the reader's attention from the word go. The ending is surprising and satisfying...A sweet, charming romance, *Sanctuary Cove* is a quick read you will remember."

—FreshFiction.com

"*Sanctuary Cove* is a gripping, second-chance-at-love romance...real and truly inspiring...I highly recommend it!"

—NightOwlReviews.com

"The first Cavanaugh Island romance is a wonderful barrier island second chance at love. The support cast is superb, especially the teens and islanders...[Readers] will enjoy visiting the Lowcountry with Rochelle Alers as their guide."

—GenreGoRoundReviews.blogspot.com

"Reading about two tattered souls finding each other and moving on with their lives is romance at its finest."

—TheReadingReviewer.com

Haven Creek

Rochelle Alers

A Cavanaugh Island Novel

FOREVER

NEW YORK   BOSTON

Forever
Hachette Book Group
237 Park Avenue
New York, NY 10017

www.HachetteBookGroup.com

Printed in the United States of America

First Edition: May 2013
10 9 8 7 6 5 4 3 2 1

OPM

Forever is an imprint of Grand Central Publishing.
The Forever name and logo are trademarks of Hachette Book Group, Inc.

The Hachette Speakers Bureau provides a wide range of authors for speaking events. To find out more, go to www.hachettespeakersbureau.com or call (866) 376-6591.

The publisher is not responsible for websites (or their content) that are not owned by the publisher.

Remember not the events of the past, the things of long ago consider not.

—Isaiah 43:18

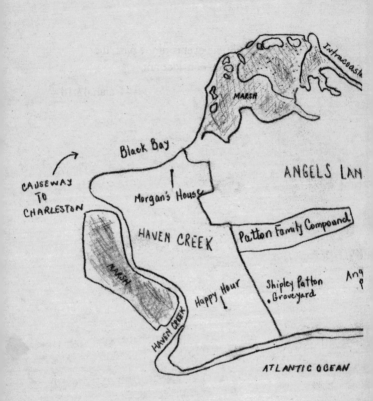

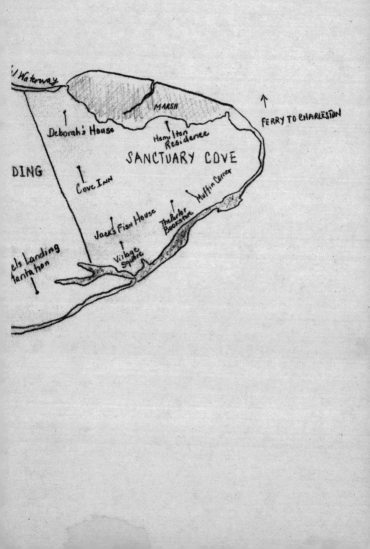

Haven Creek

Chapter One

~~~

"Didn't you tell me you were trying to get in touch with Nate Shaw?"

Morgan Dane stared at Francine Tanner, who looked as if she'd been running. She was breathing heavily, and blotches of red dotted her freckled cheeks. Morgan was one of only a few residents on Cavanaugh Island who didn't call Francine by her nickname, Red. She'd been born with bright, straight, orange-red hair. Over the years her tresses had darkened to auburn and softened into curls, but the nickname stuck. Today, Francine had ironed her hair flat, its blunt-cut strands brushing her lightly tanned, bared shoulders. Her floral-print sleeveless sundress, nipped at the waist, flared around her long legs. Morgan and the redhead had befriended each other in high school, when they found themselves in the same classes. Whenever they had an exam, they alternated between studying at Morgan's house, in the Creek, and

Francine's, in the Cove. Even after leaving the island to attend college, they'd managed to stay in touch.

"Yes, I did. Why?" Morgan asked.

"I just saw him."

"Where is he?"

Francine leaned closer. "He's sitting five rows behind you."

Morgan stood up. "Would you mind holding my seat? And don't let anyone sit in the chair with my hat. I'm holding it for David Sullivan."

Once Francine agreed, Morgan turned, scanning the crowd that had gathered under the large white tent for the man whom she'd called not once but twice, asking that he call her back. She spotted him sitting next to his younger brother. Taking determined steps, she approached Nathaniel Shaw, watching his impassive expression as she closed the distance between them. Twenty years had passed since Morgan had last come face-to-face with Nate, but time had been exceptionally kind to him.

His shoulders were broader, muscled, and there was a liberal sprinkling of premature gray in his cropped black hair. Nate wore the customary Cavanaugh Island wedding attire: slacks, shirt open at the collar, and lightweight jacket.

He rose to his feet when she stood less than a foot away. He was taller than she'd remembered, too. She extended her hand. "I don't know if you remember me, but—"

He took her hand, holding it for several seconds. "Of course I remember you, Mo."

Morgan wanted to scream at him. If he remembered her, then why hadn't he returned her calls? "Is it possible for you to put aside some time for us to talk about a project I'm involved with?" She lowered her voice, then took several steps away from the crowd. He followed her so they wouldn't be overheard by those staring at them.

"What type of project?"

"If you'd returned my calls, then you'd know." The retort came out sharper than she'd wanted, and she watched his eyebrows lift a fraction. Morgan had been a month shy of her fourteenth birthday when Nate left Haven Creek to attend college on the West Coast. No one, not even Francine, knew she'd had a crush on the tall, good-looking honor student. At the end of each school year she'd expected him to return to the Creek, but to her disappointment he'd opted to live in California. She'd heard that his father wanted him to come back after he'd graduated to help with the family's furniture-making business, and Nate's decision not to return had caused a rift between father and son lasting almost two decades.

"Did you leave a message?" he asked.

She stared up into clear brown eyes, wondering what was going on behind them. "Yes. I left a message on your voice mail at the shop. In fact, I left two messages."

A slight smile lifted the corners of Nate's mouth. "I'm sorry, but I didn't get the messages. Either my father erased them or there's something wrong with the phone. When do you want to talk?"

"Anytime that's convenient for you, Nate."

"Are you going to the reception?"

She smiled, exhibiting a matched set of dimples in her cheeks. "Yes."

"We can meet there and talk."

"Are you familiar with the layout of Angels Landing?"

He returned her smile with a mysterious one of his own. "I've been there a few times."

"If that's the case, then meet me at the duck pond at three. Are you wearing a watch?"

"No watch, but I have this." Reaching into the breast pocket of his jacket, Nate palmed a cell phone. "I'll program you in on my cell for three."

Morgan nodded. "Thank you, Nate."

"You're welcome, Mo."

She walked back to where she'd left Francine. "Thanks."

Francine gave her a wide-eyed stare. "Well? Aren't you going to tell me what happened?"

"I'll tell you after I talk to him."

Resting her hands at her waist, Francine narrowed her emerald-green eyes. "Now I know you didn't just dis your favorite girl."

"I don't want to say anything, because I might jinx myself."

Francine leaned close enough for their shoulders to touch. "Remember I'm the one who has visions."

Morgan felt a chill wash over her body despite the warm temperatures. "Stop it, Francine. You know talk about spirits scares me."

"One of these days I'm going to tell you your future." She hugged Morgan. "Let me hurry and get back before my mama sends out a hunting party. After all, we were contracted to do the hair and makeup for the wedding party."

Morgan watched Francine until she disappeared from her line of vision. Her friend's mother owned the Beauty Box, and it was Mrs. Tanner who'd suggested that Morgan cut off her braids in favor of a short, natural style. She'd worn the braids for more than three years. Although both styles were low-maintenance, Morgan realized the shorter style was nearly maintenance-free. Her new look was in keeping with the other change going on in her life. She'd recently opened her own architecture and design company.

When the awning over the small shop, bearing the legend M. DANE ARCHITECTURE AND INTERIOR DESIGN, was unfurled, people began buzzing about why she'd resigned her position with Ellison and Murphy. One of the partners at the Haven Creek firm had referred to Morgan as a young upstart. When her interview with the editor of the *Sanctuary Chronicle* revealed that she'd been commissioned by Kara Newell to oversee the restoration of Angels Landing Plantation, a property that had been designated a National Historic Landmark, a few of her former coworkers had called her disloyal, a traitor, and much too inexperienced to take on any restoration project, whether large or small. Their words had hurt her beyond belief.

At thirty-two, Morgan felt as if her life were perfect, as perfect as the day's weather was for a Lowcountry beachfront wedding: brilliant sunshine, fluffy white clouds, and a cool breeze blowing off the Atlantic. It also appeared as if all of Cavanaugh Island had turned out to witness the marriage of their sheriff to a young woman with ties to the island's most prominent family. As she looked around, she noticed there were very few empty chairs set up under the enormous white tent.

Morgan wasn't the only one who'd decided to arrive early to get a seat close enough to see and hear the cer-

emony. Most of the island's permanent residents did not
want to believe Taylor Patton had fathered a child, but
that conclusion was inevitable once it became known that
he'd left his entire estate to Kara Newell, his daughter.
The gossip escalated once Kara had managed to snag
Sheriff Jeffrey Hamilton, who happened to be one of Cavanaugh Island's most eligible bachelors. Morgan knew
some folks had come to the wedding because of curiosity,
but most were there to celebrate the joining of two families whose roots were intertwined with the history of the
island.

"I figured none of dem Pattons would show up, but
they be here in droves."

She smiled when she recognized the voice of her parents' neighbor sitting behind her. Hester Owens was an
incurable gossip, known to repeat things she'd overheard
while managing to put a spin on the news, making it her
own.

Hester's sister, also sitting behind Morgan, spoke up.
"Well, Heste , they cain't stay mad at that young gal.
After all, sh 's one of dem. She so much like Teddy that
it's downri scary, and that's why I don't know why
Harlan fix nout to claim she ain't one of dem."

Morga iked eavesdropping on the older folks, not so
much to listen to their conversations as to listen to their
occasional lapses into the language spoken for centuries
by Sea Island Gullahs.

Gertie, Hester's sister, continued, "She may look like
Teddy, but folks say she ain't mean like her grandmomma."

"You right 'bout dat," Hester agreed.

Morgan wanted to turn around and agree with Hester's

sister, too. Her grandfather had taken photographs of Theodora Patton, and the resemblance between Kara and her paternal grandmother was uncanny.

A shadow fell over Morgan, and she glanced up to find David Sullivan. She smiled at the impeccably dressed attorney. He fit aptly into the category of tall, dark, and handsome, and there was no doubt that he and Jeff were related. Both had the same warm brown eyes and cleft chin. "You made it."

David sat, leaned over, and pressed a light kiss on her cheek. "Finally. There was a fender bender on the causeway." He turned around when someone tapped his shoulder, then smiled and nodded at the elderly woman. "How are you, Miss Hester?"

Hester squinted behind the lenses of her rimless glasses. "How come you not in the wedding? After all, you and Corrine's grandbaby boy are cousins." Corrine Hamilton was the groom's grandmother and David's great-aunt.

Morgan shook her head when David mumbled something about Jeff wanting a military-themed wedding, and even though she wasn't a gambler she was willing to bet that, before the sun set that evening, there would be talk that she and David were seeing each other.

Once the Newell-Hamilton nuptials were announced, David had called to ask her if she was attending the wedding with a date. She hadn't hesitated when she said no, quickly informing him that she would meet him there. David had asked her out before, but Morgan had no intention of becoming a substitute for the woman who'd ended a long-term relationship with him because he hadn't been able to commit. It wasn't that Morgan didn't find the attorney attractive, because he was; however, she wasn't about to become David's Miss Right Now.

"You cut your hair," he said in her ear. "I like it."

She flashed a gentle smile. "Thank you."

Settling back, David crossed one leg over the opposite knee. "I asked you a question last week, and you said you'd wait until you saw me to give me an answer."

Morgan gave him a sidelong glance. Many women her age were looking for a single, attractive, intelligent, and professional man to go out with, and here she was ready to turn him down. "I can't go out with you, David, and you know it. We're friends. Besides, I know you still love Petra; you've even called me by her name a couple of times."

David met her eyes. "I guess it's going to take time for me to get over her."

She patted his hand. "Five years is a long time to see someone exclusively, so I understand what you're going through."

Reversing their hands, he squeezed her fingers. "You're a good friend, Morgan. If you need anything, I want you to call me. And that includes legal advice."

Morgan nodded. She liked David, but not in a romantic way. "It looks as if everyone on the island is here," she said, shifting the topic of conversation away from them.

David glanced around the tent. "You're right. There's hardly an empty seat."

Two minutes later, prerecorded music flowed from the speakers attached to the poles in the tent, and those standing around talking to one another craned their necks looking for empty seats.

*   *   *

It'd been a little more than six months since Nathaniel returned to Haven Creek, but sitting under the tent brought back memories of his childhood, when he'd accompany his parents to Cavanaugh Island weddings. He didn't have to know who was getting married. It was just the excitement of seeing everyone dressed in their Sunday best for the beachfront ceremony and then going to the reception that would follow, where he'd eat until his belly felt as if it would explode. That was before his mother took sick, complaining of pains in her stomach. She grew thinner with each passing day, until she barely weighed eighty pounds when she finally passed away.

There had been an open invitation to everyone from Jeff and Kara for their wedding, but Kara had broken tradition when she invited the entire island to come to the reception, which was to be held at Angels Landing. Nate had come because of Jeff. After his shift ended, the sheriff would stop by and they would share a cold beer while reminiscing about the old days. No one was more surprised than Nate when Jeff announced he was getting married. Times had changed and Nate had changed. Twenty years was a long time to be away from his family, friends, and all that was familiar.

"Hey, Nate, where have you been hiding yourself? I was expecting you to come by the club."

Rising slightly, he gave one of the partners in the Happy Hour, a local nightclub, a rough embrace. "I've been busy putting up a barn." The building that Shaw Woodworking had occupied for decades was not only too small for Nate and his father, especially when they were working on large pieces, but also needed major repairs.

Jesse Grant landed a soft punch on Nate's shoulder.

"Tell your old man to give you time off for good behavior. Look, man, I'd love to stay and talk, but I have to give my cousin a message from her mother. Come by either Friday or Saturday. That's when we have live music."

"I'll think about it," Nate said, smiling.

"I'll be looking for you, bro," Jesse said over his shoulder as he made his way toward the front of the tent.

Nate had no intention of going to a club. Not even one as innocuous as the Happy Hour. The past four years of his life had been a merry-go-round of clubs, and he'd had his fill of ear-shattering music, flashing lights, and people with plastic smiles and surgically enhanced bodies who were either too high or too drunk to remember what they'd said or done the night before.

He retook his seat, watching Jesse as he said hello to Morgan. Nate's eyebrows lifted slightly. When he'd left the Creek to attend college, she had been a shy, long-legged, wide-eyed, awkward girl. Not only had she grown up, she'd also filled out. She laughed at something Jesse said, dimples winking in her flawless dark brown face.

Nate found himself transfixed with the fluidity of her hands when she gestured and the graceful lines of her body, outlined in the fitted tangerine sheath she was wearing. He couldn't imagine why she'd called him or what she wanted to talk to him about. However, he would find out in another three hours.

"Are you really going to the Happy Hour?" Bryce asked his brother.

Nate looked at Bryce, noticing a shimmer of excitement in his large hazel eyes. "No."

"Come on, Nate. You have to go at least once."

Resting an arm over the back of his brother's chair, he

shook his head. "If I've seen one club, I've seen them all. And even if I did go, I'm not taking you with me. You have a curfew, remember?"

Bryce sat up straight. "We could get there around eight and leave in time for me to get home by midnight."

Nate shook his head. "Sorry. I'm not biting."

His twenty-two-year-old brother couldn't seem to stay out of trouble. It'd begun when Bryce went to high school on the mainland. He dabbled in drugs, got arrested for drunk driving, and the year before was arrested for disorderly conduct. In lieu of jail, he was placed on probation for two years. Bryce was required to call the Department of Probation in Charleston every night from his home phone before midnight. He was prohibited from leaving the island, and was subject to unannounced home visits from his probation officer. Nate blamed himself for not being there for his brother when he needed him most, but now that he was back to stay he knew things would be different. Their father's hypertension had put him at high risk for a stroke, and he had asked Nate to look after Bryce.

Bryce folded his arms over his chest, stretched out his legs, and crossed his feet at the ankles. "Don't you know how to have fun? You get up before dawn and work on that damn barn all day and half the night. You're not Noah building an ark because the Lord told you that he's going to send a flood to destroy—" His words were choked off when Nate's fingers tightened around his hand.

"Watch your mouth, Bryce," Nate whispered hoarsely. "You've been giving Dad a rough time, but it stops now." He increased the pressure on his brother's hand. "Since I've been back I've turned a blind eye to your smart-ass mouth. The barn will be finished in a couple of weeks, and that's when *you'll* start getting up at dawn to work with me. No more sleeping late and sitting around all day watching television. And when you speak to your mother and father, it will be with respect or I'll call your probation officer and have him violate you." Nate released Bryce's hand. "What's it going to be, bro? Are you willing to work with me, or would you prefer the accommodations at the county jail?"

Bryce gritted his teeth. "Do I have a choice?"

"Sure you do. Some guys prefer three hots and a cot to an honest day's work. Now, are you going to pick door number one or door number two?"

A beat passed, then Bryce mumbled, "I'll work with you."

Smiling, he patted the younger man's cheek. "See, that was easy."

Nate didn't like playing the bully when he'd always been Bryce's hero. Three thousand miles and twenty years made maintaining the bond with his sister and brother difficult. He called, wrote, and never forgot their birthdays, or his niece's and nephew's, and yet, despite his efforts, he had still grown distant from them. His relationship with his father and stepmother took longer to resolve, and it was the first time since Lucas married Odessa that Nate felt they were truly a family unit. It had taken time, space, and maturity to realize he couldn't change the past. His father's affair with his wife's nurse as Nate's mother lay dying had haunted him for years. Rumors and gossip were as intrinsic to the people who lived on Cavanaugh Island as their Lowcountry cuisine. He'd believed it was simply talk until he saw his father and Odessa in bed together once his mother was admitted to a mainland hospice.

Fifteen-year-old Nate took Manda Shaw's death hard; he intensely resented the woman who, three months later, had taken her place when she married Lucas. He rejected her and her claim that she was now his stepmother.

After a lengthy stint in California, he'd returned to Haven Creek a week before Thanksgiving, channeling all his nervous energy into his work. Bryce was right when he said Nate spent all his waking hours building the barn. Not only was it therapeutic, but when it was completed it would provide a place for him to live without depending on the generosity of his sister and brother-in-law, who'd permitted him to stay in their guest room.

Nate was snapped out of his thoughts when the wedding planner and her staff began motioning for everyone to take their seats. Nate checked his cell phone. It was eleven fifty-five. The ceremony was slated for twelve noon, followed by a cocktail hour at one and a buffet dinner at two.

The chamber music changed to a processional, and everyone turned to watch as two marines in their dress blues escorted Kara's mother and Jeff's grandmother to their assigned seats. The best man wore his dress blue uniform, and Kara's maid of honor was resplendent in a cornflower-blue halter-style A-line gown. She walked with the best man down the white carpet to the place where Reverend Malcolm Crawford stood next to Jeff, who was also wearing dress blues. The music changed again, this time to the familiar strains of Mendelssohn's "Wedding March." The assembly stood, turned, and stared when Kara appeared on the arm of her father.

Nate's eyes met Morgan's when she turned in his direction. A smile played at the corners of her mouth before it grew wider, her dimples deepening until they were the size of thumbprints. Unconsciously, he returned her smile, then shifted his attention to what was touted as the wedding of the season.

Chapter Two

⌒◡⌒

As he was driving to the reception, Nate followed the signs pointing the way to valet parking. Within minutes of the exchange of vows and rings, he and Bryce had left the beachfront wedding ceremony to avoid a traffic jam. There were more posted signs, these to indicate the location of comfort stations.

When Morgan had asked Nate if he was familiar with the layout of the property that had given the town its name, he hadn't lied to her. Today the historic house was surrounded by yellow tape to keep out intruders and the curious. Nate was ten when he came to the rose-colored Greek Revival–style antebellum limestone mansion with his father for the very first time. It'd been Theodora Patton who'd asked Lucas Shaw to replace the worn rosewood-and-mahogany decorative inlaid border on the living and dining room parquet floors. At that age Nate had been awestruck by the sheer size and furnishings of the largest house on Cavanaugh Island. He'd stood there gawking until his father instructed him to sit and watch what he was about to do.

He spent that summer and the next eight as an apprentice to the man who had a reputation as the most skilled furniture maker in the Lowcountry. When he'd graduated high school it had been Nate's intention, like that of so many other young men on the island wishing to escape its mundane, small-town existence, to enlist in the military. However, he'd promised his mother that he would attend college, and her deathbed plea superseded his most fervent yearning. He'd been offered a full scholarship, and despite his father's adamant protests he left South Carolina for California.

Coming to a stop, he got out of the Sequoia, leaving his jacket on the second row of seats. Bryce did the same. The valet gave him a ticket, which Nate pocketed. Shielding his eyes with one hand, he gazed out at the expanse of landscaped property, his gaze taking in a carpet of green dotted with trees and well-tended shrubs. More vehicles were maneuvering into the parking area as he and Bryce walked along a stone path leading to a trio of tents.

They encountered a quartet of elderly men belonging to the local American Legion, each holding handfuls of bright red poppies and asking for donations to assist disabled and hospitalized veterans. "Good afternoon, son. Are you or have you been in the military?"

"No, sir, but I'll definitely give you a contribution for me and my brother." Reaching into his pocket, he gave the man a bill.

"Damn!" Bryce drawled as he looked around. "This reminds me of your wedding reception."

He looked at Bryce and shook his head. He knew it

hadn't been easy for the twenty-two-year-old to find himself alienated from his friends as well as cut off from Charleston's nightlife. It was the first time in nearly seven months that Bryce had been given permission from his probation officer to attend a social function.

"Everything does look nice," Nate said noncommittally.

He didn't want to agree with Bryce, because that would conjure up memories of his own wedding, which resembled an epic movie with a cast of thousands. Unfortunately, that day he hadn't been so much a participant as a spectator at an event destined for failure. His gaze shifted to an enormous red-, white-, and blue-striped tent about the size of a traveling circus's big top. Row upon row of tufted blue chairs were pushed up under round tables covered with alternating red and white tablecloths. It was Memorial Day weekend, and in keeping with the patriotic theme, vases of blue delphiniums and red and white sweet peas adorned the center of each table. There was a smaller tent from which wafted the most delicious aromas as the waitstaff circulated with trays of hors d'oeuvres and flutes of Champagne. A third tent was set up for the DJs, who played an upbeat tune that currently topped *Billboard*'s Radio Songs chart through speakers set up around the property. Couples were already gliding across the dance floor.

Bryce draped an arm over Nate's shoulder. "Is it okay if I have a drink?"

Shifting slightly, he met Bryce's eyes. There was no mistaking the fact that they were brothers. Both were tall and slender, and shared the same complexion, high cheekbones, and even features. The only exception was eye color. Bryce's were a sparkling hazel; Nate's a clear golden brown.

"Please try not to overdo it. Remember your actions have consequences."

Bryce patted Nate's back. "I told you I'm not going to jail." He headed for the bar while Nate picked up a flute of Champagne off the tray of a passing waiter.

Nate didn't want to quash Bryce's fun, but on the other hand he didn't want Bryce violating his parole, forcing him to serve out his sentence. A knowing smile tilted the corners of his mouth when he saw his brother reach into the pocket of his slacks for his driver's license. It was apparent that Jeff had instructed the bartenders to card those they suspected were under the legal drinking age.

He'd just put the flute to his mouth when he saw Morgan with David, and wondered whether she and the attorney were a couple. He was still stunned by her transformation, but then a lot of people and things on Cavanaugh Island had changed during his absence. Although both he and Morgan lived in Haven Creek, Nate had only occasionally caught glimpses of her when she and Francine went on their early morning bike rides. But once, when he saw her walking into a shop in the Creek's business district, he'd given her more than a cursory glance, thinking that she was an anomaly compared to the casually dressed young women who lived and/or worked on the island. Everything about her radiated big-city sophistication and reminded him of the fashionably dressed women who lived in some of the large cities he'd visited.

His gaze lingered on her long, shapely legs, rising up from a pair of strappy stilettos. Nate smiled. It was apparent that Morgan was very secure when it came to her height. The sexy heels put her close to the six-foot mark. He continued to stare at her while sipping the extra-dry Champagne.

"Would you like to try the crab cakes, sir?" Nate shifted his attention when a waiter handed him a cocktail napkin. He speared a miniature crab cake slider topped with a dollop of crème fraîche and chopped green onions, then placed it on the napkin. "I suggest you also try the spring rolls. They're incredible." The waiter handed Nate another napkin.

"Thank you." Nate took a bite of the miniature spring roll, savoring the variety of spices on his tongue. If the appetizers were an indication of what the caterers had prepared for the buffet, then Jeff and Kara's guests were in for a sumptuous feast.

The tents were quickly filling up, and Nate scanned the crowd for his family. He'd planned to attend the ceremony, offer his personal congratulations to the bride and groom, and then leave. But Morgan had piqued his interest when she said she wanted to talk to him about a project. The fact that she'd left him two voice mails indicated that whatever she wanted to discuss had to be important to her.

He lost track of time reuniting with friends and classmates he hadn't seen in years, most chiding him for becoming a recluse since his return. Even the excuse that he was busy helping his father at the shop sounded hollow to his own ears. Nate's number one priority had been making certain his brother stayed out of jail. His second priority had been monitoring his father's health.

The elder Shaw's hypertension had become a concern for his primary physician, and Dr. Asa Monroe had cautioned Lucas to drastically change his diet and shorten his work hours. When his father called to let Nate know that Bryce had been arrested and was facing jail time, he knew it was time to come back to Haven Creek. The decision to leave California had been an easy one. His marriage was over, leaving him the opportunity to return home and work the family business. Now that his father had cut back on his hours Nate found himself alone in the workshop several days a week, which he enjoyed. The hard work kept his mind off other things, such as his failed marriage.

A smile spread across his features when he saw a woman he'd dated briefly in high school. Their relationship never progressed beyond the platonic stage because she was a minister's daughter, and the last thing he'd wanted was to incur the wrath of her fire-and-brimstone-preaching father by sleeping with her. Extending his arms, Nate wasn't disappointed when she came into his embrace. Lowering his head, he dropped a kiss on her sandy-brown twists, which were pulled into a ponytail.

"Hey, beautiful," he crooned.

Chauncey Bramble angled her head up at him, smiling. "You always know what to say to make a woman feel good."

Taking her arm, Nate led her away from a group of older guests who were watching them like hawks. "Have I ever lied to you?"

Chauncey was voted prettiest girl in their graduating class and had been homecoming queen. He'd read that Chauncey had married her college sweetheart a month after he was drafted by the Atlanta Hawks. He and Chauncey were similar in that they both had married high-profile celebrities whose professional *and* personal lives became salacious fodder for television shows, magazines, and supermarket tabloids.

She stared over Nate's shoulder. "No," Chauncey said after a pregnant pause. Her eyes met his. "Where did I go wrong, Nate? I should've married you instead of Donnell."

What he wanted to tell the still-attractive woman with the sprinkling of freckles dotting her upturned nose and high cheekbones and the sparkling dark brown eyes set in a face the color of golden raisins was that she didn't have to stay with a man who constantly cheated on her and was now forced to pay child support to three different women.

"Even though we can't change our pasts, we shouldn't blame anyone but ourselves if we repeat past mistakes," he said in a quiet tone.

Chauncey affected a wry smile. "You're so right. And I repeat the same mistake more times than I can count whenever I forgive Donnell for his infidelity. When I heard about the first baby it hurt me to my heart. I was shocked with the second one, but I still forgave him. Once he told me about the third I was so numb that I wasn't able to react." Her expression changed, her features seemingly crumbling before his eyes. "I wish I could be more like you."

Lines of confusion appeared between Nate's eyes. "Be like me in what way?"

"I wish I had the strength to leave my husband the way you did when you found out your wife was having an affair."

He gave her a comforting smile. "Things have a way of working out for the best." Nate didn't want to appear insensitive; however, he didn't want to talk about his past. He spied the person he'd been looking for, giving him the out he needed. He kissed Chauncey again, this time on the cheek. "My father just arrived and I need to talk to him about something."

Chauncey rested a hand on Nate's shoulder. "My kids and I are spending the summer in the Creek, so maybe I'll see you around."

"I'm sure you will."

Chauncey had mentioned the strength it took for Nate to leave his wife, but for him it had nothing to do with strength. Although he'd had trust issues, his love for Kim outweighed them. He'd known their marriage was over when he found out that his wife was having an affair with her manager. When he'd confronted Kim she glibly admitted to having several affairs during their engagement *and* throughout their marriage.

Nate wended his way through the guests who were claiming seats under the big tent now that the cocktail hour was winding down. The first thing he noticed was that his father was alone. "Hey, Dad. Where's Odessa?" It was rare that anyone saw Lucas at a social event without his wife.

Lucas smiled at his elder son. "She'll be along once she decides what she wants to wear. As long as I live I'll never understand women. Why can't they make up their minds when it comes to clothes?"

Nate returned the smile. "I don't know, Dad. You've known them longer than I have," he countered, giving his father a long, penetrating stare. Lucas pulled a handkerchief from his jacket pocket, blotting the moisture dotting his forehead. At five ten, the sixty-three-year-old Vietnam veteran had been a powerfully built man with large hands and muscled forearms, but had lost more than thirty pounds since he'd been placed on a restricted diet. He'd had to buy an entirely new wardrobe to accommodate the weight loss.

Again, the resemblance between the Shaw men was remarkable. Nate knew what he would look like in twenty-five years whenever he stared at his father. Those who lived in the Creek said you could always tell a Shaw man because all of them looked alike. Lucas had grayed prematurely and several months ago had decided to shave his head, which had prompted him to wear hats to protect his scalp against the sun's harmful rays.

Taking off his brand-new Panama, Lucas wiped his head with a handkerchief. He'd pinned the commemorative poppy on his hatband. "How long you going to hang out here?" he asked.

"I'm not sure. Why?"

Lucas set the hat on his head at a jaunty angle. "I was wondering if you were going to drive Bryce home."

"I'll take him back, but first I have to meet Morgan at three."

Lucas pressed the heel of his hand to his forehead. "Now I know I must be getting old. I forgot to tell you that she called and left a couple of messages wanting you to call her."

Nate scanned the tent for Morgan, finding her surrounded by several men, as if she were holding court. The expression on her face spoke volumes. Either she was bored or bothered by all the attention. He also hadn't missed the obvious stares directed at her from a group of young women watching the exchange.

"Yeah, I know. She let me know about it."

Lucas followed his son's gaze. "What does she want?"

"I don't know."

"You know she left Ellison and Murphy to open her own business."

Nate nodded. He'd read about Morgan going into business and setting up M. Dane Architecture and Interior Design in Sanctuary Cove. "I saw the article in the *Chronicle* saying that she's been commissioned to oversee the restoration of Angels Landing."

"That's a big job for a little girl."

"Mo is hardly a little girl, Dad."

A beat passed. "You're right about that, son." He snorted audibly. "I can't stand it."

"Can't stand what, Dad?" Nate asked.

"Just look at those guys buzzing around her like flies on a carcass. Everyone knows they acted like she didn't exist until after she fixed up her grandpa's house and bought a new luxury truck. Her daddy told me she ain't studdin' none of dem," Lucas drawled, lapsing into dialect.

Nate never liked the gossip that was so insidious in small towns, but this was one time he welcomed it. There was something about Morgan that more than piqued his curiosity. Although he wasn't that much older than she was, he'd always thought of her as a little girl. She was a freshman in high school when he'd been a senior.

"Isn't she dating Jeff's cousin?"

Lucas grunted again. "If she is, then that's news to me. I'd heard David was devastated when that girl he'd been seeing for a while left him high and dry just when he was about to ask her to marry him."

"You win some and you lose some," Nate said cynically.

"What about you, Nate?"

"What about me, Dad?" He knew his father hated when he answered his question with another question.

"Have you thought about getting married again?"

An uncomfortable silence ensued. "No."

"You're only thirty-seven, and much too young to spend the rest of your life alone. Don't you want a family?"

"I have a family: you, Bryce, Sharon, and the kids."

"Aren't you lonely?"

Nate gave his father a direct stare. "Just because I'm alone doesn't mean that I'm lonely."

"That's horseshit and you know it."

If Nate was shocked at his father's comeback he refused to show it. One thing he didn't want to do was argue with him—and especially not with an audience present. In the past they'd had their dustups, but always behind closed doors. There had been a time when Nate believed the Shaws put the "dys" in dysfunction, but after leaving the Creek he'd discovered his family wasn't that unique when it came to problems and secrets better left unspoken.

"I don't want to talk about it," he said softly.

"Avoiding the issue isn't going to solve anything."

A frown settled into Nate's features. "Come on, Dad. Not today. I came here to celebrate Jeff's wedding and have a little fun."

"Speaking of fun, what you should do is hook up with Morgan. Not only is she pretty but she's real smart. I admire her because she could've graduated college and moved away like so many of our younger folks. But she stayed, put down roots, and opened her own design firm."

Nate chuckled softly. "Since when did you start match-making?"

Lucas managed to look embarrassed. "I'm not really matchmaking, son. It's just that if you do decide to start going out again you won't have to look very far for a good woman."

"Thanks, Dad. I'll be certain to keep that in mind." What his father didn't realize was that he wasn't interested in hooking up with any woman—at least not on a permanent basis, because when it came to relationships he was batting zero. "Can we table this discussion for another time?"

Lucas ran a hand over his face. "Okay. We'll talk about it tomorrow."

Nate laughed. "Dad, I have plans tomorrow."

"We're not going to see you for Sunday dinner?"

"No. I'm going to use the rest of the weekend to finish roofing the barn."

Lucas frowned. "That can wait, Nate."

"They're predicting rain next week, and you know I can't work outdoors in the rain. I promise I'll come over next Sunday."

With the shop closed for the holiday weekend, he would have another two days not to get into it with his dad about his current marital status. Nate knew his father wanted him to get involved with a woman, but that decision would have to be his own. He'd spent half his life making his own decisions. Whether he succeeded or failed, only *he* had to live with the outcome.

"Can I get you something to drink?" he asked Lucas.

"I can't have what I'd like to drink," the older man mumbled angrily.

Attractive lines fanned out around Nate's eyes when he smiled. He knew his father liked to occasionally take a shot of bourbon after dinner followed by a cigar, but had given up both because his doctor had cautioned him about the health risks. He rested a hand on Lucas's shoulder. "If you get your blood pressure under control, then maybe you'll be able to take a nip or two."

Lucas's expression brightened. "To tell you the truth, I really don't miss it all that much."

"That's—" Whatever Nate was going to say was preempted when the volume on the music was lowered and the DJ announced the arrival of Mr. and Mrs. Jeffrey Hamilton. The sound of thunderous applause followed the announcement as Jeff, Kara, and the bridal party entered the main tent. "Come, Dad, let's go and sit down."

Lucas craned his neck, looking around him. "Where's Bryce?"

"Don't worry. He's not going anywhere." Nate escorted his father to a table that was quickly filling up with Haven Creek residents. "Put your hat on the chair next to yours for Odessa."

"Where are you going to sit?" Lucas asked when he realized every seat at the table had been claimed.

He pointed to a nearby table. "I'll be over there."

Nate walked over to a table where a group of women wearing fancy hats were seated. They looked as if they were going to a royal wedding or the Kentucky Derby. He greeted those he knew by name and nodded to the others, giving them a friendly smile. With the exception of the sheriff's clerk, all of them were over seventy. Some were widowed and a few had never married.

"Ladies, do you mind if I join you?"

His query elicited blushing and fluttering eyelids. "Please do, Nate," crooned Winnie Powell. Jeff's clerk had to tilt her head to meet his eyes because the brim of her hat obscured most of her face.

He saw his sister, brother-in-law, and niece and nephew sitting with his brother-in-law's family two tables away from where he sat. There were a few empty chairs, but it was too late to change tables. Nate's impassive expression did not change when Odessa entered the tent, searched the crowd, and then walked over and sat down next to Lucas. Looking as if she'd just stepped off the pages of a slick fashion magazine, she waved a white-gloved hand to Nate when their gazes met, he nodding in acknowledgment. His relationship with Odessa hadn't been strained until she married his father, and, not wanting to exacerbate the situation, he felt that living with Sharon and her family would be less uncomfortable than living with Lucas—not only for him but for Lucas and Odessa as well.

Nate directed his attention to the woman sitting opposite him. She hadn't changed in thirty years. Her snow-white bobbed hair, bright blue eyes, and Cupid's bow lips were still the same. "Good afternoon, Mrs. Cunningham."

The elderly woman squinted at him over her half-glasses. "Aren't you Manda and Lucas's boy?"

He nodded. "Yes, ma'am."

"Weren't you in my class?"

"Yes, ma'am," Nate repeated. "I was in your fourth grade class the year Adrienne McIntosh represented South Carolina in the National Spelling—" He didn't get to finish his statement before a pair of scented arms looped around his neck at the same time a pair of soft lips grazed his cheek.

"Promise you'll save me a dance, Nate," a feminine voice whispered in his ear.

He recognized the sultry tone of the woman leaning in a little too close for propriety. As a teenager she'd earned the reputation as a flirt, and no doubt that hadn't changed. Pendulous breasts rested on his shoulder as the perfume wafting from her body smothered him like a heavy blanket.

"Sure, Trina," he said, even though he hadn't planned on dancing with anyone. If he hadn't have promised to meet Morgan he would've left right after the bride and groom personally greeted their guests. The women at the table glared at Trina as she walked away, her generous hips gyrating rhythmically in a too-tight dress that displayed her full, curvaceous body to its best advantage.

"What a brazen heifer," Winnie spat out under her breath.

"She's always been too loose for my tastes," said Donna Shelton, a retired school librarian.

"You watch out for her, Nathaniel," Mrs. Cunningham warned. "She's already had a couple of husbands, a bunch of babies, and she's been out trolling for husband number three."

He smiled. "Thanks for the warning."

Nate lowered his head, staring at the tablecloth. Nothing had changed. Whenever it was his mother's turn to host the quilting bee, he and Sharon would sit at the top of the staircase and eavesdrop on the grown folks' conversations. If Manda knew what her children were up to, she would've grounded them for the entire school year. Some of the talk he understood, but occasionally their discussions went directly over his head. Like when they'd whispered about a woman *fixin'* her husband after she caught him *tomcattin'*. He knew what *tomcatting* meant, but not what they meant by *fixing*.

Once he'd entered adolescence, gossip wasn't even a passing thought, because Nate found other things to hold his interest, especially cars and girls. Even though he wasn't permitted to date until he turned sixteen, that still hadn't stopped him from hanging out on the beach with his friends after he'd completed his chores. His life was simple and predictable. His parents' mandate was: go to school, pass the courses, and help out in the shop. He and Lucas had struck a deal. Nate would get up early during the summer months and work in the shop for six hours. After that, he was free to do whatever he wanted.

Everything was perfect until he turned fifteen. Manda had complained of chronic fatigue along with back pain. This was followed by rapid weight loss and days when she'd been too tired to get out of bed. When Lucas finally convinced her to see a doctor, the diagnosis was devastating and life altering for the entire family. Manda had pancreatic carcinoma, and the cancer had metastasized to other organs. The oncologist predicted she wouldn't survive a year.

Manda prepared her family for the inevitable, putting on a brave face for her son and daughter. But nothing could prepare Nate for losing his mother. Manda died, and the woman who'd been her nurse and childhood friend married Manda's widowed husband three months later. Gossip was rampant that Odessa couldn't wait for Manda's body to get cold before she worked her wiles on the grieving widower. And when Bryce was born, everyone began counting on their fingers. Odessa claimed he'd come two months early, but Bryce's birth weight indicated he was unquestionably full-term.

When it came time to attend college, Nate hadn't wanted to leave Haven Creek. It meant leaving Sharon, who was two years his junior, and Bryce. His younger brother had just turned three and followed him everywhere. Nate had nicknamed him Shadow. Despite his hesitancy, though, Nate left to attend college. He needed the three thousand miles and a totally different lifestyle to mentally distance himself from his father, stepmother, and Cavanaugh Island.

"Nathaniel?"

His former teacher called his name, shattering his musings. "Yes, Mrs. Cunningham?"

"Are you sweet on some young girl?"

Leaning back in his chair, Nate smothered a curse. He didn't want to believe she'd asked him something so personal—and in front of eight other women. "No, ma'am."

Winnie placed her hand on Nate's. "If that's the case, then I'd like to introduce you to my younger sister, who lives in D.C. Lately she's been going out with a bunch of losers. I keep warning her about online dating, but she claims she likes variety."

Mrs. Cunningham shook her head. "Now, why would Nathaniel want a woman who sleeps around?"

A deep flush suffused Winnie's face. "I didn't say she sleeps around, Miss Alison."

"Well, it sounds like she does, if she's dating that many men," Mrs. Cunningham retorted.

Nate pushed back his chair. "Excuse me, ladies, but I have to meet someone."

It was apparent he'd made a mistake by sitting at a table with so many women. It was also obvious they saw him as someone they could dangle in front of their single female relatives. Well, he wanted no part of their hookup schemes. He'd never had a problem attracting a woman, and if he was interested in one he had no qualms about asking her out. Reaching into the pocket of his slacks, he took out his cell phone. He had another forty minutes before he was scheduled to meet Morgan. Glancing around, he spied her with her parents.

Taking determined steps, he approached the trio. "Good afternoon, Dr. Dane, Miss Gussie."

"Good afternoon, Nate." The elder Danes, both dentists, greeted him in unison. Everyone had taken to calling Morgan's mother Miss Gussie to clarify which Dr. Dane they were referring to. It didn't seem to bother Gussie that her patients referred to her husband Stephen as Dr. Dane.

His eyes met Morgan's. "I know we're supposed to meet at three, but is it possible for us to meet sooner?"

"Sure." Morgan nodded to her parents. "Mama, Daddy, please excuse us."

Cupping her elbow, Nate led her out of the tent and into the brilliant sunlight. "I'm sorry to intrude on you and your folks—"

"Don't worry about it, Nate," Morgan said softly. "I'll see them tomorrow for Sunday dinner."

Nate stared at Morgan's small doll-like face under the upturned brim of her sunflower-yellow straw hat. It was no wonder men were drawn to her. Everything about her was stunning! He found her wide-set eyes, flawless dark brown complexion, delicate features, and dimpled smile mesmerizing.

"Is there a problem?" Morgan asked.

"Nothing monumental, except that I had to get away from the ladies at my table."

She gave him a sidelong glance, her lips parting, dimples winking at him. "Were they trying to hook you up with their granddaughters?"

Nate stopped in midstride, causing Morgan to lose her balance. Reacting quickly, his hands spanning her waist, he held her steady. "How did you know?"

Still cradled in his embrace, her smile grew wider. "Nate Shaw," she said in a soft voice. "Either you've been away too long or you don't get out enough."

Nate stared at Morgan's mouth. Even her teeth were perfect, but he figured they would be, given that her mother was an oral surgeon and her father was an orthodontist. And he knew when she'd called him by his first and last name that it was a slight reprimand.

"Perhaps it's both."

She sobered. "You were sitting with the ladies that make up the recently formed Cavanaugh Island Beautification Committee. Their raison d'être is beautifying the Cove and Creek business districts and also some of the less than attractive homes in the Landing. But the word is they're better suited to matchmaking. They began targeting any single person from twenty to forty after an op-ed piece appeared in the *Chronicle* about high school kids who leave home to go to college or into the military but opt not to come back here to live. Jeff was the exception when he came back after his grandmother's heart attack. So when you decided to sit with them it was like walking into a minefield."

"What about you, Mo? You're still here."

"And you came back," she countered in a soft tone.

He nodded. "That's because my family needed me." A beat passed. "Have they ever tried hooking you up with someone?"

Morgan took a step backward, and he dropped his arms. "Too many times to count," she admitted as they continued to walk.

"I suppose they'll stop now that you're with David." Her gentle laughter floated in the air. "What's so funny?" Nate asked.

"What's funny is there's nothing going on between David and me. We're just friends."

He had his answer. Morgan and David weren't seeing each other, which made her fair game for the ladies who apparently were using their beautification activities as a smoke screen for a matchmaking or dating service. Nate didn't understand why it'd been so important to know her relationship status, because if he were to have a relationship with Morgan—or any woman, for that matter—he feared it would be short-lived.

He thought about what Morgan said about leaving the island. He'd been one of those who'd left to attend college, but instead of returning to pick up the reins of Shaw Woodworking he'd decided to live in California. And it'd taken nearly twenty years for him to find his way back home.

In a way, his life had paralleled that of his friend Jeff, who'd left to attend college and then went into the Marine Corps. Jeff had come back to care for his grandmother, whereas Nate had returned to look after his brother and take over the family business. Unlike Jeff, though, Nate doubted he would remarry. He'd been there, done that, and wasn't about to have his heart ripped apart again.

They were near the parking area when he said, "I want to stop and get my sunglasses."

"And I have to go to my car and change my shoes," Morgan added.

Nate glanced down at her narrow feet. Although they were sexy, the stiletto heels were not practical for walking on grassy surfaces. "It's a wonder you can walk in those things."

"I've had a lot of practice. I used to put on my mother's heels and play dress-up, so when it came time to wear them I was already a pro."

Resting a hand at the small of Morgan's back, he steered her away from the cars maneuvering into the line for valet parking. "We'll go to your car first, and then mine." Now he knew what his father had been talking about when Morgan opened her tiny purse. She pressed a button on her key fob and remotely opened the hatch on a gleaming white Cadillac Escalade. It was a full-size luxury hybrid SUV with seating for eight.

"Nice ride," he crooned. Nate found the smell of leather as intoxicating as that of raw wood.

Morgan beamed, as if he had complimented her baby. "Thank you." She exchanged her stilettos for a pair of patterned Burberry flats. Her head came up, and she glanced at him staring down at her. "I'm ready," she announced after closing the hatch.

Nate blinked, as if coming out of a trance. He felt like a voyeur because he'd found himself unable to stop staring at her legs. "Do you always keep boots in your truck?" Morgan had stored a pair of Doc Martens and a hard hat in the cargo area.

Morgan nodded. She slipped the strap of her purse over her shoulder. "I keep them around in case I have to go to a construction site."

He protectively took her hands in his and noticed her fingers were cold as ice. "Are your hands always so cold?"

Morgan smiled up at him. "Cold hands, warm heart."

Nate had no comeback for her quip, because he didn't know Morgan as well as he knew her sisters, who were closer to his age. Besides, knowing her better would only lead to trouble. He wasn't interested in getting involved with any woman in the Creek, the Cove, or the Landing. All the relationships he'd had in college and those that followed ended badly, but when he met Kim he'd believed his luck had changed. They dated for more than a year, then moved in together. Six months later they announced their engagement, and on the one-year anniversary of their first date they married in a typical high-profile celebrity Hollywood wedding, with helicopters buzzing overhead and paparazzi with telephoto lenses attempting to capture images of the private gathering.

It ended when Kim bragged publicly about her extramarital exploits. The revelation nearly destroyed him emotionally, and Nate was forced to examine himself, asking what he hadn't done to keep her faithful. He discovered he'd done nothing wrong, but her affair further proved that he had issues with trust. He hadn't trusted his father or his stepmother, or his former wife.

Nate managed to find his gunmetal-gray truck without too much difficulty. Unlike Morgan, he hadn't brought a spare key and had to wait for the valet to open the Sequoia. He plucked the sunglasses off the console, placed them on the bridge of his nose, and then returned the key fob to the waiting valet.

"Now I'm ready," Nate told Morgan, reaching for her hand again. "Why is it you never moved away again?" he asked after a comfortable silence.

Chapter Three

Morgan pondered Nate's question as she attempted to form an answer that would sound credible not only to him but also herself. How could she tell this man that she'd carried a torch for him for years? That she'd returned hoping that he would, too? That even when she met other men she'd found herself comparing them to Nate?

She was thirteen when she experienced her first crush. It began at Perry's. The small Charleston-based eatery was a popular hangout for local high school students. She'd gone to the mainland with her older sister to look for a dress for her eighth grade graduation, and when Rachel suggested stopping at Perry's, Morgan could hardly contain her excitement.

Most of Cavanaugh's grade school kids couldn't wait to attend high school on the mainland, where hanging out at Perry's was a rite of passage. There were designated sections in the restaurant for seniors, juniors, sophomores, and freshmen. And if a senior walked in and couldn't find a seat, then a lowly freshman was obligated to forfeit his. Rachel said girls were the exception; they were never asked to give up their coveted seats for any male upperclassmen.

Morgan couldn't believe the noise level: It appeared as if everyone were talking at once, even as music blared nonstop from a colorful jukebox. Her attention was drawn to Nate, who sat in a booth with her cousin Jesse. Although Haven Creek was the least populated of the towns on the island, and everyone there knew one another, children usually only interacted with those in their own age group. With Nate being four years her senior, Morgan rarely spoke to him.

But that afternoon was different. She and Rachel shared the booth with Jesse and Nate, and he asked her if she was looking forward to high school. The fact that he'd seemingly taken an interest in her had caused her heart to beat so fast that she felt light-headed. And because he was the first boy in the Creek who'd made her feel special, she'd fantasized about being in love with him.

He was so different from the junior high boys, who'd taken to calling her Olive Oyl. When she researched the name on the Internet, Morgan was devastated to see a tall, skinny animated character with long black hair rolled into a bun. Even after her body had filled out and the same boys who'd called her names asked her out, she'd rejected them because she wasn't able to forget their cruel adolescent comments.

She was a sophomore in college when she had her first date, and it was during her junior year abroad that she engaged in what had become her first serious relationship. It had taken leaving the States and falling in love with a man who wasn't an American for Morgan to acknowledge the full extent of her femininity.

She eased her hand from Nate's when they reached a meadow where a stream flowed into a large pond. Flocks of ducks and swans had settled down under a copse of weeping willow trees to escape the afternoon heat. Morgan and Nate stood under an ancient oak draped in Spanish moss, which shielded them from the sun.

"I didn't leave because I've never wanted to run away."

Nate gave her a sidelong glance. "You think folks that leave Cavanaugh Island are running away?"

Morgan turned to face Nate, wishing she could see his eyes behind the dark lenses. "Not everyone. Just those who made it known they couldn't wait to leave."

His eyebrows lifted a fraction. "Didn't you leave the state for college?"

"Yes."

He shook his head. "Why, when you could've gone to Clemson? I happen to know they have a wonderful architecture program."

She nodded, staring at a black swan flapping its raven wings as it rose majestically and landed on the water, creating widening ripples. Several gray ducklings followed the magnificent bird, swimming in a single column. "That's true, but I'd always wanted to go to Howard University because it's my parents' alma mater. I enrolled there as an engineering student, then halfway through my second year I switched my major to architecture."

Slipping his hands into the pockets of his slacks, Nate breathed out an audible sigh. "You went to D.C., but then you came back."

Morgan smiled. "I was glad to be home because I'd

spent my junior and half my senior year abroad. I left the Creek again to enroll in a graduate program at the Savannah College of Art and Design."

"I'm sure you received quite a few job offers."

"I did," Morgan confirmed. "I had a visiting professor at SCAD who'd sent my portfolio to a San Francisco firm. I flew out there for an interview, and they rolled out the red carpet. The partners were willing to pay for me to relocate and advance me enough money to buy a condo. They were also offering a six-figure starting salary with perks that included a company car and expense account."

"Why didn't you take it?" Nate asked.

"They wanted me to design celebrity mansions, but my focus is historic preservation."

"So you turned them down." His query was a statement.

"Yes."

"Did you ever regret your decision?"

She shook her head. "Not once. I was hired as an architectural assistant with Ellison and Murphy. What they paid me didn't compare to what I would've earned in California, but sometimes it's not all about money."

Nate angled his head. "If it's not money, then what is it about?"

Morgan gave him a direct stare. "It's about staying connected to my family."

"Staying connected nowadays is as easy as a keystroke," he argued softly. "If it isn't with a cell phone, then it's e-mail, instant messages, texting, or even Skype."

"Maybe I should've said I wanted to remain connected to my roots." She chewed her lower lip. "I wasn't homesick when I lived in Savannah because it's the Lowcountry, and it's only a two-hour drive between Savannah and Charleston." Morgan saw a tiny rabbit scurry across the grass and disappear into a hole under a flowering bush. "I'm certain you remember the military recruiters at the high school targeting Cavanaugh Island boys because they knew from past experience that they could easily sign them up. The number of eligible bachelors dropped so drastically that girls from the island had to resort to online dating to find a man. And when they did find one willing to marry them, they, too, left."

A hint of a smile played at the corners of Nate's mouth. "Did you go online looking for a man?"

"No," she replied much too quickly.

"Would you ever sign up for online dating?"

"I'm not that much of a risk taker. It would be my luck to hook up with a psychopath."

Nate laughed softly. "And I'm certain there are a lot of them lurking behind too-good-to-be-true profiles." He sobered. "Are you staying because you're looking for a Cavanaugh Island husband?"

She emitted a nervous laugh. "I'm not looking for a husband. And I doubt if I would ever marry a man who grew up here." Even if she'd forgiven most of the boys who'd teased and taunted her, she didn't think she would ever forget coming home, holding back tears, and locking herself in her bedroom, where she cried until she had dry heaves.

Adolescence hadn't been an easy time for Morgan. She'd towered over most boys from grade school to her last year in high school. It was a fact that girls matured earlier than their male counterparts, but for Morgan it took a while to develop the curves other girls flaunted when they were still in junior high.

She didn't want to talk about herself because it conjured up the memories she'd locked away in the farthest recesses of her mind. She wanted to know more about Nate. He'd come back to Haven Creek around Thanksgiving and had kept to himself. When she and Francine went on their early morning bike rides, they rode past the structure that had housed Shaw Woodworking for nearly a century. When she did see Nate, he was working on the roof of the barn, which was still under construction.

"If you weren't running away from Cavanaugh Island, then why didn't you come back?" Morgan knew she'd caught him off guard with her query when she heard his intake of breath.

The seconds ticked by, and after a full minute Nate said, "At that time in my life, living in California suited my temperament."

"Now that you're back, do you plan to stay?"

Pulling his hands from his pockets, Nate folded his arms over his chest. "What's this all about, Morgan? Why all the questions?"

Morgan knew that what she intended to propose to Nate would change his life as much as hers had changed when Kara Newell commissioned her to oversee the restoration of Angels Landing Plantation. "I just need to know if you plan to live here for the next three to five years."

"What if I say no?"

"Then we have nothing to talk about," Morgan said, turning and walking back the way they'd come.

Moving quickly, Nate caught her upper arm. "I give you an answer you don't want to hear and you walk away," he whispered in her ear. He dropped his hand and took a step until they were facing each other. "Did you ask me to meet you to talk about a project or did you need me to…"

"Need you to do what, Nate?" she asked when he didn't finish his statement.

"Run interference between you and your male admirers?"

Her jaw dropped, no words coming from her gaping mouth. Then she laughed, the sound shattering the stillness of the afternoon. "You've got to be kidding!"

"What am I to think?" he countered. "You claim you left two messages—"

"I did leave messages, but not to ask you to go out with me. I have as much interest in you romantically as I have in coming down with a case of poison ivy."

"Damn, Mo. That's cold."

"I'm not saying I would never go out with you, but I try not to mix business with pleasure."

Morgan hadn't lied. She wasn't that thirteen-year-old girl hoping, praying, fantasizing that Nate would fall in love with her and they would live happily ever after. Every year she'd wait for him to come back, to show him that she'd grown up. But when he didn't, her feelings changed and she was resigned to the fact that there would never be anything more between them than friendship. When the news of his engagement to a supermodel was splashed across the pages of entertainment magazines, Morgan felt nothing, and it was then she knew she had matured not only physically but mentally as well.

She tilted her chin in a defiant gesture. "I've been commissioned to oversee the preservation of Angels Landing Plantation, and that includes the house and construction of outbuildings. Artisans from the Creek will be given priority over those in the Cove, the Landing, and the mainland. Shaw Woodworking is at the top of my list as a source for skilled carpenters to recreate the slave village. I would've spoken to your father, but I've heard that he's semiretired." Morgan knew that Nate was the best there was for this project and hoped he would accept the job.

If Nate had had one wish, it would be to retract his words. There was no doubt he'd come down with a lethal case of foot-in-mouth disease. He ran a hand over his head, cursing to himself. Perhaps he should've waited to hear her out before he opened his mouth.

"I'm sorry, Mo. I don't know why I said that."

She waved a hand in dismissal. "Forget about it."

"I can't. I was out of line."

"If you're apologizing, then I accept your apology. Now, can we get back to business?"

Pushing up his glasses, Nate pinched the bridge of his nose. Restoring a house to its original state was a monumental undertaking that would probably take years to complete. Attention to detail would be vital to ensuring authenticity. He wanted to turn down Morgan's offer because he barely had time to complete the work Shaw Woodworking had already been commissioned to do. And there was still the barn, which he wanted to finish before the end of the summer. However, if he could get Bryce to assist him, then perhaps he could help Morgan with her project.

"I don't know, Morgan. I'll have to think about it."

"I don't want to pressure you, but I'm going to need your answer before the end of next week; otherwise I'll have to contact someone else. I've projected three to five years to complete the entire restoration."

He was taken aback by the sudden chill in her voice. It was apparent that Morgan was no shrinking violet. She had a business to run, and for every businessperson, time translated into money. "Can you give me a hint of what I'd be involved with if I decide to accept your offer?"

"You'll have to come by my office and I'll show you the schematic."

"What's the address?"

"It's on Main Street off Moss Alley, two doors down from the Muffin Corner. You can find me there most nights."

"What made you open an office in the Cove and not the Creek?"

Morgan laughed. "You must think I'm a traitor not to live and work in the Creek, but I didn't want to be in direct competition with my former employers. It would be like rubbing salt in an open wound. They were shocked when I handed in my resignation, and mad as hell when they found out I'd opened an office in the Cove. I only have one client, yet they bad-mouth me every chance they get."

"One client and a restoration project of historic proportions. There's no doubt when this land is fully restored it will draw as much attention as Mansfield Plantation and Middleton Place."

Morgan clasped her hands behind her back to keep from throwing her arms around Nate's neck and kissing him. Nate hadn't seen her plans for the restoration, yet he'd fully grasped her vision for the historic landmark house and land. She unclasped her hands. *He's got it!* screamed the voice in her head.

"You're really excited about this, aren't you?" he asked.

She compressed her lips. "How do you know?"

"Your eyes, Mo. They give you away."

"You have no idea how much this project means to me," Morgan admitted. "It's not about becoming my own boss as much as it is about saving a culture that makes me proud to say I'm Gullah."

Nate smiled, exhibiting a mouth filled with straight white teeth. "I understand where you're coming from. When I lived in California, people always made fun of my accent. I tried to explain that I was Gullah, but they looked at me as if I'd come from outer space."

"We may have inflections, but definitely not accents. My roommate at Howard was from Chicago, and when she came home with me during spring break she couldn't stop raving about the food and the lushness of the island. I believed she would've moved here after graduation if she wasn't engaged to a boy who lived in Houston." Morgan glanced at her watch. "I think we better get back. Thank you for hearing me out." Reaching for her hand, Nate's thumb caressed her knuckles, the calluses on the pad making her heart beat a little too quickly.

"I can't give you an answer until I see your plans, and then I'll have to talk it over with my father and brother."

"The entire restoration is projected to take at least three years. So please keep that in mind when you talk to them."

"Okay, I will."

They walked back to the parking area, where Morgan

put on her heels. When they reentered the tent she felt as
if hundreds of eyes were watching her and Nate. It was
then she realized they were still holding hands. "Let go of
my hand," she said between clenched teeth.

Nate took off his sunglasses. "Let them look, Mo.
Even if we were standing ten feet away from each
other they would make up something to beat their gums
about."

She smiled up at him, dimples flashing. "You're right
about that."

Morgan knew that gossip was as essential to the island
as genealogy. The inhabitants of Cavanaugh Island kept
detailed family records in their Bibles because they didn't
want cousins marrying cousins. Nate dropped her hand
and rested his at the small of her back. "Let's find a table
where we can sit together. Wait. I think I see one."

"Yoo-hoo! Na-than-iel! I'm coming, baby!" His name
came out in three distinct syllables as Trina, arms out-
stretched, bore down on them. Those who heard her call
Nate's name moved aside quickly, stepping out of the
way like the Red Sea as it parted. Trina's heaving, ample
bosom challenged the dangerously low-cut décolletage in
a dress that was definitely a size too small for her volup-
tuous body.

Her eyes widening in surprise, Morgan stared numbly
at him. "You and Trina!"

"There is no me and Trina," Nate spat out.

"Then why is she coming for you, *baby*?"

"I promised to dance with her," Nate said sotto voce.

"You're kidding, aren't you?"

He shook his head.

"Bad move, Nate. Trina has tentacles for arms, and

once stuck she's like fast-drying glue. Do you want me to run interference for you?" Morgan wanted to laugh even though she knew that Trina coming on to Nate was no laughing matter.

"I did promise her, and there's probably no harm in just one dance."

Morgan knew that one dance would turn into much more, and she had to decide whether to warn him or mind her own business. Her conscience nagged at her, and she knew she would be remiss if she didn't let Nate know what he was about to encounter.

"It's very noble of you to want to keep your promise. But the harm is she'll stalk you like prey."

His eyebrows lifted as he gave her an incredulous look. "It's that bad?"

"It's worse than you could ever imagine," Morgan whispered, watching Trina's approach.

Nate closed his eyes. "The beautification ladies warned me she was looking for a husband, but that was only after I'd agreed to dance with her."

"Do you want me to run interference for you?" she repeated.

"Yes, please."

"Work with me," Morgan whispered again.

His hand moved up and he put his arm around Morgan's waist. "Thank you."

She affected a warm smile when Trina sidled up to Nate, false eyelashes fluttering, reminding Morgan of the handheld fans of churchgoers during Sunday service. Some unsuspecting men found it hard to resist Trina's seductive wiles until it was too late. Like the late Liz Taylor, the beguiling woman collected husbands. She'd been labeled a black widow, yet instead of killing off her mates she traded them in for new ones whenever she grew bored with them. Several men had had to take out restraining orders to keep her from coming within one hundred feet of their homes.

Trina flashed Nate her most seductive grin as she looped her arm through his. "I thought we could dance now that everyone's eating. Hi," she said, nodding at Morgan as if she were an afterthought.

Affecting a frown, Morgan's eyes shifted between Nate and Trina. "You're dancing with *her* after you told *me* you didn't want to dance?"

Nate lifted broad shoulders under his shirt. "Look, baby—"

Bracing a hand on his chest, Morgan pushed Nate away. "Don't you dare *baby* me, Nathaniel Shaw. Tell me now. Are you *my* man?"

"You know I'm yours, baby," he crooned, then dipped his head and brushed his mouth over hers.

Trina's eyes grew wider. "You're with Mo?"

Nate nodded, smiling. "Yep."

A disappointed scowl distorted Trina's pretty face. "Why didn't you say something?"

Morgan's arm went around Nate's waist. "We decided we didn't want to go public with our relationship for a couple of months. I suppose the cat's out of the bag now."

"I won't say anything if you want to keep things on the down low," Trina whispered conspiratorially.

"Thank you," Morgan and Nate chorused. Both exhaled an audible sigh when Trina turned on her heels and walked away.

"I owe you, Mo."

She gave Nate a long, penetrating stare. "Yep, you sure do."

"I'm sorry, but I hadn't realized Trina had changed that much when I told her I would dance with her. And you're right. I have been away too long and I definitely don't get out enough. I had no idea she was looking for a husband. Maybe I should take Jesse up on his offer to come to the Happy Hour."

"The ladies at the club would love you," Morgan said teasingly. "You're single, educated, and don't have any children. They'd be on you like white on rice."

"Not if you come with me."

Morgan shook her head. "Nope—I already bailed you out once. Now you're on your own." She knew if he'd asked her years ago she would've said yes.

"Please come with me just this one time. As a friend?"

She moved to one side to let a boy carrying a plate piled high with catfish fritters pass. "I can't, Nate. I'm too busy with my project to go clubbing."

"What if I tell you yes?"

Morgan held her breath. When she'd created the list of artisans she would approach for her project, she knew she wanted Shaw Woodworking at the top of the list. Their reputation for crafting some of the finest pieces of furniture in the Lowcountry was legendary throughout the region. The Shaws' carpentry skills had been passed down through the generations, and when she researched the architectural plans of many of the homes built on Cavanaugh Island the names of Nate's ancestors appeared on documents dating back to the mid–eighteenth century. It had been a Shaw who'd laid the parquet floors at Angels Landing, not only when it was first built in 1830 but also following the Civil War, when a fire had destroyed most of the rooms on the first floor.

"I don't want you to agree to sign on to the project out of gratitude. Maybe after you see the rendering you'll know whether you have the time to devote to the work. This commission is too important to me to accept a commitment of less than one hundred percent. There are folks waiting for me to mess up. I refuse to let that happen."

"Auntie Mo," chimed a childlike voice.

Morgan glanced down at her five-year-old niece tugging on the hem of her dress. There were traces of a red substance on her chubby cheeks, and wisps of hair that had escaped the sandy-brown plaits falling to her shoulders were curling around her cherubic face. Bending slightly, Morgan picked up the child, who hugged her tightly around the neck.

"Auntie Mo, Mama wants you to sit with us." Her gaze shifted to Nate.

She dropped a kiss on the little girl's hair. "Amanda, this is my friend Mr. Nate," Morgan said when Amanda continued to stare at him.

Nate smiled. "Hello, Amanda."

Amanda hugged her aunt tighter. "My daddy says I can't talk to strangers."

"Your daddy's right. You shouldn't talk to strangers."

Amanda rested her head on Morgan's shoulder. "I talk to my friends in school."

Nate's eyes met Morgan's when he said, "That's a good girl. Mo, go sit with your family while I try and find my folks."

"As soon as I put this little munchkin down I'm going to get something to eat. And don't forget to save a dance for me, *baby*," she drawled, her voice lowering to a seductive timbre. Nate's laugher followed her as she carried Amanda to the table where the Danes had managed to find a place to sit together. Amanda wiggled to get down, running and climbing onto her father's lap.

Shrugging off her purse, Morgan placed it on the table next to Rachel. "I'm going to get something to eat."

Rachel stood up. "I'm going with you."

It didn't take Morgan long to discover why her sister, who'd had a full plate of food at her place setting, wanted to come along. She asked, "What's up with you and Nate?"

Rachel had asked the question that probably hundreds of others under the tent also wanted to know. Morgan's impassive expression did not change. "It's not what you're thinking."

Rachel frowned and rested a hand over her swollen belly. She had resigned her position as a forensic technician with the Charleston police department to become a stay-at-home mother now that she was expecting her second child. The epitome of high-maintenance, she was as beautifully turned out as a model on the catwalk even though she was three weeks from her due date. She wore a deep rose-pink linen tunic over a pair of black slacks in the same fabric.

"How do you know what I'm thinking?"

Morgan inched along the buffet line, picking up a plate, silverware, and a napkin. "Your face is an open book, Sis. You want to know what Nate and I were talking about."

Rachel grinned mischievously. "You know I'll haunt you if you don't tell me."

"We talked business."

"That's it?"

Morgan extended her plate to the server for a spoonful of red rice with sausage. She gave her sister a sidelong glance. She'd always felt closer to Rachel than to her oldest sister. Firstborn Irene was fiercely independent and solitary. No one was more surprised than Morgan when Irene announced she was getting married. And the man she'd chosen as her husband was a single father who'd adopted his twin nephews after his sister died in a traffic accident. Eight years ago Irene and her Charleston County chief medical examiner husband had a son, adding a third boy to their mixed-race blended family.

"What? Did you want me to say that Nate and I are hooking up?"

Rachel flashed a Cheshire cat grin. "That would be nice," she said, then sobered quickly. "Folks have been talking about you and David, but I think Nate would be a better match."

"I don't have time for a relationship."

"When are you going to make time, Mo? You'll be thirty-three in two months and your biological clock is ticking."

"I'll have the smothered cabbage," Morgan said to another server. "I don't need kids when I have Rasputin."

"He's a freaking cat!" Rachel shouted, garnering the attention of those close enough to have overheard her outburst.

"A cat that's loyal and doesn't give me grief," Morgan countered. "He doesn't ask where I've been, who I've been with, or when I'm coming home. I feed him, give him fresh water, change his litter box, and he's content to sit in the sun or snuggle with me on the porch."

"A cat is not a man, Mo," Rachel hissed. "Mama and Daddy should've never named you after Grandpa, because you're just like him. You living in his house doesn't help. After Grandmomma died he withdrew into his own world, walking around and taking pictures of people and old houses. You're no different except you prowl around musty-smelling old homes looking for antiques and heirloom pieces. Grandpa could've remarried, but he chose to be alone. Think about it, Mo. Do you want to end up an old woman in a house filled with cats?"

Clamping her jaw tightly, Morgan decided it was best to ignore her sister's rant rather than get into a heated discussion about her single status. Her family refused to accept that it was her choice not to become involved with a man. And it wasn't that men hadn't asked her out. She didn't have the energy to devote to a relationship—at least not at this time in her life. Once she was able to get the restoration up and running, then she would consider dating.

Her Russian Blue kitten wasn't human, yet he provided her with the companionship she needed. The feline was always there for her; he didn't talk back, and she used him as her sounding board whenever she launched into a lengthy monologue to air her ideas. No, the kitten wasn't a man, but somehow he fit quite nicely into her present lifestyle.

Morgan also didn't want to think about Nate because then she would be forced to revisit her past, when she woke thinking about him and went to sleep longing for him. She didn't know where she'd found the strength not to react like a quaking virgin when he'd held her hand, placed his arm around her waist, or kissed her. What she did acknowledge was that too much time had passed, and not only had she changed but Nate had also. A wry smile twisted Morgan's mouth as she moved along the buffet table. He'd asked her to go with him to her cousin's club and she'd turned him down. Not because she wanted to, but because she had to.

Think with your head and not your heart. Love with your heart and not your head.

It was as if she could hear her grandfather and namesake whispering to her. She hadn't come this far, sacrificed a love life to advance her career, to let her heart overrule her head.

Chapter Four

~~~~~

Morgan sat on the porch swing, one bare foot tucked under her body and the toes of her other foot pressed to the pale jade-colored floor as she swung slowly back and forth. The late afternoon sun cast long and short shadows over the landscape, turning it into an emerald forest. She smiled. Spring was her favorite season on the island. Flowers were in full bloom, afternoon temperatures peaked in the low eighties, and nighttime temperatures hovered in the low sixties, making it possible to sleep with the windows open.

Her beloved grandfather had willed her the house where her father and uncle had grown up. Even before she'd moved in, she drew up plans to update the interior and expand the rear of the house to include a solarium, an in-home office, and a spacious storage area.

Rachel had scolded her about spending too much time at home, but it was here that she was able to kick back and relax. It was where her creativity flourished whenever she had to design living spaces for a client. It was also where she went online to research historic properties and the complex contemporary and historical relationship between black and white Lowcountry families and their connections to the past.

Morgan wanted to stay longer at the reception, but after she'd returned to the table with her food she'd encountered questioning gazes from her family. She knew they wanted to know where she'd gone with Nate and what they'd talked about. The situation had become so uncomfortable that she decided to end the impasse. She kissed her mother with a promise to see her the following day, sought out the newlyweds, gave them an envelope containing a check payable to one of their designated charities, and left. Rasputin was waiting for her when she opened the door, the tiny blue cat winding its lithe body around her ankle, the sounds coming from him indicating he was glad to see her.

Morgan cleansed her face of makeup and then stepped into the shower stall. Twenty minutes later, dressed in shorts and a tank top, she'd retreated to the porch to unwind, her silver-blue feline companion asleep next to her.

Exhaling an audible sigh, she closed her eyes and let her senses take over. She inhaled the sweet scent of blooming flowers mingling with the smell of salt water; detected the buzzing of insects, and savored the warm breeze sweeping over her exposed skin. Morgan opened her eyes, smiling. Living on Cavanaugh Island, and in the Creek in particular, afforded her a sense of peace she hadn't been able to grasp in all her travels. The house and the land on which it sat represented her past, her present, and, she hoped, her future.

The sound of an approaching car's engine made her sit up straight. Rasputin also stirred, opening his emerald-green eyes. "Don't move, baby boy," she cautioned him when he stood up and jumped off the swing, landing silently on the porch floor.

Coming to her feet, Morgan walked over and opened the front door and the cat scooted inside. Although her pet was playful, he tended to be skittish around strangers. Making her way to the steps, she leaned against a white column, waving to Francine as she maneuvered her shiny red Corvette into the driveway and parked behind the Cadillac.

"I thought you would still be at the reception," she said to her friend when she mounted the stairs.

"I stayed long enough to feed my face. I'll go back later, when the crowd thins out. I asked your mother where you were and she told me you'd probably gone home." Francine removed her sunglasses, perching them atop her head. "She said either you had an attitude about something or you weren't feeling well."

Morgan bit down on her lip. "It was none of the above."

The redhead flopped down on an Adirondack rocker with a green-and-white seat cushion, her luminous eyes meeting and fusing with Morgan's. "It's about Nate, isn't it?"

"I guess you heard."

Francine emitted a delicate snort. "Miss Hannah asked me about you two. I guess because we're friends she thought I'd spill my guts."

Hannah Forsyth was Sanctuary Cove's head librarian as well as the island's official historian. Many kids described Hannah as the lady with the cotton candy hair because of its Champagne-pink color. "What did you tell her?"

"I told her I didn't know what she was talking about. This, by the way, is the truth."

Morgan returned to the swing and sat. The seconds ticked as she rocked. "I asked Nate if Shaw Woodworking would sign on to the restoration project."

Francine gave her a questioning look. "What did he say?"

"He says he'll have to talk it over with his father and brother before giving me an answer."

"What else?"

Morgan knew if she didn't tell Francine about what had happened, then her friend was certain to hear a version that wouldn't come remotely close to the truth. She told her about the beautification committee members' matchmaking attempt on Nate's behalf, his promise to dance with Trina, and her stepping in to thwart Trina's seduction.

Francine brought up her hand to stifle her giggles. "I wish I could've been there to see Trina's face when you told her that you and Nate were going together."

"She seemed to have taken it well."

An expression of seriousness replaced amusement when Francine said, "What's going to happen once word gets out that you and Nate are a couple?"

"We're not a couple."

"Didn't you just tell me he wants you to go with him to Happy Hour?"

"Yes, but—"

"Get real, Mo," Francine said, interrupting her. "If the

man's asking you out, then there's something about you he likes. And I shouldn't have to tell you that he's been MIA since he came back to the Creek. Not a day goes by in the Beauty Box that his name doesn't come up in conversation. All someone has to do is say 'Nate' and it's on like popcorn. Even the women who don't live in the Creek admit to driving by his place just to see him on the roof of the barn wearing nothing more than a baseball cap, cutoffs, and construction boots."

"He's definitely eye candy," Morgan admitted.

"He's more than eye candy. He's young, single, and loaded."

Morgan stopped swinging. "I'd read that he declined his share of community property under California's divorce laws."

Crossing her sandaled feet at the ankles, Francine combed her fingers through her hair. "Working at a beauty salon has its advantages if you want to know what's happening in other people's lives. Someone asked Sharon if Nate planned to stay in the Creek, and she said yes because he'd sold a string of self-storage facilities in Los Angeles and San Diego. She also said that Nate and his wife had a prenuptial agreement providing that whatever they'd acquired before and during their marriage was exempt from community property."

"So that proves he didn't marry his supermodel wife for her money."

"And that means he's not a parasite. That's more than I can say about some of the men I've dealt with since my divorce," Francine spat out.

"You don't have to turn on the hard sell, Fran. My interest in Nate has to do with restoring Angels Landing

Plantation, not whether he'd make a good boyfriend or husband. And even if I were interested in him, I don't have the time for a relationship."

"I think you forget who you're talking to," Francine said in a whisper after a long, uncomfortable pause. "Aside from my family, you're the only one who knows I'm psychic. You claim you don't want me to tell you your future, but that doesn't stop me from seeing visions that pertain to you."

Morgan's heart was beating so hard and fast she was certain it could be seen through her tank top. When she first met Francine, she'd found her somewhat strange, with her head of unruly curly red hair and bohemian style of dress, reminding her of the 1970s hippies in her grandfather's photographs. The kids at school said Francine was weird, but Morgan admired her because she marched to the beat of her own drum. And her offbeat style suited her dramatic talent, which far outweighed her eccentricity. An aspiring actress, Francine was also quick to remind those who questioned her ethnicity that she was Gullah despite her fair complexion, red hair, and green eyes.

One day Francine said that Morgan, her study partner, was going to get an award at graduation for excellence in math. This disclosure made Morgan uncomfortable because they weren't going to graduate high school for another two years. When Morgan asked Francine how she knew this, her response was, "I was born with a caul over my face." Gullahs believed that a baby born with a caul or veil over its head would have supernatural abilities. This included the ability to see spirits and talk to them, or become a healer. Talk of ghosts and spirits had always frightened Morgan, so she made it a point to leave the room whenever the subject came up. However, when she did receive the award at graduation for exceptional math scores, she realized that Francine was psychic.

A chill swept over her and she shuddered as if it were thirty degrees rather than eighty. Slumping limply against the back of the swing, she closed her eyes. "Talk to me."

Moving off the rocker, Francine sat next to Morgan, reaching for her hand. "You've been in love with Nate for a long time. The reason you never left the Creek was because you were waiting for him to come back."

Morgan opened her eyes. "That's where you're wrong, Francine. I *had* a crush on him in high school, but after he left and didn't come back I forgot about him."

"You were forced to forget about him because he was married."

"Are you saying I still feel something for him?"

A shadowy smile parted Francine's lips. "Not consciously."

"What about Nate? Does he unconsciously feel anything for me?"

Bright green and dark brown eyes met. "Didn't he ask you out?"

"He asked me because he wants other women to know he's not available."

"It's more than that, Mo."

"What is it, then?"

Francine shook her head. "I don't know."

"Why not?" Morgan asked.

"I haven't concentrated on him. When I do, I'll let you know."

"No, Fran. Please let it go."

"Are you sure you don't want to know?"

Smiling, she nodded. "Very sure. I've always lived my life by letting things unfold naturally. It gives me the option of dealing with it or letting it go."

"Okay. But I'm going to tell you if the spirit comes to me with a warning for you to be careful."

Easing her hand from Francine's, she hugged her. "Thank you."

"It's all good. I'm going back now. Why don't you come with me?"

"I'm too relaxed to get up and get dressed again. After I go to my mother's for Sunday dinner, I plan to relax for the rest of the long weekend."

Francine pushed to her feet, Morgan rising with her. "Are you going to any of the Memorial Day celebrations?"

Every year families gathered in the square at Sanctuary Cove for a ceremony honoring veterans who'd fought in wars dating back to the Revolution. This was followed by reenactments, beginning with the War of Independence and concluding with skirmishes commemorating the Civil War. The stagings were always held in an open field behind the church in Angels Landing.

"I don't know yet," Morgan said. She didn't want to commit to going and then back out. Her holiday weekend plans included cleaning her house, putting up several loads of laundry, and watching at least two movies from a stack still encased in cellophane. "If you want to hang out next weekend, then I'll go to Happy Hour with you."

Francine's smile was dazzling. "You know I'm partial to Happy Hour."

"Friday or Saturday?"

"Friday," Francine said as she walked off the porch and got into her car.

Resting her shoulder against the porch column, Morgan stared at the taillights of the fire-engine-red sports car until it disappeared from her line of vision. *You've been in love with Nate for a long time. The reason you never left the Creek was because you were waiting for him to come back.* She hadn't wanted to tell Francine she was wrong for fear that her friend would come up with something else she wasn't ready to accept.

When Morgan was thirteen, she wasn't in love, but she was infatuated with Nate. As an adult, she'd come to experience love, and for her the relationship was fraught with more pain than passion. She hadn't come back to live in the Creek because she was waiting for Nate; she'd come back because of the promise she'd made to her grandfather.

Pushing off the column, Morgan sat down on the top step, hugging her knees to her chest. It was her twelfth birthday when her grandfather asked her what she wanted to be when she grew up. She hadn't hesitated when she said an engineer.

He then suggested she create a wish list of all the things she wanted to accomplish, put it away, and then take it out every ten years to monitor her accomplishments. By twenty-two she'd graduated college with a degree not in engineering but architecture. That time, when she updated the list, her items had decreased from ten to six, because some of her childhood entries were unrealistic.

The day she celebrated her thirty-second birthday Morgan retrieved her list and was mildly surprised to find

that she'd attained many of her goals. What she'd found
odd was that most of what she'd aspired to was career related. Her only personal longing was to own a home, and
that had been achieved by the terms of her grandfather's
will. He'd left her his house, a parcel of land in Haven
Creek, and an extensive collection of photographs, a few
of which hung in museums around the country and several of which were sold to private collectors. He'd also
bequeathed her a collection of jazz records dating back to
the 1940s.

What was disturbing was that her wish list didn't include marriage or children. In another two months she
would turn thirty-three and there wasn't a week that went
by without her sisters reminding her that not only was
her biological clock ticking, it was also winding down.
She'd tried explaining that her love life wasn't a priority
because her focus had always been on her education and
establishing a career. It wasn't as if she hadn't had a few
relationships; however, they were usually short-lived due
to her unwillingness to commit. Her career had always
come first. She'd become so driven to achieve professional success that the running joke among her engaged
or married girlfriends was that she had become a professional bridesmaid. She'd been a bridesmaid for both her
sisters, for Francine, and for two former college room-
mates. After her fifth time as a bridesmaid she doubted
whether she would ever have her own "happily ever
after."

Morgan knew she still had time to look for Mr. Right
and settle down with a couple of children, but doubted
whether she'd ever find a husband on Cavanaugh Island.
The hurtful comments from the boys about her height and

weight wreaked havoc on her emotional stability, and the result was an inability to feel completely confident with men.

When she updated her wish list for the second time, she never could have imagined her involvement in restoring Angels Landing Plantation to its original magnificence.

Once again her love life would take a backseat to her career.

Wednesday morning, Nate punched in the code on the keypad at the entrance to Shaw Woodworking. Ironically, he hadn't realized how shabby the wooden building looked until after he'd built the barn less than a thousand feet away from the structure that had become a Haven Creek landmark.

His great-grandfather had built the one-room cabin after his wife complained about the noise coming from the shed behind their home. Elias Shaw was rarely seen in public because he'd spend most of his waking hours sawing and hammering tables, chests, headboards and footboards, chairs and servers. Elias and succeeding generations had continued the tradition of date-stamping and signing each piece.

He opened the door, inhaling the smell of raw wood, which was like life-giving oxygen to him, and chided himself for staying away so long. Returning to the Creek had healed him inside and out. He'd reconnected with his family and his roots.

Roots. The word reminded him of Morgan. It'd been her sole reason for not leaving the Creek, and it was the reason he'd returned. Nate wasn't certain how long he would've continued to live in L.A. if it hadn't been for his father's health crisis or Bryce's involvement with the law. His marriage had ended in divorce, the housing market had gone belly-up, and except for an occasional job building movie sets, his days and nights were usually spent walking along the beach.

The telephone call from Odessa telling him that Bryce was in jail and Lucas had been transported to a hospital after he'd suffered a mild stroke had galvanized Nate into action. He told his landlady he was giving up his apartment, then wrote her a check for the remaining months on his lease. He also paid her to pack up his personal items and ship them to Cavanaugh Island. Hours later he was on a nonstop flight from LAX to Charleston International. He'd taken a taxi directly from the airport to the hospital. He was relieved that his father hadn't suffered any lasting effects from the stroke, but the doctor had issued a stern directive that Lucas had to lower his cholesterol and blood pressure. He'd also advised Lucas to work fewer hours and exercise more. It all translated into semiretirement.

Nate checked the dehumidifier that ran around the clock to prolong the life and preserve the quality of the planks of wood stored on built-in shelves in the cabin. He'd gotten up early to work on the doors to an armoire. The client had requested a replica of an eighteenth-century French piece made of cherrywood. Lucas had spent countless hours sanding the padauk until it felt like satin under his fingertips. The wood was difficult to work with because of its interlocking grain. But with patience and perseverance it'd become a beautiful, rich, deep red with dark streaks shimmering over the surface.

His father had promised to deliver the armoire the week after Labor Day, and Nate knew he had to finish carving the door-panel inlay to complete the piece by the due date. Working on the barn had taken up most of his spare time, but now that the roof was installed he would shift his attention to commissioned pieces.

Flipping a switch, Nate turned on the track lighting that illuminated the space. He had been true to his word when he told Bryce that he could join the family business. Bryce's probation officer had mandated that he have full-time employment, and working at Shaw Woodworking fulfilled that requirement. But Nate's reaction to seeing Bryce carve wood was one of astonishment. His brother was to wood as Michelangelo was to marble. He was an artistic genius.

Nate had just placed a bag containing food that Sharon had prepared for him in the refrigerator when the door opened. Peering over his shoulder, he saw Lucas walk in with Bryce. "What jolted you two out of bed so early this morning?" he said teasingly.

Bryce scratched his chest, which was covered by a white T-shirt. "I made a mistake and set my clock for five instead of six."

Nate nodded. "If you come in early, then that means you can leave early. I'm glad you're here because I'd like to discuss something with both of you before we start working."

Lucas straddled a seat at the bench where they normally took their meals. "Why do you sound so ominous?"

Smiling, Nate sat opposite his father. "Trust me, Dad. It's hardly ominous." He turned to stare at Bryce. "If you're making coffee, then I'll take a cup."

"Me, too," Lucas called out.

"No coffee for you," the brothers said in unison.

"Dr. Monroe said I could have one cup a day as long as it's decaf."

"You know this ain't decaf, Dad," Bryce said.

Nate reached across the table and patted his father's hand. "I'll pick up some decaf when I go to the store later on today." He glanced away rather than watch Lucas's crestfallen expression. He couldn't imagine not being able to eat or drink whatever he wanted. "Thanks," he said when Bryce handed him a mug of steaming black coffee. Bryce had added milk to his own.

"What do you want to talk about?" Bryce asked as he straddled the bench seat.

"I'd like to restructure the business," Nate said after he'd taken a sip of the hot brew.

Lucas angled his head and narrowed his eyes. "Restructure how?"

Nate stared into a pair of eyes much like his own. "It's time we incorporate."

Pulling a handkerchief from the pocket of his coveralls, Lucas dabbed his shaved pate. "Why didn't you do this a long time ago?"

"Remember, Dad, I was never involved in the company."

"Wrong, Nate. You've worked with me since you were a boy."

"I assisted you when I was a boy," he countered. "What's different now is that I've invested in this company, and that means I'm involved. I've underwritten the cost for a new building and machinery, and I bought a new truck. Incorporating will protect you against personal loss. If anyone were to sue you you'd lose everything, including your home and land. It's different when someone sues a company—all you'd lose is the company's assets."

"What's your stake in this?" Bryce asked Nate.

"The same stake you'll have once you're off probation."

Lucas and Bryce listened intently when Nate told them that he planned to move all the supplies, machinery, and unfinished pieces of furniture into the barn. He told them he had an appointment with the family attorney, who was in the process of drawing up incorporation papers that would change the name of the company from Shaw Woodworking to Shaw & Sons Woodworking, Inc. Lucas would be listed as president and Nate as treasurer. Nate would also assume the responsibility of meeting and negotiating with potential clients. Lucas's work hours would decrease to four hours a day, any three days of the week he chose. Bryce had also been placed on the payroll. He was expected to serve a yearlong apprenticeship, and upon completion would become an equal partner in the corporation. Nate was resolute when he told his brother that he was expected to arrive on time and be ready to work.

Shaw & Sons Woodworking, Inc. It'd taken him less than two minutes to come up with the name for what locals considered a mom-and-pop establishment. As the descendant of highly skilled furniture makers whose reputation was legendary throughout the Lowcountry, Nate sought to bring the family-owned business and name into the twenty-first century.

Nodding and smiling, Bryce said, "I like it."

"So do I," Lucas said in agreement.

Nate's smile matched theirs. "The projected reorganization will not only benefit the company but the entire family."

"How much will I be paid?" Bryce asked Nate.

"That will be Dad's decision."

Lucas stared at his younger son. "I'll have to think about it."

"What's there to think about?"

"Don't push me, Bryce," Lucas retorted. "I told you I have to think about it."

Bryce's hands tightened around his mug. "I hope it's above minimum wage."

"That's enough, Bryce," Nate warned softly. He held up a hand when his brother opened his mouth to continue to challenge their father. "That topic is not open for discussion. However, there's something else I want you to know about." He told them about Morgan's restoration project.

Lucas shook his head. "That's a lot to ask from you, son. Don't you think it may be too much responsibility for you now that I'm semiretired?"

"No. I have three to five years to re-create the slave village. I'll also hire several assistants to complete it, so there'll be no cost overruns."

"I just don't want you to end up like me, Nate, working longer and harder than necessary to provide for the family."

Nate gave Lucas a reassuring smile. "You've done well, Dad." What he wanted to say is that he wouldn't have had to work so hard if Odessa didn't spend her *and* his money as if it grew on trees. As a nurse she was required to wear a uniform when at the hospital, but it was her need to have a new outfit for services every Sunday that threatened to bankrupt her husband. If Odessa didn't see a designer label on a dress, suit, pair of shoes, handbag, or piece of jewelry, then she avoided it like the plague.

Bryce drained his mug. "I could help you out whenever I'm not working here."

"I'd love to have you, brother. Now let's get to work so we can finish this wooden sarcophagus."

Throwing back his head, Lucas laughed loudly. "It *is* large enough to hide at least two bodies."

Chapter Five

Nate walked into the kitchen, smiling when he saw his niece and nephew sitting on stools at the cooking island. They were watching their mother as she cut strips of dough for a lattice-top pie. He patted his seven-year-old nephew's head and then dropped a kiss on his five-year-old niece's neatly braided hair.

"Mama's making pie for dessert," the children chorused.

Nate gave them a warm smile. "Watch your mama carefully so you can learn to cook as well as she does."

Gabrielle patted her hair. "Mama and me have the same hair," she said proudly. Her hair was styled with a profusion of braids that were pinned into a knot on the crown of her head.

Sharon Shaw Mills winked at Nate. "She's been bugging me to braid her hair, so now that school is out, I decided to oblige Miss Thang and take her to the Beauty Box with me."

Whenever he looked at his sister, it was a constant reminder of what their mother had looked like at that age. Sharon had inherited her mother's petite frame, café au lait complexion, and coal-black curly hair, physical characteristics she'd passed along to her own offspring.

"You girls look beautiful," Nate crooned.

"Momma's not a girl, Uncle Nate," Gregory piped up, correcting his uncle. "She says she's a woe-man."

Nate turned his head to hide the grin that had spread across his face. Living with his sister had taught him one important rule: Edit everything before you say it, because her children had minds like steel traps. They remembered everyone and everything.

"Thank you for reminding me, Gregory," he said in apology. "I'll see you guys later."

"Aren't you staying for supper?" Sharon asked.

"No. I have to go to the Cove."

"Do you want me to leave a plate for you?"

"No, thanks. I'll grab something at Jack's Fish House."

Nate was anxious to see what Morgan was proposing. He'd spent all day Sunday, Monday, and early Tuesday morning putting shingles on the roof of the barn. It'd taken him five months to put up the framework, including the roof and all-around overhangs, the exterior and interior walls, and the floors, windows, and doors. The structure could've been completed in under a month if he'd hired a crew to assist him. But for Nate it was a test of endurance. He'd used every waking hour for the project, dividing his time between working with his father in the one-room cabin that had served as the workshop for Shaw Woodworking for nearly a century and working on the barn site itself.

He got into his truck, started the engine, and headed for Sanctuary Cove. The paved road connecting Angels Landing to Sanctuary Cove cut down on the travel time. Cavanaugh Island had changed slightly during his absence, only adding to the island's charm.

The Creek had Happy Hour, a club catering to the under-forty crowd. It was the only bar on the island. Then there was Panini Café, another gathering spot in the Creek for the younger crowd. Both establishments were popular with local and mainland residents. Nate maneuvered slowly along the two-lane road lined on both sides with towering pine trees. He barely glanced at the sign indicating the number of miles to Angels Landing and Sanctuary Cove.

Angels Landing appeared to have been caught in suspended animation. Totally residential, it nevertheless had no new homes or subdivisions. There were the "haves," who lived in scaled-down replicas of antebellum mansions, and the "have-nots," who lived in one-story structures built on pilings off the ground. Many of these houses were in need of a fresh coat of paint as well as new windows and screens. He chuckled softly. The years he'd spent working for a West Coast developer had perfected his observational skills. He could now apply what he'd learned to his hometown.

The paved road wound through a swampland where few had ventured in the past because of quicksand, alligators, and poisonous reptiles. His gaze followed the flight of a pair of snow-white egrets who had been perched on a fallen branch resting in the murky water.

Fifteen minutes later he entered the town limits of Sanctuary Cove. Having been accustomed to speeding on California freeways, Nate had to reprogram his brain to drive less than twenty miles per hour. There were no streetlights, except in the Cove and Creek business districts, no posted speed limits, and no stop signs on the island.

Nate decelerated, maneuvering through the downtown. He'd become a sightseer: He passed Jack's Fish House, then the town square, where groups of teenagers used to gather around the fountain and the marble statue of patriot militiaman General Francis Marion atop a stallion. He stared at the Cove Inn, the town's boardinghouse. It, too, needed a fresh coat of white paint. It suddenly hit him as if he'd been jolted by electricity. This was the first time he'd been to the Cove since his return. Jesse had accused him of hiding, Bryce had asked him if he knew how to have fun, and Morgan had talked about him not getting out enough. It was apparent they were right, because he felt more like a tourist than a native.

Since his return, his routine was always the same: up at sunrise, retire to bed at midnight, which left him with little or no time for himself. And if he didn't share Sunday dinner with his family or go to the lumberyard on the mainland, Nate would've lived a monastic existence. He hoped that would change now that the barn was nearing completion.

Nate turned down a side street and drove into an area set aside for business district parking. He managed to find an empty space between a rusty pickup and a late-model roadster. The Memorial Day weekend signaled the official start of the summer season, and that meant the island's population increased appreciably, with an influx of tourists and college students. Walking out of the parking lot, he made his way down Moss Alley. Ageless oak trees draped in Spanish moss had given the iconic narrow cobblestone street its name.

Moving back to Cavanaugh Island had been a shot in the arm for Nate. Here there was no manufacturing to pollute the air and water; no traffic jams, no exhaust fumes; no fast-food restaurants, big-box stores, or strip malls. When the local kids didn't go to Charleston, they'd hang out in the town square or on the beach. There had never been a record of a vehicular fatality or a hit-and-run accident. Anyone caught driving under the influence was harshly dealt with by local law enforcement.

He strolled along Main Street, peering into storefronts. He smiled when he saw the piano in the Parlor Bookstore. The shingle above a nearby storefront read ASA MONROE, MD, CRITICAL CARE FAMILY PRACTICE. Dr. Monroe had become his father's primary physician. It was good the island now had a resident doctor and a bookstore.

Nate glanced at the clock above the building housing the *Sanctuary Chronicle.* It was 6:20. Morgan had mentioned she could be found in her office most nights, so he turned on his heels and headed back toward Moss Alley.

The sound of the doorbell chiming like Big Ben echoed throughout the space where Morgan had set up M. Dane Architecture and Interior Design. She saved what she'd typed, then walked to the front door. Peering through the beveled glass, she saw the figure of a man, then his face. Nate. Unlocking the door, she stared up at him. Her breath caught in her throat, making breathing difficult. The stubble on his jaw, and his black T-shirt, relaxed jeans, and work boots, served to enhance his blatant virility.

"You came."

Staring at her under lowered lids, Nate smiled. "I told you I would. Do you always keep the door locked?"

"I do when I'm here alone and working in the back." She opened the door wider. "Please come in." Nate walked in, the subtle scent of sandalwood aftershave wafting to her nose. *Why does he have to look and smell so delicious?* her inner voice asked. Morgan knew that if she wasn't careful, old feelings were certain to resurface, making it hard for her to maintain a professional demeanor when interacting with him. Closing and locking the door, she turned to find him glancing around the outer office.

"I like what you've done here," Nate said, staring at a trio of framed Jonathan Green prints.

Two side chairs upholstered in natural Haitian cotton flanked a low table topped with a vase of fresh flowers and succulents in small decorative pots. Twin Tiffany-style floor lamps matched one on another table, which doubled as a desk. Recessed lighting, prerecorded music flowing from speakers concealed in the ceiling, and the cool colors of blue, gray, and white created a calming effect.

Nate ran his fingers over a wall covered with blue-gray fabric. "Fiberglass?"

Morgan nodded. "You're good. How did you know?"

"I've installed panels like these in a number of houses."

"I thought you only work with wood," Morgan said, slightly taken aback by Nate's revelation.

"I spent about fifteen years working for a builder, and during that time I learned a lot about the construction business." Clasping his hands behind his back, he studied the decorative marquetry inlay and contrasting veneers on the desk in the reception area. "Where did you get this table?"

She took a step, standing close to him. "It belonged to my great-grandmother."

"Is it signed and dated?"

"The underside is stamped: Shaw 1898."

Nate gave Morgan a quick glance. "How many pieces do you own that were made by my ancestors?"

"Come with me and I'll show you."

She led the way to the back of the shop, where she'd set up her private office. She'd divided the expansive area in half, to accommodate a lounge. "The credenza is a Shaw, and so is the drop-leaf table." Morgan stared at Nate when he touched the credenza as if it were a priceless relic.

"Was this a part of a dining room set?"

"Yes. My grandfather gave away the table, chairs, and china closet when he married my grandmother. She came to their marriage with her own furniture, so he agreed to part with everything but the tables and credenza. When his mother heard what her daughter-in-law had done she never spoke to her again."

Nate crossed muscular arms over his chest and angled his head. "I've heard of families falling out over money, but rarely furniture."

Morgan stared into his clear brown eyes, which seemed not to look at her but through her. It was the same look she remembered when they'd shared a booth at Perry's, which now seemed eons ago. Had he recognized her longing gazes? Or had he thought her a silly,

awestruck girl all too eager for an upperclassman to acknowledge her?

"We Danes are reluctant to let go of our past, lest we
forget where we've come from."

Bending slightly, Nate peered closely at the photographs atop the credenza. "Living here makes it almost
impossible to forget where we've come from. Your grandfather made certain to preserve history when he took
those pictures." There were black-and-white photographs
of couples walking to church in their Sunday best, a
group of men sitting on the back of a pickup truck filled
with watermelons, a young man in a zoot suit, and girls
jumping rope.

"Grandpa was known as the Lowcountry James Van
Der Zee."

He stood up straight. "Are these photos originals?"

Morgan shook her head. "No. When Grandpa passed
away he left me all his photographs, camera equipment,
and negatives. Some of his originals are exhibited in museums and many are in private collections."

"You've done an incredible job decorating this place."

She curbed the urge to curtsy. "Thank you."

"Now that I see this place, I'd like to hire you to decorate my barn."

Morgan went completely still. "You want me to decorate a barn?"

"It's not what you think. I built a two-bedroom apartment in the loft."

"How large is the apartment?" she asked.

"It's about twenty-one hundred square feet."

"That's larger than some of the houses on the island."

A rumble of laughter came from Nate's broad chest.

"Well, it is in a barn. Will you come by and look at it?"

There was a pregnant pause before Morgan said, "Sure. But I can't come for at least two weeks. I'm currently interviewing brick masons and landscapers while attempting to complete a research project. Is that okay with you?"

He nodded. "It's fine."

"Now that we've got that settled, would you like to see the rest of the office?"

"Sure."

She opened the door to the lounge, revealing four yellow leather chairs pushed under a round glass-top table and bookcases filled with books on subjects ranging from art, African-American history, architecture, castles, gardens, and handicrafts to decorating and interior design. A wall-mounted flat-screen TV and an orange leather reclining love seat had turned it into the perfect place to unwind and relax. Open louvered mahogany doors exposed a utility kitchen with overhead cabinets, a refrigerator, microwave, and dishwasher.

"This is the office lounge. The door in the corner is a bathroom."

"Was all this here when you rented the space?" Nate asked.

"No. It was an open space with a minuscule bathroom. I had the bathroom expanded and a plumber put in a shower stall, but I can't use it because the retractable showerhead sprays water everywhere."

"Did you tell the plumber?"

"Yes, but he's on a job in Myrtle Beach. He says as soon as he's finished he'll come and adjust it."

Nate brushed past her and entered the bathroom. Sliding back the frosted doors, he looked at the showerhead. "It's probably the diverter valve. I'll come by tomorrow night and fix it for you."

"You don't have to do that."

Turning, he approached her, she taking a step backward when he stopped less than a foot away. He was too close for comfort. His eyes glittered like yellow citrines in a face deeply tanned from working outdoors in the hot sun.

"If I'm going to work for you, then you're going to have to loosen up."

Nate knew he'd shocked Morgan when her jaw dropped. He stared at her parted lips, wondering how she would react if he kissed her—a real kiss this time. It was his turn to be shocked by his thoughts. He'd never been impulsive, especially when it came to women, but there was something about Morgan that made him react differently. He knew it had nothing to do with her looks, because he'd dated his share of beautiful women. In fact, he'd married one.

Staring at her, sharing the same space, made Nate aware of things he either hadn't noticed or had forgotten. First it was her voice. It was low, sultry, and incredibly seductive. Then it was her confidence. It was unusual for a woman in her early thirties to have so thoroughly taken charge of her life and career, resigning her position at a small but very successful architectural firm to strike out on her own. And she was not only confident but also secure when it came to her marital status. Whereas many women her age were trolling clubs, joining dating sites, and asking their friends to hook them up with a man,

Morgan had admitted she wasn't looking for a husband. Especially not one who came from Cavanaugh Island. His father was right when he said men were buzzing around her like bees flitting from flower to flower. Instead of preening, she'd appeared totally bored and unaffected by all the male attention she'd garnered at last weekend's wedding reception. We're more alike than not, Nate mused as he continued his mental assessment of Morgan.

"What's the matter, Mo? Cat got your tongue?" he said teasingly when she compressed her lips.

"No," she countered, smiling. "It's just that I didn't expect you to accept my offer without seeing the rendering. And you also said you had to talk to your dad and brother."

"I discussed it with them and they're in agreement that I should work with you. I've finished the barn's construction, so that'll give me time to help you out."

Morgan pressed her palms together at the same time she closed her eyes. When she opened them they were dancing with excitement. "Thank you, Nate. Now are you ready to see the model of what will eventually be the fully restored Angels Landing Plantation?"

Attractive lines fanned out around her eyes when she smiled. He didn't know how or why, but he felt her excitement as if it were his own. "Yes."

Nate had decided to become part of the restoration project for several reasons, not the least of which was curiosity. But it was also good for his ego, and for posterity. The Shaw name was deeply ingrained in the annals of Lowcountry furniture making, and to have the name associated with the Angels Landing Plantation restoration was something his sister and brother could tell their grandchildren. Children of his own weren't part of his thinking, because he had no intention of remarrying. And becoming a baby daddy was definitely not an option or even a remote possibility for Nate.

Since his return, working with his father was a reminder of how it'd been before he left for college. Accompanying his dad to the lumberyard was like visiting a toy store. The smell of raw wood had become an aphrodisiac, and the sight and sound of the saw was mesmerizing whenever it sliced large stumps into planks or wide boards. He'd watched his father, transfixed whenever he ran his fingertips over freshly cut Western red cedar, sugar maple, Brazilian mahogany, or American black walnut. Time and again he'd found himself doing the same thing. By the time he'd turned twelve he could differentiate at a glance among the many types of wood used in furniture making.

Nate followed Morgan back into her office, his gaze following the gentle sway of her hips in a pair of light gray cropped linen slacks. She appeared cool and fresh in a silk lavender man-tailored shirt and navy blue patent leather flats. When she opened the doors to an armoire, he noticed she'd replaced the drawers with shelves.

"I'll help you with that," he offered when Morgan slid out one of the shelves. He took it from her. "Sweet heaven," Nate whispered when he saw the scaled-down model of a fully restored Angels Landing Plantation.

"You can put it on the drafting table." She pulled out two high-back stools, turned on a swing-arm lamp, and positioned a high-intensity light over the table.

He placed the board with its magnetized pieces on the table, unable to believe the meticulous detail. The antebellum mansion sat at the end of a live oak allée. The scaled-down Greek Revival model, with pale pink columns and tall, black-shuttered windows, was an exact replica of the main house. Morgan had included guest-houses, carriage houses, an English boxwood garden, a family cemetery, chapel, and outbuildings around the property; rows of cabins and another cemetery made up the slave village. He recognized the cypress swamp at the east end of the property, which bordered the slave village on three sides. She'd even re-created the pond, which was surrounded by weeping willow trees.

"How long did it take you to complete this?" Nate asked.

"Once I got the surveyor's report it took a little more than a month."

"Is that all?"

Morgan chuckled. "There were days I'd work sixteen hours just to finish it. I usually create a regular rendering on the computer, but for a project of this scope, I felt a three-dimensional representation would be a lot more visually interesting and realistic."

Nate remembered the set of toy soldiers he'd set up on an imaginary battlefield when he was a child, in imitation of the Revolutionary War and Civil War reenactments that were held during the island-wide Memorial Day celebrations. "What are these?" he asked, pointing to two buildings near a formal rose garden.

"Kara wants to turn the plantation house into a museum." She touched the larger of the two buildings. "This one will be Angels Landing Inn. It will have conference rooms, a restaurant with room for sixty guests, and twelve double-occupancy suites. The other will house a museum shop that will be restricted to local artisans. They will be able to exhibit and sell their handicrafts."

"Won't the restaurant compete with Jack's?"

"No. I've spoken to Otis and Miss Vina and they've agreed to let their daughters run it."

"You've thought of everything, haven't you?"

Morgan smiled, her dimples deepening. "I can't take the credit, Nate. After all, this is Kara's vision."

"It may be her vision, but it's your genius that will make it come alive."

"I'm hardly a genius, Nate."

"There's no need for you to be self-deprecating. You're much too good for someone else to exploit your talent. So claim your genius, Mo."

Extending her hand palm up, she then made a fist. "I just claimed it."

"That's more like it." Nate paused, staring at a large grassy area some distance from the proposed inn. "Do you have any plans for the land next to the new buildings?"

"Kara still hasn't decided whether she wants to put in a nine-hole golf course. I'm certain it will act as a perk for conference attendees wishing to unwind. I suggested building the course to halt developers looking to buy land for condos, country clubs, and private golf courses here on Cavanaugh Island, as they've done on Hilton Head and Jekyll Island and many of the other Sea Islands."

Leaning back on the stool, Nate slowly let out his breath. "I heard talk about them offering folks a great deal of money to sell out."

"They prey on us like locusts. It's gotten so bad that there's talk about putting a referendum on the ballots in all three towns in the upcoming election to restrict developers from soliciting Cavanaugh Island residents."

Nate met Morgan's eyes. He held his breath when she appeared to come closer, although she hadn't moved. She lowered her gaze, peering up at him through long, thick lashes. "Do you think it'll pass?" he asked.

"If it gets on the ballot I know it'll pass here in the Cove and probably in the Creek."

"What about the Landing?"

"One never knows about the folks in the Landing," she replied.

Morgan blinked, shattering Nate's entrancement. He wondered if she looked at all men the way she looked at him. Did she realize how seductive she was? Morgan was the total package: intelligence, incredible beauty, a flawless complexion, a dimpled smile, and a drop-dead gorgeous body.

"No lie," he said halfheartedly. "The folks who live there were always out of step with those in the other towns. What's going to be my involvement with your project?" he asked, changing the topic of conversation.

Morgan stood up, retrieved a stack of photographs off her desk, and handed them to him. "As we discussed, you will be responsible for re-creating the slave village. That means the cabins and the outbuildings, including the blacksmith shop, the winnowing barns, and the furniture for each cabin. As you can see, some of the original structures are dilapidated, but intact enough for you to get an idea of what they looked like inside. You will also be constructing another eight cabins."

A slight frown furrowed Nate's forehead. "I'm going to have to use distressed wood for the new cabins to get the same weatherworn effect as the ones that are still standing."

It was Morgan's turn to frown. "Will that pose a problem for you?"

"No. But if you're going to restore the plantation to its original state, then everything should look as it did then. And that means tearing down the old cabins and putting up new ones. It will probably be more cost-effective, too, because instead of building a structure from the ground up I can purchase them as prefabs. That's what I did with the barn. It came with engineered blueprints and calculations as well as a full lumber package—but not the concrete, nails, and roofing. I also had to purchase the windows, doors, fireplace, furnishings, fixtures, insulation, and utilities. Working alone took three times as long as it would have if I'd had a couple of assistants."

"How about cost?"

His entire face lit up as he gave her a Cheshire cat grin. "I don't think I spent more than one fifteen for everything."

Morgan blinked, then gave him a long, penetrating look. "I don't believe it. You spent one hundred fifteen thousand for a new house with more than two thousand square feet of living space?"

He nodded. "Living *and* working space. Shaw Woodworking will occupy the first floor. I ordered the package without the horse stalls to give us more working area. The final cost would've been a lot more if I'd paid for labor."

"Are you saying you'd put up the cabins by yourself?"

Nate recognized an expression of concern cross Morgan's features. "No. Building sixteen cabins and furniture for each is a herculean feat. And there are also the outbuildings. I'd have to work with at least two other carpenters."

She nodded. "I'll subcontract with you and it will be your responsibility to hire the people you want to supervise. Your crew will be the only one that will not report to the project manager." Opening a drawer under the drafting table, Morgan took out a pad and wrote down a figure. "This is my offer." He was hard pressed not to smile. Morgan was offering him a great deal more money than he anticipated. "I've factored in cost overruns for each line in the budget, so if you're going to need more money, please let me know."

This time Nate did smile. "It looks good, Mo."

Her eyebrows lifted a fraction. "Are you sure?"

"Quite sure."

She exhaled an audible sigh. "If that's the case, then I'll have David draw up a contract for you to go over with your attorney. The agreement will be between Nathaniel Shaw and the Angels Landing Plantation Preservation Foundation, and you'll receive a one-quarter advance once the contract is executed. By the way, do you have a middle name?"

"It's Phillip."

Nate was going to tell Morgan that the agreement should be between Shaw Woodworking, Inc., and the preservation foundation, but quickly changed his mind because he didn't want to commingle funds from two different enterprises. He realized his cautiousness came from not completely trusting Odessa.

When she'd first come to the Creek to care for his mother he'd overheard her asking their neighbor if there were any well-off single men on the island. He later learned she'd grown up dirt poor after her father was stabbed to death in a dice game. After that she swore she would never wear secondhand clothes or eat grits for breakfast, lunch, and dinner ever again.

Lucas wasn't wealthy but he had always earned a good living crafting custom-made furniture. Nate's suspicions about Odessa were confirmed when some of her relatives who'd come to the Creek for her wedding had whispered she'd always been a gold digger. He'd never interfered when it came to his father and stepmother's relationship, but Nate didn't intend for Odessa to inherit the monies he'd set aside for his niece and nephew's college education.

Morgan extended her hand. "It's nice to have you on board, Nathaniel Phillip Shaw." He took her cool fingers, cradling them to his chest. "What are you doing?" she asked.

She tried extricating her hand as he tightened his hold. "Let me warm you up."

"I'm not cold," she countered. "In fact, I'm quite warm."

Nate pressed his thumb to her wrist. Her pulse was beating in double time. "Are you afraid of me?" The query was out before he could censor himself.

A full minute passed before Morgan said, "Why would I be afraid of you, Nate?"

He dropped her hand. "I don't know what it is, but I feel like you're not always comfortable around me."

She let out a nervous laugh. "You're imagining things. I'm here with you alone. If I was uncomfortable I never would've asked you to become involved with this project."

He attempted to conceal a mischievous grin, deciding to challenge her claim that she was comfortable with him. "Come have supper with me. I'd planned to eat at Jack's, but if you want to go someplace a little more upscale, then I'll go home and change."

"It's ironic you mention Jack's because I was going to order a delivery from them."

"Jack's delivers?"

Throwing back her head, Morgan laughed, the low, sultry sound washing over Nate like the mist coming off the water. He stared at the graceful curve of her long neck and the silken skin on her throat, wondering what it would be like to press his mouth there. Again, his erotic thoughts returned, leaving him more shaken than he wanted when part of his anatomy reacted vigorously. He was grateful to be seated and that the drafting table concealed his growing erection.

Nate still didn't know what there was about Morgan that had him entertaining licentious fantasies. He'd always related to her as the youngest daughter of the Drs. Dane, who'd trailed behind her grandfather whenever he went out, several cameras slung around his neck, looking for new subjects to capture on film. When she was about eight she could be seen with her own camera, snapping pictures of flowers, butterflies, or anything that would stand still long enough for her to shoot them.

Even though the Shaws and the Danes lived within walking distance of each other, Nate hadn't regarded them as neighbors. It wasn't until he and Morgan rode the same bus to high school that he realized she'd changed. She was tall—much taller than her female counterparts and many of the boys her age. She'd either style her hair in a single braid or occasionally pull it up in a ponytail. He would already be seated on the bus when she would board, and she and Francine would always sit together.

He usually didn't say much to her except to acknowledge her when passing in the halls. The few times he'd engaged her in conversation she was either with her older sisters or her cousin Jesse, who treated her as if she were his younger sister.

The fact that he was four years her senior meant that she was off-limits. Nate had preferred dating girls his age or a year or two older. There was still a four-year age difference between them, but things had changed. Both were consenting adults, if either decided they wanted a relationship.

Relationship! That single word rocked him to the core. He'd told himself he would never become involved in another relationship, but here he was contemplating one with Morgan. And he knew if they did have one it would never lead to a commitment or marriage.

I doubt if I would ever marry a man who grew up here. Morgan's statement came rushing back with vivid clarity. Even though he'd been away for a long time, Nate was one of those who had grown up on Cavanaugh Island. He didn't know what it was about Cavanaugh Island boys that turned her off, but this was one time he was glad they did, because in that instant he decided he liked Morgan enough to date her—and not because she'd helped thwart Trina's amorous advances.

"Didn't I tell you that you don't get out enough?" she said teasingly. "Jack's started delivering last year, when the locals complained they couldn't get a seat at the restaurant because of the tourists. Otis and Miss Vina hired high school students to make deliveries to island residents. They begin the Memorial Day weekend and end Labor Day. Once the tourists leave everything goes back to normal. We don't have to jostle for space on the sidewalks, you can always find a parking spot in the business district, and if you take the ferry then you're not packed in like sardines. A couple of summers ago they started running two ferries instead of one between here and the mainland." She glanced at her watch. "Jack's is probably filled to capacity and you'll have to wait more than an hour to be seated. Tell me what you want and I'll add it to my order. Deliveries usually take under a half hour."

"You're right, Mo."

"What am I right about?" Morgan asked.

A hint of a smile softened Nate's mouth. "Not getting out enough. Maybe you can help remedy that."

Her eyebrows lifted inquiringly. "How can I help you?"

"Go out with me. Since I've been back the only places I go are the Charleston lumberyard and the hardware store to pick up supplies and tools."

"All work and no play, Nate. You know what they say about that?"

He nodded. "I know. It will make me dull."

She sobered quickly. "What exactly do you have in mind?"

"Well, I did promise Jesse I would come to the club."

She pushed out her lips. "And my cousin can be relentless when you promise him something." Morgan studied him with a curious intensity that made Nate believe she was about to reject his offer. A beat passed, then she said,

"Okay. I'll go with you to the Happy Hour. I'll let you know when I'm available."

Nate curbed the urge to pump his fist in triumph. He'd finally convinced her to go out with him. Maybe after spending time together he would understand what it was about Morgan that drew him to her.

"I'll go along with whatever you want, Mo." He'd agree to almost anything just to have her go out with him.

Morgan could not believe what she'd agreed to do. Had she truly lost her mind? Anyone who went to the club knew that if a group of guys or women came in together they were there for guys' or girls' night out. If she and Nate were to go together, then they would be thought of as a couple. Going to the club as a couple would only intensify the gossip that had begun at Kara and Jeff's wedding reception.

"I'm going to give you my business card," she said, her voice shaded in neutral tones as she stood up and walked to the desk. Picking up a pen, she jotted down a number on the reverse side. "I'm also including my home number. If I don't pick up, then leave a voice mail."

Nate stood up. "The shop's voice mail is working now. Please give me your cell phone and I'll program it with my numbers." Morgan handed him the card and her cell phone. "Are there any new dishes on Jack's menu?" he asked.

"No. The only change is smaller children's portions. Other than that it's the same." Morgan watched him tap the screen as he programmed several numbers into her phone. "How many numbers do you have?"

Glancing up, Nate smiled at her. "I'm giving you my

cell. Also my sister's number, because I've been living with her until my apartment is ready, and my dad's cell."

"Haven Creek isn't so big that I won't be able to find you. What do you plan to do? Go MIA?"

"No." He handed her back the iPhone. "I didn't bust my hump for the past five months putting up that barn to cut and run. I plan to be around for a very long time." Nate squinted at Morgan. "I hope you weren't thinking I was going to run out with your money. You don't trust me, do you?" he said before she could answer.

"Of course I trust you."

"I was just checking."

Pinpoints of heat stung her cheeks once she realized that Nate was teasing her. After all, it wasn't her money but Kara's. The newly married Mrs. Jeffrey Hamilton—a direct descendant of Shipley Patton, the original owner of Angels Landing—had put up more than five million dollars to begin the restoration of the property that had been in her family since the 1830s.

Morgan didn't know Nate well enough to have witnessed this side of his personality. When most boys were, as the older folks would say, *cuttin' the fool,* he'd always been rather serious, something she'd attributed to the fact that he had lost his mother. Morgan hadn't attended Manda Shaw's funeral, but those who did talked about it for a long time. Lucas and Sharon had been inconsolable, while Nate hadn't shed a tear. Miss Hester claimed someone in the family had to be strong for the rest of the Shaws.

Three months later, gossip spread across the island like a lighted fuse attached to a stick of dynamite when Lucas married Odessa. Morgan had been too young to understand what all the talk was about when Nate's younger brother was born. And if there was one rule in the Dane household that was enforced to the letter, it was not repeating gossip. Neither Morgan nor her sisters were permitted to talk about their friends or what they'd overheard. Just this week, when she and her sisters had joined their parents for Sunday dinner, Rachel had been abruptly silenced with a disapproving glare from her mother when she opened her mouth to repeat what she'd heard about Morgan and Nate.

"If we're going to work together, then we have to learn to trust each other."

"I do trust you, Mo. Otherwise I never would've given you my word about re-creating the slave village."

Morgan studied his face feature by feature, searching for a hint of guile. Even if the feelings she'd had for Nate resurfaced, she knew they would always take a backseat to the rebuilding of Angels Landing Plantation. Updating her wish list kept her focused.

"As long as we understand each other, I know we'll get along well."

"As long as we keep in mind it's only business and nothing personal then we should get along famously," Nate countered. "And that includes going to Happy Hour together," he added.

"I never mix business and pleasure."

Morgan hadn't lied to Nate. Unfortunately, she'd discovered the wisdom of this principle when she studied abroad. She'd had an affair with her professor, and when it ended she realized she wasn't the first female student he'd seduced. She'd wanted more and he didn't. And for her, it'd become once bitten, twice shy.

If she hadn't been on the rebound from what had proved to be a relationship in which her heart had over-ruled whatever common sense she had at the time, Morgan never would've become involved with the much older and more worldly professor. It'd taken years before she felt comfortable dating again, and none of those relation-ships progressed beyond the platonic stage.

"Now that we've settled that, what do you want to or-der from Jack's?" she asked.

"I'd like neck bones and gravy with a side order of per-low rice."

"Smoked or fresh bones?"

"Fresh," he said, smiling.

"Those are my favorites, too," Morgan said as she scrolled through her cell's directory for the number for Jack's Fish House. "Every order comes with a container of sweet tea and biscuits. Do you want dessert?"

"No, thank you."

Even though she cooked for herself, Morgan ordered from Jack's at least twice a week. She didn't know what it was that made their dishes so exceptional. Whenever someone asked Otis or Luvina Jackson their secret for concocting some of the best dishes in the region, their answer was their pots. The rice pots, cast iron skillets, and Dutch ovens were seasoned from years of preparing recipes that had been passed down through countless gen-erations of Lowcountry Gullahs.

She added Nate's order to her own shrimp cakes and crab cakes with a side of potato salad. "Make sure to de-liver it to M. Dane Architecture."

"Is that off Moss Alley in the Cove, ma'am?"

"Yes, it is."

"Someone will be there in about twenty minutes."

"Thank you."

Morgan hung up. "Twenty minutes." She waved away the two large bills Nate had taken out of his pocket. "Jack's sends me a statement at the end of each month."

Folding his arms over his chest, Nate gave her an incredulous look. "You order that much food from them?"

"I order whenever I have a meeting, and I provide lunch for my receptionist, Samara Lambert."

"Last week she and her husband, Nelson, rented the vacant house across the road from my dad's."

"Jeff hired Nelson as a deputy sheriff, and as a condition of his employment he had to move from the Cove to the Creek. Now we have resident law enforcement in all three towns. Nelson got back from being deployed last year, and even though Samara is a teacher she was having a hard time making ends meet with him gone. Samara offered to work for me as a part-time receptionist now that her kids are on summer break."

"What are you going to do when school starts again?" Nate asked.

Morgan paused. It was a question she'd asked herself many times. "I'm hoping to find someone with some interior design experience. They don't have to be full-time, because I spend most of my time in the office."

"What if you have to leave?"

"I try and schedule appointments to go to furniture warehouses or textile shops on weekends. Do you know anyone willing to work at least twenty to twenty-five hours a week?"

Nate shook his head. "I'm sorry, but I can't think of anyone."

"It would be easy if I'd opened an office in Savannah because I could always get a student from SCAD."

"So you have a degree in architecture from Howard and a graduate degree in interior design from Savannah College of Art and Design?"

"I also have a postgraduate degree from SCAD in historic preservation."

"No wonder you're not married," Nate remarked glibly. "You've been a professional student most of your adult life."

His words had the same effect on Morgan as they would have if she had taken hold of a rosebush with her bare hand. The thorns stabbed and drew blood. "I wouldn't be able to balance marriage, motherhood, and a career at this time in my life."

"Women do it every day. Look at my sister and yours."

"My sisters stayed home for two years after their children were born, and that's something I wouldn't be able to do even if I were married right now. If I did marry, then I would have to delay becoming a mother until Angels Landing is completed. And you're a fine one to talk, Nate. You're pushing forty and I don't see you with little Shaws running around." If looks could kill, there was no doubt that Morgan would've dropped dead the instant Nate glared at her.

"I wanted children, but my ex-wife didn't, because her career was more important than our marriage."

"I'm . . . I'm sorry—"

Nate put up his hand. "There's nothing to apologize for, Morgan. The topic is moot."

Her temper flared. "You were the one who brought it up."

"I know and am I'm sorry I did. Can we call a truce?"

Crossing her arms under her breasts, Morgan turned her back. "I'll think about it."

Taking two steps, Nate pressed his chest to her back. "How long are you going to think about it?" he whispered in her ear.

Morgan couldn't think, not with his body touching hers so intimately. "Don't!" she screamed, laughing uncontrollably when he tickled her ribs. "Stop!"

"Have you thought about it?"

"Yes!"

"What say you?" he asked, his hands moving up her rib cage.

"I give up! Truce." Tears were streaming down her face from uncontrollable laughter. She managed to put some distance between them when he finally dropped his arms. Wiping the moisture with her fingertips, Morgan glared at Nate. "One of these days when you least expect it I'm going to pay you back."

A wide grin parted his lips. "Is that any way to talk to a friend?"

The doorbell rang, preempting what she wanted to tell him about friendship. Friends didn't tease friends. Brushing past him, she walked in the direction of the front door. Nate's fingers tightened around her upper arm and stopped her retreat.

"Stay here, Mo. I'll get it."

Morgan was still in the same position when Nate returned, carrying two bags with Jack's logo on them. "This one is yours."

"Please put it on the table in the lounge. I'll eat it later."

"You're not going home?"

"Not yet. I still have some research to finish and print out before I leave."

"How late do you work?" he asked.

"I usually try to leave before it gets dark." She had never gotten used to driving at night because none of the roads was lit. The alternative was to take the ferry at the Sanctuary Cove landing back to Charleston, then pick up the causeway.

"I'll wait with you," Nate volunteered.

She shook her head. "That's not necessary."

"Mo, please don't fight me on this. I know you leave before nightfall because you probably don't like driving in the dark. And that means I'll wait."

Resting her hands at her waist, she angled her head. "You're not giving me much of a choice, are you?"

"Not tonight."

If he'd been any other man, Morgan would've thought he was trying to dictate what she should and should not do. That was what the last man she fell in love with attempted to do.

"Okay, Nate. Let's eat first."

Chapter Six

Morgan washed her hands before covering the table with a white linen cloth, then set it with round placemats made of bulrush sewn with strips of saw palmetto. Then she set out napkins, plates, silver, glasses, serving dishes, and spoons. She emptied the large containers of sweet tea into a pitcher.

Nate, having washed his hands in the bathroom, stood watching her. "Do you do this every time you sit down to eat?"

She glanced up at him. "Of course."

"Aren't you making a lot of work for yourself when you could just eat from the carton?"

"Don't you ever eat at the table?"

He moved behind one of the chairs, resting his hands on the back. "When you work at a construction site, you sit on the ground and eat whatever you've brought with you." Nate pulled out the chair. "Come sit down, Mo." He seated her before taking a chair on her left.

Morgan handed him the dish containing a crab cake and a shrimp cake. "Please take one of each."

"Only if you'll have some of the neck bones I ordered."

She ladled a spoonful of neck bones onto her plate, along with a serving of potato salad. They ate, concentrating on the delicious cuisine. Morgan broke the comfortable silence when she said, "Tell me about the work you did in California."

"There's not much to tell," Nate said as he picked up a light, fluffy golden biscuit.

Morgan stared at Nate's profile. The contours of his face reminded her of Michelangelo's statue of David. Her gaze shifted to his large hands, with their long, slender fingers and clean, blunt-cut nails. She recalled the calluses on his palms, indicating he was no stranger to hard work.

"I still want to know."

"Why?"

Resting her chin on the heel of her hand, she lowered her gaze. "I'm curious as to why you stayed away so long."

Picking up his napkin, Nate wiped his mouth. "Money."

She blinked. "Money?" she repeated.

He nodded. "I'd gotten a full academic scholarship to attend several colleges, but I decided on San Diego because a widowed aunt lived there. She'd married one my uncles, and because she never had any children she invited me to live with her. Despite not having a lot of money, she bought me a secondhand car so I could commute to and from campus. Halfway through my freshman year I got a job with a local contractor building custom kitchen cabinets. Whenever he paid me I took out enough for gas and incidentals and gave what was left to my aunt. It wasn't until my father called to ask me whether I was selling drugs that it hit me that Aunt Lizzie had called him. He went on and on, threatening to come to San Diego and beat me if I'd gotten involved with drug dealing. I had to explain that I'd taken a part-time job, while still keeping my grades up."

"What was your major?" Morgan asked in between bites of the expertly prepared fish cakes.

"Business. I continued making cabinets even after I'd graduated. That's when a developer approached me to work for him. It was the beginning of the housing boom and he was in demand, putting up mini-mansions and subdivisions in southern California, Arizona, and Nevada. I put in an average of sixteen hours a day building cabinets and designer doors. I carved a set of doors for a house in Vegas made of Brazilian mahogany that sold for two million dollars."

Her jaw dropped. "You're kidding, aren't you?"

"I wish. The client owned a share in one the casinos."

"Talk about conspicuous consumption." There was a hint of revulsion in Morgan's voice.

"The price was obscene, but he never batted an eye when he wrote the check. I'd made so much money that the IRS owned my soul, so that's when I decided to invest it. I ran into a guy I knew from college who'd gone on and on about building self-storage units similar to those used by commercial companies. He nagged the hell out of me until I agreed to sit down with him, and we worked out a financial feasibility plan. We started with one location in L.A. Two years later we had six in Los Angeles and three in San Diego. Collectively we owned more than two dozen sites when I sold my share earlier this year. I was amazed at the number of people who are hoarders. And they're not like the folks you see living in filth, like those on reality TV shows, but people who are loath to throw anything away."

"Were you affected when the bottom fell out of the housing market?"

"No, only because I was an independent subcontractor—not a developer who buys land, builds homes, then waits for someone to purchase them at outrageously inflated prices. When everything went bust I was living in L.A."

"I can't thank my granddaddy enough for willing me his house, because there is no way I would've been able to afford to buy a house on my former salary. I did update the plumbing and wiring and expanded it to suit my lifestyle."

"Is the showerhead operable?"

Morgan screwed up her face. "You know you're not right."

He smiled from ear to ear. "It's just that when you pay someone to do work for you it should be done right the first time."

"Have you never had to go back for a do over?"

"Never. Only because I had an incredible teacher. My father would make me cut and sand a piece of wood over and over until I was ready to clobber him with it. He said he couldn't in good conscience take folks' hard-earned money and do a half-assed job. There's an old sign on the wall in the shop that reads IF IT'S NOT PERFECT, THEN IT'S

A SIN. I don't know how long it's been hanging there, but it's become a Shaw credo."

"Are you going to put it up in the barn?"

"I'm not overly superstitious, but something tells me if I take it down it'll bring bad luck."

Nate was more than lucky. He'd been blessed. In addition to his college degree, he had inherited a skill that went beyond anything he could learn from books. It was almost inconceivable that someone would pay him two million dollars for a set of doors. But for those who had more money than they knew what to do with, it was little more than a drop in the bucket. He'd become the fortunate recipient of their folly.

"If it ain't broke, then don't fix it," she intoned.

"You're right about that," Nate said in agreement.

Morgan glanced at her watch. It was a lot later than she realized. The research she wanted to finish would have to wait until she got home. "I think I'm going to call it a night."

Pushing back his chair, Nate stood. "What about your research?"

"If I'm not too sleepy I'll do it at home."

She rose to her feet, reaching for the dishes. Nate had answered her question as to why he'd elected to live in California, but there was another question she wanted answered: how he'd met his model-actress wife. That might have been too personal, and she didn't want to cross the line and jeopardize their newfound working relationship. Even though he would be an independent subcontractor, she still held the purse strings.

Nate reached for the serving dishes. "I'll clean up the table while you take care of your office."

"There are containers in the cabinet over the sink for the leftovers. You can take home whatever you want."

Nate met her eyes. "What about you?"

She managed a tired smile. "I have food at home."

Morgan hadn't realized how fatigued she was until she stood up. She'd gotten up at dawn to go cycling with Francine. Her friend always biked from the Cove to meet her, and then they returned to the Cove before Morgan biked to the Creek, cycling along the causeway's bike lane. The early morning ride always left her invigorated. Occasionally they would walk down to the beach and watch the sun rise. After a leisurely shower, fortified with her usual breakfast of fiber, seasonal fruit, and a cup of herbal tea, Morgan was ready to meet the challenges of the day.

Most times she could be found in her office hours before the business district was beginning to stir. The exception was when she decided to stop off at the Muffin Corner. Lester and Mabel Kelly always opened early for customers looking to buy freshly baked bread, doughnuts, and other bakery items.

"Are you sure you don't want save some for tomorrow's lunch?" Nate asked as he walked into the kitchen.

"I try not to eat the same thing two days in a row."

"You don't eat leftovers?"

"If I eat chicken today, then I won't eat chicken again until Friday."

"Picky, picky," he mumbled under his breath.

"I heard that," she called out to his broad back. "Just rinse the dishes and I'll stack them in the dishwasher."

She'd gone through a phase when she'd not only been a picky eater but also ate only enough to keep from being malnourished. On one occasion, she'd gotten sick after she'd gone to a restaurant with her family to celebrate her father's birthday. Her illness had become so severe her parents had to take her to the hospital. Unfortunately the doctors were unable to identify what had gotten her sick, which frightened Morgan so much that she was afraid to eat for fear of a violent reaction. Once she got over her phobia she monitored everything she put into her mouth in the hope that she would be able to identify what made her sick if she were to experience a similar reaction.

"I do know how to use a dishwasher," Nate called out as he emptied the remains of their dinner into glass containers.

"So you're not one of those helpless bachelors?"

"Far from it. I can cook, clean, change baby diapers, and put out the trash without being told."

Sitting in front of her computer, Morgan logged on, printed what she'd saved, then logged off. She had no comeback to Nate's claim that he didn't need a woman to take care of his daily needs.

She'd gathered her tote bag when he joined her in the office. "Aren't you going to take the leftovers?"

Nate shook his head. "I'll get them tomorrow when I come back to fix the shower." He glanced around the office. "Are you ready?"

"Let me check the back door and make certain the transom is closed."

Five minutes later she sat in her Escalade following Nate as he drove slowly along Main Street. The streetlights had come on, and most of the businesses had closed. The lights ringing the town square highlighted the young people who'd gathered around the fountain.

Once she drove past the Cove Inn, blackness descended as though someone had pulled down a curtain. A sweep of headlights from an oncoming vehicle illuminated the road. She focused on the taillights of the Sequoia as Nate maneuvered along the road, seemingly having memorized every curve.

Morgan let out an audible sigh when she saw the lights from Oak Street in the distance. It would've been preferable for her to set up M. Dane Architecture and Interior Design along the Creek's main street, but the town's charter wouldn't permit two businesses offering the same services to open within one thousand feet of the other. She also didn't want to anger her former employer. Traditionally, businesspeople who lived in the Creek operated their businesses in the Creek, and it was the same in the Cove. Those living in the Landing were given the option of doing business in either town.

She accelerated, pulling alongside Nate as she tapped lightly on her horn. She lowered the passenger-side window. Leaning to her right, she said, "I can make it home from here."

Nate stuck his head out his window. "That's all right. I'll see you to your door."

Before Morgan could reject his offer he drove off. When they reached Morgan's street the solar lights she'd installed on the porch shone brightly in the darkness. Nate was out of his vehicle when she maneuvered under the carport and cut off the engine.

He opened her door and extended his hand, helping her to exit. "The bugs are vicious tonight," he remarked, swatting at one that had flown too close to his face.

Morgan reached for her tote and handbag, then raced

to the porch before she became a feast for the insects. She unlocked the screen door and then the inner door. Nate, who'd followed her, held the door open.

"Rasputin!" Morgan screamed when the cat launched himself at Nate. The cat stopped short of attacking Nate's leg, then sat, staring up at the tall man standing next to his mistress. The brilliance of the feline's eyes was reflected in the light coming from a table lamp.

"What the hell..." Nate swore under his breath. "You didn't tell me you had an attack cat."

She dropped her handbag and tote. "He's more a scaredy-cat than an attack one. He runs every time someone comes to visit. My nieces and nephews have never seen him because he hides as long as they're here."

Hunkering down, Nate picked up the kitten, who continued to give him the evil eye. "Please don't tell me your mama named you after the mad monk."

"He's a Russian Blue shorthair."

"Just because he's Russian doesn't mean you should've given him the name of a crazy man."

Morgan couldn't believe Rasputin had permitted Nate to hold him. The kitten bared his teeth and claws whenever she took him to the vet for his checkups. "I didn't want to name him Boris, Ivan, Nicholas, or Alexander, so I thought Rasputin suited his fickle personality."

Nate ran a finger over the cat's head. "He could've been Peter the Great."

"Peter's too common. And who ever heard of a cat named Peter?"

Rasputin purred softly. "Yeah, I know, Blue. You're neurotic because you were saddled with a name that makes everyone believe you're crazy. I should kidnap you and bring you to the shop, because every once in a while we have field mice that come to visit because of the wood shavings."

Morgan held out her arms. "Give me back my cat. You're not taking him anywhere."

Nate dropped a kiss on the cat's soft fur. "You've got a selfish mama, but don't worry, Blue, when I come back for a visit we'll have to talk over a few things. And when you're ready to have a girlfriend I know one you're going to like." He placed the purring cat into Morgan's out-stretched arms.

"I don't plan to mate him."

"Come on now, Mo. Do you think that's fair?"

"What's not fair is having stray cats running around the island."

"My sister has a short-haired cat that looks a lot like Rasputin. I'm certain if they were bred they would have a litter of adorable kittens."

"What breed is she?"

"I think she's called a Snowshoe."

Morgan knew exactly the breed of cat Nate was talking about. When she'd decided she wanted a cat, it had taken months of research before she'd settled on the Russian Blue. The Snowshoe would've been her second choice. And because the breeds weren't widely known, their price tag made them affordable only to an exclusive club of cat owners.

"I'll have to see her before I decide to introduce Ras to her."

The clock on the parlor table chimed the hour. Dipping his head, Nate pressed his mouth to Morgan's cheek. "It's getting late. I'll see you sometime tomorrow."

Morgan stared up at him, committing everything about his face to memory. "Call me before you come."

He nodded. "Good night and thank you for dinner. I'll be certain to return the favor." Turning, he opened the door and closed it softly behind him.

"Good night," she whispered.

She hadn't realized she'd been holding her breath until she locked the door. When she'd gotten up earlier that morning Morgan never would've predicted how the day would end. Nate had agreed to re-create the slave village, he wanted her to decorate his apartment, she'd agreed to accompany him to Happy Hour, and her pet had bonded with another human being, something he'd never done.

Perhaps Ras knew that his mistress cared for Nate more than she was willing to admit.

Sitting on his sister's enclosed back porch, Nate watched lightning illuminate the darkening late afternoon sky. He was house-sitting. The Millses had embarked on their annual road trip, this year stopping in Colonial Williamsburg, Washington, D.C., and Philadelphia.

He'd begun spending several nights at the barn, sleeping on an air mattress. He was still awaiting Morgan's call about when she would come by to see the apartment and get decorating ideas. As promised, he'd stopped by her office and repaired the showerhead. Unfortunately, he hadn't been able to return the favor of buying dinner for her because she was in a meeting with her project manager. However, she'd stepped away to tell him that whenever she was able to clear her calendar she would call him.

Nate caught movement out of the corner of his eye seconds before Sharon's cat sprang up from the floor and settled down on the cushion beside him. His sister liked cats, whereas he was partial to dogs. After his divorce, he'd regretted moving into a complex that wouldn't allow pets of any kind, but he planned to get a dog in the coming months.

Running his fingers over the soft shorthair, he thought about Morgan's cat. She may have named him for a Russian monk and purported mystic, but he thought Big Blue was a much more suitable name for the exquisite feline. Another flash of lightning lit up the sky, and Patches meowed softly as she slipped onto his lap.

"It's just a little lightning," he cooed, hoping to soothe the agitated cat. Mother Nature was putting on her own light show, although there was no thunder or rain.

He shifted, attempting to get into a more comfortable position. Nate felt a restlessness he hadn't experienced since his return. Perhaps it had something to do with his finishing the barn's construction and needing another challenge. He'd installed kitchen appliances and the bathroom's plumbing fixtures. All that remained was to decorate the two bedrooms, the living and dining area, and the kitchen and bathrooms.

A wry smile tilted the corners of his mouth. It would be the first time he would live in a home that would suit his personal tastes. When he'd attended college, he'd lived with his aunt, then it was motels and furnished apartments when he worked for contractors and developers. Once he married Kim, it was the mansion her father had given them as a wedding gift. Not only was the ten-thousand-square-foot house much too large for two people, but its furnishings were as ostentatious as their over-the-top lifestyle. And after the divorce, it was another furnished apartment.

Living above the workshop was a win-win situation. There was no commuting to his place of business, and he could work at odd hours without disturbing anyone. When he'd decided to restructure Shaw & Sons Woodworking, Inc., he'd also revised the hours of operation. After he conferred with Bryce, they'd decided to begin their workday at six in the morning and end at two in the afternoon, when daytime temperatures reached their zenith. This arrangement suited his brother because he had most of the afternoon and evening to himself.

Bryce had revealed that he'd reconciled with his longtime girlfriend, who'd ended their relationship following his arrest. The elementary school teacher had convinced him to reenroll in college so that he could finish the twenty-two credits he needed to earn his degree. His brother had spoken to his probation officer, who would have to approve his leaving the island to attend classes at the College of Charleston. Nate was relieved that Bryce was finally getting his life back on track.

Another flash of lightning lit up the sky, and Patches stood up, arching her back. It was obvious the cat was feeling the effects of the approaching storm. She jumped off the love seat and hid under a corner table. Nate remembered the storms that swept across the island when he was a child. His mother would gather him and his sister in her bed, where she would read to them to take their minds off what was going on outside the house. It wasn't until years later that he suspected Manda was more frightened of the storms than her children were.

Sinking lower on the love seat, Nate wondered what

Morgan was doing. Was she sitting on her porch with her cat, watching the lightning display? Was she out on a date? Or was she home working well into the night on the restoration project? It'd been more than a week since he'd last seen her, and he couldn't get the images of her dimpled smile and the sound of her sultry voice out of his mind.

His cell phone vibrated on the table next to where he sat. Picking it up, he punched in his pass code. "Nate here," he drawled—his usual greeting.

"Hello, Nate, this is Morgan. I'm sorry I didn't get back to you before—"

"There's no need to apologize," he said, interrupting her and sitting up straight. It was as if thinking about Morgan had conjured her up.

"I did promise to get back to you before now."

He smiled. "Whatever you were occupied with had to be more important than looking at my place." A throaty chuckle came through the earpiece.

"Now who's being self-deprecating?"

Nate felt properly chastised when he remembered accusing Morgan of being self-deprecating. "That's something I've never been accused of."

There was a distinct pause before Morgan said, "I didn't call about your apartment, but to ask you if you wanted to go to Happy Hour with me." Nate clenched his teeth to keep from shouting for joy at the same time he pumped his free fist. "I know, the weather looks bad, but I figured it would keep a lot of folks from coming out."

"You're probably right about that. What time do you want me to pick you up?"

"Eight is good. I'll call Jesse and tell him to save us a table."

"I'll see you at eight."

"Thanks, Nate."

He shook his head. "No, Mo. I should be the one thanking you."

She laughed again. "What if we thank each other?"

"That'll work." Nate ended the call, then stared at the time on the phone's display. It was after five, and that meant in less than three hours he would see Morgan again. It had been a long time since he'd felt this excited about seeing a woman.

Chapter Seven

Morgan sat on the porch swing with her eyes closed and took a deep breath. Her stomach was doing flip-flops. She was going out on a date with Nate, and if she didn't steady her nerves she was certain to have a meltdown. First things first. She had to decide what to wear. It should be feminine but not too sexy, and her makeup had to be subtly dramatic.

Get a grip, Mo. Everything is going to work out just fine. Counting slowly to ten, Morgan managed to listen to her inner voice long enough to gather her wits. All she had to do was let everything unfold naturally.

She couldn't hide the fact that she was anxious to get in touch with Nate after spending four hectic days in New York City looking at wallpaper patterns. Her usual vendor had closed up shop without notifying her, and when she called a shop in Atlanta the proprietor told her the patterns she'd inquired about had been discontinued.

Morgan realized that wallpaper was nearly passé when

it came to decorating residential interiors. However, there were textile companies that continued to manufacture it for commercial clients. She'd made the rounds to several firms until she finally found what she wanted.

Once the workmen began stripping the walls at Angels Landing, she realized that the layers of wallpaper were so dry and rotted it was impossible to distinguish one pattern from another, so she decided to choose a new pattern that resembled that of the last layer, a velvet-flocked damask. Fortunately, she found samples and colors that would complement the furnishings in the mansion. She'd taken photos of the samples with her digital camera, left her business card with the salesman, who'd patiently answered all her questions, and promised she would get back to him once she reached a decision.

She was exhausted after walking all over Manhattan looking for materials. And because she hadn't booked a return flight, she had to take a red-eye, arriving in Charleston at four in the morning. She fell asleep in the taxi on the ride back to Cavanaugh Island and didn't wake up until the driver stopped in front of her house.

After a quick shower, she crawled into bed and fell asleep again. The telephone woke her sometime after three in the afternoon. It was Irene, checking to see whether she'd arrived home safely. She'd suspected her sister wanted to bring Rasputin back because she wasn't overly fond of cats. Morgan would've left her pet with Rachel if she hadn't been pregnant. Rachel's obstetrician had cautioned her not to come into contact with a cat's litter box because of possible harm to her unborn baby.

She'd retrieved the office's voice mail and there was a

message from Kara, asking to meet her Monday morning for breakfast. After Irene dropped off Rasputin, Morgan called Francine to see whether she wanted to hang out at Happy Hour, but her friend declined, saying she had plans to meet her grandmother. So then Morgan called Nate.

She knew she'd piqued Jesse's curiosity when she asked her cousin to reserve a table for two but wouldn't tell him whom she was bringing. There was no doubt many would be surprised, if not shocked, to see her and Nate together, but she was past caring what people said about her. Surviving a hellish adolescence had taught her that sticks and stones might break her bones but names would never hurt her. It had taken a while, but she was now immune to disparaging remarks.

It had taken a long time, but she'd come to accept what she wasn't able to change. Morgan wasn't as secure as she let on, but that was something she would never reveal to anyone; it probably would take the rest of her life to feel completely comfortable when interacting with the opposite sex. Pushing off the swing, she went inside the house to prepare for an evening with a man who was unaware that a teenage infatuation was back, and this time it was stronger than it had been then—what seemed like a lifetime ago.

When Nate maneuvered up to Morgan's house and saw her rise from where she'd been sitting on the front porch waiting for him, his foot hit the brake so hard that the truck skidded to a sudden stop. In that instant he would've actively campaigned for her to win the title of sexiest woman alive. Slipping out from behind the wheel, he met Morgan as she approached him.

Reaching for her hands, he kissed her fingers. "You look incredible."

The off-the-shoulder dress, patterned in vertical black-and-white stripes, hugged her body like a second skin. His gaze moved slowly from her face to her feet, encased in a pair of black-and-white pin-striped stilettos. He stared at the smoky shadow on her lids, which made her large, dark eyes appear mysterious, before letting his gaze slip down to the shimmering raspberry lip gloss that high-lighted her sensual mouth.

Morgan smiled and lowered her lashes. "Thank you."

Tucking her hand into the bend of his elbow, he led her around to the passenger side of the Sequoia. Opening the door, he caught her off guard when his hands went around her waist, lifting her effortlessly. Her arms looped around his neck as he set her on the leather seat. Morgan's eyes appeared abnormally large in the glow coming from the porch lights and lanterns lighting the path leading to the house.

"Thank you," Morgan repeated.

Waiting until she was belted in, he came around the SUV and took his seat behind the wheel. Nate wanted to tell himself that he wasn't affected by Morgan, but that would be a lie. There had been women before and after his marriage, yet he hadn't thought about any of them as often as he thought of Morgan. It hadn't even been that way with Kim.

"I'm sorry for calling you at the last minute," Morgan said apologetically as he backed out of the driveway.

He gave her a quick glance. "I'm glad you called. I would've spent the night hanging out with my sister's cat."

"At least she's a female."

Nate smiled. "You're right about that. But she's the wrong species."

Morgan stared through the windshield. "That's where we differ. I enjoy Rasputin's company."

"More than that of a man?"

"Now you sound like my sisters." There was an accusatory tone in the statement.

Downshifting, he turned onto the road leading to the club. "Why? What do they say?"

"They tease me about growing old in a house filled with cats instead of a husband and kids."

Nate's chuckle reverberated inside the vehicle. "I don't see you that way at all."

"How *do* you see me, Nate?"

"You're going to marry a man who will love everything about you, and the two of you will share a house with at least three kids and several cats and dogs."

It was her turn to laugh. "You left out the white picket fence."

"That, too."

"Is that what you wanted when you married?" Morgan asked him.

Nate exhaled an audible breath as he concentrated on navigating the dark roadway.

"It was, but I knew within minutes of exchanging vows I wasn't going to get it."

"You went into something knowing it was doomed?"

"Crazy, isn't it?"

"No, Nate. I don't think you were crazy."

"What do you think I was?"

"You were in love," Morgan whispered. "And love can make you do crazy things."

The sweep of the Sequoia's headlights lit up the club's parking lot when Nate pulled into an empty space and shut off the engine. Resting his right arm over the back of Morgan's seat, he unbuckled his belt and then shifted to face her. "Were you ever afflicted with the love crazies?"

Releasing her seat belt, she turned to give him a direct stare. "Twice. I didn't learn the first time, so I was doomed to repeat it."

His eyes met hers in the dim light. "Were the men from Cavanaugh Island?"

"No. Why?"

"I thought they would've been, since you claim you'd never marry a man who grew up here."

Affecting a wry smile, Morgan shrugged her shoulders.

Cradling the back of her head, Nate pressed his mouth to her ear. "Do you want to tell me about it?"

"It's a long story."

"And we have all night."

Her eyelids fluttered. "You're right. I think we'd better go in, because Jesse is holding a table for us."

Jesse was standing near the door when Morgan and Nate entered the club. He pulled her close, kissing her cheek. "I guess it's true," he whispered.

Morgan went stiff as she stared at her cousin, who was built like a football linebacker. In fact he did play college football, and had been drafted by the NFL, but quit after his first season to care for his younger brother and sister after their parents were killed by a drunk driver. Jesse married a girl from the Landing, was now the father of two boys, and had opened the Happy Hour with his brother-in-law.

"What is?" she whispered back.

"You hooking up with Shaw."

She wasn't given the opportunity to reply before her cousin released her to slap Nate's hand before pounding his back. "Hey, man. It's good seeing you out and about," Jesse said.

Nate gave him a sheepish grin. "I have to admit I was going a little stir-crazy spending so much time alone." He curved an arm around Morgan's waist, pulling her close to his side. "If it wasn't for Mo, I'd still be living a monk-ish existence."

Morgan went completely still when he said "monkish," hoping and praying that Jesse wouldn't misinterpret the word to mean "celibate"—and therefore that she and Nate, having abandoned his monkish ways, were sleeping together.

Nate reached into the pocket of his slacks, taking out a money clip, but Jesse shook his head. "There's no cover charge for family."

"Did you save us a table?" she asked her cousin.

"Yes." He beckoned the hostess. "Please show my cousin and her boyfriend to their table."

She opened her mouth to tell Jesse that Nate wasn't her boyfriend, but the words died on her tongue when Nate squeezed her hand. "Let it go, baby," he said in her ear.

"How did you know what I was going to say?"

"I told you before that your eyes give you away. People are going to draw their own conclusions because we're together. I really don't care and neither should you. We're both consenting adults, so let's enjoy each other."

Morgan knew he was right, but that didn't explain the internal conflict that had her nerves on edge. She wished she could be as indifferent to the situation as Nate was. He wanted friendship, while she wanted more. The problem was Morgan was uncertain what the "more" was. She knew that sleeping with Nate would be disastrous. It would be the same as her first relationship. Even after she and her boyfriend had split, she continued to see him every day because they took many of the same classes together.

"This place is nice," he said as they followed the hostess to a table in a corner that provided a modicum of privacy while permitting them to view the stage, where a quintet played a soft, bluesy piece. He pulled out a chair for Morgan, then sat opposite her.

She glanced around the dimly lit club. The U-shaped bar was the Happy Hour's centerpiece, and its mirrored walls made everything appear bigger. Tables with seating for two, four, and six were positioned closely together to maximize the club's capacity. It was after eight and the place was only half filled, but by the time the waiter took their drink orders several large groups of patrons had arrived. The waitstaff, who wore white shirts with black ties, armbands, slacks, and shoes, was polite and efficient.

Morgan stared across the table at Nate. He was dressed entirely in black, reminding her of New York City, where everyone seemed to favor that dramatic color. The glow from the candle on the table threw long and short shadows over his clean-shaven jaw. The gold from the flame was reflected in his golden orbs, which stared openly at her.

"Are you glad you came?" she asked, smiling.

Nate returned her smile, his gaze fixed on her parted lips. "I'll let you know later."

"I have to assume it's a little different from the L.A. clubs."

"It's a lot different."

"How?"

Lacing his fingers together, he leaned back in his chair. "Folks here seem to come to have a good time, while I found those in L.A. usually go to be seen."

Morgan placed her hand over his. "How often did you visit the clubs?"

Nate reversed their hands, tightening his hold when she attempted to pull away. "Too many times to keep count. Kim loved clubbing."

"When we read that you were engaged to Kimberly Mason, it was headline news. Most of us in the Creek were preening because you were one of ours. Miss Odessa couldn't stop bragging that her stepson was marrying a world-famous supermodel. After a while folks got a little tired of her talking about what she planned to wear to the wedding."

Nate released her hand and pressed a fist to his mouth. "Would you believe she changed twice during the reception?"

Morgan's eyes grew wider. "No!"

Struggling not to laugh, Nate nodded. "Odessa had a captive audience, so she intended to make the best of it."

"What about your father?"

Sobering, he glanced over her shoulder. "My dad knew I was making a mistake, and he tried being diplomatic when he said, 'If you ever get tired of this circus, remember you can always come home.'"

"It was that bad, huh?" Morgan's voice was soft, coaxing.

"It had become a nightmare," he said after a pregnant silence. "The first two years of my marriage were a continuous round of photo shoots, fashion shows, parties, red-carpet appearances, and exotic vacations."

"Weren't you working with a developer?"

"The housing market was just beginning to slow down, so I decided to take a break and support Kim. Traveling with her gave me an opportunity to visit places I'd only read about. It also exposed me to people and places I probably would've never experienced if I'd stayed in the Creek. But after a while it truly had become a circus. There were nonstop parties with enough booze and drugs to get every inhabitant of a small country high for at least a month."

Morgan stared without blinking. "Did you get into drugs?"

"Never. My dad told me about soldiers who went to Vietnam and got hooked on drugs. Many of his close friends died from drug overdoses. He preached to me day and night that if I ever got caught up with drugs—and that included selling them—he would beat the hell outta me. My father didn't believe in hitting his kids, but there was something in his voice that said he wasn't issuing an idle threat.

"I must have had my head in the sand, because it was a long time before I realized Kim was snorting and freebasing coke. She claimed it suppressed her appetite, and the only way she could continue working was if she didn't gain weight."

This revelation shocked Morgan. She'd read about the

supermodel's infidelity, but not her substance abuse. "What did you do?"

"There wasn't much I could do. I told her to get clean or we were through. She checked into a private rehab near the Santa Ana Mountains, but left after two weeks, declaring she'd kicked the habit by going cold turkey."

"Had she?"

"I didn't follow her twenty-four seven, but it appeared she was telling the truth. Her publicist told the media she'd checked into the posh center because of exhaustion. Everyone seemed to believe it because she was so fright-fully thin. I managed to get her to put on some weight, and her agent signed her up for several modeling gigs overseas. This time she didn't want me to go with her. Kim's manager promised me he would look after her. I got a job building movie sets to keep from going stir-crazy. We'd celebrated our third anniversary when I told Kim I was ready to start a family. She asked that we wait a year because she had been selected as the spokesperson for a major cosmetics company and it would entail some traveling.

"I agreed to wait the year, but then the news broke that she'd been sleeping with her manager. When I finally got to confront her she didn't lie about it. In fact, she admitted that she'd been sleeping with him before we met, during our engagement, and, of course, after we were married. But he wasn't the only one. It was as if all the venom poured out when she revealed she never wanted children."

"Had you told her you wanted children?"

Nate nodded. "Yes."

"Would you have married her if she'd told you she didn't want kids?"

"No. First marriage and then children is what I consider a normal progression."

"I'm sorry it didn't work out for you."

"I'm not sorry, Mo." His eyes seemed to pin her to her seat. "It's my past and something I don't intend to repeat."

Morgan hadn't realized she'd been holding her breath. "You can't be turned off by all women because of one bad one."

A flash of white shone in his face when he smiled. "Trust me. I'm not turned off by women. I just don't plan to marry again."

The voice in Morgan's head told her to let it go, but she ignored it, saying, "Don't you think you're being unfair? You may meet someone who might become the perfect wife and mother for your children. Are you willing to forfeit personal happiness because of one selfish woman?"

Nate's smile didn't falter when he said, "Are you angling for the position?"

Heat stung her cheeks. "Of course not! I told you before that at this time in my life I wouldn't be able to balance marriage and a career."

He leaned closer. "What about two or three years from now? Do you think you would change your mind?"

Morgan thought of her wish list. There was nothing on it that pertained to marriage and children. Still, she said, "I probably will."

"It's something…" Nate's words trailed off when the waiter set coasters on the table, then their drinks. Reaching into his pocket, Nate tipped the man, who surreptitiously pocketed the bill.

The waiter smiled. "Thank you. Would you like to order from the menu or would you prefer the buffet?"

Nate winked at Morgan when she mouthed, "Buffet."

"We'll have the buffet," he said to the waiter. As soon as the man walked away, Nate suggested, "Why don't you go first while I wait here?"

Leaving her tiny purse on the table, Morgan got up and joined those who'd lined up near the tables groaning with trays of hot and cold food. A voice came from behind her. "What brings you out, Mo?"

Turning, she smiled at someone she hadn't seen in a long time. "Hey, you," she said to a man who'd gone to school with her. Dylan Hoyt had left the Creek after graduation and joined the army.

The skin around Dylan's dark blue eyes crinkled when he smiled. "Don't you think I deserve more than a 'Hey, you' after all these years?" He extended his arms and Morgan moved into his embrace. Hugging her tightly, he landed a kiss close to her mouth. "Now, that's better. How have you been?"

The four-inch heels she was wearing put her head level with his. "I'm good. How about you?"

"I'm home on an extended medical leave. I got shot during an ambush in Afghanistan. I spent a couple of months in a military hospital in Germany before they sent me back here. My mom's been bugging me to go out on a medical discharge, but I love the military."

She stared at the dirty-blond stubble on his cheeks, through which she detected tiny scars. "It's not easy to please everyone when you feel you have to follow your passion."

"That's what I've been telling her. She claims I need to stay in one place, settle down and get married, and of course give her some grandbabies."

Morgan smiled. "That's sounds familiar." Even though her parents were grandparents of four and were expecting their fifth, they'd professed to want at least ten. "How often do you come here?"

"This is my first time since I've been back. I ran into Jesse, who told me he welcomes all active military. We get to eat free, which includes two drinks." A flush darkened his face. "That's an offer I'd be a fool to refuse."

"You have to know how patriotic everyone on Cavanaugh Island is. Practically every home on the island flies an American flag." She always put up her flag on Memorial Day, the Fourth of July, and Veterans Day.

Dylan nodded. "I would've been back in time for the Memorial Day weekend reenactments if my paperwork hadn't been held up."

"Are you here alone?"

"No. Robyn's here with me."

Morgan glanced around to see if she could spot the Charleston native Dylan had dated off and on for years. As she moved along the line Morgan was greeted by several other Creek and Cove residents who congratulated her on her new venture. She finally picked up a plate and flatware, filling the plate with an assortment of salad greens and hot and cold hors d'oeuvres. Nate had drunk half his beer by the time she returned to the table.

Rising to his feet, he stared at her plate. "Everything looks delicious."

She smiled. "It is. The chef is awesome."

"I'll be back," Nate drawled in a spot-on Arnold Schwarzenegger imitation.

Chapter Eight

~~~

Morgan slapped at Nate's hand when he attempted to spear a piece of calamari from her plate, but she wasn't fast enough. He popped the morsel into his mouth. "Go get your own," she said.

"There wasn't any left when I got there. Where are you going?" Nate asked, rising with her as she pushed back her chair.

"I'm going to tell Jesse to have the kitchen staff put out some more."

"Sit down, Mo. Please." He exhaled when she complied. "I'll make certain to get some the next time we come."

Morgan gave him a long stare. "You want to do this again?"

"Of course. Good music, delicious food, and a beautiful date. That makes for an awesome trifecta."

Propping her elbow on the table, Morgan supported

her chin on the heel of her hand. "What happened to your 'Please come with me one time as a friend'?"

"Do you remember everything I say?" he asked.

"Just about."

"Don't tell me you have a photographic memory."

"Just about," she repeated. Pressing his fist to his mouth, Nate smothered a curse. "I heard that, Nate," Morgan drawled.

"Must I monitor everything that comes out of my mouth whenever I'm around you?"

"Of course not. The only thing you have to remember is not to say something you don't actually mean."

Crossing his arms over his chest, Nate angled his head. His initial reluctance about going to a club vanished within seconds of walking into the Happy Hour. There were similarities and distinct differences between it and the clubs he'd visited in the past. In other clubs, it hadn't mattered whether the music was rap, pop, or techno, it was always loud. The music at the Happy Hour was loud, but not so loud that he couldn't hear what Morgan was saying. Here, the clubbers were mostly college students and professionals in their twenties and thirties looking to unwind at the end of the week.

The food, music, and camaraderie all paled in comparison once he thought about the woman who'd accompanied him. Her beauty and intelligence aside, Nate found Morgan outspoken and unpretentious. He hadn't been able to take his eyes off her when she'd stood in the buffet line, but he'd experienced unease when she hugged Dylan Hoyt.

He didn't want to think of it as jealousy, because that emotion had never been a part of his personality. It hadn't bothered him when Kim wore next to nothing on the runway, because it was a part of her profession. Not only was she selling the garment, she was also selling her body. He'd lost count of the number of times she'd reminded him that her body was a hanger from which to display a designer's garment. He also accepted the fact that men gawked at her, but only because there was little he could do about it. Nate believed he knew who his ex-wife was when he married her. Once she disclosed the number of men she'd slept with, though, what she'd become rocked him to the core.

He shook his head, as if to banish all thoughts of Kim. What he didn't want to do was think about his ex. Thinking and talking about her was like reopening a wound that had healed. Nate stood and rounded the table, offering Morgan his hand. "May I have this dance?" The band was playing one of his favorite songs.

Morgan rose gracefully to her feet, looping the strap of her purse over her body. "Yoo-hoo! Na-than-iel. I'm coming, baby!" she said teasingly as he led her out to the dance floor and eased her into a close embrace.

Pulling her even closer, he fastened his mouth to the column of her neck. "Why did you have to bring that up?"

She giggled. "Don't forget you still owe Trina a dance."

He swung her around and around. "That's not going to happen, because she believes I'm your man."

"The truth is you're *not* my man."

"What if I were, Mo?"

Easing back, she met his eyes. "What are you talking about?"

"What would you expect from a man if you decided you wanted a relationship?"

"That's easy. He has to be willing to let me be me."

Nate was taken aback by Morgan's response. "What about fidelity?"

"Isn't that a given?" She'd answered his question with one of her own.

They swayed in unison, their feet barely moving. Tightening his hold on her waist, Nate buried his face in her short, curly hair. The curves of her tall, slender body fit perfectly against the contours of his physique; their bodies were molded together like puzzle pieces. The scent of her perfume complemented her sensuality. It was subtle, hypnotic, and wholly alluring.

"Not with some couples."

"It is with me," she said quietly, her moist breath sweeping over Nate's ear. "I know firsthand what infidelity feels like, and I don't have to tell you it cuts like a knife."

"If I were your man I would never cheat on you, Mo."

Morgan's fingers dug into his shoulder blades. "And I wouldn't cheat on you. But that's something we don't have to worry about."

"Why?"

Her mouth grazed his jaw. "Because we're friends, Nate."

He smiled. "Why do you sound so confident about that?"

"Because that's what I want," Morgan countered.

"What about what you need?"

Morgan stopped swaying, her eyes meeting his. "It's never about need, because it interferes with my focus."

Nate wanted to laugh. He never would've predicted he would find himself attracted to a woman who wanted friendship without the entanglement of a commitment, and at this time in his life he wanted *and* needed the same.

He lowered his head and brushed a light kiss over her parted lips. "We're now officially friends."

This was the second time that night Morgan questioned her sanity, asking herself if she could maintain a friendship with a man who reminded her of why she'd been born female. Even when she'd experienced her first sexual encounter, it'd been Nate's face and not the one of the man sharing her bed she'd fantasized about. It had been Nate's mouth kissing and tasting her exposed skin. It had been his hands that made her aware of areas on her body she'd come to recognize as erogenous zones. And it had been fantasizing about Nate during lovemaking that helped her physically transition from girl to woman.

Crazy or not, she had to remind herself that she was no longer that wide-eyed, hero-worshipping girl who hung onto Nate's every word and took a corridor that led away from her classroom just so she could bump into him in the hall. Even if he didn't speak to her, Nate would always nod or smile. The one time he said she looked pretty, Morgan believed she'd been hallucinating because she had worn a dress she'd relentlessly hounded her mother to buy for her. It was a simple sundress in a sunny yellow with criss-crossing straps that bared her back. A pair of black patent leather ballet flats with a grosgrain bow pulled the winning outfit together. It was at that point that her infatuation with the honor student turned to love. Not only had he acknowledged her, but he'd also thought her pretty.

Morgan knew at the time that Nate was too old for her and that her parents would never permit her to date an eighteen-year-old boy, but that didn't stop her from filling up the pages in her diary about what he wore, what she'd overheard him say, and what she felt when she found out that he was dating Chauncey. Morgan hated Chauncey; she thought she was hideous and wished her dead. Years later, when she reread what she'd written, she got down on her knees and prayed to God to forgive her. Fast-forward nineteen years: Now Nate had asked whether they could see each other, albeit as friends—but it was tantamount to dating, to an ongoing relationship free of commitment.

As much as Morgan would've wanted the situation to be different, she knew that whatever they would share had to be commitment-free. That way there would be no pressure and no hard feelings. Any illusion of falling in love, becoming engaged, getting married, and setting up a household with a husband had fled. As a professional businesswoman, her focus was on growing her business. Kara had entrusted her with a multimillion-dollar historic restoration and preservation venture, which she planned to see to fruition. It was a challenge Morgan sought the first time she'd visited a historic site, one that was not far from Newburyport, Massachusetts. She'd dreamed of it, yet had no idea it would become a reality when she reached thirty-two years of age.

"Friends," she repeated. Her response seemed to please Nate as he spun her around and around in an intricate dance step. "Wait a minute, Twinkle Toes. Don't tell me you're practicing for *Dancing with the Stars*."

Nate dipped her low. "I'll have you know I took dance lessons back in the day."

"You're kidding," she said, staring up at him.

He eased her upright, then led her back to their table and seated her. "Nope. My aunt Lizzie had been a professional dancer. She'd come along when not many of our people could get roles in the movie musicals that were so popular in the forties and fifties, but with her so-called exotic looks she was able to get parts denied other black performers. She continued to work until she married my uncle. He was a Communist sympathizer who'd convinced her to attend several meetings with him. Her name was one of many that appeared on the Hollywood blacklist during the McCarthy witch hunts. Her career ended abruptly, and no casting agent would let her through the front door."

Totally intrigued by the story, Morgan was unaware that she'd bitten her lip until she felt it throbbing with her pulse. It was then she realized she knew nothing about the Shaws other than that they had produced a long line of carpenters and furniture makers. "What happened after that?"

"Once the word circulated he and his wife were commies, my uncle was summarily dismissed from his job with a building maintenance company. The only position Aunt Lizzie could find was cleaning houses, and Uncle Phillip got by doing odd jobs. A woman who was a professor at UCLA and wrote articles for the *Daily Worker* under a pseudonym hired her as a live-in housekeeper and my uncle as a landscaper. When the woman discovered my uncle's skill as a carpenter, she commissioned him to make built-in bookcases, furniture for the formal dining room, and several guest bedrooms. My uncle died from a ruptured aorta a few days after he celebrated his fiftieth birthday. Fortunately he'd taken out a modest life insurance policy, naming Aunt Lizzie as the beneficiary. She handed in her resignation, rented an apartment, and then set up a dance studio, offering lessons to neighborhood kids."

Morgan heard the huskiness in Nate's voice when he talked about his aunt having to give up teaching once she was diagnosed with an arthritic hip. That's when he accepted the scholarship to attend San Diego State University and her offer to come live with her. On days when she was able move around without too much difficulty, she taught him to fox-trot, waltz, quickstep, tango, and rumba. She also taught him how to cook. He told Morgan how she would fuss with him about spending all his free time with an old woman when he should've been out with his friends, but as a full-time student who worked another twenty hours a week making cabinets, he'd been too exhausted to socialize.

A wry smile pulled down one side of Nate's mouth. "Our roles were reversed when her arthritis worsened and I became the caretaker. After I graduated I tried convincing her to move to Las Vegas with me, but she didn't want to leave her old neighborhood. She wound up in a skilled nursing facility after she was diagnosed with Alzheimer's, and I made it a practice to visit her every weekend."

"Where were you living?"

"Vegas."

Morgan's eyebrows shot up. "You drove from Las Vegas to San Diego every weekend?"

He nodded. "The two cities are only three hundred miles apart. The other residents would tease her, saying her son must really love her to visit so often. I played along with them after I heard her tell another patient I was her son. That's when I started calling her Mama."

"What ever happened to her?"

He stared at the flickering candle on the table. "I'd gone to see her for her birthday and she was lucid for the first time in weeks. We talked about when she met my uncle after he'd gone to see her perform in an all-Negro dance revue when it came to Charleston. She talked for hours, and I listened. Then she said she was tired and wanted me to leave. I kissed her, told her I loved her, and said I would be back the following day. She said I was the son she'd always wanted. The nursing home called me six hours later to tell me she'd passed away in her sleep." Nate closed his eyes, his chest rising and falling heavily. "It was the second time in ten years that I'd lost a woman I loved."

Morgan placed her hand over his fisted one. "She's at peace, Nate."

He opened his eyes, the light from the candle reflected in his golden orbs. "I know that, and I try not to dwell on it."

"I shouldn't have asked."

"Come on, Mo. If we're going to be friends, then we should feel comfortable talking about anything." His expression brightened. "Do you want another glass of wine?"

"No, thank you. If I have another glass you'll have to carry me out of here."

"I could carry you under one arm like a football."

Resting her hands at her waist, Morgan glared at him under lowered lashes. "What's that supposed to mean?"

"Don't get huffy, baby. You're hardly a heavyweight."

Nate talking about her weight had aroused old fears and insecurities about her body—the ones she had when she was the brunt of boys' adolescent jokes. "Maybe you'd prefer I look like Trina?"

Without warning, Nate's face went grim. "Where is all this coming from, Morgan? I meant it when I said you're beautiful. No, I take that back. You are *stun-ning*! In case you didn't notice, more than half the men had their tongues hanging out when you stood up to go to the buffet table. Hoyt was cheesing so wide that if this place were any brighter, I know I would've been able to see his molars."

Morgan hesitated, torn by conflicting emotions. Was Nate actually jealous? And if he was, did that mean he felt something that went beyond friendship? Or was it simply male posturing?

"Dylan's not interested in me. He's here with his girl-friend."

Nate grunted. "Since when has that stopped a dude from hitting on another man's woman?"

Her eyes drank in the sensuality of the man who was separated from her by the small span of the round table. It was she who'd stared at Nate when he'd gotten up to get his food, too engrossed in him to notice whether other women were staring at him. "Don't you mean another man's friend?"

Nate waved his hand. "It doesn't matter whether it's a girlfriend, fiancée, lover, or wife. There's an unwritten rule among dudes that you never cross that line. And Hoyt crossed it when he kissed you."

Morgan's confusion increased when she replayed Nate's rationalization over and over in her head. She didn't want to read more into it, because then she would have to conclude he was jealous, and there was definitely no reason for him to be jealous of her and another man. They'd laid down the ground rules. They would be friends without a physical relationship. And for Morgan, that meant that she was free to pick and choose whom she wanted to date or sleep with.

"Did we not establish that we would be friends and nothing more?"

"I'm not debating that, Morgan. How would you feel if we were out together and some woman pushed up on me and then kissed my mouth?"

Not wanting to get into an argument with Nate as to their prearranged relationship, Morgan chose her words carefully. "It wasn't a real kiss, Nate. He just missed my cheek. Honestly, I don't know how I would react, especially if I didn't know her. I'd probably be more surprised than anything else. But you know Dylan."

"Remember I've been away for a long time, so I don't know your connection to him."

"There is no connection other than we graduated the same year. There are a couple of things you should know about me. I'm not a jealous person and I'm not your ex-wife. In other words, you can trust me not to screw around on you if we decide to take our friendship to the next level. And if we don't and I meet someone with whom I want more than friendship, then you'll be the first to know."

A beat passed. "You don't bite your tongue, do you?" Nate asked.

She smiled. "Not when it comes to defending my actions or beliefs," Morgan countered. "It's different when you're the youngest in the family. Not only did I have to fight not to be treated like a baby, I had to fight for my independence. I come from a family of scientists who expected me to follow in their footsteps. My parents are dentists, Rachel has a degree in forensic science, and Irene is not only a medical examiner but she also married one. They see me as the oddball artist who spends her time drawing and decorating grown-up dollhouses. So if you feel you're going to have a problem dealing with my frankness, then I suggest we stick to a solely business relationship."

Slumping back in his chair, Nate's gaze met and fused with hers. "I don't have a problem with you being outspoken. It's one of the things, along with you being unpretentious, that I like about you."

Bowing her head slightly, she smiled. Most men she met were usually turned off or intimidated by her directness. She'd spent too many years hiding, retreating, cowering, and praying she wouldn't become a target of their ridicule. "Thank you."

"There's no need to thank me. I like the fact that you're confident enough to accept who you are."

It'd taken a long time for Morgan to accept who she was. Once she decided she wanted to become an architect rather than an engineer, it signaled a turning point in her life. Whenever she accompanied her grandfather on his photo shoots, it was the old buildings she loved photographing. Peering through the viewfinder at a dilapidated structure, she'd tried to imagine who'd lived there and what their lives had been like. She was very confident in her career. Much more confident than she was when it came to interacting with men.

"I think there's one more thing you need to understand before I take you home tonight."

Nate's ominous tone caught Morgan off guard. "What's that?"

"You're nothing like my ex-wife."

"Should I take that as a compliment or an insult?"

A hint of a smile played at the corners of Nate's mouth. "It's definitively and unequivocally a compliment." He signaled a passing waiter, asking that he bring the check for their drinks. "Are you certain you don't want another glass of wine?" he asked Morgan.

"I'm going to pass because I made plans to go into the office tomorrow."

"You work six days a week?"

"It's more like five and a half. I open at ten and close around two on Saturdays." Morgan had to shout in order to be heard over a group of men and women who had entered the club cradling large decorative bags filled with gaily wrapped gifts. The hostess sat the party of twenty at a long table only a few feet from Morgan and Nate. The sounds of shrieking, laughter, and the booming bassline beats coming from the powerful sound system made it impossible for her to hear what he was saying.

Pushing back his chair, Nate rounded the table. "Let's get out of here," he said in her ear. He paid the waiter, telling him to keep the change.

Morgan needed no further prompting. The noise had escalated to an ear-shattering level. Nate held onto her hand as he pushed his way through the throngs of people standing at the bar. It was apparent the impending storm had held off long enough for Happy Hour regulars to come out and enjoy a night of live music, food, and exotic drinks. They managed to make it to the front door, where a line of young men and women waited at the entrance, hoping to gain admittance. "I'm glad we decided to come early," Nate remarked as he led Morgan to his truck.

"I've told Jesse and Dwayne to expand the club to include a room for private parties. That way they won't have to turn away people at the door. Jeff is a nitpicker when it comes to overcrowding. One time he came by on patrol and there were so many people in the club folks could hardly move. Jeff told Jesse he had to shut down immediately and warned him that the next time he was cited for overcrowding, he would have to appear in front a judge and face the possibility of having his liquor license suspended."

Nate helped Morgan up and then came around and sat beside her. "Sharon tells me Jeff is a straight-up, no-nonsense sheriff. I don't see it, because whenever we talk he seems so laid-back."

"He takes his job very seriously," Morgan said in confirmation. "After spending twenty years in the Marine Corps as a military police officer, he's not to be played with. Did Sharon tell you what happened a couple of years back, when he first took over as sheriff and he had a run-in with some kids from the mainland who'd come over on the ferry to get high?"

"No. What happened?"

"They confronted him and ended up a sorry sight by the time the EMTs took them to Charleston for medical attention."

Pressing the button to start the engine, Nate shifted into reverse and backed out. He'd barely cleared the space when a low-slung two-seater nearly hit his bumper as the driver swerved into the parking space.

"What did he do to them?"

"When Jeff confronted them in the Cove's schoolyard, one kid came at him with a bat while another pulled a gun. Then the fight started, with Jeff coming out the winner. He grabbed the bat and broke the arms of the boy with the gun, and then he punched out the wannabe baseball player. At first we heard there were six kids, but the official report said there were only four."

"With four against one they definitely had the advantage."

"They would've had the advantage against someone not trained in hand-to-hand combat."

Nate's deep chuckle echoed in the close confines of the vehicle. "It sounds like they had a death wish."

Morgan's sultry laughter joined his. "I'm certain a few of them were wishing for death or anything to stop the pain. That's when the word circulated that Cavanaugh Island has a badass sheriff who'd rather bust heads than talk. It must have worked because we haven't had any problems with kids starting trouble."

"I wish he would've been the one to straighten Bryce out. It's different when someone you know is breathing down your neck twenty-four seven."

Morgan stared out the windshield as Nate accelerated along the narrow road leading back to her house. "How's he doing?"

"So far, so good. He's working with me now. Bryce is truly gifted. Unlike Dad and me, who usually sketch our patterns before we begin carving, Bryce will pick up a wood chisel and start right in. Right now we're working on the doors to a replica of an eighteenth-century French armoire."

"I would love to see it!" Morgan couldn't hide her excitement. It wasn't often she got to see handcrafted pieces before they were finished.

Nate gave her a quick glance. "When?"

"Now?"

"Baby, the place is full of dust and I wouldn't want you to ruin your dress and shoes."

Morgan placed her hand over Nate's as he gripped the steering wheel. She wondered if his calling her baby was said unconsciously or whether it was deliberate. "Then when can I see it?"

"What about early Sunday morning?"

She grimaced. "I usually go to early service on Sunday, and it's also my turn to host Sunday dinner. My mother and sisters rotate preparing dinner and I'm usually the second Sunday in the month." Morgan pursed her lips. "I just thought of something."

Nate maneuvered into the driveway to Morgan's house, stopping under the carport. "What is it?"

"Come and eat with us. That is, if you don't have prior plans. Then after dinner I can change—"

"I promised Dad I would see him Sunday," Nate said, cutting her off. "But there's no reason why we can't get together later in the evening."

Morgan nodded. "We're usually finished around seven. Is that too late?"

Reaching over, Nate's forefinger grazed the short curls on the nape of her neck. "No, it's not too late."

Unbuckling her seat belt, Morgan leaned to her left and kissed his smooth cheek. "Thanks for tonight. I really enjoyed myself."

"Same here." Nate caught her chin, angled his head,

and touched his mouth to hers. "I'll walk you to your door."

There was no passion in the kiss, but the joining was enough to remind her of long-forgotten desire. "That's okay."

Nate was already getting out and coming around to assist her. Resting a hand at the small of her back, he walked her to the door. Morgan unlocked it, and as if on cue Rasputin sat there waiting for her.

Bending slightly, Nate scooped up the cat. "Hey, Blue. What's up? Are you ready to meet your girlfriend? She's a little older than you, but cougars are in vogue and no one will care if you sleep with an older queen."

Morgan tried not to smile. "Go home, Nate, and stop trying to turn my cat into some kind of feline stud."

He handed Morgan her pet. "You may not have a say once he meets Patches."

Her dimples winked at him when she smiled. "Good night, *friend*."

His warm smile matched hers. "Good night."

Morgan waited until the sound of the engine faded before closing and locking the door. She didn't know what to make of the time they'd spent together. It was as if Nate were saying, "Come to me," and when she did he would put up a barrier telling her to go away. He'd professed to want friendship, but then it seemed as if he wanted more than that when he complained about Dylan kissing her.

Although Morgan hadn't wanted a relationship in the past, she could see herself having one with Nate, which frightened her because none of her previous relationships had worked. It couldn't be a friends-with-benefits relationship, because she'd harbored feelings for Nate for far too long. It had to be all or nothing for Morgan, and since Nate told her he had no interest in getting remarried, she didn't want to waste her time or get hurt.

Think with your head and not your heart. Never were her grandfather's words more prophetic than now, when her teenage wish had come true. Morgan's eyelids fluttered wildly as she attempted to blink back tears. Heaviness settled in her chest, making breathing difficult. She realized life had thrown her a wicked curve. The adage "Be careful what you wish for" was standing on her chest *and* staring her in the face.

Nate tossed restlessly on the bed. Before leaving the house he'd closed all the windows, and the buildup of heat was smothering. Tossing back the sheet, he reached up and touched the light switch, turning on the ceiling fan. The blades rotated slowly until they reached maximum speed, dispelling some of the hot air. He'd tried sleeping, but his mind was a jumble of confusing thoughts that had everything to do with Morgan.

He didn't understand why he'd disclosed things to her he hadn't told anyone else. Nate knew his father resented his sister-in-law, blaming Lizzie for seducing his twin brother, who had walked away from the family business to follow her to California. And when Nate announced he was going to San Diego to live with his widowed aunt while attending college, for Lucas, it'd been history repeating itself. His late brother's widow had worked her wiles again. This time she'd lured his son three thousand miles away instead of encouraging him to attend a local college, as Lucas had wanted him to.

Nate hadn't told his father that he was not only running away but also looking for someone to replace his mother, and that someone wasn't Odessa. Lizzie offered Nate the emotional stability he needed to accept his mother's untimely death as well as Lucas and Odessa's deception and the anxiety of being separated from Sharon and Bryce.

Nate had studied Morgan's expression when he'd talked about his aunt and uncle. Not only had she hung onto every word, she had also empathized with him when he'd mentioned Lizzie's declining health and death. The one time he'd attempted to tell Kim about his aunt, she said she didn't want to hear about dead people.

Nate knew he'd overreacted when he saw Dylan and Morgan hugging and kissing. The encounter was a blatant reminder of the times he'd witnessed his ex-wife hugging and kissing men, men she'd subsequently admitted to sleeping with.

Closing his eyes, he ran a hand over his face. Nate had to remember his reason for coming back to Haven Creek. It wasn't to become involved with a woman—even one as beautiful and intelligent as Morgan. It was to pick up the pieces of his life and reconnect with his family.

She'd talked about staying focused, but that wasn't easy for him. When it came to the family business, he had tunnel vision. However, it was becoming more and more difficult to live in virtual isolation. His interaction was limited to his family: Lucas, Odessa, Bryce, Sharon, Webb—his federal air marshal brother-in-law—Gabrielle, and Gregory. Going to the Happy Hour, talking and dancing with Morgan, was a nagging reminder that he was too young to spend the rest of his life cut off from the world.

Nate felt comfortable enough with Morgan that he could be himself. There wasn't a need to try to impress her. She was a good listener, something he'd found lacking in some of the women he'd become involved with. She asked questions, and he hadn't hesitated when answering them.

It was apparent that neither wanted a relationship. He was committed to Shaw & Sons, and she to M. Dane Architecture and Interior Design.

Turning on his side, he closed his eyes. Minutes later he fell into the comforting arms of Morpheus, then slept soundly until Patches jumped on the bed and lay across his chest. He opened one eye, then the other. The cat stared at him for a full minute, her bright blue eyes glowing eerily in her dark face. She meowed softly, and Nate knew the cat wanted him to get up.

He rose on one elbow. "You're not a dog that needs to be walked, so please do me a favor and go back to your bed and let me catch a few more winks."

Patches meowed again, and he knew if he didn't get up, the cat would continue to meow. "Okay, I'm coming." He got out of bed, reached for the cutoffs he'd left on a chair, and slipped into them.

It hadn't taken Nate long to see why Patches had come into his bedroom. A large bug with a hard shell lay on the middle of the kitchen floor, its wings fluttering. He pulled a sheet of paper toweling off the roll, picked up the bug, opened the back door, and released it.

Stretching his arms above his head, he inhaled a lungful of moist salt water. He stared up at the watercolor-painted sky. The sun was just coming up. He decided to go back to bed. "I took care of it, Patches," he said to the cat when she rubbed against his bare leg. The Snowshoe blinked as if she understood what he was saying.

He returned to the bedroom, Patches following. He'd finished the barn, and there was no need for him to get up at dawn. Nate knew he'd been running on adrenaline when he'd worked sixteen-hour days to put up the new home for Shaw & Sons. He fell facedown onto the bed.

"Go away, cat," he groaned when Patches jumped on the bed and snuggled against his thigh. He usually kept the bedroom door closed to keep her from getting into bed with him. If he wanted to share his bed with someone, he certainly didn't want it to be a cat. It'd been more than six months since he'd made love to a woman. The statistic was a blatant reminder of his self-imposed celibacy.

Nate groaned again, this time when the flesh between his legs stirred. He'd told himself he didn't need a woman to ease his sexual frustration; there were alternative methods for obtaining sexual release. But now that alternative didn't seem so appealing, and he chided himself for asking Morgan for friendship. He could've easily asked to date her. After all, she'd mentioned the possibility of taking their relationship to the next level.

Turning over and flopping on his back, he stared at the whirling blades, waiting for his erection to go down. When it did, he was able to go back to sleep, his dreams filled with images of Morgan smiling and staring up at him from beneath lowered lids.

Chapter Nine

⁓

Morgan studied the wallpaper samples she'd uploaded to the desktop in her home office. The previous owners of Angels Landing had decorated all six bedrooms in shades of green: bottle green, fern green, moss green. Wall hangings, seat cushions, bed linens, and rugs all claimed some version of the color. When Kara mentioned the replication of the shade, Morgan decided that the bedrooms with dark furniture would have wallpaper and chair fabrics in a light palette, and that the opposite would be true in rooms with lighter-colored pieces.

She entered notes for the palette for the upholstered armchairs, a daybed, and a round pedestal table she'd identified as Swedish country with classic French provincial influences. The four snow-white pieces were now stored in the attic, along with all the furniture that had occupied the master bedroom's sitting area.

When Nate referred to his brother as an artistic genius, Morgan felt he was being modest about his own talents.

Even though she hadn't seen his work firsthand, there was no doubt Nate was more than capable of continuing the furniture-making tradition begun generations before him. Her gaze shifted to the pedestal table made by Nate's grandfather. She could imagine him working with wood in natural or painted-white tones.

Closing her eyes, she recalled the gentle press of his soft lips on hers. It wasn't just the joining of mouths that had sent shivers of awareness up and down Morgan's spine; it was also the lingering fragrance of his cologne, which complemented his body's natural masculine scent. It was all she could do not to throw her arms around Nate's neck, pull his head down, and drink in his kiss until she was sated.

Morgan continued adding notations along the palette column for the white French-inspired furniture: *White curtains in sheer or lightweight material. Upholstery patterns in toile de Jouy, stripes, and checks.*

"No green," she whispered, chuckling under her breath. The minutes became hours as Morgan selected fabric and wallpaper for each of the six bedrooms. She still had to make selections for the two two-bedroom guesthouses. The longtime groundskeeper and his wife lived in one, and Kara and Jeff had decided to reserve the other for their personal use.

The cell phone on the desk chimed and Morgan glanced over at the display. She punched the button for the speaker feature. "What's up, Fran?"

"Where are you, Mo?"

"I'm home. Why?"

"I'm on my way." She glanced at the time on the phone. It was after five. The Beauty Box took its last customer at two o'clock on Saturdays, closing and locking its doors promptly at that time.

The line went dead, and Morgan wondered what it was Francine wanted to see her about. They went bike riding rain or shine, Monday through Friday, catching each other up on what had happened over the past twenty-four hours. Sometimes they rode in complete silence because they had nothing to say. The bike rides offset the need for her to work out at a sports club. The notion of setting up an in-home workout room was scrapped in favor of the solarium, where she spent many hours reading, relaxing, and listening to music.

Morgan was grateful for Francine's distraction, because she needed to begin preparing for Sunday's dinner. Walking on bare feet, she made her way down a narrow hallway to the renovated all-white kitchen. The pristine color was broken up by hanging palms and ferns in black-and-white checked glazed ceramic pots drinking in the light and sun in front of a trio of mullioned windows.

The contractor had installed state-of-the-art appliances: a refrigerator-freezer, dual dishwashers, a built-in microwave, cooktop, and double ovens with warming drawers. She placed five pounds of peeled white potatoes and three eggs in a large pot, covering them with cold water. Whenever it was her turn to host Sunday dinner she alternated between preparing pork, chicken, beef, or fish as the main dish. This time she would make the baby back ribs she'd purchased from one of two Haven Creek pig farmers. One advantage of living in the Creek was the ready availability of farm-raised chickens, eggs, and hogs. Some of the residents had established a cottage agricultural industry: On Tuesday mornings, they brought their products to a farm stand, selling homemade honey and homegrown fruits and vegetables. Jars lining the shelves in Morgan's pantry were filled with jam, jelly, preserves, pickles, relishes, and seasoning sauces made by women who learned the tradition of canning from their mothers, grandmothers, and great-grandmothers.

The doorbell chimed, its bells echoing throughout the house, and Rasputin, who'd been reclining on a mat at the side door, scooted out of the kitchen and into the pantry. Morgan went to answer the door. Francine appeared to be agitated as she paced back and forth.

The redhead stopped pacing. "I went by your shop figuring I would see you, but the door was locked." Her profusion of auburn curls moved as if they'd taken on a life of their own.

Morgan opened the door wider. "Come on in. Rasputin is hiding," she said when she noticed Francine glancing around the parlor. Her cat and best friend were like oil and water. Francine didn't like cats, and Rasputin knew it. She left the solid oak door open, but latched the screen door.

"Your pet is possessed," Francine mumbled.

"Easy, easy," Morgan drawled. "You're talking about my baby."

Francine's expression brightened. "Speaking of babies, that's why I'm here."

"What's wrong, Fran?"

Looping her arm through Morgan's, Francine led her to the yellow floral love seat and pulled her down beside her. "Remember I told you that I hadn't concentrated on

Nate?" Morgan nodded. "Well, I did earlier this morning. And when he came to me in a vision, I was more than a little shocked."

Morgan stared at her best friend, thinking about their long-lasting friendship. Francine was awarded a full scholarship to Yale as a drama student, graduated, and moved to New York City as a trained stage actress. She fell in love with a fellow struggling actor, and after a six-week courtship they were married at City Hall, with Morgan in attendance as a bridesmaid and witness.

Morgan didn't have to be psychic to know that Aiden was using her friend. It was the Tanners who sent a check every month to cover the couple's living expenses so they wouldn't have to subsist on instant noodles. Francine's parents had achieved financial success after they'd opened a number of fast-food restaurants, and Mavis Tanner realized her longtime dream of owning and operating a full-service unisex salon when she opened the Beauty Box.

After Aiden secured a recurring role in a prime-time soap opera, he filed for divorce, citing irreconcilable differences. A week after the divorce was finalized, Aiden married one of his co-stars. As Aiden's star rose, Francine's fell, and she resorted to making commercials to keep up her acting skills. Her dream to become a stage actress faded, and she returned to Cavanaugh Island, enrolled in cosmetology school, and joined her mother at the Beauty Box.

"What about Nate and babies?" Morgan asked.

Biting on her lip, Francine stared straight ahead. "I saw him holding one."

"You saw him holding a baby?" she asked, bewildered. "What does that have to do with me, Fran?"

"You were also in my vision. You were standing next to Nate."

Morgan took in short, shallow breaths, her mind in tumult. Even though she'd told herself over and over that she didn't believe in ghosts and spirits, her gut said otherwise.

"That means nothing, Fran. You see me, Nate, and a baby in your dream—"

"It wasn't a dream, Mo," Francine said, interrupting her. "I wasn't asleep, and that means it was a vision."

"Is there a difference?"

"Of course there's a difference. You dream and I can see the future."

"I stand corrected," Morgan said facetiously. "Okay. It was a vision, but what I don't understand is why you're going on about me and Nate."

"Did you not go out with him last night?"

Morgan's eyes narrowed. "So you know about that? Or should I say you *heard* about it?"

"The Beauty Box wasn't open a half hour before folks started gossiping about seeing you and Nate at Happy Hour together. A few of them had the audacity to ask me if you and Nate were a couple, and you know yours truly didn't part her lips."

Massaging her temples with her fingertips, Morgan met Francine's eyes. "That's because you have my back, and also your mama would fire you on the spot. You know she doesn't allow gossip in the shop."

"Word," she drawled. "After that incident when Selma repeated something she'd heard about Miss Cindy's husband fooling around with some young girl from

Charleston and Miss Cindy came into the shop waving a pistol while screaming, 'I'm going to kill the lying heifer,' my mother established the no-gossip policy."

"Gossip or not, there's nothing going on between me and Nate except friendship."

"You know there're different levels of friendship, Mo."

"We are *just* friends."

"Are you going to go out with him again?"

"Yeah," Morgan said, drawing out the word. "But it's not what you think. We'll be busy with work."

Stretching her legs, Francine stared at the navy blue polish on her toes. "All it takes is one time."

"One time for what?"

"For you to sleep with Nate and get pregnant."

Morgan emitted a groan of exasperation. "I told you Nate and I are friends. He doesn't want a relationship, and neither do I."

"Maybe not now, but it's coming, and I promise not to say, 'I told you so.'"

"Can we please change the subject, Fran?"

"Sure, Mo."

"Are you doing anything?"

"When?" Francine asked.

"Now."

She sat up straight. "No. What do you have in mind?"

"I'll make dinner for you."

Combing her fingers through her curls, Francine tucked them behind her ears.

"What's on the menu?"

Morgan stood up. "What do you feel like eating?"

Francine pushed to her feet. A mysterious smile parted her lips when she stared at Morgan.

"It's been a while since I've had steak."

Morgan smiled. "You're in luck, because I happen to have a couple of rib-eye steaks in the freezer. Now that it's getting cooler we can grill and eat outside."

"You'll grill and I'll eat," Francine said teasingly.

"Let's go, Red."

"Hey," she said to Morgan's back as she walked out of the parlor. "You never call me Red."

"I'm going to start calling you that until you learn how to cook."

"As long as I have friends and relatives willing to feed me there's no need for me to spend time sweating over a hot stove."

"What are you going to do when you have kids? Fill them up with fast food?"

Francine followed Morgan into the expansive gourmet kitchen. "Their grandmomma will feed them like my grandmomma feeds me."

"Well, if you want to eat tonight, then you're going to have to sing for your supper."

Climbing up on a stool at the cooking island, Francine watched Morgan as she opened the freezer and took out a plastic bag containing the butcher-paper-wrapped steaks. "What do you want me to sing?"

"A few tunes from *Porgy and Bess, Evita,* and *West Side Story.*"

"Hey, that's a lot of singing."

Morgan flashed her charming dimples. "I'm offering three courses: salad, entrée, and dessert. And I'm also willing to offer you a choice of beverages."

Resting her elbows on the black granite countertop, Francine lifted her eyebrows. "What are my choices?"

"Latte, frappé, cappuccino, wine, margarita, piña colada, espresso, and tea."

"Well, damn! With choices like those I don't mind singing for my supper."

The two women dissolved into a paroxysm of laughter that left tears rolling down their cheeks. Despite whatever was going on in their lives, they could always count on each other for support.

Nate opened the screen door, holding it so it wouldn't slam against the frame, and entered the house where he'd spent the first eighteen years of his life. Since returning to the Creek he hadn't been able to think of it as home. It looked and smelled different from what he remembered. It wasn't that Odessa had changed the house much since she'd become its mistress. However, her subtle touches were apparent. The pale blue walls his mother favored were now white. The beautiful parquet floors his father had laid before he brought Manda home as his bride were now concealed under area rugs, something his mother would've never done.

There were additions to the photographs that lined the fireplace mantel in the living room, chronicling the family's milestones over the years: Lucas and Odessa's wedding picture, Sharon's college graduation photo, and Bryce's high school graduation picture. Framed photos of Sharon's children rested on a credenza, along with a couple of bonsai trees.

Nate walked past the dining room and its table set for six, wondering who else Odessa had invited to eat with them. Voices raised in laughter came from the kitchen, and he headed in that direction. He was mildly shocked to find his father, Odessa, Bryce, and two young women who were obviously sisters. Both had the same ash-blond hair and large gray eyes. Odessa was busy basting a roasting chicken while Lucas peered into a pot on the stove.

Nate stood in the entrance to the kitchen, staring at Odessa. Why hadn't he noticed it before? Now he knew why his father had been drawn to his second wife. She was Lucas's type: petite, sophisticated, and outgoing. Although he'd tried, Nate still didn't think of Odessa as his stepmother. She was his father's wife and his brother's mother.

Odessa glanced up, smiling. The skin around her brown eyes crinkled when she smiled. The glow from an overhead light fixture reflected off the gray in her short black hair. "Nate. I'm glad you decided to join us." Everyone in the kitchen turned to look at him.

"I told Dad I was coming."

Wiping his hands on a towel, Lucas approached Nate. Placing his arms around his shoulders, he pulled him close. "Thanks for coming," he whispered in his ear.

He smiled. "Thanks for inviting me."

Lucas eased back. "You know you don't have to wait for an invitation. This house is as much yours as it is mine."

Nate wanted to tell his father it wasn't his house. It stopped being his home the day he left Cavanaugh Island for college.

He handed Lucas a shopping bag. "I picked up some dessert at the Muffin Corner."

Lucas looked into the bag. "What did you bring?"

"Strawberry shortcake."

The older man swore softly under his breath. "They

don't call Lester Kelly the cake man for nothing. You know," he continued in a normal tone, "I've cut down on dessert, but I'm certain Bryce will eat my share."

Odessa set the roasting pan on a rack in the oven, adjusted the temperature, and closed the door. "Bryce, please introduce your friends to Nate."

Bryce came to his feet and gave Nate a rough embrace. He was grinning from ear to ear. "Ladies, this is my brother, Nate. Nate, the one in the red is my girlfriend, Stacy Butler. And that's her sister, Amber."

Nate extended his hand, shaking hands with Stacy and Amber. He'd found both women attractive, but it dawned on him that he was more estranged from his family than he'd realized. Six months ago he'd finally gotten to know his niece and nephew, and now, for the first time, he was meeting a woman Bryce was dating. He'd missed his brother coming to him to talk about girls and maybe even ask his advice when it came to sex.

He'd stayed in his marriage much too long, and perhaps because of this he admired Stacy for breaking up with Bryce. It was obvious she hadn't condoned his behavior and she wasn't going to let him crash and burn, taking her with him. Nate had encountered women who continued to support their incarcerated boyfriends, husbands, and baby daddies even if they were serving multiple life sentences. He understood they didn't want to completely abandon the men they loved, but the downside was that these men were going to die in jail, and the women should begin planning their own future without them. If Stacy was going to be the catalyst who would help Bryce redirect his life, then Nate had to applaud her.

Odessa wiped her hands on a dish towel. "Why don't

you young folks go and sit on the back porch? It's going to be at least twenty minutes before we eat."

"Are you certain you don't need any help?" Nate asked. Unconsciously, he'd slipped back into the patterns of the past, when he'd ask his mother whether she needed help in the kitchen, especially on occasions when she'd complain that she felt tired after coming home from her position as a school nurse.

Odessa, in a completely unexpected gesture, stood on tiptoe and kissed his cheek. "Thank you for asking, but I have everything under control. And thanks for bringing dessert."

Not waiting for the others, Nate walked out of the kitchen and down a wide hallway that led to the back porch, plagued by emotions that swept him up in a maelstrom of confusion. He had become part of a family unit, even though he sometimes wanted to reject it because he felt he was being disloyal to his mother's memory.

He'd lost count of how many times he'd tried to imagine Manda's reaction to Odessa marrying her husband. Would she approve? Or would she think of it as an act of betrayal that while she lay dying her childhood friend was in her bed making love to her husband?

For years Nate had blamed Odessa, yet he knew his father shared equally in the blame. After all, he was married, and he had the audacity to fornicate under the same roof where he lived with his children. There was one thing he was certain of, and that was that Kim had never cuckolded him in their bed. She'd been forthcoming when she admitted to sleeping with her lovers in a small apartment she'd kept for her rendezvous in a less-than-desirable neighborhood in East L.A.

Nate slowed, waiting for Amber and Stacy to precede him out to the back porch. He sat on a cushioned love seat beside Amber and gave her a sidelong glance. Upon closer inspection he realized she was older than Stacy, who appeared closer to Bryce's age. There were tiny lines around her eyes and tightness at the corners of her mouth. Her fingers were bare, leading him to believe she wasn't married or engaged. There were other things he'd noticed about her. Amber's skin was reminiscent of a ripe peach, a pinkish gold. It was the perfect complement for her pale hair.

Bryce sat opposite them, his arm around Stacy's shoulders. "Hey, Nate, Stacy and I are going into the Cove to catch a movie afterward. Maybe you want to come along with Amber."

Suddenly it all made sense to Nate. It was obvious that Bryce had invited Amber to join the Shaws for dinner because he'd wanted to pair him up with his girlfriend's sister. "Sorry, bro. I have plans for later on tonight."

Amber leaned closer, pressing her shoulder to Nate's. "You don't remember me, do you?"

"No, I don't," he replied.

Amber gave him a wide grin. "That's where we differ, because there's no way I'd forget you. I was part of the press corps that covered your wedding."

Nate found himself temporarily mute. What were the odds that he would meet someone on Cavanaugh Island who'd attended his wedding? "Who do you write for?"

"I'm a freelance journalist. I have a syndicated column that appears in several papers across the country."

"Did you come here expecting me to give you an interview?"

Amber chewed her lip as if deep in thought. "Look, Nate, I'm going to be truthful. When Stacy called to tell me she'd reconciled with your brother, the name Shaw piqued my interest because I'd remembered that you were born on Cavanaugh Island. Even though she hadn't met you, Bryce told her you were once married to Kimberly Mason. And when she told me she was planning to eat with your parents I figured I'd tag along, hoping to get lucky."

"What do you mean by lucky?"

She leaned closer. "I'd like to interview you."

Nate was annoyed that his brother had attempted to set him up with a reporter looking for a story. "I'm sorry, but I don't give interviews."

Amber slumped back, folding her arms under her breasts. "Have you kept in touch with your ex-wife?"

Nate went still. He'd told Amber he didn't grant interviews, yet she'd persisted. "No comment."

"You're really going to make this difficult for me, aren't you, Nate?"

"It wouldn't be difficult if you respected my decision not to give interviews."

"Not even for family?"

"What are you talking about?"

"Isn't it obvious?" Amber whispered. "My sister told me she and Bryce are talking about getting married."

Nate didn't want to believe Bryce wanted to marry his girlfriend at this point in his life. He was still on probation; he could only leave the island if it was business related; he lived with his parents, and he had only recently begun to draw a regular paycheck. It wasn't a solid foundation on which to begin married life. However, whatever his brother decided, Nate knew he would have to support him.

"My answer would be the same."

"Are you always this stubborn?" Amber asked Nate.

He smiled. "I'm as stubborn as you are tenacious."

She rested a hand on his arm. "We'd make a good team if we decided to hook up. That is, unless—" Her words stopped abruptly when Lucas stuck his head through the partially opened door.

"Y'all come on in now."

Nate wasn't certain what Bryce had said to Amber about him, but his brother had to know he wouldn't talk to anyone about Kim. Even when Bryce had asked about her, he'd told him he didn't want to talk about his ex-wife.

He walked into the dining room, seated Amber, and then returned to the kitchen to help bring out the serving dishes. Glancing at the clock on the microwave, Nate estimated dinner would last a couple of hours, followed by coffee and dessert.

He knew it was customary to sit after dinner and talk, but this night he would break with tradition. Nate was not only waiting for Morgan to call him, he was also looking forward to seeing her again.

Chapter Ten

Sunday dinner at the Danes' had become a relaxed and somewhat festive affair. Rachel was teased because she claimed she didn't want to know her baby's sex, and she hadn't selected names for a boy or a girl. Irene said she'd dreamed of Rachel holding up a fish in each hand and, according to superstition, dreaming of fish translated into a pregnancy. And two fish was an indication that Rachel was carrying twins. All the talk about pregnancy and babies did little to assuage Morgan's unease, and once dinner concluded she breathed a sigh of relief, claiming she had work to do before meeting with a client the following day. Her assertion was truthful, because she'd promised Nate she would look at his apartment to offer decorating ideas.

Francine's vision continued to nag at Morgan as she stood on the porch watching the taillights of her parents' car disappear in the distance. She'd spent a restless night tossing and turning, dreaming about babies. Her friend's prediction had even hounded her at church, making it difficult to concentrate on the pastor's sermon, and she'd been so distracted during dinner that even her mother asked her if she was coming down with something. She'd reassured her mother that she was okay, and just had a lot on her mind. When Gussie asked what could be so absorbing that she had to repeat herself several times before Morgan heard her, her daughter offered everyone an update on the Angels Landing Plantation restoration. Both her parents warned her not to get in over her head, and said that if she needed help she should hire an assistant. She didn't need an assistant as much as she needed to purge her head of Francine's unsettling prediction, because having Nate's baby wasn't even a remote possibility. Becoming a mother was not on Morgan's wish list.

She reached into the back pocket of her jeans for her phone, then punched the speed dial for Nate's cell. He answered after the second ring, his low greeting caressing her ear. "How was Sunday dinner?" she asked.

"It was interesting."

"I can't wait to hear about it."

"How was yours?" Nate asked.

"Probably not as interesting as yours, but entertaining enough," Morgan replied, going inside the house, where she adjusted the thermostat for the air-conditioning and plucked her house keys out of a small sweetgrass basket on the parlor side table.

She smiled when his sensual chuckle came through the earpiece. "Are you ready for me to come and get you?"

Morgan locked the front door. "Forget about coming. I'm on my way. I'll be on foot."

"I'll meet you halfway."

"Nate—" Whatever she was going to say died on her lips when the cell phone signal faded. Morgan had decided to walk the short distance between her house and Shaw Woodworking. The building was a familiar landmark to anyone living in the Creek and to those who called Cavanaugh Island home. It was visible from the road leading directly into the Creek's business district.

It was the perfect night for a walk. The sweltering afternoon temperatures had dropped almost fifteen degrees, and a light wind coming off the ocean made it comfortable. Morgan had chided Nate about leaving the Creek to live elsewhere, when at one time she'd been equally guilty of occasionally entertaining the notion.

Whenever she traveled to another state or abroad, she tried to imagine living there permanently. But there was something about Cavanaugh Island that kept pulling her back. There were times when she understood what Al Pacino's character in *The Godfather Part III* meant when he said he was being pulled back in. Although not prone to bouts of sadness, Morgan realized she'd suffered from some form of melancholy the year she'd lived abroad. It was on the island where she felt alive, inspired.

She moved closer to the shoulder of the road with the sound of an approaching car, then stopped and waited for it to pass. The driver slowed, rolled down the driver's-side window, and waved to her. Rap music was blasting from his muscle car's speakers.

"Do you need a ride?" the young man with the colorful tattooed arms shouted over the cranked-up volume.

Morgan shook her head. "No, thanks," she said to the grandson of the man who owned one of the Creek's last remaining pig farms.

She wanted to tell the teenager that he'd better lower his music before entering Haven Creek. The mayor was a stern enforcer when it came to disturbing the Creek's quality of life. He'd persuaded the town council to pass a resolution prohibiting horn honking, except in cases of dire emergency, and loud music. Whether the music came from residences or vehicles, the consequence was the same: an initial warning followed by a hefty fine for the second offense.

She continued walking, and ten minutes into her walk she saw Nate in the distance. A smile parted her lips with his approach. He wore a white T-shirt, ripped jeans, and construction boots. Her stomach did a flip-flop when she noticed skin showing through the torn fabric. As he grew closer she saw the five o'clock shadow on his jaw, knowing Nate would have to shave every day to remain clean-shaven. Her gaze shifted to his forearms and bulging biceps, remembering the rock-hard, solid feel of his body pressed to hers when they'd danced together at the club.

Morgan didn't want to be this affected by Nate, but the way her body was reacting to the sight of him made it impossible not to be. Her pulse was racing, her stomach muscles were tight, and her throat was suddenly dry. Nate was a living, breathing work of art. He had it all: face, body, and brains. It was no wonder one of the world's most beautiful women had claimed him as her own, and Morgan knew that if Nate and Kim had had children they would have produced incredibly attractive offspring.

If he were food, he definitely would've been dessert: frothy, sweet, and best eaten slowly, while savoring every morsel, a feast of oral gratification.

Heat swept over Morgan's face and chest with her licentious musings. Either she'd been without a man for far too long or she was lusting after someone beyond her reach. Nate had laid out the ground rules: friendship only. Maybe it was good that he had established the limits for their association beforehand, if only to prove to Francine that her vision was wrong.

Nate extended his hand, taking Morgan's and pulling her to his side. Dipping his head, he kissed her cheek. "How are you?"

"Good."

"You look adorable." She wore a pair of skinny jeans, a tank top, and running shoes.

She laughed. "I look like I should be hanging out at the mall."

"I love seeing you dressed down. You appear less intimidating."

"Come on, now, I can't imagine you being intimidated by anyone."

He smiled at her. "Maybe I should've said you appear more relaxed."

"Do you think my clients would take me seriously if I dressed casually? It's very different for male architects. They can wear jeans and a hard hat and no one would think anything of it."

"Are you speaking from personal experience?"

There came a comfortable silence broken only by the sounds of birds and a rustling in the underbrush bordering the road. This was Nate's favorite time of the day, when every living thing on the island appeared to slow down to welcome the stillness and solitude that accompanied dusk. Vehicular traffic decreased, and people gathered on front and back porches to escape the heat that came from the kitchen, where they'd prepared Sunday dinner. It was also a time to relax and wind down from weekend activities in an attempt to prepare for the coming workweek. School was out, and that meant children could stay up far beyond their school-year curfews. Many of the older kids took either the causeway or the ferry to Charleston to party without having their eagle-eyed relatives monitoring them.

"I had a problem with a few male clients when I was first hired by Ellison and Murphy. I could've filed sexual harassment charges, but that probably would've derailed my career. When I approached the partners with what I was going through, they decided I would handle only their female clients from then on. It worked out well, because that's how I met Kara. She asked how long it would take for me to move up at the firm, and I told her about ten years. That's when she decided to commission me to oversee the restoration and preservation of Angels Landing Plantation. One of the conditions was that I had to resign my position at E and M and set up my own firm."

"Good for you." Nate gave her delicate fingers a gentle squeeze. "Talk about girl power."

Morgan glanced up at him, smiling. "You guys have the old boy's club, so we do whatever we can to help a sister out."

Slivers of waning sunlight coming through the canopy of trees slanted over Morgan's flawless dark skin. Nate felt as if he'd been punched in the gut when he looked at her face. He couldn't pull his gaze away. His physical attraction to Morgan was never more apparent than it was the night he'd come to her office. And if he hadn't been sitting at the drafting table, Morgan would've thought him no better than the male clients who had come on to her. Nate couldn't believe he'd waited to get to this age to find himself lusting after a woman. Even as an adolescent, he'd learned to control his urges.

"I promise not to sexually harass you," he said glibly.

Morgan made a sucking sound with her teeth. "I'm not worried about you, Nate."

His eyebrows shot up. "Why would you say that?"

"I doubt if you'd risk dishonoring your family's name by getting arrested for harassing a woman on the island."

"You're right, Mo. I would never bring that kind of disgrace on my family."

"By the way, how is Bryce doing?" she asked, deftly shifting the conversation to a safer topic. She didn't want to talk about their relationship.

"He's okay. He's working with me now."

"How did you get him to do that?"

He eased Morgan off the road when he heard a car coming from behind them. They stood closely together under the trees until it passed. "I told him he had two options. Either straighten up or I was going to call his probation officer and have him violated."

Morgan gave him a wide-eyed stare. "You would've done that?"

Nate nodded. "I wasn't issuing an idle threat. His reckless behavior was also affecting my father and stepmother." *Stepmother.* It was the first time he'd uttered the word aloud. In the past it had always been "Odessa" or "my father's wife." "I remind him constantly that his actions have consequences. He could spend the next two years of his life behind bars for one mistake. It's not that hard to do the right thing, Mo."

"You make it sound simple."

He frowned at her. "You must think I'm a monster."

"It's not that."

"Then what is it?" he shot back.

"For you it's, like, all or nothing. Don't you leave room for compromise?" Morgan asked.

"Compromise is for business deals, not for people's lives or their futures. If my father had died from a stroke as a result of Bryce going to jail, it would've impacted all of us, especially Gregory and Gabrielle, who worship the ground their grandfather walks on. It's not just about Bryce and what he wants, so if I have to play bully badass to keep him out of jail, then I'll do whatever I have to do."

Silence descended on them again, and Nate wondered if what he'd said to Morgan would affect their working relationship. He wasn't as concerned about their professional relationship as he was about their personal friendship. He hadn't wanted to lie to her about Bryce. There were times when he'd had to threaten or intimidate his brother, but it was for Bryce's benefit.

There were also occasions when Nate had wanted to lash out or confront his father about what he'd witnessed between him and Odessa, but something wouldn't permit him to do it. He'd kept all his hurt inside, where it'd festered for years, nearly eating him alive. As he matured he realized he should've confronted Lucas instead of living with the demons that wouldn't allow him to trust anyone.

Crossing the road, Nate led Morgan along the path leading to the workshop. Several hundred feet away stood the newly erected barn. Working alone to put up the struc-

ture had offered him the solitude he needed to begin the
process of healing and forgiveness. The day he finished
putting on the roof, he carved a plaque with words from
one of his favorite books of poetry: *Between Tears and
Laughter* by Alden Nowlan. He wasn't certain where it
would hang, but it was a constant reminder of how far
he'd come in his quest for maturity.

"Why do you keep that old wagon and pickup truck on
the property?" Morgan asked as he punched in the security code, unlocking the door.

"My great-grandfather used that wagon to haul the
wood that had come from the mainland. The pickup belonged to my grandfather. It was built in 1947 and is
considered a classic. If you look closely you can see the
words *Shaw Woodworking* painted on the doors."

"I suppose you keep them here as a reminder of where
you've come from."

Nate stepped inside the air-cooled cabin and punched
in another code to disarm the security system. Track
lighting illuminated the space, making it as bright as day-
light. "The first time I mentioned getting rid of them, my
father went ballistic. I think I was around eight at the
time, but I still remember it." He smiled when he saw
Morgan run her fingertips over one of the half-finished
pieces. She caressed it lovingly, and it filled him with
pride that she understood his passion, because that was
something his ex-wife never appreciated.

Morgan stared at the workshop's many built-in shelves,
from which hung every conceivable carpentry tool. The
room also contained a large wooden table with benches
on either side, sawhorses, cans of paint and varnish, and

finished chairs, tables, and cabinets affixed with tags bearing the names of those who'd ordered the pieces. She noticed a small refrigerator, a table with a microwave, and door in a far corner with a sign indicating a restroom.

"You have a lot of space here. It looks to be about fifteen hundred square feet."

Nate met her gaze. "You've got a good eye. It's exactly fifteen hundred square feet. My father expanded it to twice its original size because we didn't have enough room to store the wood we wanted to keep on hand."

Pushing her hands into the pockets of her jeans, Morgan walked over to a large piece of reddish wood resting on a pair of sawhorses. "The wood smells wonderful."

"It's like an aphrodisiac," Nate said as he moved next to her.

Her jaw dropped when she realized what she was staring at. It had to be one of the doors to the replica of the eighteenth-century French armoire Nate had mentioned. "May I touch it?" She couldn't disguise the awe in her voice.

"Of course."

The wood was cool under her fingertips. "How long did it take to bring out the patina?" she asked, rubbing her bare arms as the cool air raised goose bumps on her flesh.

"Are you cold, baby?"

It was the fourth time Nate had called her baby, and Morgan shrugged it off as a slip of the tongue. "A little."

Wrapping his arms around Morgan's waist, Nate pulled her back against his body. "This is my dad's project. The client wanted cherrywood, so we knew the wood had to be padauk. It's an exotic wood that's bright orange when freshly cut, but later oxidizes to a darker, rich, purple-brown over time."

Morgan tried not to react to the warmth of the hard body molded to hers, wondering if Nate was aware of what he was doing. "The grain is slightly wavy." She had to say something, anything, in an attempt to ignore the pleasurable sensations coursing through her.

"It's called interlocking, and that's what makes it difficult to work with. The dust from this type of wood can pose a health risk to carpenters. It can cause respiratory problems, swelling of the eyelids, and itching if precautions aren't taken beforehand."

Looking over her shoulder, her gaze met and fused with Nate's. "How would you know that if it's first time you worked with it?"

"Before I work with unfamiliar wood I read everything I can about it. The Shaws have an unwritten rule that everyone must wear long sleeves, protective eyewear, and dust masks. We keep it cool here year-round to preserve the wood." He dropped his arms. "Come with me next door. I can assure you it's a lot warmer there."

He was right. The barn was warmer than the workshop. The first floor consisted of an open space abutting a built-in shed. Nate said the shed would be used to store lumber. There were workstations fitted with grinders, sanders, chisels, vises, and clamps. An industrial vacuum sat in a corner among at least a half dozen sawhorses.

"How many windows did you install?" she asked, glancing upward.

"Seventeen in total. The plans came with or without horse stalls."

"And you opted for the one without the stalls."

"Not having the stalls gives us more work space. And even if I raised horses I couldn't see myself sleeping under the same roof with them."

Morgan scrunched up her nose. "Don't like the smell of horseflesh and hay?" she said teasingly.

"Nope. Remember when the Creek had a lot of pig and chicken farms? Whenever the wind blew everyone had to close their windows."

She shuddered noticeably. "Please don't remind me. That's when the smell of salt water was like an expensive perfume."

"Come upstairs with me and I'll show you the apartment."

Nate opened a French-style door leading to a staircase and cedar balcony. Morgan was impressed with the design and layout of the building because of the separation of the barn and the residence. There was a set of French doors at the end of the balcony leading into an expansive living and dining space. Her mind was churning with ideas about how to decorate the area. Nate stopped in the middle of what would become the living room as she made her way into the kitchen. She'd counted nine windows, three spanning the width of the balcony and six running the length of the living room to the kitchen. Nothing excited her more than decorating a residence flooded with natural light.

The black-and-white kitchen, with its double stainless steel sinks, dishwashers, ovens, microwave, and an island with a cooktop and grill, was a chef's dream. The pantry, utility closet, and laundry room were concealed behind louvered doors. She opened the sliding glass doors leading out to a deck with a cedar railing. The vistas were spectacular, offering an unobstructed view of the island and the steeples of the many churches dotting Charleston's landscape. To the left of the deck was the staircase that led to the first floor.

Morgan continued exploring Nate's apartment, opening the door to a bathroom with a shower, vanity, and commode, a smaller bedroom that could be used as a guest bedroom or home office, and a master bedroom with an adjoining full bathroom and a wall of walk-in closets. Selecting furnishings for the apartment was certain to become an interior decorator's dream.

Leaning against the wall separating the living room from the master bedroom, Nate gave her a hopeful look. "What do you think?"

"I'll do it."

"You'll do it," he repeated.

Her dimples winked at him. "Yes."

Morgan wasn't given time to react before Nate swung her up, holding her above his head as if she weighed no more than a small child. "Please, Nate! Put me down."

His response to her desperate plea was to spin her around while singing the theme to *Rocky,* "Gonna Fly Now."

"Now!" she screamed.

"Don't worry, baby. I'm not going to drop you." He spun her around several more times, then slowly lowered her until her feet touched the floor at the same time he brushed his mouth over hers, deepening the kiss until her lips parted under his. When the kiss ended, he kissed her again, this time on the forehead.

Morgan was certain Nate could feel the runaway beating of her heart against his chest. "Don't ever do that again."

"Pick you up or kiss you?"

"Both."

"But I wanted to thank you."

"What are you thanking me for?" she asked.

"For agreeing to decorate my place."

She shook her head. "Kisses fall into the benefits category."

"Not to me. It's a perk."

"Perks and benefits are one and the same."

"A benefit is payment or a subsidy, while a perk is an incentive, privilege, or even a freebie."

Her lips twisted with a cynical smile. "You made that up."

"No, I didn't." The warmth of Nate's smile was reflected in his voice. "Anyone with a degree in business knows that."

"Well, I happen not to have a business degree."

"Well, I do," he countered.

"You don't have to be so smug about it."

"I'm not smug, baby. I just know I'm not going to be the one to break our friends-without-benefits agreement."

"So what about that kiss?" She slapped his arm playfully.

"That doesn't count."

Morgan rested her hands at her hips. "Put up or shut up."

Cupping his ear, Nate gave her a wide grin. "Oh," he drawled facetiously. "Do I hear a challenge?"

"Bam!" she retorted, holding her hand in front of his face. "Yes, you do!"

Nate captured her wrist. "Why don't you concede now?"

"You want me to give up?"

Staring deeply into her eyes, he nodded slowly. "Either you give up now or suffer the humiliation of defeat."

Morgan narrowed her eyes as she looked up at the man she'd spent years fantasizing about; the man she'd wanted to introduce her to a world of sexual pleasure; the man who still had the power to make her heart beat fast. She wanted to beg him to make love to her the same way an addict pleads for a fix.

"What constitutes defeat?"

"The repeal of our agreement and..."

"And what, Nate?" she asked when his words stopped.

"We become friends *with* benefits."

She laughed, the sound bubbling up from her throat. "It's only been two days. Why are you changing your mind?"

Nate released her wrist. "There's something about you that makes me crazy. You're beautiful, intelligent, sexy, and you make me laugh. Going to the Happy Hour with you told me I could have a normal friendship with a woman. I'd only agreed not to sleep with you because that's what you want."

"I said that because I don't want sex without dating."

"Is that what you want, Mo? You want me to date you?"

She closed her eyes for several seconds. Why did he make it sound as if he was going to do her favor? "I can't afford to get caught up and get so involved with you that I'll lose focus on the restoration project."

"That doesn't have to happen."

"Because you say so?" she asked. "I've waited a long time for something like this to come along, and having a sexual relationship with you will complicate things. Remember we have to work together, and if we break up we'll still have to interact with each other. You know that will be uncomfortable."

"Why are you putting up roadblocks even before you give me a chance to prove that I want to date you and only you? It's not about sleeping with you as much as it is getting to know you better, to see where things could lead." A wry smile twisted his mouth. "There will be no other women, I promise, Mo."

A beat passed. Resting her hands over Nate's heart, she leaned into him. "Okay, but it has to be on my terms. Which, by the way, are nonnegotiable."

Staring at her under lowered lids, Nate said, "What are your terms?"

"*If* there comes a time when we do sleep together, you *must* use protection." Francine's baby prediction had become a permanent tattoo on Morgan's brain. "And if we decide to end it there can't be any histrionics."

Nate successfully curbed the urge to laugh at Morgan. Since becoming sexually active, there wasn't a time when he hadn't used protection, except when he was with his wife. He also wasn't opposed to an amicable split. "That's easy. Is there anything else, boss lady?" He did laugh when she wouldn't meet his eyes.

"That's it."

"That's it," he repeated. "All wrapped up with pretty paper and a bow."

"I'd like to believe we're being very adult about everything."

"Adult or anal, Morgan?"

"Adult," she insisted. "We live in the same town and

will be working together on several projects, so I think it's important we establish the ground rules beforehand."

Nate saw Morgan in a whole new light. She exhibited a maturity usually not seen in a woman her age. Establishing the ground rules was something he and Kim had neglected to do, and in the end it was as if they couldn't agree on anything.

"It is very important." His arms went around her waist. "You're quite the businesswoman—"

"Businessperson, Nate."

He inclined his head. "I stand corrected."

"I'll forgive you this time, baby."

Attractive lines spread out around Nate's eyes when he smiled. "So now I'm your baby?"

"Don't you play yourself, Nate. I should've called you on it the first time you called me baby."

An expression of unadulterated innocence crossed his features. "I did?"

"Yes, you did, and you know it. Do you call every woman baby?"

"Nah," he drawled, winking at her. "Just the ones I like."

Morgan patted his stubble. "Enough talk about who likes who. I need you to think about how you want to decorate your house. Do you plan to paint the walls and ceilings? And what style of furniture, rugs, and artwork do you prefer?"

Nate studied Morgan, unable to believe she could go from talking about their sleeping together to furniture and knickknacks. But she had reminded him more than once of remaining focused. "I don't know," he said. "You make the selections and I'll let you know if I like them."

Pushing against his chest, she forced him to release her. "Okay. I need to know if you want it to look like a bachelor pad or if you would prefer a style that's more family-oriented."

He lifted his shoulders under his T-shirt. "Family sounds good."

Morgan crossed her arms under her breasts, bringing Nate's gaze to the soft swell of flesh rising above the neckline of her top. "Do you have a budget for what you want to spend?"

"No."

"Not even an estimate?"

"Nope."

She exhaled an audible breath. "You're not making this easy for me." A beat passed as they stared at each other. "Did you make any modifications to the blueprints?"

"Not structurally," Nate replied. He'd built a half bath with a slop sink next to the shed and installed soundproofing throughout the entire first floor.

"I'll need to see the prints to verify the dimensions. I've downloaded a design program and decorating catalogs on my computer, so all I have to do is click and drag the furnishings and accessories onto the floor plans. I should have several of them completed in a couple of weeks."

Nate nodded. "I'd like to be in a bed by the end of the summer." Right now he was sleeping on an air mattress, which he stored in the walk-in closet along with several changes of clothes.

"I'll work up the bedroom first." Morgan lowered her arms, glancing at her watch. "I'd better get home. I have a breakfast meeting tomorrow."

"After I get you the blueprints, I'll drive you home."

* * *

As promised, Nate drove Morgan home. They stood together on the porch, his arm braced over her head as she leaned against the door frame. "When am I going to see you again?"

Morgan lowered her eyes, staring at his chest. "Wednesday. I'll call you after I return from my bike ride and invite you over for breakfast. Which do you prefer? American or continental?"

He moved closer, her moist breath feathering over his throat. "Come on now, Mo. I'm Gullah. You shouldn't have to ask me that."

"American," she said in singsong.

His large hands cradled her face, holding it gently as his head came down as if in slow motion. Nate's lips brushed against Morgan's. He continued to nibble at her lips as if she were freshly whipped sweet cream until the sound of scratching shattered the quiet. His head came up and he saw Rasputin with his front paws pressed on the window screen.

"Pardon the pun, but Rasputin is a Peeping Tom."

Morgan giggled. "He knows I usually give him his snack around this time." She kissed Nate's chin. "Good night. I'll call you," she said over her shoulder as she walked to the door.

Nate stared at her retreating back. Despite his bad luck in the past, he looked forward to dating Morgan. He hoped this time would be different.

Chapter Eleven

❧

Morgan was relieved when Francine called to cancel their bike ride. She wanted to sleep in late. The Beauty Box's summer hours were now in effect, so the unisex salon and spa was closed on Sundays and Mondays. Most of the businesses on the island kept summer hours, too, because of the extreme heat, and were closed between the hours of twelve and two.

Sitting at the makeup table in a corner of her bedroom and wielding a sable makeup brush, Morgan applied a light dusting of powder to her face. Adjusting the light coming from the tiny bulbs circling the mirror, she looked closely at her handiwork. Eyeliner and mascara brought out her eyes, and a coral lip gloss accentuated her mouth. Using her fingertips, she fluffed up her short curls. Standing, she walked over to the walk-in closet, selecting a long, loose-fitting slip dress in coral and a pair of straw-colored espadrilles. When she'd gotten up earlier that morning and turned on the television, the meteorologist had predicted temperatures in the midnineties. Morgan decided not to wear her usual office attire, which consisted of a pencil skirt or tailored slacks with her ubiquitous stilettos. She added a pair of silver hoop earrings and three matching bracelets, completing her bohemian look for her breakfast meeting with Kara.

Rasputin lounged near the closet, staring at her feet. "Yes, baby, I'm going out." Whenever she put on her shoes, the cat would eye her with what Morgan interpreted as contempt because she was leaving him alone. The cat meowed softly. "When Mama comes home for lunch she'll play with you for a while." Instead of eating in the office, she would come home for the two-hour island-wide siesta.

Picking up a straw tote, Morgan checked to see if she had her keys. Rasputin followed her to the door, his plaintive meows continuing even after she'd closed and locked it. In that instant she wondered if she should get another cat to keep her pet company. Then she thought about what Nate had said about his sister's cat. Maybe she would ask Sharon if Rasputin could visit with her cat so she could see if he was able to get along with another of his species.

Getting into her truck, she backed out from under the carport and headed for Sanctuary Cove.

Punching a button, she increased the cool air flowing through the Cadillac's vents. It wasn't officially summer, but the temperature didn't reflect that. The numbers on the dashboard displayed an outside temperature of eighty-eight degrees, and it was only 7:40 in the morning. There were days when as a child she would spend most of the day at the beach, cooling off in the water. She smiled. The beach was the perfect place to relax after she closed the office.

Morgan and Kara had agreed to meet at least once a month to confer about the progress of the restoration. Kara and Jeff had gone up to Myrtle Beach for what they called a mini-honeymoon. Jeff wanted to wait until after the fall elections before he took his bride away on an extended honeymoon to somewhere exotic. The newlyweds divided their time between Jeff's grandmother's house and a guesthouse at Angels Landing. This morning she would meet Kara at Corrine Hamilton's house.

She drove along the road connecting Haven Creek to Angels Landing, then maneuvered onto the new two-lane road connecting the Landing with the Cove. Morgan and practically everyone else on Cavanaugh Island had breathed a collective sigh of relief once the county had built the road connecting the two towns. Very few were brave or foolish enough to travel on the foot trails, which were surrounded by swamps filled with poisonous snakes, alligators, and quicksand.

Local environmentalists opposed the draining of the swamp because it would upset the ecological balance, yet after years of debate they were willing to compromise. The South Carolina Department of Transportation drained enough to build the road without disturbing the wildlife's natural habitat. It had taken Morgan a good three months after the road was paved to get over her fear of seeing a snake or a gator.

She entered the town of Sanctuary Cove. Many of the businesses along Main Street were closed, with the exception of the supermarket. She drove past the bookstore and the Muffin Corner, slowing and rolling down the window. She waved to Lester, who was hosing down the sidewalk outside the bakeshop. "Good morning, Lester," she called out. He glanced up, smiling.

"Mornin', Mo," the pastry chef called back.

Raising the window, she turned onto the road leading to Waccamaw Road. A few of the older residents were sitting on rockers on their porches, catching the morning air before the heat chased them indoors. When her grandfather was alive, a lot of the older folks were reluctant to install air-conditioning units in their homes. Ceiling or box fans were enough for them. That all changed when eight elderly residents died from dehydration after a heat wave that lasted more than a month. An island-wide fund-raiser produced enough money to purchase air-conditioning units for any island resident over the age of seventy who couldn't afford to buy one. The electricity in a few of the homes had to be updated to accommodate the additional wattage.

Morgan parked in front of a house with white vinyl siding and dark green shutters. Corrine Hamilton sat on the front porch reading a newspaper. She set the newspaper on a side table and rose to her feet with Morgan's approach.

"Good morning, Miss Corrine," Morgan said. The seventysomething former school principal was still a very attractive woman. She was tall and slender, with smooth skin the color of café au lait and short silver curls. The Yorkshire terrier sharing the rocker with Corrine raised his head briefly, stared at Morgan, and then rested his muzzle on his front paws.

"Good morning to you, too," Corrine said with a warm smile. "Look at you." She patted her own curls. "We have the same hairdo."

Morgan nodded before leaning forward to hug Jeff's grandmother and kiss her soft cheek. "How have you been?"

Corrine met a pair of eyes as dark as her own. "Can't complain. Jeffrey's married and Kara is the granddaughter I always prayed for. Go on in. You'll find her in the kitchen."

Morgan opened the screen door and walked into the house, where everything appeared to be in its place. Throw pillows were positioned at the correct angle, table-tops and wood floors were spotless, and mouthwatering aromas wafted in from the kitchen.

She stood at the entrance to the modern kitchen, watching Kara as she cracked eggs with one hand. The newlywed's usual tawny complexion was several shades darker. "I'm impressed."

Kara turned, her hazel eyes shimmering with amusement. She'd pulled her shoulder-length hair into a pony-tail. Light from a hanging fixture reflected off the diamonds in the engagement ring and wedding band on her left hand. "I learned that trick from watching the cooking shows." Wiping her hands on a towel, Kara came over and hugged Morgan. "You look so cool in that dress."

"If you don't have to go out, then don't. The weather's brutal."

Kara pulled the oversized T-shirt she was wearing away from her chest. "I've been wearing Jeff's tees because my shorts and slacks are too tight. Please sit down." Waiting until Morgan pulled out a chair and sat at the kitchen table, she went back to cracking eggs.

Morgan noticed a mysterious smile playing at the corners of the former New York City social worker's mouth.

Kara had come to Cavanaugh Island after the reading of her late father's will and never left. She'd been as shocked as everyone to discover she was the biological daughter of Taylor Patton. The late owner of Angels Landing Plantation had left his secret love child the historic house, two thousand acres of prime property, money, and worldly goods worth millions. However, Kara's unexpected fortune had come with a proviso: She was required to make Angels Landing her legal residence for five years and restore the property to its original condition. Not only had Kara stayed, she fell in love with the island's sheriff and married him after a whirlwind courtship.

"What aren't you saying, Kara?"

"Jeff and I are expecting our first baby early next year. We decided to start trying before the wedding because we're both getting older and want to have another child soon."

Morgan nodded. So that's why Kara had mentioned her too-tight slacks and shorts. "Congratulations to the both of you."

Kara shared Morgan's smile. "Thank you."

"Jeff disappointed a lot of the single women around here when he announced he was marrying you."

"I'm sorry about that. But not really," Kara said quickly, grinning from ear to ear. "He grew up here, went away, and then came back to live. What's the expression? 'When you're slow you blow'? It's apparent they were slow, so when I realized that he was one of those special men you don't meet every day, I knew I wanted to spend the rest of my life with him."

"He's one of the good guys. Even though we didn't grow up in the same town, I've never heard anything bad about him. His high school record of sacking opposing teams' quarterbacks still hasn't been broken to this day."

"He rarely talks about that. If I have to be jealous of anything, then it's the Marine Corps. Hardly a day goes by when one or two of his buddies don't call him. They were planning a getaway for the Labor Day weekend until I told him about the baby. I insisted he go, but he claims he doesn't want to leave me alone until after I give birth." Kara shook her head. "I don't understand men, Morgan. I'm going to need him more *after* the baby than before."

"You're lucky you have Miss Corrine."

"Gram is a gem. I think she was more excited than Jeff when I told her about the baby. Enough about me. What about you, Morgan? Are you still seeing David?"

Morgan gave Kara a prolonged stare. "Why does everyone think I'm going with David?"

Kara returned the stare, her gold-green eyes appearing lighter in her sun-browned face. "Didn't you guys come to my wedding together?"

"Yes, but we're just friends. Don't get me wrong, Kara. David is a wonderful catch, but he's still hung up on his ex."

"I thought he was over her."

"No; he's still hurt by the situation. Besides, I'm just not interested in him in that way."

"What if you saw each other as friends?"

Morgan already had a male friend: Nathaniel Shaw. "I don't think that would work."

"You don't want to get married?"

"I'm not saying I don't want to be married or have children."

"What *are* you saying?" Kara asked.

"It can't be now," she replied after a pregnant pause. Morgan thought about her wish list. "I have too many things I'd like to accomplish before becoming a wife and mother."

"I'm going to say what you just told me about Jeff. David is one of the good guys. And I'm not saying that because he's Jeff's cousin."

"When are you and Jeff going to tell everyone about the baby?" Morgan asked, smoothly changing the topic.

"We're waiting until the Island Fair, and then we'll make the announcement."

The annual island-wide celebration began July 1 and ended with a spectacular fireworks show at midnight on July 4. The carnival-like events included amusement park rides, picnics, and fun and games for all ages.

"How are you feeling?" Morgan asked Kara.

"Other than having a rapidly expanding waistline and feeling hungry twenty-four seven, I'm okay. Jeff has threatened to handcuff me to the bed because I get up in the middle of the night to raid the refrigerator. One night he came home during his dinner break to find me sitting in front of the fridge with the doors open, eating left-overs."

Morgan laughed until she had to hold her ribs. "You're worse than my sister Rachel. Her doctor told her to stop eating ice cream sundaes because there's no more room for the baby to grow and that's why she's so uncomfortable."

"Some women crave pickles and ice cream, but I crave watermelon. If there's no watermelon in the fridge, I literally have a meltdown."

"How is Jeff taking impending fatherhood?"

"I believe he's going to be certifiably crazy by the time I give birth. He went to the Parlor Bookstore and bought every book on pregnancy and babies Deborah Monroe had in stock. He rolled his eyes at me when I asked him if he planned to deliver his own son or daughter."

"What do you want? A girl or a boy?"

Kara turned on the cold water faucet as she diced onions. "It doesn't matter. Personally, I would love to have twins."

"Do twins run in your family?"

"I don't remember my mother talking about twins on her side of the family. I know you mentioned researching the shared histories of the black and white Pattons. Did you find any evidence of twins on either side?" she asked Morgan.

"Not yet. I'm still collecting slave bills of sale, records of property ownership, and estate inventories. It will take a while before I get around to checking birth and census records."

Over a leisurely breakfast of spinach omelets, fresh melon, and corn muffins, Morgan and Kara chatted comfortably about Angels Landing. She told her Nate had agreed to re-create the slave village, including the winnowing barns and blacksmith workshop. She also gave her an update on the problem she'd had with the discontinued wallpaper patterns.

"I'm going to stop by Angels Landing after I leave here to check with the project manager. He says it's going to take time stripping the paper because he doesn't want to damage the walls. Even though I'm looking to complete the restoration in three to five years, I still don't want him to milk us with cost overruns."

Peering at Morgan over the rim of a glass of freshly squeezed orange juice, Kara took a deep swallow. "Didn't you tell me he came highly recommended?"

"Yes, I did. But when people see dollar signs, the greedy gene takes over. I'm glad David suggested you include the termination-at-will clause in his contract. If his workers are slacking off, then he's at risk for losing his job." Morgan dabbed the corners of her mouth with her napkin. "Maybe Bobby Nugent needs a little shake-up. I'm going to ask Nate if he would act as an inspector."

Kara's fork was poised in midair. "Isn't he a carpenter?"

Morgan smiled. "He's more than a carpenter." She told Kara about the barn. "I'll call and ask him if he's willing to meet me at Angels Landing tomorrow morning."

"What are you going to do if Bobby's been purposefully slowing down?"

"I'll fire him on the spot," Morgan replied.

Kara stared, wide-eyed, at the architect. "Who will you get to replace him?"

"Me. That is, until I can find someone qualified to fill the position. I'll be at Angels Landing every morning around seven thirty to monitor who's on time and who's late. The workers are paid to begin working at eight. They're entitled to a lunch hour, two ten-minute breaks— one in the morning and another in the afternoon—and are scheduled to work until four. If I have to install a time clock for them to punch in and out, then I will."

"Come on, Morgan. It's not that critical."

"Yes it is, Kara. My reputation is on the line here. You're paying me to fulfill the conditions stated in your father's will. Stripping wallpaper isn't like restoring the ceiling and frescoes of the Sistine Chapel."

Kara held up both hands. "I'm out of this. Do whatever you have to do."

Morgan nodded. "Thank you."

Kara pushed back her chair, rising to her feet. "Do you want coffee or tea?"

"Can you make iced coffee?"

"Sure, I'll make you some. I've sworn off coffee, tea, pop, and of course anything alcoholic. It's just fruit juice, water, and milk."

"Think of how healthy you and your baby will be," Morgan said.

"Now you sound like Jeff."

Morgan stood up and began clearing the table. "I brought my laptop with me so I can show you the wallpaper samples. I need you to tell me which ones you like so I can order the quantities I need for each room before they're discontinued."

"We'll look at them in the sunroom."

Morgan entered M. Dane Architecture and Interior Design through the rear door. The soft chiming of a bell alerted the receptionist that someone had come in. Seconds later, Samara Lambert appeared in the open doorway to Morgan's private office. In deference to the heat, Samara had brushed her shoulder-length brown hair off her face, holding it in place with a red-and-white striped headband. With her freshly scrubbed face and white sundress, banded with candy-cane stripes at the hem, she looked as if she were in her early twenties rather than her midthirties. A pair of red ballet flats completed her look.

Samara's lips parted in a knowing smile. "I know I

look like a little girl, but this is the coolest thing I could find in my closet. It's one of my matching mother-daughter dresses."

Morgan placed her tote on a chair. "You look adorable, Sam."

"That's exactly what Nelson said to me before he left for work this morning." Pulling a crumpled tissue from her pocket, Samara dabbed the back of her neck. "And you look like the princess of cool."

"I had to search my closet to find this dress."

"I nearly melted before I got here. The air went out in my car last night and I had to drive from the Creek with all the windows rolled down." There were red splotches on Samara's pale cheeks.

"You can't drive around in this weather without air-conditioning," Morgan said.

"I know. I left the car at the service station, and one of the mechanics told me he's going to try to get to it today. If not, then it won't be until tomorrow."

Walking over to the thermostat, Morgan lowered the temperature so more cool air would flow through the vents. "Are we scheduled to see anyone today?"

Samara shook her head. "No, but a messenger delivered an envelope before you walked in."

"Maybe we'll—" The doorbell chimed, interrupting Morgan.

Samara turned on her heels. "Let me see who that is."

Morgan sat down at her desk, picking up several letters. She noted the return address on the envelope that had been hand-delivered. It was from Sullivan, Webster, Matthews and Sullivan. She opened the envelope and read the cover letter, signed by David. He wanted Nate to go over the enclosed contract, sign it, and return it to him within ten days.

Samara returned, handing Morgan a single sheet of paper. "Someone from the mayor's office delivered this."

Morgan scanned it quickly. It was a power-outage alert, warning businesses to conserve energy until further notice. The power company planned to have rolling brownouts to prevent a potential island-wide blackout. There was also a recommendation that businesses extend their midday siestas by two additional hours until further notice.

Her head popped up. "Instead of closing between twelve and two, we'll have to remain closed from twelve until four."

An expression of panic crossed Samara's face. "That means I'll only get two work hours."

"Don't worry about it, Sam," Morgan said, in an attempt to put her at ease. "Your pay will remain the same, and you'll get to spend more time with your children."

"What are you going to do?"

"Any calls that come into the office will be forwarded to my cell."

"How long do you think this is going to last?" Samara asked.

Morgan remembered the last time the island lost electricity. It was during a thunderstorm earlier that spring. The power had gone out and wasn't restored until late the following morning. She wasn't affected because she'd had a backup generator. The year Cavanaugh Island was hit hard from a series of tropical storms, many of the island's residents bought generators.

"I don't know, but I prefer brownouts to blackouts.

Why don't you pack up and go home? After I make a few calls, I'm also leaving."

Excitement shimmered in Samara's brown eyes. "Are you sure?"

"You can stay if you want, but after I finish what I have to do I'm going to the beach."

"I'm gone!" Samara shouted as she rushed to put her desk in order. "I'll see you tomorrow."

"Don't you need a ride?" Morgan called after her.

"I'm going to call Nelson and have him pick me up."

Morgan waited for Samara to leave, locked the front door, and then turned its sign around so that the CLOSED side faced the street. She reprogrammed the telephones to go to her cell. Slipping the contract into her tote bag, she adjusted the air-conditioning, turned off all the lights, and locked the rear door.

Outside, the heat hit her as though she had opened the door to a blast furnace, and the humidity wrapped around her like a weighted blanket. Although Morgan was used to the Lowcountry's subtropical climate, temperatures between ninety-five and one hundred degrees in June were not the norm.

She got into her vehicle, started the engine, and rolled down the windows, waiting for the interior to cool enough to drive off. Reaching for her phone, she punched the speed dial for Nate's cell. It rang four times.

"Hey, baby."

Morgan smiled. "Hello, Nate."

"What's up?"

"I'm calling to let you know I'm going to drop off your contract. David says he has to have it back within ten days."

"I won't be there."

Her smile faded. Was Nate about to renege on their agreement? "Why not?"

"Right now I'm sitting in the airport. I'm on standby, waiting for a flight to L.A. My former business partner's sister called to tell me he was shot when someone jacked him for his bike."

Morgan bit her lip. "Is he all right?"

"All I know is he's in the ICU."

"Oh, no."

"I'm not certain how long I'm going to be away. As soon as I find out where I'll be staying, I'll text you the address. Overnight the contract to me. I'll sign it and overnight it back to you."

"Thank you, Nate."

His chuckle caressed her ear. "There's no need to thank me, Mo. I gave you my word."

"I suppose I needed to hear it again."

"Why? Don't you trust me?"

"Of course I trust you." Her voice had gone up an octave.

"Hold on, Mo. They just called my name. I think I have a seat. Gotta go."

"Okay. Have a safe flight."

"Thanks. Bye, baby."

"Bye," she whispered.

Shifting into gear, Morgan maneuvered out of the parking lot. Mixed feelings surged through her. She felt a sense of loss at knowing Nate was leaving. When had she begun to lean on him? He'd questioned whether she trusted him, and somehow, despite being away from each other's lives for more than two decades, she did.

Chapter Twelve

Nate walked into the hospital room, stopping abruptly when he saw Dwight Wickham sitting up in bed. The machines monitoring his vitals were gone, leaving only the IV taped to the back of his hand.

"Well, look at you."

Dwight extended a fist, smiling when Nate gave it a bump. "I'm baaack."

His friend had spent the past eleven days in a medically induced coma to bring down the swelling where a small-caliber bullet had lodged in his brain. Nate had promised Dwight's sister he would stay in L.A. until the neurosurgeon deemed it time to reverse the coma.

Jacqueline had called him, hysterical, when she'd discovered Dwight lying unconscious in his driveway, his top-of-the-line BMW motorcycle missing. She'd apologized, saying she'd called Nate because Dwight had listed him as a secondary contact in the event of a medical emergency.

Sitting on the chair at the foot of the bed, Nate stared at Dwight. Not only were they friends and former business partners, they were also kindred spirits, sharing the same birth date. His friend always joked about being born in the wrong decade, because he would've loved living as a hippie. But that didn't stop him from looking like one: full salt-and-pepper beard, waist-length ponytail, tie-dyed shirts, and bell-bottoms.

"How are you feeling?"

Dwight's left hand trembled slightly when he reached up to touch his bandaged head. "Except for a bitch of a headache, I'm good. You know the SOBs cut my hair and beard? It took me more than twenty years to get it that long."

Crossing one leg over the opposite knee, Nate leaned back in the uncomfortable chair, where he'd spent hours watching Dwight hooked up to beeping machines. He'd told Jacqueline he wanted to be there when her brother woke up.

"It'll grow back, DW." He didn't want to tell the eccentric self-made millionaire that he'd looked like a homeless person with his long hair and unkempt beard.

"I'll have to see what I look like with a shaved head before I decide whether to grow it back. Women claim men with bald heads are sexy." He flopped back against the pillows cradling his shoulders. "I don't know why, but I feel as if I've lost twelve years of my life rather than twelve days."

"You're alive, DW. That's all that matters."

"If they'd wanted the damn bike I would've given it to them. In fact, I would've taken them to the dealer and bought both of the bastards a new one. The young one with the gun threatened to shoot me before I handed over the keys."

"Would you recognize them if you saw them again?"

Dwight's eyelids fluttered. "No. I installed closed-circuit cameras around the house a couple of months ago. There's no doubt the police will be interested in seeing the footage." Dwight's large gray eyes stared at the ceiling. "When I looked down the bore of that gun, it was as if I saw my life flash before my eyes, Nate. I tried remembering the names of the women I'd slept with and realized there were too many to count. There were a few I loved enough to marry, but I didn't want to change or stop what I was doing." His gaze swung back to Nate. "I envied you when you married Kim, because you seemed so happy. That's when I proposed to Nicole."

"You never told me that."

A wry smile twisted Dwight's mouth. "That's because she said she couldn't introduce me to her conservative right-wing parents with me looking like a blast from the seventies. All she did was ask me to cut my hair and beard, and I refused."

"Do you keep in touch with her?" Nate asked.

"We still exchange Christmas and birthday cards."

"Is she married?"

"No."

"Are you still in love with her?" Nate asked.

A beat passed. "Yeah. I always think of her as the one who got away."

Nate pointed to the telephone on the bedside table. "Call her, DW. Call her and let her know you're ready to meet her folks."

"I don't want her to come back to me just because I'm lying in this bed."

"It shouldn't matter where you are. If she loves you then she'll take you lying down or standing up."

"I'll think about it," Dwight promised. "If I do call her, it'll be after I'm discharged."

Nate uncrossed his legs, planting both feet on the floor. "I'm going to make one request."

"What's that?"

"I want to be your best man."

Dwight laughed. "Not only will you be best man, you'll be the godfather to my firstborn." He sobered quickly. "What about you, man? Are you seeing anyone?"

Nate thought about Morgan. He hadn't spoken to her since the day he left. He'd kept his promise to text her the address of the hotel where he'd been staying. Two days later he received the envelope with the contract. He'd wanted his lawyer to look it over before he signed it, but three thousand miles and the ten-day turnaround time made that impossible. He'd scrawled his signature across all three copies, and, using the hotel's concierge, mailed them back to Morgan.

He'd lost count of the number of times he'd stopped himself from picking up his cell phone to call her just to hear her sultry voice. "Yes and no."

"What's that supposed to mean?"

"Yes, I'm seeing a woman. But it's not serious."

"You're friends?" Nate nodded. "That's a good sign. Nicole and I dated for almost a year before we slept together."

Nate pushed to his feet. "It's time I leave so you can

get some rest. Now that you're okay, I'm going to head back home." He walked to the side of the hospital bed. "I'll probably see you once more before I leave." Resting a hand on Dwight's arm, Nate gave it a gentle squeeze. "When you're back on your feet I want you to come to Cavanaugh Island for a little R-and-R. The invitation extends to Nicole. I just built a place with an extra bedroom, so you have no excuse."

Dwight covered the hand on his arm with his. "I promise I'll come, with or without Nicole."

"I'll haunt the hell out of you if you don't keep your promise."

Waiting until he was seated in his rental car, Nate took out his cell and tapped the keys for Morgan's number. It was a little after eleven on the East Coast. He sat up straight when his call was connected.

"M. Dane Architecture and Interior Design. This is Samara. How may I help you?"

Nate hesitated. He'd dialed her office number when he'd wanted her cell. "Hello, Sam. This is Nate. Is Morgan available?"

"I'm sorry, Nate, but she's not here. She's meeting with Bobby. He's the project manager. Do you have the number to her cell?"

"Yes, I do."

"I think you should call her."

There was something in Samara's voice that made the hair stand up on the back of Nate's neck. "I will. Thank you, Sam." Scrolling through the directory for Morgan's numbers, he tapped in the right one this time.

"Hi, baby," came her throaty greeting.

"Hi back to you," he said, grinning.

"I couldn't believe it when your name came up on the display. I'd thought you'd dropped off the face of the earth."

"Never happen, baby. I didn't call you because I know you're busy with all your projects." She laughed, the sound sending shivers up Nate's back.

"You know I'll always make time to talk to you."

"Is everything all right, Mo?"

"Yes. Why wouldn't it be?"

"I heard something in Sam's voice when she said you were meeting with the project manager."

"You spoke to Sam?" Morgan asked.

"I called your office by accident."

"What did she tell you?"

A frown appeared between Nate's eyes as he squinted through the windshield. "Nothing. What's going on between you the project manager?"

"It's nothing I can't handle."

"Let me be the judge of that. Talk to me, Morgan."

Nate listened as she told him about the wallpaper issue. "There's a faster method that uses fabric softener and water to loosen the old adhesive."

"I told him that, but he says he prefers using metal putty knives."

"That's old school, Morgan."

"Well, it's apparent that Bobby is old school. What he's going to be is fired if he doesn't finish all the stripping by the end of the month."

"Did you tell him that?"

"Not yet."

"Do you want me to talk to him?" Nate asked.

"No. I'd wanted to talk to you about different stripping methods, but I researched it on my own."

"I'm coming home as soon as I can reserve a flight. If you don't mind, I'd like you to show me plans for the house before you take me on a walk-through. I've worked on enough old buildings and houses to judge how long it should take to restore something."

"We'll talk about it when you get here."

He heard a soft beeping that indicated his phone's battery was low. "Before I hang up I'd like to ask whether you'd attend the Island Fair with me."

"We'll talk about that, too, when you get here."

"Did someone else ask you first?"

"No, Nate. You're the first one."

"If that's the case, then why won't you give me your answer now?"

"Hold on, Nate. David just walked in with your check and a copy of your executed contract."

"You talk to David. I'll see you when I get back."

Nate ended the call without saying good-bye. A shadow of annoyance swept over his face, turning it into a mask of stone. Law firms had messengers on staff to deliver and pick up important documents. Why, he mused, did David feel the need to play messenger boy? Was it a ruse to continue to see Morgan under the guise of business?

Even though he wasn't prone to listening to or repeating gossip, Nate remembered the talk about someone noticing that David's Lexus had been parked overnight at Morgan's house. *What's funny is there's nothing going on between David and me. We're just friends.*

Why, he mused, did he remember her words as though

she had said them minutes ago instead of weeks ago? Nate wanted to believe Morgan, but David's name came up much too often for them to be just *friends*. Nate had come to detest the seven-letter word. Children were friends. And David and Morgan were no longer children.

Sitting in the car, he cursed to himself. Nate felt pain shoot through his right hand, and when he looked down he realized he'd gripped the tiny phone so hard it'd left an impression on his palm. Gritting his teeth in frustration, he started the car and drove out of the hospital parking lot faster than the posted speed. He had to get back to his hotel room, pack, and check out. After he turned in the rental car he would try to secure a flight to Charleston. He'd have to see Dwight on his next trip out.

Morgan came awake when she heard the doorbell. Sitting up, she stared at the clock on the bedside table. It was after two in the morning. Swinging her legs over the bed, she practically ran out the bedroom, Rasputin following close behind. She couldn't imagine who would come to her home at this hour.

Peering through the partially closed blinds, she saw Nate leaning against the porch column. Counting slowly to ten, she tried slowing down the runaway beating of her heart. Her hands were shaking uncontrollably when she was finally able to open the door.

"What wrong?" The two words came out in a breathless whisper.

Taking two long strides onto the porch, she found herself in his arms, his mouth coming down on hers in a kiss that stole the breath from her lungs. Her arms circled his neck, holding him close as her lips parted under his. She

moaned as their tongues touched. Holding her aloft, Nate
carried her inside the house, kicking the door closed behind them.

Morgan felt as if a part of her had left her body, leaving
her in suspended animation as she tried to understand
what was happening to her. Was she dreaming, fantasizing about Nate making love to her? Cradling his face in
her hands, she gave in to the wonderful sensations coursing through her body. It was only when she felt Nate's
growing erection against her middle that she was jolted
back to reality.

"Don't." The single word of protest sounded weak
even to her ears. However, it was enough to make Nate
raise his head. His breathing was labored, as if he'd run a
grueling race.

"Nothing's wrong," he moaned in her ear.

"Then why are you here at this hour?"

"I missed you."

"You come to my house at two in the morning to tell
me that you missed me?" She laughed softly when Nate
placed tiny kisses all over her mouth.

"Yes."

"You could've called and told me that."

Nate angled his head. "Aren't you glad to see me?"

"Of course I am."

"Then what's the matter?"

Morgan covered her mouth to keep from blurting out
how much she'd missed Nate. Missed seeing him, hearing
his slow, drawling cadence, inhaling his cologne, and
waiting for his kisses.

She lowered her hand. "When I saw you standing there
I thought something had happened."

Nate dropped his arms. "Like what?"

"I don't know."

"You don't know," he repeated softly. "I'm sorry if I woke you, but I need to know now if you're going to the Island Fair with me."

Morgan was even more confused than before. Nate claimed he missed her, yet she'd gotten only one telephone call and two texts from him in two weeks. She also knew that going to the Island Fair with him would be like taking out a full-page ad in the local paper announcing they were a couple. It had been a tradition among island teenagers that whomever you attended the fair with would become your boyfriend or girlfriend for the summer.

"What's the rush, Nate?"

"The rush is I want to ask you before someone else does."

"Even if they do it doesn't mean I'm going to go with them. Now please go so I can get some sleep. I plan to go to the early service tomorrow."

Nate touched her thigh, his hand sliding up her bare hip under a cotton nightgown. "I'll see you tomorrow."

It wasn't until he left, closing the door behind him, that Morgan slid to the floor. She pressed the back of her hand to her mouth to muffle cries of sexual frustration. She was shaking so hard her teeth chattered.

Everything she'd dreamed had come true, and for reasons she didn't understand she couldn't tell Nate that she had missed him. That she didn't want him to stop kissing her, and that if he'd asked she would've let him make love to her. But she feared he wouldn't continue to date her or be willing to take things to the next level once they slept together.

She also didn't know why she hadn't given him an answer about the fair. Maybe it was because going with him would mean that they were more than just two people hanging out. She'd been lying to Nate, Francine, and herself. She wanted to fall in love. She wanted marriage, and she definitely wanted her own family.

Spending time with Kara and watching her face when she talked about Jeff was mesmerizing. The joy in her eyes was almost palpable. Kara had come to Angels Landing to accept her birthright, unaware she would find the love of her life.

Rasputin crawled up on Morgan's lap and settled down to sleep, forcing her to open her eyes. She had to get up and try to go back to sleep or she would be out of sorts for the rest of the day. It was Irene's turn to host Sunday dinner, and Morgan had promised she would come to her house to help her make a few side dishes.

"I'm sorry to disturb you, Ras, but I have to get up." The cat jumped off her lap, heading for his own bed in the alcove off the pantry. Unlike a lot of cats, her pet preferred sleeping in his own bed to hers.

She got back into bed, fluffing up the pillow under her head. Morgan stared at the whirling blades of the ceiling fan until her eyes grew heavy. She slept fitfully, erotic dreams assaulting her like missiles, until she got out of bed and lay on the love seat on the screened-in back porch to wait for the sun to rise.

The warmth of the rising sun came through the screen, filtering over Morgan's face. It was the heat that woke her. Smiling, she realized she had managed to grab snatches of much-needed sleep. The birds were singing, hopping from branch to branch, as Rasputin sat on a perch in the corner watching them.

Sitting up, she stretched her arms upward at the same time she rolled her head on her shoulders to relieve the tightness. Morgan knew a leisurely soak in the bathtub would help start her day off right, followed by a full breakfast that would tide her over until she ate later that afternoon. Walking on bare feet, she made a mental note to call the Beauty Box to schedule a full-body massage. The tension holding her in a punishing vise was what wasn't on her wish list.

Morgan acknowledged the people she'd known all her life as she entered the Haven Creek Baptist Church. She walked to the pew where generations of Danes had sat since the small church had been erected. She stopped short when she spied Nate sitting between Irene and Rachel. She stared numbly at his strong jaw and chin when he lowered his head to hear what Rachel was saying. She'd remembered Nate attending services with his father, mother, and sister, but he'd stopped coming to church after his mother passed away.

Why, she mused, was he sitting in her family pew when the Shaws had one of their own? And had he come to church because she'd mentioned she was coming? Well, she thought, she would find out soon enough. Morgan entered the pew, sitting on Rachel's right.

"Hey," she whispered to her sister.

Rachel's head came around at the same time Nate turned to smile at her. "Hey," Rachel said. "I told Nate he could sit with us because his family usually attends the later service."

Morgan stared at Nate, wondering why she hadn't noticed the length of his lashes before now. "Good morning." Her voice was shaded in neutral tones that belied the turmoil roiling inside her at that moment.

A crooked smile touched his strong mouth. "Good morning, Mo."

Irene leaned forward. "I invited Nate to join to us for Sunday dinner."

If she hadn't been in the house of the Lord Morgan would've told her sisters what she thought of their very transparent scheme. Instead, she settled back and picked up a hymnal. The church was quickly filling up with worshippers.

Cavanaugh Island was eight square miles, with Sanctuary Cove claiming four of those miles, Angels Landing three, and Haven Creek a mere one. The Haven Creek Baptist Church had once been used as a one-room schoolhouse, and had a capacity of fifty. An addition expanded the church to include a Sunday school. It had become the norm for fathers to attend the later service while their children received Sunday school instruction. This ritual permitted their womenfolk to attend the early service, then return home to begin preparing the most important meal of the week.

The corpulent organist sat on the bench, his thick fingers poised on the keys. A melodious chord filled the church, soaring to the rafters as the voices of the choir joined in. Morgan cast a surreptitious glance at Nate, smiling when she saw his lips moving as he sang along. It was apparent he hadn't forgotten his religious upbringing.

The one thing Morgan could count on during the summer months was that the service would begin and end on time. The lack of air-conditioning was definitely a factor. Ceiling and portable fans did little to dispel the humid air and the heat generated by the crush of human bodies.

Reverend Hightower's sermon, about King Nebuchadnezzar and Daniel's ability to interpret the king's dreams, was particularly moving for Morgan when she recalled her conversation with Francine, who had said, *You dream and I can see the future.* She couldn't tell anyone that her dreams about Nate were triple-X-rated.

The service ended with a recessional hymn, and Morgan walked to the lot set aside for parking. Nate followed, his arm around Rachel's shoulders as she waddled slowly. She was a week past her due date.

Morgan turned to face her sister. "You look like you're ready to pop."

Rachel cradled her belly. "I know; I feel like it, too. I'm going home to lie down."

"Are you in pain?" Morgan asked.

"No. I'm just uncomfortable."

Morgan glanced around the lot, looking for Rachel's minivan. "Where's your car?"

"Irene picked me up."

Morgan saw her oldest sister talking to the assistant pastor. "I'll take you home." Rachel lived with her daughter and Charleston PD husband in a newly constructed four-bedroom West Ashley duplex apartment.

"No," Rachel said in protest. "You have to help Irene with dinner. Drop me off at Mama's."

"I'll take you to your mother's house," Nate volunteered.

Rachel held her belly with both hands. "Have you ever delivered a baby, Nate?"

He smiled. "Not yet." He led Rachel to his truck, physically picking her up and settling her on the seat.

"Where's Rachel?"

Morgan turned. She hadn't heard Irene come up behind her. "Nate's taking her to Mama's. She should know she's too close to having that baby to go gallivanting."

Irene sucked her teeth. "No one can tell Miss Know-It-All a thing. I told her to stay home, but she wouldn't listen. Poor James threw his hands up. He told me on the down low that everyone at the Charleston PD has been alerted to expect a nine-one-one call from his wife."

"There's something I need to know from you."

"What is it?" Irene asked as she took a pair of sunglasses from her handbag.

"Why did you invite Nate to dinner?"

"I saw him sitting alone, so I asked him to join us. Is that a problem?"

Morgan's smile didn't reach her eyes. "Not for me."

Irene affected a smug smile as she settled her glasses on the bridge of her nose. "Good. It also isn't a problem for Nate."

"I know what you're up to, Irene."

The elegant medical examiner's eyebrows shot up. "And that is?"

"You're trying to set me up with Nate."

Irene fingered her key fob. "No, I'm not. You did that already. You know Mama hates gossip, so I'm going to let you know what I've heard. There's talk that you and Nate were seen together at Happy Hour. His truck was parked in your driveway, and someone claims they saw you walking together on Southern Pines Road. If you're going with Nate, then you hit the jackpot. Every girl in high school had a crush on him, yours truly included."

Morgan's mouth dropped open. She couldn't believe she wasn't the only Dane girl to have a crush on Nate. "You're kidding."

"No, I'm not."

"Why are you waiting until now to tell me this?"

"I just want you to know that Dane women have impeccable taste when it comes to men."

The emotion eddying through Morgan was so strange and foreign that it took a full minute before she was able to identify it. The harder she'd tried to ignore the truth, the more it'd tormented her.

She was still in love with Nate.

Chapter Thirteen

❧

Morgan watched Irene as she added two cups of water to a large pot containing smoked turkey necks and bay leaves before she covered it with a lid. "Lower the flame and let it simmer until the necks are ténder," Morgan said. Both women had covered their short hair with colorful bandanas. It was a habit they'd adopted from their mother, who wore one when cooking to keep her hair out of the food.

Irene gave Morgan a sidelong glance. "Maybe with you talking me through each step, I'll be able to make a palatable gumbo."

"It's all prep work. Now we'll slice the sausage and chop the bell pepper, celery, white and green onions, and okra while the smoked meat is simmering."

"Are you going to chop the garlic clove?" Irene asked.

Morgan shook her head. "No. You'll add it to the chopped ingredients that you'll sauté in a cast iron skillet. Do you have a cast iron skillet?"

Irene glanced up at the pots and pans hanging from a rack suspended over the cooking island and stove top. "I was certain I had one."

"That's okay. I'll go home and get mine," Morgan volunteered.

Irene rested a hand on her sister's arm, stopping her retreat. "Let me call Mama and ask her to bring hers."

"Mommy, Daddy wants to know when we're going to eat." Irene's youngest son had come into the kitchen, handing her an empty bowl.

Irene ruffled his coarse sandy-brown hair. "Tell him we'll eat when the food is done."

"Mommy says when the food is done!" Ethan Snell shouted loudly.

"Ethan! What were you told about yelling in the house?" Irene said.

"Sorry, Mommy," he whispered.

Irene looked teasingly at Morgan. "See what you have to look forward to? I have two teenage sons who have bottomless pits for bellies and an eight-year-old who pretends he's a secret agent when he spies on his older brothers. Let me call Mama before I forget."

Even though her sister occasionally complained about her sons, Morgan knew she was very proud of them. The twins were honor students, and Ethan was a musical prodigy. Irene and her husband had sold their Charleston town house for a house in the Creek, which they renovated to accommodate their growing family. It wasn't far from the house where the older Danes had raised their three daughters.

Irene finished her call. "Mama said she's going to bring the skillet."

"What's up with Rachel?" Morgan asked.

"James came to Mama's and took her home. When he tried to put Amanda in the car she threw a hissy fit, so Daddy told him to leave her."

There came a roar of deep voices, and the sisters exchanged a knowing look. Nate and the Snell men had gathered in the family room to watch a baseball game. Morgan had made the introductions when Nate arrived with a decorative shopping bag filled with wine. He'd bought red, white, and rosé because he wasn't certain what Irene was serving. Nate and Dr. Anthony Snell bonded quickly once they discovered they liked the same sports teams.

Morgan raised the lid on a Dutch oven, which held two cut-up stewing chickens. There still wasn't enough liquid to add the dumplings. "Can you check to see if the greens are tender?" Irene asked her.

Mouthwatering aromas filled the kitchen when Morgan took the top off the pot of collard greens. Whenever it was Irene's turn to host dinner, she prepared a variety of dishes because her sons and husband had prodigious appetites.

"Mom, are you making biscuits?" A mop of sun-streaked light brown hair fell over a gangly teenager's forehead.

"Yes, Brandon. Now tell your father to stop sending you kids in here."

Brandon blushed. "Yes, ma'am."

Gussie walked into the kitchen, kissing Brandon's cheek as he ducked his head. "You need a haircut, baby." Irene took the shopping bag containing the skillet while Morgan hugged and kissed her mother. "What's this I hear about Nate Shaw joining us?" she whispered.

"I invited him, Mama," Irene said.

"That's real nice of you."

"I'm glad you approve," Irene quipped.

"How's Rachel?" Morgan asked her mother, hoping to defuse a potentially heated verbal exchange between her and Irene. Of the three Dane sisters, Irene had been the one who had most often challenged her mother, usually without much success.

"She was complaining of back pain."

Irene laughed. "It won't be long now. I can't wait to hold my little niece or nephew."

The three women launched into a debate about whether Rachel was going to have a girl or a boy, while Irene insisted she would have twins because of her dream.

Two hours later, Morgan sat between her identical twin nephews, Brian and Brandon, and across the table from Nate in the formal dining room. Everyone bowed their heads while Anthony blessed the table. Conversations started up again once the soup tureen filled with gumbo was passed around the table.

Gussie swallow a mouthful. "Who made this?"

"Irene."

"Morgan."

The sisters had spoken in unison.

Irene shook her head. "It's Morgan's recipe."

Brian elbowed Morgan. "This is so good, Aunt Mo."

Morgan patted his back. "Thank you, Brian." The twins were seven when their uncle Anthony Snell married Irene Dane. Irene had sat them down, telling them they were going to be a family. Anthony would no longer be Uncle Tony but Dad, and Irene would be Mom.

"I believe your gumbo is better than Jack's, baby

girl," Stephen Dane announced proudly. "It's definitely a winner."

"I agree," Gussie said, confirming her husband's assessment. "You should enter it in the one-pot category at the Island Fair."

"Don't forget her potato salad," Irene added.

Gussie stared directly at Morgan. "Do you plan to go to the fair this year?"

Thank you for putting me on the spot, Mama, Morgan thought. "Yes. Nate and I are going together." She felt the heat from countless pairs of eyes on her with the announcement.

Stephen cleared his throat. "Won't this be your first fair since you've returned to the Creek?" he asked Nate.

Nate knew his smile spoke volumes. Unknowingly, Morgan's mother and father had been instrumental in Morgan's decision to go with him. "Yes it will, Dr. Dane."

Stephen waved his hand. "There will be none of that Dr. Dane business. If you're dating my daughter, then I'd like you to call me Stephen."

Nate was gloating and he didn't care who knew it. "Thank you, Stephen."

When Morgan had asked to speak with him at Jeff's wedding, he never anticipated the effect she would have on his life. She'd gotten him to come out of his shell since his very public marriage and divorce. When he thought about the other women he'd dated, Nate could honestly admit he'd never been friends with them.

Being in a relationship with Morgan would be deeper than any he'd had before, because he and Morgan could be friends as well as lovers.

He met Morgan's eyes. "You definitely should enter the gumbo in the fair's food-tasting contests."

A secret smile trembled over her lips before they parted. "I'll have to think about it."

Anthony swallowed a spoonful of gumbo, chewing slowly on a tender shrimp. Brian and Brendan looked enough like him to have been his sons rather than his nephews. "What's there to think about, Morgan? I went to med school in New Orleans and had my share of gumbo. But this is the best I've ever eaten."

"I'll act as your sous-chef," Nate volunteered.

"What's a soup chief, Grandpa?" Amanda asked.

Everyone at the table laughed. Stephen dropped a kiss on his granddaughter's hair. "He or she is an assistant chef, Grandbaby girl."

Amanda's mouth formed a perfect O. "Wow. That's cool."

Stephen kissed Amanda again. "Morgan bringing home a ribbon would be cool. The last time we had a ribbon was when my mother won first place for her peach cobbler. And that was more than forty years ago."

"Hear, hear," everyone around the table chorused as they raised their glasses.

"Don't forget I still have to help Mama roll out crusts for her pies," Morgan reminded those sitting around the table.

Nate smiled at Morgan. "I told you I'll act as your sous-chef when you make the gumbo, so that should give you time to make the crusts."

Gussie pressed her palms together. "That settles it. This year the Dane women are going to enter several contests. Morgan will make her gumbo and I'll make my sweet potato pies. Of course she'll make the crusts because I can never roll them that thin."

"That's cool," Amanda repeated.

Nate wanted to say it was more than cool. Eating dinner with the Danes had become a time for healing and reflection. Today was the twenty-second anniversary of his mother's death, and he'd felt the need to connect with her spirit before visiting her grave. Manda had been very involved with Haven Creek Baptist Church, serving on several of the many committees dedicated to improving the spiritual and physical health of its members.

Sitting at the table with Morgan's family made him feel as if he were truly a part of their family unit. That was something he was still working on with his own. His gaze had fused with Morgan's, and he wondered if she was aware of how much he liked her, how often he wanted to see her.

Everyone took second helpings of gumbo before filling their plates with collard greens, stewed chicken and light, flavorful dumplings, and fluffy, buttery biscuits. A glass of ice-cold milk sat at Amanda's place setting, while the other children drank freshly squeezed lemonade. The adults were given the option of choosing sweet tea or wine.

After a dessert of coconut lemon cake, the table was cleared, dishes were stacked in the dishwasher, and containers were filled with leftovers for those who wanted them. Brian and Brandon protested loudly when Irene gave their grandfather a container of gumbo. They managed to look embarrassed when their mother opened the refrigerator to show them several large containers filled with it.

Nate shook Anthony's hand, and then hugged Irene. "Thank you again for inviting me."

Leaning back, she stared up at him with eyes that reminded him of Morgan's. "Now, don't you be a stranger."

"I promise I won't."

He exchanged handshakes and fist bumps with the twins. Nate stared at Amanda, who clung tightly to her grandfather's leg. Holding out his hand, he smiled at her. "Good-bye, Amanda."

The little girl stared at his hand for at least thirty seconds before she touched his fingers. "Good-bye."

Walking into the kitchen, he found Morgan wiping down the cooking island. Smiling, she closed the distance between them. "You're leaving?"

"Yes. Dinner was wonderful."

"We enjoyed having you."

Lowering his head, he kissed her cheek. "May I come by and see you later?" he whispered in her ear. He heard the hitch in her breathing with the query.

"Yes."

He kissed her again. "Good night, Mo."

Her eyes moved slowly over his face. "Good night, Nate."

Morgan was sitting on the porch steps when Nate drove up. He stuck his head out the driver's-side window. "Lock up the house and come get in."

She rose to her feet. "Where are we going?"

He smiled at her. "It's a surprise."

"Do I have to change?" she asked Nate, holding out her arms at her sides.

"No. What you have on is perfect."

Turning, Morgan climbed the steps and retrieved her house keys from the basket on the parlor table. Like so many island residents, she didn't lock her doors unless she was out or it was time to go to bed. During daytime hours, even if the doors weren't standing open, they were usually unlocked. It'd been a while since there had been a reported burglary or break-in. Maybe that was because everyone knew each other, or because all-seeing eyes were always on the alert for anything out of the ordinary—such as when Nate's truck was parked in her driveway. It wasn't as if it'd been there overnight. She wondered if there was a clandestine citizens watch group, in addition to the deputies who patrolled the towns around the clock, that went around peeking in windows or monitoring cars.

Nosy neighbors were definitely a downside of living in a small town. But that wasn't enough for her to consider moving. Living in Haven Creek made Morgan feel connected and protected. And going out with Nate was a plus. She knew his family. He knew hers, and there wasn't much he could attempt to conceal from her.

She locked the front door, pushing the keys into the pocket of her shorts. She'd come home, showered, shampooed her hair, and changed into a pair of shorts, an oversize T-shirt, and flip-flops. Rasputin had followed her around, making strange growling sounds until she picked him up. Her cat was an anomaly, because most cats were solitary and independent.

Nate was standing outside the vehicle watching her approach. She smiled. He was similarly dressed, in cutoffs, a white T-shirt, and sandals. Morgan enjoyed the feel of him when he held her close, kissing her mouth. This kiss was different from the others they'd shared. It was an intimate caress.

He ended the kiss, pressing his mouth to her eyelids. "You don't know how much I wanted to kiss you today. I'm glad I was seated across from you instead of next to you, because I'm afraid my hands would've done things under the tablecloth that would've been unquestionably inappropriate while dining."

Morgan was grateful they hadn't been seated together. It would've proven much too tempting to inadvertently have their shoulders touch or for her to lean into him. She'd never been one for public displays of affection, especially in the presence of her family. When Nate held her hand at the wedding reception, she knew why the gesture had elicited talk among her relatives.

"Are you ready to tell me where we're going?" she asked when he helped her up into the Sequoia.

"If I tell you, then I'll ruin the surprise."

Morgan didn't have to wait long to discover what the surprise was. When Nate pulled into the area at the beach set aside for parking, it was obvious he wasn't the only one who'd made the same plans. She counted eleven other vehicles.

Nate retrieved a wicker picnic basket, blanket, a boom box, and two solar-powered lanterns from the Sequoia's cargo area. She picked up one of the lanterns and the blanket as they made their way down to the beach. This is what she'd wanted so many years ago. She'd fantasized about sitting on the beach with Nate while pouring out her heart and telling him of her love for him.

The sun was enormous, shimmering in the darkening sky over the pounding surf. The heat of the day was

offset by the setting sun and the wind coming off the
ocean. They found a spot away from the other beach-
goers, spreading a blanket on the sand and anchoring
the corners with the boom box, lanterns, and picnic basket. Morgan took off her flip-flops and sank down to the
blanket on her knees. She watched as Nate sat opposite
her, opened the basket, and removed its contents. There
were plates, silverware, wineglasses, and bottles of red
and white wine. There were also clear glass containers
with hard and soft cheeses, grapes, and sleeves of stone-
ground crackers.

"Where did you get this?"

Nate gave her a sidelong glance. "I bought the basket
from the Pick Nick. I was in luck because it was the
last one. Velma said they were selling like hotcakes. The
cheese, fruit, and crackers came from the deli at the
Cove's supermarket."

Although smaller and less populated than the Cove
or the Landing, Haven Creek was an artist's paradise.
Oak Street was lined with tiny shops selling canned preserves and vegetables, handmade quilts, and sweetgrass
baskets; a number of shops sold paintings, sculptures,
and handicrafts produced by local artists. Every Tuesday
the vegetable stands in the open lot behind the church
brimmed with fresh produce grown by local farmers. A
portable refrigerated shed was set up for hog and chicken
farmers selling fresh corn-fed chickens, eggs, ham, bacon, ribs, and whole and half pigs.

"What about the wine?" South Carolina was still a blue
state, which prohibited the sale of alcohol on Sundays.

"I have an extensive wine collection in a cooler at my
sister's house."

She watched him quickly and expertly uncork a bottle of red wine. "I'd never figure you for a wine connoisseur." Morgan remembered Nate had ordered beer at Happy Hour.

"I'm more of a collector. Before I started going on the Napa Valley wine tours I didn't know a Syrah from a Cabernet Sauvignon." He half filled a wineglass with the Pinot Noir, handing it to her. He repeated the motion, handing Morgan the other glass as well. Then he opened the container of cheese, topping the crackers with Gruyère, Port-Salut, and Swiss. He retrieved his glass, touching it to Morgan's. *"Salud!"*

She inclined her head in acknowledgment. *"Salud!"* Morgan took a sip of the wine, savoring the medium-bodied, fruity wine and its woodlike flavor on her tongue. Morgan popped a grape into her mouth, chewing it slowly. "The wine is excellent."

The brilliance of the setting sun turned Nate's white T-shirt a fiery orange-red. "It's one of my favorite reds."

"I can see why." It was the perfect complement to the fruit and mild-flavored cheeses.

Morgan couldn't believe she was in love with a man who wasn't willing to give her a happily ever after…again. And in a couple of days all of Cavanaugh Island would speculate about their being an item once they attended the fair together. What would she do when the affair ended? When he decided things were getting too serious?

She shook her head as if to clear it. She couldn't think about that right now. Instead, she would try and enjoy this time with him.

Nate shifted position, sitting beside Morgan, she resting her head on his shoulder. They sat together, sipping wine, nibbling on fruit, crackers, and cheese, while listening to the music coming from the boom box. The voice of the blues singer was pregnant with raw emotion when he sang about finding the love of his life, then losing her to another man. The lyrics were so heartbreaking she wondered if Nate identified with the vocalist.

"Do you hate your ex for what she did to you?" Morgan felt the muscles in Nate's shoulder tighten.

Nate couldn't believe Morgan wanted to talk about another woman when he'd wanted it to be just the two of them. Easing her down to the blanket, he lay behind her in spoon fashion. "No, I don't, and I don't want to talk about her. Not tonight."

"What do you want to talk about?"

"You."

"What about me, Nate?"

"I want to get to know you better. For instance, why did your parents give you a boy's name?"

"It was a peace offering from my mother to her in-laws. My grandparents never forgave my father for marrying a woman who wasn't Gullah."

"I don't know why, but I always thought she was Gullah."

Morgan laughed softly. "After being with Daddy for more than forty years, she's picked up a lot of the traditions and vernacular."

Nate held his breath when Morgan moved, pushing her hips against his groin. "How did your parents meet?" he asked.

"They were both students at Howard. My grandmother

thought my mother was stuck-up. Grandpa gave them a gift of a quarter acre of land on the Creek for their wedding. It wasn't until after they'd set up a practice in Charleston that they were able to save enough money to build a house. Mama and Grandmomma weren't bosom buddies, but they dealt with each other because of Rachel and Irene.

"When Mama discovered she was pregnant again, everyone kept saying she was going to have a boy, and in an effort to extend an olive branch to her in-laws she promised to name the baby Morgan after my grandfather, whom she adored. I was obviously not a boy, but the name stuck."

Nate pressed his mouth to the nape of Morgan's neck, breathing a kiss there. "I remember you trailing behind your grandfather."

Morgan covered his hand, which was resting on her belly, with hers. Her fingers gave his a gentle squeeze. "He was the most incredible man I've ever known. He'd only graduated high school, yet he knew so much because he was a voracious reader. But it was what he did with his camera that put him on the map. Grandpa would tell me to look at a house and let him know what I saw. I would say windows, steps leading up to the front door; then he would stop me, telling me to look beyond the obvious. That's when he'd point out the grain in the wood, how the steps were worn down on one side from countless footsteps, and that the paint on one side of the house was more faded than the other because it faced direct sunlight.

"Whether Grandpa was taking photographs or listening to his prized collection of jazz records, I was always in awe of the stories he'd tell me about back in the day. After my grandmother passed away, I'd come over to clean his house while he cooked. It was when he showed me photographs of the Brooklyn Bridge that I decided I wanted to be an engineer."

"How old were you?" Nate asked.

"Twelve. I was in awe of the fact that the bridge was designated a National Historic Landmark and was listed on the National Register of Historic Places, because I'd thought only homes or buildings were chosen for that designation. I later learned the bridge was also named a National Historic Civil Engineering Landmark."

"Why did you give up engineering for architecture?"

"Once I started looking at homes and office buildings the way my grandfather saw them through his camera lens, I knew I wanted to design structures rather than build them. After Grandpa left me his house, I drew up plans and expanded it. I've been thinking about adding a second story, but that would entail raising the roof."

"That's easy enough to do."

Morgan raised her head, staring at him over her shoulder. "Maybe in the future."

Nate chuckled. "Tomorrow is the future."

"Very funny, Nate."

"You know, I've never really been inside your house."

"Yes, you have."

"No, I haven't, Mo. No farther than your parlor. By the way, I like how you decorated it."

Turning around, Morgan faced him. "When you take me home I'll be certain to give you a personal tour. Speaking of decorating, I've completed the floor plans for your apartment."

Nate tried seeing her expression, but there wasn't enough light coming from the lanterns. "I thought you said it would take you a couple of weeks just for the master bedroom."

Morgan buried her face between Nate's chin and shoulder. "I'll admit I'm a tad bit obsessive-compulsive. Once I start a project, I usually don't stop until I finish it."

"How is Mr. Blue?"

Morgan laughed, the sultry sound caressing Nate's ear. "Spoiled rotten."

He cupped her hips, pulling her closer. "You should think of saving some of that spoiling for your future children."

Morgan laughed again. "Don't worry. There will be more than enough spoiling to spread around."

"Speaking of babies, Rachel was *very* uncomfortable when I drove her to your parents' house. I prayed she wouldn't go into labor and I'd have to try to deliver her baby."

"Most babies don't come that fast, Nate. I don't know why they feel the need to make their mamas suffer before they make their appearance."

Nate's hand moved lower, his fingers caressing the skin on Morgan's smooth thigh. He felt her tense up at the same time she caught her breath. "It's okay, baby. I'm not going to do anything you don't want me to do." She relaxed under his light touch. "Doesn't that go back to the Bible, where it was Eve's punishment for tempting Adam to sin?"

"He didn't have to sin," Morgan argued in a quiet voice. "After all, he was put in charge of the garden, and he knew the rules. He should've been strong enough not to permit himself to be tempted."

"Sometimes it isn't that easy. I don't think you women are aware of the power you have over men. You make us do things we professed we'd never do. The next thing we know you have our noses wide open."

"Oh, no, you're not going to go there!" Morgan protested. "You're no better than Adam when he blamed Eve for making him sin."

"Well, she did," Nate countered. "If she hadn't been looking so hot he would've been able to resist her."

Throwing back her head, Morgan laughed hysterically at the same time Nate's deep chuckle rumbled in his chest. "What makes you so certain she was hot?"

"Look at you, Mo. It's been proven that Eve was a sister, and if you're a daughter of Eve, then she had to be hot."

Without warning Morgan pushed against his chest, and he released her. What had he said to make her withdraw? Nate thought maybe he'd come on too strong, or...His thoughts trailed off as he remembered another time when he'd mentioned her beauty and she'd appeared visibly uncomfortable.

Scooting over on the blanket, he pulled her closer to him, so that she was sitting between his outstretched legs. "Did I say something wrong?"

Morgan swallowed the lump in her throat. She knew she had to tell Nate about her insecurities when it came to men or she would never be able to move forward. She opened her mouth and the pain she'd held on to like a badge of honor came pouring out. Morgan spared no details as she told Nate about the hurtful comments other kids directed at her regarding her height and weight. She told him that she'd prayed to be invisible whenever she walked into Perry's because she knew no boy would ever invite her to sit with him. And that the very boys who made her adolescence a living hell weren't interested in her until she became a homeowner and had set up her own business.

"That's when they came sliding around, talking about how hot I was, when years before they'd called me names. One even had the audacity to apologize because he'd told me he wouldn't sleep with a bag of bones even if I'd offered it to him for free."

"They were young and silly, baby."

"They were mean and evil, Nate. I hated men until I got to college and discovered that guys either liked me because I was an engineering student and smart, or because I was lucky enough to have my own apartment and car."

Nate's arms tightened around her middle. "Is that why you said you'd never marry a boy from Cavanaugh Island?"

Morgan watched the increasingly high waves and rough surf wash up on the sand. "Yes. If it hadn't been for Francine I wouldn't have had a single friend in high school. She understood what I was going through because a lot of kids teased her about her curly red hair. We made up a gossip column and got our frustrations out by writing salacious stories about girls who were known for sleeping around. Of course we embellished it, then laughed our asses off when we read them to each other. Each week we would try and top the one before, but it stopped when the news got out that one of the girls we wrote about discovered herself pregnant and didn't know who'd fathered her baby. Her parents were so devastated her mother had a breakdown and had to be hospitalized for a couple of months." She couldn't tell Nate that Francine had written what she did after seeing it in a vision.

"What's the expression about one's actions having consequences?" Nate said in her ear. "Her getting pregnant had nothing to do with what you'd made up about her in your gossip column."

"I know, but that didn't stop me from feeling sorry for her."

"That's because you were nothing like her."

Tears pricked the backs of Morgan's eyelids, but she managed to blink them back before they fell. "I know if I'd dated you in high school I would be different now."

Lifting her effortlessly, Nate shifted Morgan so that she was straddling his lap. "You were too young then. And knowing how your father feels about his baby girl, he would've come after me packing heat."

"Why would you say that? We wouldn't have slept together."

"I know that and you know that. But would your father have believed it? Before I asked Chauncey out her father made me sign a note stating that I wouldn't sleep with his daughter."

Morgan's jaw dropped. "You're kidding."

"No. He raised his daughters to save themselves for marriage, and if he found out they weren't virgins, then he would have made certain that whoever they'd slept with would never father children after he blasted them with his shotgun. Talk about scared. I never told my father about it because he would've gotten in Reverend Dobson's face, and whatever ensued, Dad would've blamed his behavior on the PTSD he'd gotten after serving in Vietnam."

"Shame on him. All this coming from a man of the cloth."

"He was a father first and a man of the cloth second. It took me a while to understand that. I probably wouldn't be any different if I had a girl."

"You would shoot some boy because he slept with your daughter?" There was no mistaking the fear in Morgan's voice.

"I would if he took advantage of her."

It was only when she saw the flash of Nate's teeth in the diffuse light that Morgan realized he wasn't serious. And she knew if she continued to sit on his lap it would lead to something she wasn't emotionally ready to deal with. At least not at this point in their relationship.

"Are you ready to see the mock-up of your decorated apartment?"

Bracing himself with one hand, Nate stood, bringing Morgan up with him. "Yes."

Chapter Fourteen

Nate felt like a hypocrite, telling Morgan to forgive and forget when he was still dealing with his own unresolved issue of forgiving Odessa. Without conferring with a therapist, he knew it all had to do with the fact that Odessa and his mother were childhood friends. Where, he mused, was the trustworthiness? Couldn't Odessa have waited until after her friend died to go after Lucas?

Lucas had been forty, an age when virile men have physical needs, but what Nate didn't and refused to understand was his father's audaciousness. Had he experienced any guilt while sleeping with another woman in the same bed where he'd slept with his wife? Or had he been blinded with lust? Or perhaps his inability to make love to his sick wife left him vulnerable.

He pulled his thoughts away from his past as he followed Morgan through her sunny parlor, past its wall-mounted flat-screen TV and into a nearly all-white living room that opened out into a dining room claiming the same palette. White walls provided the backdrop for the creamy upholstered modern sofa, love seat, and club chair. A collection of black-and-white photographs was displayed on one wall. Crystal vases on the white coffee and corner tables cradled bouquets of fresh flowers that added color to the serenity of the space. Light from the crystal chandelier overhead reflected warmly on the glossy wood floor.

Though the living room was formal, the dining room had a welcoming feel. The table, with seating for ten, was made of white planks of bleached pine. Matching ladder-back chairs had blue-and-white pin-striped seat cushions. A profusion of dried hydrangeas in varying hues ranging from creamy white to deep purple filled a trio of blue Depression glass vases on an antique buffet server. Nate noted that the floors in the dining room, which were rubbed with white paint and glazed, sparkled under the overhead ceiling fixture. The windows in both rooms were draped with white-on-white awning-striped voile that let an abundance of natural light into the space.

Morgan met his gaze when he turned to look at her. "All the furniture in the living and dining rooms belonged to my grandmother." She gave him a knowing smile. "You already know the tables and buffet server were made by your people. I had to replace the chairs in the parlor because they were too worn to repair. My grandparents only entertained in the living room on special occasions."

"How many bedrooms do you have?" he asked.

"Three. Come with me and I'll show you the kitchen," she said, leading him down a narrow hallway. "This is the only room I remodeled."

As in the other two rooms, Morgan had again used

an all-white palette. Two of the four walls were exposed brick. The brick color and pattern were repeated in glazed tiles on the floor. Nate found the modern space, with its hanging live palms and ferns, pristine and homey. A round table surrounded by four chairs matched the one in the dining room. Nate didn't have to look at the underside to know it was built by a Shaw.

"You can do some serious cooking in here."

"This is one of my favorite rooms in the house. Whenever I have company everyone gathers here."

"You don't use the dining room?" he asked.

"I do only if I host Easter or Christmas. I gave up trying to get everyone to eat in the dining room. I bought a couple of folding tables with chairs that I use whenever it's my turn to cook Sunday dinner."

"Am I invited?" he asked teasingly.

"Of course, Nate. If Daddy told you to call him Stephen, then that means he thinks of you as family."

Nate angled his head. "Did he tell your brothers-in-law to call him Stephen when they were going with your sisters?"

"No, but that's only because they didn't come from Cavanaugh Island."

"So I get special treatment because I'm a native?"

"He knows you, Nate. And he knows your family. That goes a long way with my dad. Daddy wasn't too happy when he heard Irene was marrying a man with a ready-made family, but that all changed once he met Anthony and the boys. Daddy loves fishing and he always takes Brian, Brandon, and Ethan with him. Maybe because he had three girls, he really enjoys doing guy things with his grandsons."

"You have a wonderful family."

"We have our problems, like any other family, but I love each and every one of them."

Nate wished he could echo Morgan's sentiments. Her family had embraced Anthony's nephews as if they were blood, while he still couldn't totally embrace Odessa as his stepmother even though she'd given birth to his brother.

"I'll show you the bedrooms before you see the space I added."

"Where's the bathroom?" he asked.

"There's a half bath off the pantry and one outside the bedrooms. The first bedroom is mine."

Standing at the entrance to the master bedroom, Nate found out everything he needed to know about the woman who'd managed to slip under the barrier he'd erected to keep women at a distance. She was a romantic.

What originally had been curiosity was now an increasing need to spend as much time with her as possible. Yet every moment he was with her, he couldn't help wanting to kiss her and touch her, but he knew that doing so could push her away and ruin things before they really got started. The notion shocked him, because even as a bumbling adolescent with raging hormones he'd never been so lacking in self-control. Thankfully, Morgan had asked whether he wanted to see the floor plans for his apartment before she'd detected his erection.

Her bedroom exuded an air of gentle Southern charm. It had a king-size mahogany four-poster draped in a sheer white fabric. The pale shade was repeated in the bed's delicate antique linens. An oval mahogany table and two pull-up chairs were positioned near a trio of windows from which hung white lace panels. She'd removed the doors to a white chest-on-chest to reveal shelves filled with stacks of blue-and-white sheets, blankets, and pillowcases. Light from bedside table lamps bathed the entire room in gold.

"It's lovely."

Morgan scrunched up her nose. "You don't think it's too frilly?"

Nate looped his fingers through hers. He smiled. "Your hands are warm tonight. And to answer your question, no, it's not too frilly."

"When I was a girl I always wanted a four-poster draped in netting, but I had to share a bedroom with Rachel. She was afraid of thunderstorms, so she would always get out of her twin bed and get into mine. We'd huddle together until it was over."

Raising her hand, Nate pressed a kiss to her knuckles. "Are you afraid of storms?"

The corners of her mouth lifted when she smiled. "No. But I am afraid of snakes."

Letting go of her hand, he hugged her. "Snakes would rather retreat than attack."

Morgan curved her arms under Nate's shoulders. "Tell that to someone else. I think my fear came from seeing one sunning itself in the backyard when I was a kid. I thought it was a branch until I almost stepped on it. I started screaming and couldn't stop. Daddy came out of the house with his gun and killed it. Ever since he told me it was a Carolina pigmy, and that most people don't hear its rattles until it was too late, I've harbored an intense fear of snakes. A kid was bitten last year after he'd tried to chase one that had gotten into his daddy's chicken's coop.

If Dr. Monroe hadn't had a supply of antivenom on hand he would've been airlifted to Charleston."

Nate rubbed her back in a comforting gesture. "Stop it, baby. You're getting yourself worked up over something that may never happen."

Leaning back in his embrace, Morgan stared up at him. "I know I'm being silly..."

"No, you're not. You have a fear of snakes. Everyone is afraid of something."

"What are you afraid of?"

"Nothing," he lied smoothly. He was afraid of liking her too much, afraid that their easygoing relationship would become more than he would be able to deal with emotionally.

Nate's vow not to become involved with a woman was shattered the instant he'd shared a dance with Morgan at the Happy Hour. For the first time in a very long time he'd gone out on a date that didn't involve sex. After he'd separated from Kim, there had been a string of nameless, faceless women who'd come in and out of his life until he woke up one morning and asked himself what he was doing. He knew he couldn't continue that lifestyle, because each time he put a woman into a taxi to send her home he felt as if he were losing a little part of himself. His having to come back to Haven Creek had saved him both physically *and* emotionally, because it was only a matter of time before he would have become a bitter, jaded middle-aged man blaming everyone except himself for the turn his life had taken.

When Manda was told she would not have long to live, she'd sat him down and lectured him about what she wanted and expected from him. Her only mandate: Take your time to find that special woman to love and protect, as his father had loved and protected her. He'd thought that woman was Kim, but she hadn't wanted his love or protection. That was something she'd gotten from her manager.

Nate glanced around the bedroom. "Do you sleep here?"

"Of course I sleep here. Why would you say that?"

"It's looks so sterile. There's not a speck of dust anywhere. And the bed looks as if it's never been slept in. It reminds me of those displays you see in furniture warehouse stores."

Reaching for his hand, Morgan pulled him over to the bed. She sat on the side of the mattress, kicking off her flip-flops. "Take off your shoes and get in."

"What?"

"Come get into the bed with me."

Nate's face clouded with uneasiness. "Why?"

"To prove to you I'm not as anal as you believe I am."

"I really didn't mean it when I called you anal."

"Yeah, you did, Nate. Nothing comes out of your mouth you don't mean to say."

She lay on the pillow staring up at him, unaware of how much he wanted to share a bed with her. He wanted to make love to her. There was something about her that had changed him—profoundly. Her artistic outlook on life was refreshing. And she'd gotten him to come out of his shell. That was something no woman had been able to do since his divorce.

"What's the matter, Nate?" Morgan said, goading him. "Are you afraid I'm going to jump your bones?"

Smiling, Nate cupped his ear. "Is that a challenge or a promise?"

Morgan patted the mattress. "Get in or go home."

"I thought it was go big or go home," he said, kicking off his sandals. "Move over, gorgeous." Morgan scooted over as he lay beside her. "Nice mattress." Rolling over on her side, she faced him, resting a bare leg over his.

They lay together, their breathing coming and going in a slow, measured rhythm. Morgan thought she would've felt a panic sharing the bed with Nate, but it was just the opposite. Cuddling with him on the bed had become a continuation of their beach outing. Never had she felt so relaxed, so confident with a man. Maybe it was because she and Nate had decided beforehand that their relationship would be based on friendship.

"How often do you do this?" Nate asked after a comfortable silence.

"Do what?"

"Invite men to your bed?"

"You're the first one."

"Lucky me."

She laughed softly. "It's not all that lucky."

"Let me be the judge of that. I don't usually get into a woman's bed unless I'm making love to her."

Snuggling closer, she wrapped her arm over his waist. "Why can't I be the exception?"

Removing her arm, Nate turned to face her. "You can't be the exception, Mo."

Her smooth brow furrowed. "Why not?"

"We talk about being friends like ten-year-olds, but we're not kids. I can't continue to kiss and touch you while pretending that I don't want more."

Morgan could hear her heartbeat in her ears. It was

beating so fast she was grateful to be lying down. "What is more, Nate?"

He smiled. "You're a very bright woman, Mo. Figure it out."

"Tell me exactly what you want."

"I want to make love to you." Pressing his forehead to hers, Nate kissed the bridge of Morgan's nose. "But I don't want to put pressure on you."

"Are you certain that sex won't complicate things between us?"

"Why should it?" Nate asked.

"I don't know. I enjoy your company and I love being your friend. I just don't want that to change." Morgan couldn't afford to get caught up, knowing that what they had would never end in a happily ever after. At least not for her. And she didn't want a repeat of what she'd had with her art history professor. During their relationship she'd lost track of the number of times he'd told her he loved her and wanted to spend the rest of his life with her, but everything came crashing down around her when she found out he'd told several other students the same thing. Once bitten, twice shy had become her mantra. The difference between Leonardo and Nate was that she knew exactly where she stood with the latter. He'd been forthcoming when he said he had no intention of getting married again. For that she was grateful because she wouldn't be blindsided.

"Were the men in your past bad to you?"

Morgan shook her head. "No. They didn't do anything to me I didn't permit them to do. My first serious boyfriend was a fellow college student, and I slept with him for all the wrong reasons. I wanted to know what it felt like to have a boyfriend, and I was more than willing to give up my virginity to him."

Morgan hadn't been completely honest with Nate. There were a number of things that led to the breakup, but she was too ashamed to admit that her first lover had asked her to become involved in a ménage à trois, if only to put some excitement in their sex life after he'd slept with her study partner. The final straw came when Morgan called her lover Nate in the throes of passion. Prior to that, the only time she'd been able to climax was when she'd fantasized about Nate making love to her.

"Were you in love with him?"

"No." *I was still in love with you,* her inner voice answered. "I had another relationship. This one was with my teacher when I lived abroad. He was older, very erudite, and to say I was in awe of him is an understatement."

Nate rubbed Morgan's short hair between his fingertips. "That's understandable, baby. A lot of young women have similar experiences. I saw that firsthand when I lived in Europe. I'd thought it was a fad, but someone told me many female college students have affairs with their instructors or men they've met in the cities or countries where they were studying."

Morgan laughed. "Well, I was one of those starry-eyed female students. I don't regret becoming involved with Leonardo, because I believed I was an adult when I met him. I finally acknowledged that I was a girl in a woman's body."

"Were you in love with him?" Nate asked again.

A wry grin twisted her mouth. "I believed I was. So much so I was ready to give up everything I had here to live in Europe."

"What happened, Mo?"

Morgan chewed her lip as she thought about what she wanted to disclose to Nate. "I found out that our relationship wasn't the first time he'd slept with a student, stringing her along then summarily dismissing her when it was time for her to return to her home country. A couple of students who knew Leonardo said I was luckier than the others because he'd actually asked me to live with him. Of course that didn't make me feel any better, but I remembered something my grandfather lectured me about."

"What's that?"

"Think with my head and not my heart. Love with my heart and not my head. With Leonardo I was thinking with my heart. He called me a silly little girl because I should've accepted what he was offering, but this silly little girl wasn't about to become a paramour to a man who could trade me in when he took up with someone new."

Nate kissed her forehead. "Good for you," he whispered. "Sometimes we have to go through a little adversity to knock us into reality."

"Are you talking about your marriage?"

"Yes."

Morgan listened intently as Nate told her about meeting Kimberly at a party he'd attended with his friend Dwight Wickham. Dwight's father worked in the film industry, and he'd invited his son and Nate to a wrap party for an independent film directed by Kim's father. The attraction had been instantaneous. Nate and Kim became an A-list couple, dating for a year before setting up house together.

"Six months later we were married in a circuslike

spectacle. I should've known it wasn't going to last because we spent the first two weeks of our marriage living apart."

"Oh, no!" The two words were out before Morgan could stop them.

"Oh, yes," Nate responded. "The wedding and reception were held on her father's estate. When it came time for us to leave for our honeymoon, Kim didn't want to because she was having too good a time with the guests. We were scheduled to sail to Hawaii and stay there for ten days before flying back to the mainland. I went and she stayed in L.A."

"I'm sorry your marriage didn't work out."

"I'm not," Nate countered. He sat up, swinging his legs over the side of the bed. "Can I see the floor plans for my apartment now?"

Despite what she had said, Morgan wasn't sorry his marriage hadn't worked out. He was back, and life had thrown her a vicious curve. She had intended to hire Shaw Woodworking for the project, but instead of Lucas being the supervisor it was Nate. She'd convinced herself that what she'd felt for Nate was nothing more than a lingering childhood crush, a crush that was now a conscious desire for him to make love to her.

Slipping off the bed, she led Nate into her office.

"Why does this room remind me of Paris?" he asked.

She looked at Nate over her shoulder after she'd turned on several table lamps. "That's because the style is known as Euro-eclectic. The writing table is a classic European-style desk, and the oval-back chair is a Louis XVI–inspired piece. I found the plaques at an estate sale in Savannah. When I bought them I had no idea what

I'd use them for, but after I added this room I decided to decorate the walls with them."

"Did you find the shades at the sale, too?"

Morgan stared at the Roman shades covering the quartet of windows. The gold, orange, and red hues in the exquisite hand-painted wall plaques were repeated in the shades, which were stamped in red with scenes from a Chinese village. This room, like the others, was filled with potted plants and vases of fresh flowers.

"No. I had them custom-made."

Nate met her eyes. "I like that each room is a different style with its own personality."

Morgan glanced at her watch. "It's getting late, so I'll show you the solarium when you come back. I'll boot up the computer so you can select which floor plan you'd like. Please pull up a chair."

Over the next three-quarters of an hour she watched Nate as he stared at a series of floor plans for each of the rooms in the barn house. "I'd like the second bedroom to be an office," he said, pointing to a plan. All the furnishings were reminiscent of the British colonial and French Regency influences found throughout the Caribbean.

"Okay, you want the entire apartment to have the same island-influenced style," she said, jotting down the numbers she'd assigned to each of the plans.

"Cavanaugh Island is subtropical, so I'd like to bring the outdoors inside. How soon can I expect delivery after you place the order?"

"Probably three to six weeks. I've chosen manufacturers that have most of the pieces in stock."

Nate placed an arm around Morgan's shoulders. "Tally

up everything and let me know how much I owe you. Don't forget to include your commission."

Morgan checked off the floor plans she wanted to print, then clicked the Print icon. "I'm not charging you anything."

"Why not?"

"Because I don't charge friends."

"What if we weren't friends?"

"Nate, please. I don't want to talk about it."

"Well, I do. I'm not going to take advantage of you, Mo. I know it didn't take fifteen minutes for you to work these up. Either you add your commission or I'll go to another decorator."

"No, you won't," Morgan countered confidently. "There's no time. You said yourself you wanted to be moved in by summer's end."

His hand tightened around the nape of her neck. "So," he whispered in her ear. "You think you know me *that* well?"

Turning her head, Morgan stared deeply into the golden orbs holding her captive. "No, but I'm getting to know you."

He leaned closer. "I wish you'd been older in high school so I would've had the opportunity to take you out."

"I don't need you to feel sorry for me, Nate. I'm past that."

"No, you're not."

Her eyebrows shot up. "Why would you say that?"

"Because you said you'd never date or marry a man from the island. If you were truly past it, then you would've changed your mind."

"Am I not dating you?"

Nate nodded. "Yes, but—"

Morgan pressed her mouth to his for a quick kiss. "No ifs, ands, or buts. Thanks to you I've turned a corner."

"Big corner or itty-bitty corner?" he whispered against her parted lips.

Inhaling his warm, moist breath, she smiled. "It was a corner of titanic proportions." Morgan shivered when Nate placed tiny kisses over every inch of her mouth, lingering at the corners. "Now please go home before I beg you to make love to me. And if there's one thing I don't like, it's begging."

Nate groaned as if he were in pain. "Morgan, do you have any idea what you're doing to me?"

Her expression reflected her innocence. "What's the matter?"

Nate closed his eyes. "I'm probably going to spend a restless night fantasizing about you." He opened his eyes, meeting her wide-eyed stare. "It's called teasing."

Her dimples winked at him when she pursed her lips. "I didn't mean—" Whatever she was going to say died on her lips when Nate pulled her to his chest and kissed her again, his tongue slipping into her mouth. It ended as quickly as it'd begun, leaving Morgan visibly shaken.

"Good night, Mo. I hope you sleep well."

She stood there a full minute before she was galvanized into action. Morgan made it to the porch in time to see Nate speeding away. At the last possible moment he put his hand out the window and waved to her. Although she returned his wave, she doubted whether he saw her because he was driving much too fast.

She sank down into the rocker instead of going inside. Trying to figure Nate out was like opening a puzzle box that held more than a thousand tiny pieces. He'd talked about wanting to make love to her, but when she echoed his words he had come undone and accused her of teasing him.

Unwittingly, he'd teased her, too. Her dreams weren't exactly G-rated. There were mornings when she woke up with her heart pounding and the area between her thighs pulsing with need.

Morgan knew she and Nate would eventually share a bed and each other's bodies, but the question was when— and where would that leave them?

Chapter Fifteen

It'd been two days since Morgan had implored Nate, *Please go home before I beg you to make love to me,* and since that time he hadn't been able to get a restful night's sleep. Rolling over, he opened one eye, peering at the clock on the bedside table. It was 2:17. He punched the pillow under his head, not wanting to acknowledge that he was turning into an insomniac.

Nate had told Morgan that she'd been too young for him when they were in high school and if given the opportunity to date her he knew for certain he wouldn't have slept with her. He hadn't needed her or Chauncey for sex because he'd been secretly sleeping with an older woman, who'd not only taken his virginity but had also introduced him to a world of sensual pleasure.

He punched the pillow again, turning over on his belly. He closed his eyes and attempted deep breathing with the hope he would drift off to sleep. The cell phone he'd left on the bedside table vibrated, the buzzing sound reminding him of an annoying insect. Nate sat up, reaching for the phone. He couldn't imagine who was calling him so late. The display shone brightly in the darkened bedroom. His sister had left him a text message saying that they were going to drive from Philadelphia to New York and spend two days there visiting the Intrepid Sea, Air, and Space Museum, the Statue of Liberty, and taking in a show at Radio City before heading back to Cavanaugh Island for the Island Fair.

Nate froze when he saw Odessa's name and number. "What is it? Talk to me!" he shouted when sobbing came through the earpiece.

"Please come, Nate."

"Is Dad okay?"

"Yes. Just come."

The next ten minutes were a blur. Nate pulled on a pair of jeans and pushed his feet into a pair of sandals at the same time he pulled a T-shirt over his head. Grabbing his keys off the dresser, he raced out of the house, stopping only to lock the door. It appeared as if he'd just started the SUV when he came to an abrupt stop, tires spewing gravel, as he punched the button to cut off the engine. The sound of deep male voices could be heard through the open windows, and Nate knew why Odessa had called him. His father and brother were yelling at each other. The scene that greeted him would be one he would never forget. Bryce stood nose-to-nose with Lucas, the veins in the necks of both men bulging.

"Bryce!" His brother, reacting in slow motion, turned to stare at Nate. "Outside." Though spoken softly, the single word had the same impact as if he had shouted it. Waiting until Bryce preceded him out to the porch, Nate closed the door with enough force to rattle the windows. He pointed to a chair. "Sit down. Please, Bryce." Pulling over a matching chair, Nate straddled it. "Tell me why you felt the need to disrespect our father in *his* home."

"Stacy's pregnant."

Exhaling an audible breath, Nate showed no visible reaction that he was about to be an uncle for the third time. "Was it planned?"

"What do you think? Hell, no, it wasn't planned."

Running a hand over his face, Nate felt his temper rising. He counted slowly to ten. "First thing, calm down. Whatever problem you're facing is *your* problem. It's not mine, Dad's, or Odessa's, so dial down the attitude."

Lowering his head, Bryce stared at his bare feet. "I'm sorry, Nate. I don't know what I'm going to do. I'm not ready to become a father."

Nate curbed the urge to hug his brother. He wasn't about to lecture Bryce about the fact that if he hadn't been ready for fatherhood, then he should've taken the necessary steps to prevent an unplanned pregnancy.

"I take it Stacy plans to have the baby."

"Yeah."

"If that's the case, then you have to get ready. She didn't make this baby by herself, so you're going to have to step up."

"It's...it's not that I don't love her, but..."

"But what, Bryce?"

"We talked about getting married."

"Okay. So what's the problem?" Nate asked.

"Stacy plans to teach until the baby comes, and together we make enough to rent a place in Charleston, but

there's not going to be much left over for food, health insurance, and things we'll need for the baby."

"You can't live in Charleston. Remember, Bryce, the
terms of your probation mandate that you live here."

"Can't I get my probation officer to change that?"

"Is that what you really want?" Nate asked his brother.
"The reason you're on probation is because you weren't
able to stay away from your crackhead friends. All they
have to hear is that you have a place where they can hang
out and Stacy will bring either your son or your daughter
to visit you in the county jail."

"That's not going to happen."

"So you say. Wake the hell up, Bryce. You're twenty-
two years old and you're about to become a husband and
father. That means you can't hang out with your friends
whenever they call. And trust me, they're going to come
calling. You were always the one with the car and a little
spare change. You were the only one who finished high
school and went to college. They are who they are—
certified bums who will bring you down. Do you think they
care how many times they've been arrested? For them it's
become a badge of honor to say they've done a bid. Shaws
don't do jail." He'd clearly enunciated the last four words.

Bryce threw up a hand. "That's all I hear from Dad.
Shaws don't do this or Shaws are expected to do that."

Bracing his arms on the back of the chair, Nate glared
at the younger man. "Don't forget your girlfriend is carrying a Shaw. Stacy only got back with you after you'd
promised her you would go back to college, get your degree, and complete your probation. That sounds like a
woman who not only loves you but also has a lot of faith
in you. Please, Bryce, don't prove her wrong."

"This is not about Stacy," Bryce countered.

"Yes, it is. You have to stop thinking about yourself. It's about you, Stacy, and your baby." Nate reached out and held his brother's arm. "I envy you, Bryce. You're going to have what I always wanted."

"Why would you envy me? You have everything, Nate. You have money up the wazoo and you can come and go whenever and wherever you please. What more do you want?"

A beat passed as Nate tried swallowing the lump that had formed in his throat. "A woman who loves me as much as I love her. The happy anticipation of starting a family."

A sheepish expression crossed Bryce's face. "I never looked at it that way. I'm sorry your marriage didn't work out."

Nate's hand tightened on his brother's arm before releasing it. "I'm not. Now I get to be here to bounce my new baby niece or nephew on my knee. I missed that with Gregory and Gabrielle."

Leaning back in the cushioned chair, Bryce closed his eyes. "I'm sorry I got in Dad's face, but I've had enough of him telling me to grow up." He opened his eyes. "In case he hasn't noticed, I am grown. What he doesn't get is I can't be like you. You've always been the good son, while I can't seem to get anything right."

"That's where you're wrong, Bryce. I've had confrontations with Dad, but the difference between you and me is I never disrespected him. Don't tell me you're sorry. Tell him."

Bryce exhaled an audible breath. "I will."

The seconds ticked by as the brothers stared at each

other. "I think I can help you out," Nate said, breaking the silence.

"How?"

Nate could hear trepidation in the query. "After you and Stacy marry, you can live in the apartment in the barn until you finish probation."

Excitement fired the gold flecks in Bryce's eyes. "But that's not going to be for another sixteen months."

"I happen to know how long it is."

"What about you, Nate? Where will you live?"

"I'll live there, too, but in the smaller bedroom." Nate had to tell Morgan his plan to convert the second bedroom into a home office would have to be scrapped. And that meant he would have to reconfigure an office space on the first floor.

"You would do that for us?"

"Come on, Bryce. Wouldn't you do the same for me?"

"Yeah, I guess so."

Nate's eyebrows lifted. "You guess so?"

"Of course I would."

Nate smiled. "That's better. I've ordered furniture, but it won't be delivered for at least another three weeks. Have you and Stacy talked about setting a wedding date?"

"No."

"I suggest you start planning your future. I'm not going to charge you rent, so that will allow you to save some money. I am going to establish a few rules, though."

Bryce narrowed his eyes. "What kind of rules?"

"You and Stacy will not move in until you're married." Bryce nodded. "And you have to keep it clean." Nate had overheard Odessa arguing with Bryce about cleaning up his bedroom.

"That's not a problem. Stacy's a neat freak."

"How in the world did she hook up with you?"

"I read somewhere that romance is about the little things. I suppose it's the little things Stacy likes about me."

Nate nodded. Bryce was right. It was the little things he liked about Morgan. It was her smile, her laugh, her quick comebacks, her dedication to her family and career, and the sensuality he suspected she was totally oblivious to.

"You've got a lot going for you, Bryce. You've got skills me and Dad will never have. Making furniture by hand is like weaving sweetgrass baskets. If it wasn't for Shaw Woodworking and Miss Rose over in the Cove and some of the other older ladies here in the Creek giving lessons, both would cease to exist here on the island. I've heard Sharon tell Gregory that even if he doesn't want to make furniture, as soon as he's old enough to use a carving knife he's going to learn to work with wood. And who better to learn it from than you, Bryce?"

"I think I'd like to have Gregory as my apprentice."

Throwing back his head, Nate laughed. "There you go." He sobered quickly. "After you get your degree you may decide you want to do something else, but remember there are always people with money willing to pay for something made exclusively by hand."

He told Bryce about the businessman who'd paid him two million dollars for the ornate doors into which he'd carved Greek and Roman mythical creatures, Gothic-inspired gargoyles, and kings and saints from the Old and New Testaments, making the wood into a work of art.

"Damn," Bryce drawled. "I had no idea you could make that much money working with a piece of wood. How long did it take you to complete it?"

"It took me two years."

"Why so long?"

"I was still working for a developer, and I'd taken on this project as an independent contractor. I'd rented space in a warehouse, and whenever I had a few hours to myself I'd work on it. Now I know what Michelangelo must have felt like when he lay on his back for four years painting the Sistine Chapel. There were a few times when I was going to call it quits, but something wouldn't let me give up. It was the first and last time I ever took on something of that size and scope. But I bet it's something you'd like, because you love to draw."

Bryce ran his fingertips over his chin. "You've given me an idea. Maybe I could carve a few doors in my spare time and try to sell them."

Nate stood up. "It sounds ambitious. Remember you're going to have a wife and child to look after in the not-too-distant future, so you may not have too much spare time."

"I'll find the time. Even if it's only an hour a day."

"And I'll help out whenever I can. Once you and Stacy work out what you're going to do, then let me know. I'm going inside to talk to Dad before I go home." Nate held out his arms and he wasn't disappointed when Bryce rose to hug him. "Congratulations, little brother."

Bryce pounded Nate's back. "You're the best brother a dude could have."

"You say that because I'm your only brother. I want you to wait until I leave before you go in and apologize to Dad."

Nate left Bryce on the porch when he opened the door and walked into the living room, where his father sat with Odessa. He gave both a warm smile as he sat across from them. "Everything's going to work out. Bryce is talking about marrying Stacy, and I've offered to let them live with me until they get on their feet."

Odessa covered her mouth with her hand. She blinked back tears. "Bless you, Nate."

He turned his attention to his father. "Dad, you're going to have to lighten up on Bryce until he moves out." Nate held up a hand when Lucas opened his mouth to interrupt him. "Please, let me finish. I told him about disrespecting you, and I don't think that's going to happen again."

"He's always been somewhat of a wild child," Odessa said.

"He is what you've allowed him to be," Nate countered. "You can't wait until he's an adult and then try to establish boundaries. It's much too late for that. He's going to have to inform his probation officer that he's getting married and that he's also changing his address."

Lucas nodded. "I'll go with him."

"I'll do that," Nate volunteered. "After all, he'll be living with me." He stared at his stepmother. Her eyes were red and puffy from crying and his heart turned over in empathy. He smiled and she returned it with a tentative one. "Congratulations, Grandma."

Clasping her hands together, Odessa bit her lip to still its trembling. "Thank you, Nate. And thank you for coming so quickly."

He gave her a long, penetrating stare. "We're Shaws, Odessa. You call and we'll come. That's what we do."

Odessa went completely still. "Are you saying I'm not a Shaw?"

The accusations Nate wanted to fling at her died on his

lips. He knew this wasn't the time or the place to attack her, to finally rid himself of the bitterness he'd carried for years. "No, I'm not saying that. You're as much a Shaw as Bryce, Sharon, or me. And especially now that you're going to become a grandmother to another generation of Shaws." He stood up, and fatigue descended on him like an anchor pulling him down to the bottom of the ocean. "I'm going to sleep in my old bedroom, because right now I don't think I can make it back to Sharon's house without falling asleep behind the wheel."

Odessa jumped up. "I'll get it ready for you."

Lucas rose to his feet. "Thanks, son."

"It's all right, Dad. Just think about your new grand-child."

"That's all I've been thinking about. I'm hoping Bryce is mature enough to take on a family of his own."

Nate rested a hand on his father's shoulder. "If he's not, then he has time to mature. Stacy seems to be a level-headed woman, and that means she'll be good for him."

Lucas blew out a breath. "You're right. She convinced him go back to school."

"They'll work it out, Dad. Most young couples do."

Lucas's light brown eyes were fixed on his firstborn. "I'm sorry it didn't work out for you."

"Come on, Dad. You know and I know that it wasn't going to last. So please stop apologizing."

"I kind of blame myself because I feel I put the mout on your marriage." Lucas had slipped into dialect.

"You did nothing of the sort. It was what it was. Now, if you'll excuse me I'm going to bed."

"Do you know something?" Lucas asked when Nate turned in the direction of the bedrooms.

He stopped, but didn't turn around. "What is it?"

"This will be the first time you slept here since you've been back."

"Yeah, I know." Nate walked into the bedroom as Odessa walked out. "Good night—or should I say good morning?"

She gave him a tender smile. "Good morning. What do you want for breakfast?"

"Anything."

"That's not saying much."

"Grits, eggs, bacon, or ham. And lots of black coffee," he said to Odessa's departing back. Nate closed the door to the bedroom where he'd spent his childhood, stripped off his clothes, and got into bed. He fell asleep as soon as his head touched the pillow.

"Morgan, I'm going home for lunch."

Her head popped up and she nodded to Samara. "I'll see you later." The heat wave was over, and the island mandate for businesses to close down from twelve to four had been rescinded. Morgan would've gone home herself if she didn't have a one o'clock meeting with Bobby. It was only days from the beginning of the Island Fair, and she wanted to start rolling out crusts for her mother's pies. She also had to go to the supermarket to buy the ingredients she needed for her gumbo.

"Do you want me to lock the front door?" Samara asked.

"Please."

Leaning back in her chair, Morgan stared at her to-do list. She had to call the furniture manufacturers to order the pieces for Nate's apartment. She also had to call Mr.

Fletcher at the Harbor Fishery to place an order for shrimp for the gumbo. She'd modified the traditional recipe, omitting the crabmeat and oysters.

Her cell rang and she picked it up when she saw Rachel's number. "What's up, Sis?"

"My water just broke."

"Where are you?"

"I'm at home."

Morgan closed her eyes. "Please don't tell me you're alone."

"I am," Rachel squeaked. "James dropped Amanda off at his mother's this morning."

"Did you call him?"

"Yes. He's on his way. But I don't think I'll be able to hold on until he gets here."

"You have to hold on, Rachel. Where are you?"

"I'm lying on some towels on the bathroom floor."

"Are you doing your breathing exercises?"

"They aren't doing me much good right now," Rachel admitted. "I feel like someone is stabbing me. After I have these babies, I'm through."

These babies. Morgan's grin was so wide her face hurt. So Irene was right when she dreamed about Rachel holding a fish in each hand. Their sister had concealed the fact that she was carrying twins.

"Talk to me, Rachel. It'll keep your mind off the pain."

"Wait a minute, Mo. James and the EMTs are here."

"Tell James to call me when—" The line went dead, and Morgan knew she would have to wait to find out whether she was going to be an aunt to nieces, nephews, or one of each. The office phone rang and she picked up the receiver. "M. Dane Architecture and Interiors."

"Good afternoon, Ms. Dane."

A shiver of excitement eddied over her when she recognized Nate's voice. "Good afternoon, Mr. Shaw. How may I help you?"

Reaching for a pen, she scribbled down notes on a legal pad. Nate had decided not to use the smaller bedroom as an office. "You still want the office furniture?"

"Yes. I'll subdivide space on the first floor for an office."

Morgan wondered what had happened to make Nate change his mind. "What size bed do you want in the second bedroom?"

"What do you suggest?"

"A queen, because anything larger will overpower the space." She pulled up the floor plans for his apartment. "I'm sending pictures of the styles you like to your cell." Morgan didn't have to wait long for Nate to tell her his choice. "You caught me just in time, because I was going to call the warehouse today."

"You still haven't told me how much I owe you, Mo."

She made interlocking circles on the pad. "I'll let you know once the order is confirmed, and you can pay them directly." Her hand stilled as she closed her eyes. She thought back to the night she'd told Nate to leave before she begged him to make love to her. She wanted him; wanted him so much she found it hard to sit still. "I know I promised you breakfast," she said, biting back a smile. "Are you available Thursday morning?" Thursday was July first, the beginning of the Island Fair.

"For you, I'll be available every morning."

And for you I'll be available every night. The heat that began in her face spread to her chest, settling in her belly when she tried to imagine waking up with Nate beside her. "Let's start with one morning."

"Oh, so there're going to be a lot of mornings, Mo?"

"We'll have to wait and see, now, won't we?"

"There's one thing you should know about me."

"What's that?"

"I'm a very patient man."

Morgan couldn't help but laugh. "And there's something you should know about me, Mr. Nathaniel Phillip Shaw."

"Whatever it is must be serious if you're calling me by my government name."

She laughed again. "I just wanted to tell you I'm the most patient woman on Cavanaugh Island." She'd been waiting far too long for him to make love to her.

"Patience is bitter, but its fruit is sweet."

"Are you a philosopher or a carpenter, Nate?"

"You can say I'm a little of both. You recognize Rousseau?"

"I love his work."

Nate's deep laugh caressed Morgan's ear. "My girlfriend is an intellectual as well as an artist."

"I'm your girlfriend?"

"Of course, baby, you're my girlfriend. What else would you be?"

"I'm not the presumptuous type."

"I repeat: I didn't know my girlfriend was an intellectual and an artist."

"You can say I'm a little of both," she admitted. "I'm going to have to hang up because I have to make several calls. I'll see you Thursday morning, if I don't talk to you before then."

"What time do you want me to come?"

"Eight." Morgan chatted with Nate for another thirty seconds, then rang off. She pumped her fists in the air. Maybe Nate was coming around. He'd admitted he wanted to sleep with her, and now he'd acknowledged she was his girlfriend. She hoped beyond hope that this relationship would go far, because she was so in love with him her heart hurt.

The Island Fair ranked second to Christmas when it came to celebrations. Shopkeepers set up stalls and tables outside their shops, exhibiting their products to locals and tourists. And because Morgan sold services and not goods, she planned to close for the duration of the fair.

Four days—ninety-six hours, or 5,760 minutes—that she hoped to share with Nate.

Chapter Sixteen

Morgan took a quick glance at the clock on the kitchen wall. It was July 1 and the first morning of the fair. She stared at the photographs on the refrigerator door. She'd uploaded the images of her sister's twin sons, whom Rachel and James had named Stephen and Dennis to honor their respective fathers, printed them out, and affixed them to the fridge with tiny ladybug magnets. The newborns would stay in the hospital until they reached the requisite five pounds, at which point they would no longer be deemed preemies.

She'd gone to the hospital to see her nephews, her heart swelling with love when she'd stood with Rachel, watching the tiny identical boys sleeping peacefully in their incubators. When she'd asked her sister why she hadn't told anyone she was carrying twins, Rachel admitted it'd been touch and go during the first two trimesters, which prompted her and her husband not to discuss her pregnancy.

Morgan had ordered Nate's furniture, sent him an invoice, which he paid with his credit card, ordered the ingredients she needed for the gumbo, and had rolled out six pie crusts for her mother's celebrated sweet potato pie. This would be the first time in years that two Dane women would enter the fair's food competition.

Soft meowing garnered her attention. Rasputin raised his nose, sniffed the air, and then meowed again. "I'm sorry, Ras, but you have your own fish." When she'd placed her fish order, Morgan had also asked Mr. Fletcher to fillet several pounds of whiting. It'd been a while since she'd had fish for breakfast.

"Nate's coming for breakfast," she said, continuing her monologue with her pet. "The last time he came over you hid from him. I hope you're not jealous, because you're still the number one man in my life." When Rasputin purred as if he understood what she was saying, she murmured, "Yes. You're my baby."

She smiled when the cat turned and walked over to the mat at the side door and settled down to lick his paws. Although cats are instinctive climbers, Morgan had trained Rasputin not to jump on the table or countertops, because she didn't want cat hair in her food.

Nate had teased her about being anal, which she vehemently denied. She liked having a neat house, and that meant dusting and vacuuming several times a week to keep cat hair at bay. What she intensely detested was clutter and disarray, because they upset her sense of balance. The solarium had become her sanctuary; glass walls brought the outside in, but because they were made of one-way glass, they provided a modicum of privacy.

The doorbell chimed throughout the house. Morgan

smiled. Nate had arrived. "Come on back. I'm in the kitchen," she called out.

Morgan's head popped up, and the person she saw standing in the middle of her kitchen was not the person she had expected. "Francine." There was no mistaking the surprise in her voice.

The redhead flopped down on one of the stools at the cooking island. "That's me." Her green eyes narrowed. "Who were you expecting?" She held up a hand. "No; please don't tell me." Francine pressed her fingers to her forehead. "Nate, right?"

"Very funny, Fran. It doesn't take a psychic to discern that."

Sitting up straight, Francine affected a smug grin. "Psychic or not, you know I'm right."

Morgan stared at her friend. An apple-green halter sundress with matching flats was the perfect outfit for her coloring and the humid, overcast weather. She'd managed to tame her wayward curls by pinning them into a bun atop her head.

"What are you doing here?"

Folding her hands at her waist, Francine rolled her eyes upward. "Is that any way to talk to your BFF?"

Morgan affected a facetious smile. "Sorry."

"No, you're not, but I'll accept your apology this morning only because I'm feeling rather magnanimous."

Resting her hip against the countertop, she met Francine's eyes. "Pray tell why you're in such a forgiving mood."

"I have a date for the Island Fair."

Morgan stared at Francine, then seconds later they were hugging and screaming like adolescent girls at a

Justin Bieber concert. "Who is he?" Morgan asked when she'd recovered from the shock of her friend finally showing an interest in a man. "Come on, give me the details."

A blush suffused Francine's face. "David."

The seconds ticked as the two women looked at each other. "David as in Sullivan?" Francine nodded. "He asked you to go with him?" Morgan questioned.

Crossing one leg over the other, Francine stared at the toe of her shoe. "It really didn't go down like that."

"How did it go down, Fran?"

"He'd come to the Cove to see Kara and Jeff, then decided to come to the Beauty Box for a haircut because he had a dinner meeting with a client later that evening."

Morgan's eyebrows lifted questioningly. "He told you all of that?"

"Yes, as I was cutting his hair. Everyone in the shop was talking about the fair and he asked me who I was going with. When I said no one, he asked if I'd go with him."

"Is this a one-time thing, or are you looking for more from him?" Morgan didn't want Francine to get her heart broken, because she knew David was still pining for his longtime ex.

"I know where you're going with this, Mo, and I appreciate your concern. I'm not feeling David like that. We're just hanging out for the Fair."

"You know what folks are going to think."

Francine sucked her teeth. "Folks can think or say anything they want. Now, what's up with you and Nate?"

"We're still together."

"I know that. Have the two of you become more than friends yet?"

Morgan had to decide whether to withhold the information or tell the truth. She decided on the latter, because eventually Francine would tell her what she'd seen in her visions. "Not yet."

"And why not? I told you I saw you and Nate with a baby."

"That's not going to—" the doorbell chimed again, stopping Morgan's rebuttal. "Excuse me. That's probably Nate."

Francine slipped off the stool. "That's my cue to exit stage left."

"Stay and eat with us."

"Really?"

"Don't play yourself, Fran. Of course I want you to stay."

Morgan went to open the door for Nate. Rasputin slipped from under the dining room table and trotted after her. Nate stood on the other side of the screen door holding a large shopping bag. Her gaze swept over his clean-shaven jaw, lingering briefly on his sculpted mouth. He smelled of aftershave and clean laundry. He was wearing a pair of well-worn jeans and a white short-sleeved shirt that he'd elected to wear outside the waistband. A pair of running shoes had replaced his construction boots.

She held the door open for him. "Please come in."

Dipping his head, Nate brushed a kiss over her parted lips. "I see Francine's here," he whispered in her ear. Francine was the only person on Cavanaugh Island with a red Corvette.

"She's joining us for breakfast."

"That's nice."

Morgan gave him a skeptical look. "Are you being facetious?"

"Of course not. I happen to like Francine." He handed her the shopping bag. "There's something in there for you, for Blue, and for your sister's twins."

She looked into the bag to find a large red shoe made of soft fabric. It had three peekaboo holes and a giant shoelace. Nate had brought Rasputin a cat playhouse. "I can't believe you actually bought something for Ras."

Smiling, Nate cocked his head at an angle. "Why not?"

"Because I think you're trying to bribe me into letting Ras mate with your sister's queen."

Reaching into the bag, he removed the playhouse. "This is not about you, baby. It's about me bonding with Blue. You know we dudes have to stick together."

Morgan shook her head. "I had you figured for a dog lover."

Wrapping an arm around her waist, he pulled her to his side. "I love dogs, but there's something about Blue that I really like. Maybe it's because I like his mama so much."

Something wouldn't permit her to tell Nate how much and how long she'd liked him. "His mama also likes his new friend."

He smiled, attractive lines fanning out from his eyes. Nate set the playhouse on the floor and within seconds Rasputin jumped in, poking his head through one of the holes.

Morgan didn't know what to make of her pet. He hid from everyone who came to the house except Nate. What was it about him that Rasputin liked? Perhaps the feline knew how much she liked him.

"Come," she said, reaching for Nate's hand.

"How's Rachel?" Nate asked as they made their way to the kitchen.

"She's home, but she hangs out at the hospital all day to feed the babies."

Nate gave her a sidelong glance. "Have you seen the twins?"

"Oh, Nate, they're adorable. I have photos of them on the refrigerator door. They're identical, so I can't tell Stephen from Dennis."

Throwing back his head, he laughed. "So the Dane tradition continues. Your sister named them after their grandfathers."

Morgan released Nate's hand when Francine came over to hug him. He kissed Francine's cheek, lifting her effortlessly off her feet. "How's it going, Red?"

Francine returned the kiss. "It's all good, Nate."

He held her at arm's length. "You look very nice."

Francine turned a vivid scarlet. "Thank you."

Morgan placed the shopping bag on a stool, then opened the refrigerator to take out two glass dishes containing the fillets she'd seasoned the night before. "We're having fish, grits, and corn muffins." She smiled when Nate and Francine bumped fists. "I seasoned some with Old Bay and some with Zatarain's. Let me know which one you want."

"I'll have both," Francine said.

Nate concurred. "Me, too."

"Plain or cheese grits?" Morgan asked.

"Cheese," Francine and Nate chorused, laughing uncontrollably.

"Is breakfast always like this?" he asked, looking over Morgan's shoulder as she removed the plastic lids covering the fish. "Wow, that smells incredible." The aroma of the marinated fish filled the kitchen.

Francine laughed. "Morgan missed her calling. She should've been a chef instead of an architect."

Nate stared at Francine. "Do you cook, Red?"

She lowered her gaze. "No."

He gave her a look of disbelief. "Not at all?"

"Leave her alone," Morgan whispered.

"I just—"

"Let it go," she said between clenched teeth, defending her friend's lack of culinary skill. What Francine lacked in cooking ability she more than made up for as a stylist and actress. Francine had given herself until thirty-five to "find herself." And it wasn't as if she didn't have options, because she could always revive her acting career.

Francine hopped off the stool. "Can I help with anything, Mo? Nothing that pertains to cooking, of course."

Morgan winked at her. "Sure. You can put out another place setting on the dining room table."

Forty minutes later Morgan, Francine, and Nate sat in the dining room eating crispy oven-fried fish, grits mixed with grated cheddar cheese and topped with minced chives, and buttery corn muffins. Nate couldn't believe Morgan could improve on her gumbo, but she had. Francine was right. Morgan had missed her calling.

He reached for another piece of fish. "I don't know which I like better—the Old Bay or the Zatarain's."

Francine, who'd just swallowed a mouthful of corn muffin, nodded. "I've eaten fish with Old Bay, but there's just enough kick in the Cajun seasoning to make my taste buds sing the 'Hallelujah Chorus.'"

"No lie," Nate said.

Morgan pushed back her chair. It was the first time she'd used the spicy seafood seasoning, and it had been a rousing success. She had always liked spicy food, but she wasn't certain whether Nate would like it. "Who wants coffee and who wants tea?"

Francine sighed. "I'm going to pass." She pressed both hands to her middle. "I'm about to explode."

Nate stood up. "I'll make the coffee." He helped the women clear the table, and then made coffee after Morgan showed him how to use the espresso machine.

Francine hugged him, then she hugged Morgan. "I'll see you two later this afternoon at the fair." Turning on her heels, she walked out of the kitchen.

Sitting at the cooking island with Morgan, drinking freshly brewed coffee liberally laced with heavy cream, Nate rested a free hand on the nape of her neck. "Is this what I can look forward to every morning if we have breakfast together?"

She gave him a direct stare before smiling. "I don't think so. If I ate this much every day I wouldn't be able to move."

"What about weekends?"

Morgan rested her head on Nate's shoulder. "What constitutes your weekend?"

He kissed her short, fragrant hair. "Friday night to Sunday night."

She laughed softly. "I'll only agree to see you one of the three days."

"What if you fix breakfast one day and I reciprocate on the other?"

"That's still two days, Nate."

Nate kissed her again, this time on her forehead. "Okay, baby. One day." He wanted to tell Morgan he was willing to agree to anything just to spend time with her. "I started painting the apartment."

"What colors are you painting the bedrooms?" Morgan asked.

"One wall in the master bedroom is a carnelian red. The other three walls, the ceiling, and the closet doors are antique white. All the walls in the smaller bedroom are celadon with white accents."

Morgan nodded, smiling. "Very, very nice. What about the living room and dining area?"

"I'm considering a light gray called Harbor Mist."

"That's going to work well with the furniture, too."

Nate wrapped his hands around the coffee cup. "My brother's going to move in with me around mid-August. He and his girlfriend are getting married."

Morgan eyes widened. "Is it the same girl he's been dating for a while?"

"Yes. Marriage and fatherhood may be what Bryce needs to finally get himself together."

"So you're going to become an uncle again?"

"It looks like it. Hopefully he and Stacy won't have twins, as Rachel did."

Frowning, Morgan pushed out her lower lip. "I'm still mad at her for not telling anyone. I should've known, because Irene dreamed that Rachel was holding up two fish. And then when she and James bought a house with four bedrooms, that was also another clue."

"What are the odds that both of your sisters would have a set of twins?"

"It is a little eerie. Both Irene and Rachel claim they're

not going to have any more kids. But when Amanda heard that she had two new baby brothers she threw a hissy fit because she wanted one of them to be a girl."

Nate groaned. "I'd love to be a fly on the wall to see her reaction when Rachel and James bring the twins home."

"I hear you," Morgan intoned. "My mother promised Amanda that she's going to take her with her when she goes to a spa for a few hours of pampering. Of the six grandchildren, Amanda is the only girl. So that alone makes her special."

"Maybe one day you'll give them another granddaughter," Nate said teasingly.

"Maybe." There wasn't much conviction in the single word. Morgan jumped up like a jack-in-the-box.

"Where are you going?"

"I want to see what you bought me."

Nate sat watching Morgan as she unwrapped the rectangular package he had brought, first carefully removing the bow and then methodically peeling off the decorative paper. She glanced up, smiling. "I know you didn't wrap this."

His expression was impassive. "How do you know that?"

"It's wrapped too neatly."

Nate returned her smile. "You're right. If left up to me it would've had a thousand pieces of tape on it." Her eyes widened when she saw the leather-covered tablet computer inside the box.

Morgan threw her arms around his neck. "Thank you, baby."

Holding her close, he pulled her back so that she was

sitting between his knees. "I didn't know if you had one."

"I do now."

"Turn it on," Nate urged. "I registered it in my name, but you can always deregister it and transfer it to yours."

Morgan pressed a button, turning on the iPad. She touched the Books icon, and two titles appeared on the screen. Her eyelids fluttered. "I don't believe it. You got me *Civil Disobedience* by Henry David Thoreau and *Discourse on Inequality* by Jean-Jacques Rousseau." Nervously, she ran her tongue over her lower lip. "I love it and I love you."

Nate pressed his mouth to the nape of her neck, inhaling her essence. He didn't want to interpret her "I love you" to be more than an expression—one that was bantered about much too loosely. And he didn't want to go there and try to imagine himself falling in love with Morgan.

He liked her a lot, but falling in love was definitely not an option. He'd acknowledged that she was nothing like Kim, yet something wouldn't permit him to open his heart again to the inevitable pain he was sure would follow.

Nate had loved his mother unconditionally, and he'd unknowingly transferred that love to Kim. He'd wanted to take care of her, but what she'd done in the dark had come to light when photographs of her and her manager in a compromising position were splashed across tabloid papers by relentless paparazzi.

Distrust had reared its ugly head, and Nate knew he could never trust a woman again with his heart. A wry smile twisted his mouth when he recalled Morgan's grandfather's sage advice about thinking with his head and not his heart. He didn't know if Morgan was the woman with whom he could spend the rest of his life, but Nate wasn't willing to risk it.

"How can I thank you for the tablet?"

Her soft query shook Nate from his reverie. "You did already."

Morgan flashed a demure smile. "I'm not talking about saying thank you."

Nate turned Morgan to face him, giving her an intense stare. "You did when you put down a dollar as your commission for decorating my place."

"Don't you know how to be gracious, Nate?"

"A dollar, Morgan. That's ridiculous."

"I'll charge you the going rate the next time we do business."

"Is there going to be a next time?" he asked.

"Of course. Would you be amenable to a barter to offset the one-dollar commission?"

Nate squinted at her. "What are you proposing?"

"I'd like you to make a mini-mansion dollhouse for Amanda's sixth birthday."

"No fair, baby. That still won't equal your commission."

Leaning closer, she brushed her mouth over his. "Then I'm going to think of something else I'd like you to do for me. Right now, talking about money is boring the heck out of me. Can we drop the subject?"

Nate shook his head. "No." There was no way he was going to take advantage of his relationship with Morgan.

Her expression stilled, her eyes narrowing. "Either you let it go or we're done, Nate. I mean it."

This was a side of Morgan Nate hadn't seen before. He'd always viewed her as easygoing, someone with whom he could talk about anything. It was apparent he'd underestimated her tenaciousness. He was only willing to let the subject drop because he wasn't ready to let her go.

Not yet.

"Okay," he conceded. "Consider the topic dropped."

"Thank you."

He eased the tablet from her hand, set it on the countertop, then scooped her up in his arms. "I need to lie down and wait for some of this food to digest. What can I do to convince you to join me?"

Morgan wrapped her arms around his neck to keep her balance. "All you have to do is ask."

"Where are we napping?"

"In the solarium." She buried her face against the column of his neck. "It's next to the office."

Nate carried Morgan into the solarium, stopping abruptly when he stared through the glass structure. The backyard was a riot of flowers, and beyond that he could see Haven Creek, the meandering body of water that had given the town its name.

The room was furnished with a white wrought iron daybed, a white wicker love seat, and a chaise with floral-patterned cushions, all atop a natural sisal rug. Royal blue, yellow, and bright green glazed pots overflowing with flowers, ferns, and palms turned the space into an indoor oasis. A trio of white wrought iron étagères was stacked with books, vinyl records in their colorful sleeves, black-and-white photographs, and a small stereo system. The gurgle of falling water over stalks of bamboo, from an indoor waterfall in the corner, was soothing and hypnotic. Nate knew without asking that this was where Morgan spent most of her time.

"This is nice," he drawled.

"It's my sanctuary."

He put her down to the daybed, then walked over to the wall. Nate recognized the glass. He could see out, but no one could see in. It was the perfect place to make love while viewing the splendor and majesty of nature.

Turning, he saw Morgan staring back at him. He smiled. "You could run around here naked as a jaybird and no one would be able to see you," he said.

She returned his smile with a dimpled one of her own. "I wouldn't know, because I've never done it."

"Why not?"

"I'm not that uninhibited."

"You're an artist. I thought most artists were."

She folded her hands in her lap. "Not this one."

Striding across the room, Nate reached down and gently pulled her to her feet. "We're going to have to do something about that." Morgan raised her head, their gazes meeting and fusing. "What do you want, baby?"

Morgan wanted to beg Nate to make love to her, but she didn't want him to believe she was weak and vulnerable. She wanted to come to him as an equal in a journey in which she no longer needed a man to take her virginity or restore her confidence in her femininity. But in a moment of weakness she'd confessed to Nate that she loved him.

Leaning into his hard body, she looped her arms around his waist. "I want you to make love to me," she whispered in his ear.

Nate tightened his hold on her upper arms. "Here?"

"Yes."

"Now?"

"Yes," she repeated.

His hands shifted from her arms to her face, cradling it gently between his callused palms. "I'll take it slow. If there's anything you want me to do, then let me know."

Her dimples winked at him. "I want you to stop talking."

Nate slanted his mouth over hers, deepening the kiss until her lips parted. She gasped when his tongue curled around hers, then moved in and out of her mouth.

Her breathing quickened as the area between her legs throbbed with a need she hadn't thought imaginable. Morgan felt like she was having an erotic dream. But holding Nate, tasting him, feeling his hardness pressed against her thighs, said otherwise. *Patience is bitter, but its fruit is sweet.* Rousseau's words were never more fitting than at this moment. She'd waited years for this moment, and now she was about to experience the sweetness she'd craved for longer than she could remember.

Chapter Seventeen

Together she and Nate took the bolster and throw pillows off the daybed, removed the slipcover, and pulled out the trundle, converting it into a queen-size bed. Sheets covered with sprigs of rosebuds matched the slipcover.

Sitting on the mattress, Morgan watched, transfixed, as her soon-to-be lover undressed. It appeared as if he were moving in slow motion when he unbuttoned his shirt, leaving it on the chaise. She held her breath when she saw the tattoo over his heart. The artist had inked MANDA in small, neat cursive.

Morgan didn't know why, but at the moment she felt like crying—crying for Nate, who hadn't been able to cry at his mother's funeral. She was grateful she hadn't attended Manda Shaw's funeral because the look on Nate's face probably would've haunted her for years. There were times when she'd caught glimpses of sadness in his eyes, but it was only fleeting. He kicked off his running shoes, bending slightly to remove his socks. Before placing his jeans on the chaise he removed a condom from one of the pockets.

When Nate talked about his brother's upcoming wedding and fatherhood, she realized Francine's vision wasn't about her and Nate; it was about Bryce and Stacy. Although Nate had promised to use protection, she had to take responsibility for her own reproductive future, and that meant taking an oral contraceptive.

Thoughts were tumbling over themselves in her head, because Morgan didn't want to think about what she was going to embark upon. She'd spent so many years fantasizing about Nate—that they'd fallen in love, he'd given her his mother's engagement ring, they'd exchanged vows at Haven Creek Baptist Church, and that she would tuck their children into bed, kiss them good night, and then slip into bed bedside him and they would make endless love until they, too, fell asleep.

She noticed the smile tilting the corners of Nate's mouth as he pushed his boxers off his hips and stepped out of them. Morgan felt as if oxygen had been siphoned from her lungs, leaving her gasping for her next precious, lifesaving breath. Fully erect Nate was larger than any man she'd seen. The fear must have shown on her face when he moved closer, sat down, and embraced her.

It had been a long time for Morgan, much too long.

She closed her eyes, resting a hand on his smooth chest, while feeling the strong steady beating of his heart under her palm.

Morgan let her senses take over when Nate deftly unbuttoned her blouse, unhooked her bra, and cupped her breasts. She gasped, and then sucked in her breath when his mouth replaced his hands. He suckled her breasts, worshipping them, and the moans she sought to suppress escaping her parted lips.

Nate's tongue worked its magic, circling her nipples, leaving them hard, erect, and throbbing. Waves of pleasure washed over Morgan when his teeth tightened on the turgid tips, and she felt a violent spasm grip her core.

"Nate," she moaned, his name becoming a litany. Hot tears pricked the backs of her eyelids. She was drowning in a haze of passion threatening to pull her under to a place where she'd never been. What she was experiencing surpassed every fantasy she'd ever had. The pleasure was so intense it was akin to pain, a pain she didn't want to stop.

Morgan felt as if she were having an out-of-body experience. She'd stepped outside of herself as she watched Nate slip off her shorts and, finally, her panties. She didn't think she would ever forget the look in his eyes when he stared at her.

"Mo, Mo, Mo," he crooned. "Shame on you for hiding such deliciousness with clothes." She reached down to cover her neatly shorn mound, but Nate caught her wrists, pulling her hands above her head. "No, baby, there's no need to hide from me, because there's not going to be one place on your body that will go untouched."

True to his word, Nate began with light, feathery kisses along Morgan's hairline. He forced himself to slow down when the need to penetrate her had become an all-consuming obsession.

Nate wasn't certain when it had begun. Perhaps it was seeing her at the reception, where there had been men who'd tried too hard to get her to notice them. Or maybe it was when he looked at her in her office—really looked at her for the first time, not as a girl but as a woman. The impact had been as unexpected as the hard-on that wouldn't permit him to stand up lest she notice it.

Whether it was her sultry voice, her laugh, or even the graceful curves of her tall, slender body, he had to admit to himself that he'd fallen for Morgan, hard. He'd told himself that what he felt for her was lust because he refused to acknowledge that he was falling in love with her. And for Nate, love and trust were one and the same, indivisible. In a moment of madness and insanity he'd lowered his guard and fallen in love with Kim, and she'd shattered the remnants of the fragile trust he'd managed to cobble together for her. And unfortunately Morgan had become collateral damage in a drama not of her choosing.

It should've been Nate and not Bryce planning a wedding and preparing for fatherhood. It should've been Nate and Morgan announcing their engagement, planning to marry in another two or three years. There was no doubt they would work well together—she designing homes and interiors and he building them.

He would come home every night to a house filled with mouthwatering aromas, the sounds of barking dogs, and children shrieking and laughing when he played toss with them. He wanted that and so much more, but Nate knew it would take years, if not forever, before he could trust another woman again.

He fastened his mouth along the column of Morgan's neck, wishing he could nibble there, but he didn't want to bruise her skin. He loved her skin—its color, smell, and texture. He loved her short hair, which smelled like coconut or a field of wildflowers, depending on which shampoo she used. Nate never tired of staring into her large eyes, seeing her dimpled smile, or watching her walk. Her litheness and grace never failed to send his libido into overdrive.

Still holding onto her wrist, Nate charted a path with his lips and tongue over Morgan's throat, shoulders, breastbone, belly, and, still lower, to the apex of her thighs. He felt her trembling as he used his knee to part her legs with the ferociousness of a starving man. He staked his claim on her wet, quivering sex. Morgan's pleas for him to stop faded, becoming moans that caused the hair on the back of his neck to stand up. Nate was relentless, nibbling and suckling her like a hungry newborn.

Morgan suffered through the erotic torture, fearing she was going to faint from the pleasure that raced headlong from the top of her head to the soles of her feet. Currents of passion flowed through her as if she'd touched a live wire. She went completely still before bucking and thrashing with the orgasm that seized her, holding her captive. It released her momentarily before sweeping her up again in a maelstrom of pleasure so intense it stopped her heart for several seconds. In the midst of her free fall, she felt Nate easing himself inside her, sliding in slowly and filling her with his hardness.

He'd released her hands, and Morgan wound her arms around his neck, luxuriating in the enjoyable sensation of his filling every inch of her. His unhurried lovemaking revived her as she rose and fell in concert with his pumping hips. He cupped his hands under her hips, allowing for deeper penetrating. A keening echoed in the room, and it took a moment for Morgan to realize it'd come from her. This was the first time since becoming sexually active that she'd really and truly been made love to.

She was forced to let go of Nate's neck when he raised her legs, anchoring them on his shoulders. An expression of carnality swept over his features as his gaze met hers, and she rose to meet his body in a moment of uncontrolled passion. A moan of ecstasy slipped past her lips as she climaxed over and over, drowning in the sweetest agony she'd ever known as Nate's deep groans overlapped hers when he found his own release.

They lay motionless, heart to heart, and Morgan wanted to revel in the peace and contentment that made it impossible for her to move or draw a normal breath. She'd waited nearly twenty years to sleep with Nate, but her happiness was overshadowed with the reality that she may never have a future with this man.

"Did I hurt you, baby?"

"No."

Lifting his head, Nate stared at her. "Are you sure?" he asked.

Morgan forced a smile that didn't reach her eyes. "Very sure."

His kissed her forehead. "You were wonderful."

"So were you." She let out an audible gasp when he pulled out.

"I'll be right back," he said, tugging off the condom.

Rolling over on her side, she pulled her knees to her chest and waited for Nate to return. She couldn't control the thoughts running through her head. How long would they continue to be lovers before she was forced to tell

Nate that she wanted more than he was willing to give?

There might come a time when she would be able to balance marriage, motherhood, and a career, but there was one thing for certain. Nate would not be her husband or the father of her children.

He returned, kissing the nape of her neck. "Turn over on your back so I can clean you up a little."

She closed her eyes when he drew the warm, damp cloth between her legs. Try as she might, Morgan couldn't halt the tears filling her eyes. Nate was the perfect tender, gentle, and considerate lover.

"Hey, Mo. Why the tears?" he whispered.

"Can't a woman cry because she's happy?" she lied smoothly.

His expression was impassive. "I have a confession to make."

"What is it, Nate?"

"I'd rather face a charging bull than see a woman cry."

She swiped at the moisture on her cheeks. "I'm sorry."

Leaning closer, Nate pressed his mouth to hers. "Please don't apologize for being happy, because right about now I feel good enough to pick you up and run around outside as naked as the day we came into the world. And I wouldn't care who saw us."

Morgan giggled like a little girl. "And the good citizens of Haven Creek would run the both of us out of town for public lewdness."

"Have you ever wondered what it would be like to be a bad girl?"

"No! Why would you ask me that?" she asked Nate.

His right eyebrow lifted a fraction. "I'd thought about being a bad boy when I was younger. I didn't want to get arrested, but raise just enough hell to let out some frustration."

"Did that frustration have anything to do with you losing your mother?"

Nate's demeanor changed like quicksilver when he smiled. "Forget I mentioned it." He kissed Morgan. "I'll be right back," he promised again.

Morgan didn't know how she knew it, but she didn't have to have Francine's gift of sight to know that Nate's frustration stemmed from his mother's death. Had he blamed himself for not doing enough for her while she was alive? Or...her thoughts trailed off. No, she didn't even want to think that Lucas Shaw had Manda taken off life support so he could marry Odessa.

She mentally berated herself for believing the gossip that had spread across Cavanaugh Island like wildfire. People were saying that someone had hexed Manda, because one day she was the picture of health and the next she looked like the walking dead. And all fingers pointed to Odessa, who'd coveted her friend's husband and had come to the Creek to hasten Manda's passing.

Morgan realized she'd been too young to understand the dynamics or the superstitions, but what she'd overheard was disturbing enough for her to ask her mother about it. That was when Gussie sat her three daughters down and warned them that if they repeated gossip about Lucas, Manda, or Odessa they wouldn't be able to leave the house except to go to school until they were grown and out on their own. Not being Gullah, Gussie never wanted to get caught up with talk about family roots and conjuring.

Morgan hadn't thought about it until now, and she

wondered if Nate had knowledge about or believed what others had said about his parents. He'd opened up to her about his ex-wife, and if he trusted her with that he might eventually open up about his family. One thing she didn't intend to do was pry. She knew if she hoped to have a positive relationship with Nate, then there had to be mutual trust and respect, something that had been missing in her past two relationships.

Nate walked into the solarium carrying two pillows and a sheet he'd taken from the supply in her bedroom. He handed her the pillows. "I figure we should get some sleep if we're going to be up late tonight."

The first day of the fair didn't begin until 6:00 p.m. All week, workers had been setting up booths and various rides for kids and adults in an open lot in Angels Landing. There were games and contests, with prizes of large stuffed animals. There were booths selling corn dogs, pizza, hot dogs, hamburgers, corn on the cob, beer on tap, funnel cakes, sausage and peppers, cotton candy, and an assortment of candied apples.

Over the next three days, shops in the Cove and Creek would open their doors at six in the morning and remain open until midnight. The farmers' markets would set up in the Haven Creek Baptist Church parking lot, where locals and tourists would fill bags and baskets with locally grown fruits, vegetables, honey, and meat. On July 4, the Cove's town square would be the gathering place for those entering their cakes, pies, one-pots, casseroles, and barbecue in contests that would be judged by chefs and cooks from some of South Carolina's finest restaurants. Home-cooked meals would be made available for sale in all three island churches.

During the Island Fair, the population on Cavanaugh Island usually swelled to more than two thousand on any given day, and plainclothes police officers from Charleston were recruited to monitor suspicious persons and activities. Except for a few arrests for public intoxication, the four-day event usually went off without incident.

Morgan smiled as Nate spread the sheet over her body. Then he got into bed with her. "Does the sunlight bother you?" she asked when he pressed his groin to her hips.

"No." He kissed her shoulder. "Go to sleep, otherwise I'm going to want seconds."

"Aren't you the greedy one?"

"You didn't know? You smell good and taste even better. And when I'm inside you I feel like we're the only two people on the planet."

She closed her eyes, thinking about her lover's pronouncement. "We're only two when we're behind closed doors. Once we open them, we have to be ready for those who may want us together and many others who'd rather see us with other people."

"I don't want anyone else, Mo. I want you."

"You have me, Nate," she said—but he didn't have her in the way she wanted him to have her. She wanted him not just today, not just tomorrow, but forever. Although she hadn't included it on her wish list, she did want a happily ever after.

Pausing, she swallowed the lump rising in her throat. She hoped what she was about to reveal wouldn't shatter their fragile trust, but Morgan knew she had to let him know what lay in her heart. "I had a huge crush on you in high school."

A comfortable silence ensued. "Do you still have a

huge crush on me?" Nate asked, his voice lowering seductively.

Another beat passed. "I think it's a bit more than a crush."

One second she was lying beside Nate, and seconds later she was on her back with him straddling her. "You could've told me how much you liked me, Mo."

"Okay; I tell you that I've had feelings for you since high school, and then what?"

"I'd do this." He kissed the nape of her neck. "And this," Nate crooned, his mouth moving to a place under her ear, breathing a kiss there. "And of course this." His mouth covered hers in a kiss that was a caress. He surprised her when instead of making love to her again, he gathered her close and then lay down beside her.

Morgan fell asleep in his arms, reveling in how much she loved being there.

Morgan could feel the excitement in the air as she and Nate made their way to the fairgrounds. Small children who normally would've been getting ready to go to bed stared, seemingly transfixed, at the lights ringing the carnival, while teenagers screamed excitedly as they met up with friends. She found the carnivallike atmosphere infectious as she clung to Nate's arm.

They'd spent the rest of the morning sleeping, awakening to make love again, and then returning to sleep some more well into the afternoon. Nate wanted them to shower together, but she'd opted for a warm bath to soothe muscles she hadn't used in a long time. They'd shared a passionate kiss before he left, and he promised to return at seven to take her to the fair.

Morgan always liked the first night because the crowds were thinner. Cavanaugh Islanders referred to it as island night, only because most tourists waited until the following morning to visit. Experienced visitors had learned to leave their vehicles in Charleston and take the ferries to the island. Extra ferries were added to the schedule, so that there was a departure and arrival every twenty-five minutes. Free jitney service was available to drive folks around the island. Those wishing to spend all four days on the island reserved rooms at the Cove Inn, Sanctuary Cove's boardinghouse, and it wasn't uncommon for residents in Angels Landing to turn their homes into temporary bed-and-breakfasts.

Local shopkeepers always looked forward to the Island Fair as a chance to exhibit their wares. The revenue derived from the four days provided additional income, ensuring financial viability until the next summer season.

Morgan knew that once the restoration of Angels Landing Plantation was finished, it would generate even larger crowds—not just for the four days of the fair or during the summer months, but year-round. Angels Landing Plantation would mirror Colonial Williamsburg in its authenticity. The mansion, slave village, and outbuildings were certain to bring history buffs and school groups to the island, and the conference center, museum, and inn would attract corporate groups and those looking for a destination wedding.

"Do you want to go on the rides or eat first?" Nate asked as they neared the perimeter of the fairgrounds.

Morgan had informed him that she wanted to ride the carousel, bumper cars, and the Ferris wheel. "If you're hungry we can eat now and ride later." She glanced up at his profile, still awed at his resemblance to Michelangelo's David. He appeared dramatic and sexy in black jeans, a T-shirt, and running shoes.

"Don't you mean hurl later?" Nate said teasingly.

"I beg your pardon! I'll have you know this girl is tougher than she looks," she retorted.

Nate pointed to the roller coaster whirling wildly around the track. The riders were screaming hysterically. "Are you willing to go on that?"

She shook her head. "I don't do roller coasters."

Leaning into her, he pressed his mouth to her ear. "Are you afraid you'll hurl, baby?"

Resting her palm on his chest, she pushed him back. "No."

"Put up or shut up, beautiful."

Morgan wasn't certain what Nate sought to prove by getting her to agree to ride on the roller coaster. "What are you wagering, handsome?"

Nate glanced around, then dipped his head and whispered a secret in her ear. "If you agree, then nod your head. If not, then say no."

If she took him up on his offer it would be a win-win not only for her but for Nate, too. Affecting a sexy moue, she nodded. Throwing back his head, he laughed heartily, the sound rumbling in his chest.

"Do you mind letting us in on the joke?" asked a familiar female voice.

Morgan and Nate turned at the same time. Francine and David stood less than a foot away, watching them. Francine had exchanged her green sundress for a white halter top and black stretch cropped slacks. David was dressed down in a pair of khakis, slip-ons, and a short-sleeved white shirt.

"Hey, you guys! How long have you been here?" Morgan asked.

David extended a hand to Nate. "We just got here."

Nate released David's hand. "Mo and I were going to get something to eat. Do you want to join us?"

Francine and David shared a look. "Sure," she said.

The two couples headed to the area where people were lining up in front of food trucks. Nate rested a hand at the small of Morgan's back. "Why don't you and Red get a table while David and I pick up the food?"

"But you don't know what we want," Morgan said to Nate.

Laugh lines fanned out around David's deep-set dark eyes when he smiled. "Don't worry, ladies, Nate and I will get a little of everything."

Nate winked at Morgan. "Yeah. *We've* got this."

Francine's eyes narrowed as the two men walked away. "Since when did they become buddies?"

Morgan lifted her shoulders under her tank top. "Since Nate finally realized there's nothing going on between me and David," she said, heading for the picnic area, which was dotted with dozens of long tables. A group of teenagers had opted to eat sitting on the grass.

Francine swung her leg over an empty bench, placing her handbag on a space beside her, while Morgan sat opposite her, resting her bag next to her. "There was a time when I thought you and David would become a couple."

"David's too uptight for me," Morgan admitted.

Shifting slightly, Francine gave Morgan a long, penetrating stare. "And Nate isn't?"

"No. Once you get to know him you'll find he's rather laid-back. I think he's more complex than uptight."

Francine leaned over the table when several women sat down at the opposite end. "I not only noticed but felt the heat between the two of you at breakfast this morning. And please don't insult my gift when you talk about being friends," she whispered. "I should've told you even before Nate came back to the Creek that you were going to get involved with him."

Morgan felt a shiver snake its way down her back. "What's next, Fran? You'll see us married and with a house filled with children, cats, and dogs. Speaking of cats, do you still have keys to my place?"

Francine narrowed her green eyes. "Yes. Why?"

"I'm going to need you to come over tomorrow afternoon and check on Rasputin." Morgan held up a hand when Francine opened her mouth. "Please don't say anything until I'm finished. Nate and I are going over to Sullivan's Island tonight. We don't expect to get back until late tomorrow afternoon. You don't have to worry about changing Rasputin's water, because I have the automatic pet waterer and preset feeder. He'll probably run and hide when you come in, but knowing someone is in the house will ease his anxiety of being left alone for so many hours."

"Who or what's on Sullivan's Island?"

"I don't know. Nate says it's a surprise." Morgan had told Francine a half-truth. She'd been shocked when he'd mentioned Sullivan's Island, but there was no way she was going to tell Francine what he'd planned for them.

"You and your neurotic cat. What you need is to marry Nate and have a few—"

"Enough about me marrying Nate," Morgan said, interrupting her. "It's not going to happen, so please don't mention it again."

"Why not?" Francine asked, ignoring her entreaty.

Chewing her lip, Morgan stared at a nearby table, which was filled with the women who made up the beautification committee. "Nate told me he's never getting married again."

The redhead snorted delicately. "And you believe him."

"Of course I believe him, Fran. Why shouldn't I?"

"Have you heard of people changing their minds? I do it at least two or three times a day."

Morgan shook her head. "Folks don't change their minds about something as serious as marriage. Either you want to do it or you don't. And Nate has been very vocal about not doing it again."

Lines of frustration creased Francine's smooth forehead. "You can't tell me he's going to close himself off from women because his ho of an ex-wife opened her legs like an ATM spitting out cash. I can't begin to imagine his humiliation once she revealed the number of men she'd slept with, but at least he came away looking like a good guy, which is more than I can say about most of the male celebrities who've been caught with their pants down."

"I don't think he was concerned about his image," Morgan said in defense of her lover. "Something tells me he doesn't trust women."

"Why on earth would you say that, Mo? Men who don't trust women use them. And I doubt very much if he's using you."

"No, he isn't, and if he tried I'd be gone so fast he'd

forget what I looked like. There's no way I'm going to allow another man to use me."

"Now you sound like me, Mo. Marrying Aiden was a big mistake, but I'm not going to blame all men because I'd fallen in love with a parasite."

"Are you saying you're ready to get married again?" Morgan asked Francine.

"I'm not actively looking for a husband, but I realize I'm not getting any younger, and if I want a couple of babies I have to start viewing the men I date differently."

"What you need to do is learn to cook," Morgan said with a twinkle in her eye. "At least enough so your husband and children don't starve."

Francine rolled her eyes. "I don't need to learn if he cooks."

Morgan smiled, her straight white teeth contrasting with her dark skin. "What are you going to do when you meet someone you like? Ask him whether he can cook?"

"That's not funny, Mo," Francine said. She sobered quickly, a slight frown appearing between her eyes. "I'm looking for someone with whom I can have a good time. If it leads to marriage, then that would be great. But if I don't marry again before my biological clock stops ticking, then I'll adopt. There are too many of our babies languishing in foster care who need a permanent home. I'm also not going to apologize when I say I plan to spoil the hell outta them."

Morgan shook her head. "I know children aren't perfect, but if your children turn into Bay Bay's kids, then please don't ask me to babysit."

Morgan was always available to babysit Amanda whenever Rachel and James wanted to spend quality time

together. One weekend, she had all her nephews and her
niece over for an extended slumber party. She'd taken re-
quests for their favorite foods, movies, and board games.
There was nonstop noise, and the doors were constantly
opening and closing whenever they came into or left the
house. Brian and Brandon assisted her on the gas grill,
while Amanda and Ethan were given the task of setting
and clearing the picnic table. Morgan enjoyed spending
time with her niece and nephews, but was left thoroughly
exhausted from the ongoing activity. After the weekend
she had a newfound respect for women who had to care
for children *and* work outside the home.

Francine patted Morgan's hand. "Now, you know
you're going to love my babies even if they're off the
chain. All I have to tell them is their Auntie Mo is going
to cook for them and they'll camp out on your front
porch, crying until you open the door."

Clamping a hand over her mouth, Morgan laughed so
hard that her sides hurt. Even if she was feeling down she
could always count on her friend to cheer her up. And
Francine could always count on Morgan to be there for
her. Morgan wondered what her friend would say when
she finally admitted she'd fallen in love with Nate, and
that Francine's vision had come true after all.

Chapter Eighteen

$\backsim\!\!\!\!\backsim$

Morgan watched Nate and David approach. "What on earth did you buy?" she asked them. Nate carried a cardboard drinks holder containing large cups of beer and lemonade while cradling four aluminum-covered paper plates to his chest. David also held a number of plastic containers. Morgan slid over, making room for Nate as he sat beside her. They shared a smile when he kissed her cheek.

"We got burgers, fries, pizza, sausage-and-pepper sandwiches, buffalo wings, and corn on the cob."

David sat down next to Francine and uncovered his containers. "And we have fried calamari, shrimp cocktail, soft-shell crabs, and beef and fish tacos."

Francine stared at David, her mouth gaping. "Who's going to eat all this food?"

"We are," David and Nate chorused.

There was no way four people could eat that much in one sitting. Nate placed a cup of lemonade in front of her along with a foam plate and plastic utensils, while David put out a stack of napkins and more plastic forks and spoons.

"We're going to give some of this away. I wouldn't want any of it to go to waste," Morgan stated. Rising slightly, she picked up a box containing two single-serving pizzas and set it aside. Then she covered the containers with two sausage-and-pepper heroes and another brimming with chicken wings. Stacking them, she stood up and walked over to a table where a young woman was sitting with three tweens. "Hey, Queenie. Nate bought too much food, so I'd like to give it to you and your children."

The family would've been homeless if Queenie's elderly parents hadn't taken them in. Willie Evans had waited until New Year's Eve to inform Queenie that he was leaving his family for a woman he'd met on the Internet. His defection was short-lived, because the woman reconciled with her boyfriend soon thereafter. Even though Willie begged Queenie to take him back, she refused. The former stay-at-home mother had gotten a part-time job as a salesclerk at the Cannery. Whenever Morgan shopped at the store, which offered local canned fruits and vegetables, she made certain to give Queenie the sale because it added to her commission.

Queenie's eyelids fluttered as she attempted to blink back tears. "I can't take charity, Mo."

"It's not charity, Queenie. It's food that's going to go to waste. And I shouldn't have to remind you that folks here liken throwing away food to a sin. So please take it."

"What do you say, kids?" Queenie asked her children.

"Thank you, Miss Mo," they said in unison.

Pushing her long, brunette hair behind her ears, Queenie took the containers. "Thank you, Mo."

Leaning over, Morgan kissed her former classmate's cheek. "You're welcome."

Morgan felt the heat from Nate's gaze when she returned to sit next to him. "Please don't say anything," she whispered.

Nate pressed his mouth to her ear. "You never cease to amaze me."

She met Francine's eyes, and the two shared a barely perceptible nod.

Dusk descended over the island as the fairgrounds filled with people. Children's screams and laughter blended with the sound of barkers inviting revelers to try a game of chance. In between bites of food, Morgan, Francine, David, and Nate kept up a steady stream of conversation, ranging from the latest Hollywood gossip to the upcoming local elections.

She noticed Nate was silent once they'd begun discussing celebrity reality shows, and she wondered if he was reliving the years he'd spent in L.A. He became more animated when the topic segued to sports, and even more so when it came to the election.

"Do you think Alice Parker can beat Spencer White?" Morgan asked.

David nodded. "Even though I don't live here, I've heard a lot of talk on the mainland that she has a good chance of becoming mayor of the Cove."

"That's because Jason Parker is her husband," Francine said. "After all, he does represent us in Congress."

"And don't forget they're loaded, so I'm sure she has a lot of money backing her campaign," David added. "What about you, Nate?"

Nate swallowed a mouthful of beer. "What about me?"

"Who would you vote for if you lived in the Cove?"

"It would probably be Alice. She's a lot prettier than Spencer," Nate drawled, deadpan.

Morgan gave him an incredulous stare. "You'd vote for someone because of the way they look rather than the issues?"

"It's all about appearances. Correct me if I'm wrong, David," Nate stated.

The attorney nodded. "Nate's right. Jason won his first term based on his looks. Luckily for him, he proved to his constituents that he also had the intelligence to go along with his face and body." He looked at Francine. "Are you going to vote for Spencer because he's one of the island's most eligible bachelors?"

Francine rolled her head on her neck. "No." The single word was pregnant with indignation. "FYI, Spencer isn't the only eligible bachelor. What's Nate? Chopped liver?"

"Nate is *not* an eligible bachelor," Morgan said.

Shifting slightly, Nate turned to give Morgan a long, penetrating stare. "Are you saying I'm out of contention?"

Pinpoints of heat stung her face. "No...um," she stammered. "That's not what I meant and you know it."

Francine touched a napkin to the corners of her mouth. "Please explain yourself, Mo."

Morgan's gaze shifted from Nate to Francine. "Whose side are you on, anyway?" She looked back at Nate. "You're not out of contention, but I'd like to believe you're temporarily unattainable to other women who may have romantic designs on you."

Smiling, Nate raised his cup. "Well put, baby."

She raised her cup, touching it to Nate's. "Thank you, sweetheart."

A comfortable silence followed the endearments as Morgan and Nate shared a smile. He'd told her when he'd whispered in her ear what he wanted her to do to him and what he was willing to become, and Morgan's mind was filled with the endless possibilities she'd conjured up, all of which would make their night one to remember. Then she sat up straight when she saw a familiar face. She almost hadn't recognized Bobby Nugent without his paint-spattered coveralls and painter's cap. He stood several feet away, waving to her.

Resting a hand on Nate's shoulder, Morgan pushed to her feet and stepped over the bench. "I'll be right back. I want to talk to someone." She and Bobby moved away from the table. "Good evening, Bobby."

He inclined his salt-and-pepper head. A network of tiny lines fanned out around his blue-green eyes, which were set in a deeply tanned henna-brown face. "Miss Morgan. The men told me about the Island Fair and I thought I'd come by and see what they were talking about."

"What do you think?" she asked.

He smiled, exhibiting a mouth filled with tobacco-stained teeth. "It's a real nice tradition you have here. I called my wife and told her to drive down from Savannah and hang out with me until the Fourth."

When Morgan first met the contractor, he told her he'd been married for forty years, and this job would be his

last because his wife had been nagging him to retire. An
avid fisherman, he'd bought a boat. His future plans included sailing to the Caribbean, where he would live with
his in-laws during the winter months.

She touched Bobby's shoulder. "I want to you meet the
carpenter who will supervise the rebuilding of the slave
village."

Nate stood up when Morgan beckoned him, then shook
hands with Bobby when she introduced him as the manager for the restoration project. "You've been entrusted
with a tremendous responsibility."

Bobby nodded. "You've got that right. It appears you'll
have your share with the village."

Crossing his arms over his chest, Nate studied the man.
"It shouldn't be too difficult," he said confidently. "I've
built homes from the ground up, renovated apartments,
and restored others to their original state. In fact, I intend
to survey the site one day next week. If you don't mind,
I'd like to come by and take a look at what you've done
to the main house."

Bobby nodded. "I'd love to have your opinion on a few
things. We had a devil of a time stripping the wallpaper."

Nate smiled. Bobby had just given him the opening
he needed to broach the topic Morgan had complained
about. "I've found using fabric softener and water helps
loosen the old adhesive. But when working larger jobs
I rent a wallpaper steamer. The advantage is the water
never cools, making the job go by more quickly."

Bobby scratched his stubble. "I guess you can say I'm
old school. I tried the machine and fabric softener once
with disastrous results."

"Are you finished stripping?"

"We have one more bedroom."

Nate detected Morgan's perfume as she moved closer to his side. "Don't start it. I'll rent the steamer and show you how it's done. That way you'll know for the next time."

"I told Miss Morgan there's not going to be a next time. I'm retiring after this job."

"If there's anything I can do to help out, just tell Miss Morgan and I'll come by," Nate volunteered. She didn't know it, but he would do anything to ease her anxiety about the project.

Bobby extended his hand. "Much appreciate the offer. I'll leave you folks to finish your food, 'cause right about now my belly is talking to me."

Reaching for Morgan's hand, Nate laced their fingers together. "I thought you told me he came highly recommended," he said when Bobby was out of earshot.

"He was," she said in confirmation.

"I have a feeling he's distracted. He probably spends most of his day thinking about what he's going to do when he retires."

"I can't fire him until I find someone to replace him."

"You don't have to fire him, Mo. He's already agreed to let me stop by and see what he's doing. As he said, he's old school." Morgan met his eyes when he stared down at her. "Give me another twenty years, I'll probably be old school, too."

"You can't say that about your father."

"That's because carpentry is not the same as building a house. With construction, there's electrical, plumbing, insulation, roofing, siding, windows, walls, floors, and painting. Wood is wood, whether it's natural, treated, native, or exotic."

"It's the same with textiles."

He smiled. "There you go."

Morgan squeezed Nate's hand. "I need to walk off some of this food."

David and Francine had cleared away the remains of the food by the time Nate and Morgan returned to the table. "What are you grinning about?" Morgan asked Francine, who gave her a Cheshire cat grin.

Francine glanced at David. "David has invited us to come to his place next Saturday night for dinner and cocktails."

Morgan started. "It's my—"

"I know it's your birthday, Mo," Francine said, cutting her off. "That's why we want to get together. That is, unless you've planned something." She gave Nate a look of feigned innocence. "I'm sorry, Nate. Did you want to do something special with Mo?"

"I didn't even know about her birthday."

David placed his arm around Francine's shoulders. "Then you don't mind if we celebrate it together?" he asked Nate.

There came a beat. Even though David appeared to be enthralled with Francine, Nate couldn't rid himself of the nagging notion that David liked Morgan for more than just friendship. He had to hand it to the dapper attorney; he had exquisite taste. David, he mused, would bear watching closely.

"No, I don't mind." He didn't mind because he had time to come up with something special.

"I guess that does it," David practically crowed.

"Francine will let you know once we finalize everything."

"No clowns," Morgan warned.

Nate snapped his fingers. "Damn, baby. You shot down my surprise."

She squinted at him. "If you bring a clown around me I won't be responsible for what happens to him."

"Remember, David, no clowns," Nate repeated. "Mo and I are going to walk around before we go on a few rides. What are you guys going to do?"

Francine looped arms with David. "We're going to the Bingo tent before tackling the rides."

Nate nodded. "If we don't see you later, then have fun."

David and Francine headed for the Bingo tent, while Nate directed Morgan along a row of colorful booths, each of which offered a passerby the chance to play a game and win a prize. He stopped in front of one that had a line of mechanical ducks against the back wall. "Do you want a stuffed animal?"

"Yes."

He pointed to rows of stuffed bears, monkeys, and penguins. "Which one do you want?"

"I want the sock monkey with the long arms and legs," Morgan said. Nate paid the vendor and then picked up an air rifle. Her dimpled smile grew wider with the pinging sound of the pellets hitting the ducks in rapid succession. Nate had hit every one of them dead center.

He put down the rifle, pointing to the upper shelf. "I'd like the large monkey."

Picking up a pole with a clawlike end, the vendor grasped the toy, handing it to Nate. "Nice shooting. And you're lucky, because it's the last sock monkey I have."

"Thanks." Nate wrapped the toy's long arms around Morgan's neck. "Are you going to give him a name?"

"Caesar."

He shook his head, not wanting to laugh. "Is he Augustus or Julius?" Morgan did laugh. The sound was as sensuous as her smile. "What's so funny?" he asked.

"He's not a Roman emperor; he's the genetically engineered chimp from *Rise of the Planet of the Apes.*"

"Are you talking about that movie with the monkeys that run amok?"

She laughed again. "Yes. I love that movie. Have you seen it?"

It was Nate's turn to laugh. "I'm afraid I missed that one."

"I have the DVD at home. Whenever you have some time we'll watch it together."

Curving an arm around Morgan's waist, he pulled her to him. "Do you think Rasputin will resent Caesar?"

"Not if I put him on the bed. Ras knows he's not allowed to jump on the countertops, tables, or beds."

"How do you train a cat not to climb when it's the most natural thing for them to do?" he asked, leading her away from the crowd that had gathered at the booth.

"Actually, I read that using cookie sheets keeps them down, and it worked. I think the noise it made when it fell to the floor bothered him. In the beginning he ran and hid before coming back to try it again. After a while he learned to stay down."

"That's ingenious."

"Training him to stay off the bed was easier. I bought a motion detector that expels compressed air whenever he comes too close. One shot of air and he'll take off like a rocket. It's a lot more humane that squirting him with water. There's a window perch and a climbing tree in the area off the pantry for him to climb on. He stays there as long as sun comes through the window. Otherwise he sleeps on the mat at the side door."

"Have you changed your mind about mating him with Patches?"

"I'll agree, only if I can have the pick of the litter."

Nate tightened his hold on her waist. "That's a promise." He stopped abruptly when their path was blocked by a young girl glaring at them. She'd rested her hands at her waist. Without warning, she opened her mouth and emitted a bloodcurdling scream.

Morgan and Nate looked at each other. "What's wrong with her?" she asked.

The child's chin quivered. "I want a monkey!"

Nate smothered a curse when he realized the girl wanted Morgan's sock monkey, and then he remembered the vendor saying it was the last one. The child wasn't much older than his five-year-old niece. He'd witnessed Gabrielle's hissy fits on more than one occasion. Sharon usually stood her ground with her willful daughter, while Nate gave into her to stop her tears.

Seeing the child was an aching reminder of all the times he'd seen his mother crying. She'd asked everyone not to feel sorry for her, because she was going to a better place, but he knew she was afraid. Manda would often deflect the conversation about her deteriorating health, saying her only regret was leaving her children without a mother. She'd made Nate and Sharon promise not to judge their father harshly if or when he decided to remarry.

Nate knew there was the possibility that his father could remarry, but he never thought it would happen within months of Manda's passing. However, it all made sense when Lucas announced he was to become a father for the third time. Only his mother's warning about respecting his father kept Nate from blurting out the reason for the fast nuptials. Odessa had found herself pregnant with Lucas's baby as Manda lay dying. Nate shook his head as if to free himself from the memories. He didn't want to dwell on past hurt, but instead cherish the good times he had with Morgan.

Morgan reached up and unhooked the Velcro fastenings on the sock monkey's arms. Hunkering down until her face was even with the child's, she extended the toy. "I'm going to give this to you on one condition. Do you understand what I'm saying?" The girl nodded and Morgan smiled. There was something about the child's face that reminded Morgan of photographs her grandfather had taken of her when she was that age. They had the same complexion and features. Her mother had parted her hair in the middle and styled it with two thick braids.

"Keisha! Oh, there you are," said a woman who was obviously the child's mother. Keisha was a miniature version of her mother.

Keisha tugged on the woman's hand. "The nice lady is going to give me her monkey, Mama."

"Oh, no, she's not, baby. You can't go around asking people to give you what doesn't belong to you. Maybe she has a little girl she wants to give it to."

Morgan didn't recognize the woman or her daughter, so they were either newcomers or tourists. "It's all right.

I don't have a little girl and I do want to give it to her. But Keisha is going to have to promise me that she will always listen to her mama, or the monkey will come back to me."

Keisha puffed out her narrow chest. "I always listen to my mama and daddy," she said proudly, not seeing her mother cut her eyes at her.

"If that's the case, then you can have the monkey."

"What do you say, Keisha?"

"Thank you, Mama."

"Don't thank me. Thank the pretty lady."

Keisha's large dark eyes sparkled in reflection of the lights that lit up the fairgrounds. "I don't know her name, Mama."

Morgan swallowed the laughter bubbling up in her throat. "It's Morgan."

"Thank you, Miss Morgan."

"You're welcome, Keisha."

Keisha clutched the monkey to her chest in a deathlike grip. "Does he have a name?"

"Yes. It's Caesar."

The child laughed hysterically. "That's the monkey from the movie, Mama!" Everyone laughed, including Nate.

Keisha's mother extended her hand. "By the way, I'm Georgia."

Morgan took the proffered hand. "You know who I am. This is Nate Shaw. He won Caesar for me."

Nate took a step and shook Georgia's hand. "Your daughter is precious."

Georgia smiled. "Keisha is what I call my miracle baby. My husband and I tried for more than ten years to have a child, but once we talked about adopting I got pregnant. I know she's a little spoiled, but I'm hoping to change that before she starts school next month."

"There's nothing wrong with spoiling a child," Nate said.

Morgan gave him a sidelong glance. She remembered him saying that he'd wanted children. She recalled his words as vividly as if he'd just uttered them: *I wanted children, but my ex-wife didn't, because her career was more important than our marriage.*

Did he still want them? Since he didn't want to marry, would that mean he was okay with having a child out of wedlock? He seemed adamant about never fathering a child without the benefit of marriage. Staring at Keisha, Morgan felt something so foreign she thought she was hallucinating. She felt the pull of motherhood for the first time. She shook her head as if to banish the thought, yet it persisted. She wanted a baby—and not any man's baby: Nate's.

"That's what my husband says." She gave a Morgan a warm smile. "I thank you again for being so selfless."

"You're welcome. Enjoy her."

"Thank you."

Morgan watched the mother and daughter walk away, and then let out an audible sigh. "I guess it wasn't meant for me and Caesar to live together."

Nate wrapped both arms around Morgan, pulling her to his chest. "I didn't know you were masquerading as Mother Teresa. First you give away food and now your sock monkey. What's next? Rasputin?"

"That's where I draw the line, Nate. Ras is my baby. My grandpa taught me if you have enough, then you can always afford to give some away."

Cradling her face, he met her eyes. "Your grandpa was a very wise man. What about a real baby, Mo?"

Ignoring curious stares coming from those watching their interchange, Morgan anchored her arms under Nate's shoulders. "That will happen eventually."

His expressive eyebrows lifted. "When?"

A beat passed. "When I meet the man who'll love me as much as I love him."

A hint of a smile tilted the corners of Nate's mouth. "It's going to happen for you."

She smiled. "What's makes you so certain?"

"Don't you know you're the total package? You're everything a man wants in a woman, with a little extra thrown in."

Morgan couldn't help but laugh. "Is the extra a perk or a benefit?"

"It's definitely a perk."

"Shame on you. Get a room, brother."

Bryce stood a short distance away, watching them. Morgan managed to extricate herself from Nate's embrace. "Hello, Bryce."

Bryce nodded, smiling. "Hey, Mo. How are you?"

"I'm good," she said.

He clapped Nate on the shoulder. "I called you earlier this morning to ask whether you were coming here tonight, but it went to voice mail."

Nate patted the pocket of his jeans, where he kept his cell phone. "I haven't checked my messages today. Where's Stacy?"

"She wasn't feeling well, so she decided to stay home tonight."

"Who did you come with?" Nate asked Bryce.

"Mom. I left her in the gaming tent. Don't worry, Nate. I'm not going to do anything that—"

"Don't worry, bro, I trust you. Is there anything you need to tell me? Because Mo and I are leaving."

"Where are you going?" Bryce asked, looking at Morgan and then his brother.

Nate put an arm around Bryce's neck, holding him tightly while he rubbed his knuckles over his head. "Do you really expect me to answer that? I didn't think so," he added when the younger man slipped out of the loose headlock. "Tell Dad and Odessa I'll stop by the house and see them after the fair. Webb, Sharon, and the kids are back, so if you don't see them tonight there's no doubt they'll be here tomorrow."

"Did you tell her she's going to become an aunt?"

"No. I'll leave that for you and Stacy to tell her."

"Mo, did Nate tell you that I'm getting married?"

Morgan had to decide whether to pretend she didn't know about the upcoming nuptials or to be truthful. She decided on the latter. "Yes, he did. Congratulations to you and your fiancée."

"Are you coming to the wedding?"

She glanced at Nate. "I will if I get an invitation."

Bryce looked confused. "You don't need an invitation if you're coming with Nate."

Before she could say anything, Nate responded. "Of course she's coming with me. Who else would I bring?"

Bryce gave Nate a rough embrace. "Don't start me lying, brother. I'm going to find Mom and let her know I'm going home."

"How are you getting there?" Nate asked.

"I'll hitch a ride with someone going back to the Creek."

"Forget it, Bryce. I'll drop you off. Meet us in the parking area."

Morgan knew she would have to wait for another night to go on the carnival rides as she walked to the place where Nate had parked his truck. "What did you tell your brother about me?" she asked.

"We don't discuss you."

"Then why would he assume I would attend his wedding?"

"Isn't it obvious, Morgan?"

"Not to me, Nate."

"I've been back more than seven months and this is the first time anyone's seen me with a woman."

"It's possible you could've been seeing someone on the down low."

"That's something I did when I was a teenager. At thirty-seven I'm much too old to sneak around."

"What kind of down low were you into?"

Nate stopped when they reached his truck. His hands circled her waist, pulling her so that she was leaning against him. "Do you really want to know?"

"Of course I want to know."

Nate raised his head, staring up at the nearly full moon. "The year I turned sixteen I started sleeping with an older woman. She was divorced and highly sexual, and I was a randy teenage boy ready and willing to give her what she wanted. "

"Do you still keep in touch with her?"

"Come on, Mo, no more questions about that."

"Why not?"

"Because I don't want to talk about her."

Morgan stared at his face. His expression looked

macabre in the silvery moonlight. "Who do you want to talk about?"

"If it's not about you, then there's nothing to discuss. Why dig up the past?"

"Okay. If that's the case, I want to tell you something I've been thinking about for a short while now." She took a deep breath. "I want to fall in love and I want children, but I know you don't want either because you're afraid of what happened in the past."

"I'm not afraid, Mo," he countered defensively. "I just don't want to deal with the heartbreak again."

There came a beat. "I can understand that." Morgan gave Nate a forced smile, but inside she was truly hurt. She thought what they were building was strong enough to change his mind.

Chapter Nineteen

⟜⟶

Nate maneuvered up the driveway to the beachfront B and B. Decelerating, he followed the narrow road leading to one of two guest cottages on the expansive property. He'd found Morgan unusually quiet during the drive from Haven Creek to Sullivan's Island, and wondered if perhaps she now had reservations about accompanying him.

He'd suggested going there to minimize gossip about his truck being parked at her house overnight. Jeff told him about the gossipmongers who had initiated rumors when he'd stayed over at Angels Landing, not because he was sleeping with Kara but because he was protecting her after several kids threw bricks through her windows. He didn't know why people felt the need to spy on their neighbors. Perhaps their lives were so unremarkable they had to divert attention away from themselves.

His own life was also predictable, but he lived it by his own rules. Nate divided his nights between sleeping in Sharon's guest room and in his apartment on the air mattress. He got up before dawn to paint until it was time to go to the workshop. Most mornings Bryce was there when he arrived, and they worked together through the early afternoon. Morgan had become a welcome distraction from what others may have considered a humdrum existence. Besides himself, only Bryce and his father knew the intense gratification of working with wood. He'd become addicted to its different smells and gloried in the feel of the grain under his fingertips. Once a piece of wood began to take shape, just looking at it was akin to a rush.

Nate pulled alongside the cottage and shifted into park, but didn't turn off the engine. Resting his arm over the back of the passenger seat, he turned to stare at Morgan. She was so still she could've been carved out of marble. "You don't have to do this if you don't want to."

Morgan turned her head, staring at him. "I never said I didn't want to."

He unbuckled his seat belt. "It's what you're not saying, Mo. You look like you've been sentenced to life in prison without the possibility of parole. I thought you would be a little more animated."

She gave him a too-bright grin. "Is that animated enough?"

Nate was not amused. "Something's wrong, and we're not getting out of this car until you tell me what's bothering you."

"I feel comfortable telling you whatever is on my mind, and I'd hoped you would do the same," she said.

Nate rested his hand alongside her cheek. "I want to open up to you, but I can't right now, baby. I should've warned you when you agreed to go out with me that I'm carrying a lot of baggage."

Her hand covered his. "Aren't you tired of holding onto it?" The query was whispered.

He closed his eyes, taking a deep breath. "Sometimes I am." Nate reopened them, the light from the dashboard casting long and short shadows over his face.

Morgan leaned in as close as her seat belt would allow, their lips only inches apart. "You can't heal unless you're willing to let go of the hurt, darling."

"Now I'm your darling?" he said, smiling.

Morgan flashed a dimpled smile. "You're my BBD."

"What's that?"

"My baby, boo, *and* my darling."

"Now, that sounds real serious."

Morgan shook her head. "You don't know how serious I am." She wanted to tell Nate that her earlier confession of love wasn't a slip of the tongue, but that she was truly in love with him. But she didn't want to spoil what they had with declarations of love.

"I like you, Morgan," he whispered. "Much more than I want or need to."

"So it's not about sex?"

He went completely still. "Is that what you think? That I pursued you because I wanted to sleep with you?"

She stared at him through lowered lids. "Why else do men seek out women?"

"The same reason why women chase men," Nate countered.

"Usually it's because we want an emotional *and* physical relationship." Morgan knew she'd shocked him when he eased back. "The initial attraction is always physical.

When I walked into Perry's for the first time and I saw you sitting with Jesse, it was like I was coming face-to-face with my favorite idol. My heart was beating so fast I thought I was going to faint. And when Jesse invited us to sit with you I was certain you could see me shaking."

"Rachel told me the more popular boys usually played football or basketball, but you were an anomaly because you were consistently on the high honor roll and were offered an academic rather than an athletic scholarship."

Her mother had preached to her daughters that when it came time to fall in love or marry, the requirement should be intellect, not good looks. Well, Morgan had proven Gussie wrong, because she'd fallen in love with a man who had both.

"I always thought you were cute, Mo."

She laughed softly. "Yeah, right. Like a little-kid cute."

"By the time you'd grown up, I was living on the West Coast. Maybe if I'd come back things would've been different between us. If I'd decided to stay, we could've been married with a couple of kids by now."

"Maybe, but there is one thing no one has ever been able to do."

"What's that?" Nate asked.

"Go back and change the past." Slumping in his seat, Morgan watched as he pressed his head to the headrest.

"I would willingly give up a kidney to be able to change my past."

She unsnapped her seat belt, leaning into him. "Even if you can't change your past, you do have the power to determine your future."

Nate took a deep breath and blew it out. "There was a time when I believed I'd mapped out my future. That was before my mother died. Then everything changed. Instead of coming back to Haven Creek after graduating college to take over the family business, I stayed in California. My father—" His cell phone rang, the familiar number of the caller appearing on the dashboard's screen. "Excuse me, but I have to take this."

He punched a button, activating the Bluetooth. "Hey, DW. What's up?"

"I asked Nicole to marry me and she said yes."

He smiled. "Congratulations. It took you two long enough to come to your senses."

"No shit," Dwight drawled.

"Watch your mouth, Dwight. I have a lady with me and you're on speaker."

"Sorry about that. You promised if I married her you would stand in as my best man."

"And I always keep my promise. Let me know when and where and I'll be there."

"This coming weekend in Vegas."

Nate hesitated. "Which day?"

"Friday night."

Saturday was Morgan's birthday, and Nate had promised David and Francine they would get together to help her celebrate it. "Can't you put it off until the following weekend?"

"No can do. Nicole's folks are flying in from Milwaukee. It's the only weekend they can get off until October."

"Hold on, Dwight," Nate said, when Morgan touched his arm. "What is it, baby?" he whispered.

Morgan pressed her mouth to his ear. "Go to Vegas. We can celebrate my birthday when you get back."

"Are you sure?" he whispered.

She mouthed, "Very sure."

Nate kissed her parted lips. "DW?"

"What's up, Nate?"

"You've got yourself a best man."

There came a pause. "Thank you."

"Anytime, buddy."

"I'm sending a private jet to Charleston to fly you out and take you back. I'll call you in a couple of days with the schedule. Look, Nate, I gotta go. Nicole and I are going out to dinner with her sister. We'll talk later."

"Later," Nate replied, ending the call. He cocked his head. "I'm so sorry, Mo."

She smiled at him. "Stop apologizing, Nate. It's not every day you become a best man."

"Wrong, baby. Bryce also asked me to be his best man."

"Lucky you."

Nate rested a hand on Morgan's knee. She'd exchanged her jeans for a pair of shorts. "You're right. Lucky me."

She slipped her hands between his thighs, laughing softly when she cupped his sex over his jeans. "My, my, my. What do we have here?"

"You're going to make me embarrass myself if you don't stop feeling me up."

"I never suspected you would embarrass so easily."

"You'd better stop, Mo, otherwise I'll take you on the rear seat. And who knows who could be watching?"

Nate cut off the engine. "Come on. Let's go inside."

He got out and came around to assist Morgan, then retrieved their bags from the cargo area. Nate set the bags down and searched under a planter. He found the keys

Lucy Granier had left for him. Twin lights flanking the front door provided enough light for him to open the two dead bolt locks. Inside, the glow from table lamps bathed the white walls in a soft gold.

It was as if time had stood still for Nate. Nothing had changed. The guesthouse was one continuous living space. It was furnished with a queen-size wrought iron bed topped with colorful quilts and tucked in a corner under a window, a bistro table and two chairs, a love seat covered with red-and-white striped ticking, and a white wicker partition, which concealed the door to a bathroom with a freestanding shower, commode, and basin. He'd always felt more comfortable here than in a room at a five-star hotel. The unpretentious room was imbued with a sense of casual comfort. He stepped aside, and Morgan walked in, glancing around the small guest cottage.

"What do you think?"

Morgan walked over to the bed and turned back the quilts to reveal crisp white sheets. "It's charming."

"There's no radio or television."

She patted the mattress. "That doesn't matter. Come and sit with me."

Nate locked the door and tossed the keys on the small round table near the door. He paused, closing the shuttered windows. He kicked off his running shoes and sat next to Morgan. He lay back, bringing her with him. "What are you thinking about?"

Shifting on her side, Morgan braced an elbow on the bed, cradling her head on the heel of her hand. "What makes you think I'm thinking about something?"

He ran his finger down the length of her short nose. "Didn't I tell you that your eyes give you away?"

"What are they saying?"

"You tell me, Mo."

"Right now I feel as if we are the only two people in the world."

Moving quickly, Nate straddled her body. "There's no reason why we can't pretend. It's just you, me, and the beach. Brunch is available until noon, so we can sleep in a little late."

Morgan wound her arms around his neck. "I can't believe I've lived here all my life and this is the first time I've ever been to Sullivan's Island."

"I used to come here with my father when I was a kid and he was delivering furniture to the snowbirds who were buying and renovating the island's abandoned houses."

"Will we have time tomorrow to do a little sightseeing?"

Nate raised his head. "That depends on what time you want to get back to the Creek."

"There's no rush. I've asked Francine to look in on Rasputin."

He pressed a series of light kisses along the column of Morgan's neck. "I suppose that means I can make love to you again and again and some more."

"Hold up, Superman. I'm in charge tonight."

"What do you have in mind?"

"Everything."

Nate rolled off Morgan and sat up. He was momentarily speechless. "What happened to your inhibitions?"

Morgan went to her knees. "I gave them the night off," she whispered, undoing the buttons on his shirt. "Just sit back and enjoy the ride."

"You're going to have to let me up."

Morgan sat back on her heels. "What's the matter?"

He kissed her nose. "I need to get protection."

Moving off the bed, he opened his bag, removing several condoms.

Morgan was still in the same position when he returned to the bed. She extended her arms and he went into her embrace. "Where were we?" he asked.

"I was undressing you." She pressed a kiss to the base of his throat. "Please lie on your back."

Nate smiled. "Yes, ma'am."

Those were the last two words he remembered after he gripped the iron bedposts, closed his eyes, and surrendered to Morgan's deft touch. She managed to undress him with minimum effort. Never had he felt more exposed, more vulnerable, as he lay motionless, waiting to submit to whatever she had planned for him.

All Nate's senses were magnified: He felt the velvety brush of Morgan's smooth skin once she removed her clothes, the moist feel of her breath feathering over his throat, and the haunting, sensual scent of her perfume as she lay on top of him, skin to skin, heart to heart.

"Am I too heavy for you?" she asked.

He smiled. "I hardly feel you." Nate wanted to laugh. He probably weighed twice as much as she did. He drew in a sharp breath. Morgan had reached between his thighs, gently massaging his flaccid penis. He hardened quickly.

"Do you like that, baby?"

Nate gasped. "I love it." She handed him the condom and he slipped it on.

He gasped again when her mouth covered one breast, and then the other. Morgan was making it difficult for him to breathe. Between her tongue suckling his nipples and her hand pumping him vigorously, he didn't know how long he would last. She caught his nipple between her teeth, increasing the pressure when he reached down to pull her hand away from his erection.

"Please let me do this," she hissed, applying more pressure.

Nate didn't know whether to cry out or moan. The slight pain was so pleasurable he believed he was close to fainting. In that instant he forgot every woman he'd ever touched, kissed, or slept with. The pleasurable torture was short-lived. Her mouth had replaced her hand and he did lose control, bucking and rising off the mattress. The muscles in his arms bulged as he gripped the headboard as though it were a lifeline. With his heart pounding painfully in his chest, Nate surrendered to the explosive ecstasy that was spiraling out of control. He saw brilliant lights behind his closed lids, and then darkness when he experienced *la petite mort* for the first time in his life. For several precious seconds his heart stopped, and he died in the throes of the sweetest, most selfless act any woman had ever offered him.

Morgan released Nate's penis, and then rested her head on his thigh. It wasn't her intention when she took him into her mouth to make him come so quickly. However, it was the first time since she'd slept with a man that she'd felt totally in control. And she liked it.

"Nate?" His response came in the form of a moan. "Are you all right, baby?"

"I don't know. I can't move." His disembodied voice sounded as if he were across the room.

"You don't have to. I'll clean you up."

She slipped off the bed and went into the bathroom. A wicker table held an ample supply of towels and face-cloths, as well as tiny bottles of shampoo, conditioner, bath gel, and body lotion. Turning on the hot water in the basin, she squeezed a dollop of gel on a facecloth, then wrung out the excess water.

Nate lay on his back, one muscular arm thrown over his head. He shuddered when she removed the condom and drew the cloth over his groin. "What on earth did you do to me?"

Morgan smiled. "I hope I made you feel good."

He shook his head. "You did more than that. Now I want to reciprocate."

Perhaps in some intimate way she'd communicated to him what lay in her heart. It'd begun as a childish crush, blossomed into unrequited love, and then faded when she realized she'd lost him to another woman. It was the love she'd selfishly withheld from the other men in her life.

"You can do that later," she said.

Nate took the cloth from her, dropping it on the pile of discarded clothing. "Come lie next to me."

Morgan paused. "Let me turn off the lights first."

She picked up the cloth, leaving it in the bathroom, and then walked around flicking off the lamps. After she'd gotten into bed, Nate turned off the bedside lamp, and the cottage was plunged into complete darkness. Morgan smiled when he pressed his chest to her back. They cuddled, spoonlike, his heart beating in a slow, measured rhythm against her back.

Nate blew his breath on the nape of her neck. "Thank you for giving your inhibitions the night off. The roles reverse tomorrow, when I do the same with mine."

"What do plan to do to me?"

"I'm not going to tell you," he said with a laugh. "I just have to make certain you'll enjoy it."

There came a noticeable pause before Morgan asked, "How often do you come here?"

"This is the first time since I moved back."

Morgan closed her eyes. "Why now?"

"Because of you," he answered. "I could've spent the night with you in the Creek, but seeing my truck parked at your house or yours at my place would exacerbate the talk about us."

"I don't care what people say about me, Nate."

"But I do," he countered. "A man can do something and people say that he's just being a man. But it's different with a woman. Folks talk about how many times Trina has been married, but no one opens their mouths about Harry Hill's boy making babies with different women all over the county. He's—what?—twenty-five or twenty-six, and he's fathered at least nine kids."

Morgan shifted into a more comfortable position. "I don't blame Harry Junior as much as I do his baby mamas. First of all, he's too old to live at home. His parents know he's trifling, and so do the women he sleeps with. What I can't understand is why these women are willing to risk their health by having unprotected sex with him. And I'm shocked that they all know one another. Harry Junior don't work, don't want to work, and will never work as long as his mother takes care of her grown-ass boy."

Nate whistled softly. "Whoa, baby. I didn't mean to rile you up."

"I can't help but get riled up when men don't step up

and take care of their children. If you don't want to take care of them, don't have them."

"Please don't put me in the same bag as Harry Junior. I don't know about the future, but one thing I do know for certain is that if I get a woman pregnant, I *will* marry her and take care of my child."

"You'd marry her knowing you don't love her?" Morgan asked.

"If I'm sleeping with her for any length of time, I'd have to have feelings for her, Mo. As for love…that's a word that's bandied about much too glibly. I love my car. I love my job, etc., etc., etc. Two people can always grow to love each other if there is trust and respect."

"Unfortunately, there are too many men who don't think like you do, Nate. Look at who they admire. Basketball and football players; rap stars who are embroiled in paternity suits with their baby mamas. I have no problem with being a single mother, but I don't plan to become a baby mama."

"What's the difference?" Nate asked.

"A single mother could be divorced or have adopted her children."

"Why would you adopt when you can have your own children?"

"I might end up not getting married or being too old to have a child."

Nate's arm tightened around her middle. "I'd be willing to father a child with you."

Morgan's mind reeled in confusion. He'd talked about never becoming an unwed father, and not wanting to remarry, so why was it okay to talk about getting her pregnant?

"That's not going to happen, Nate," she said softly.

"Why not?"

"Because that would mean us getting married."

"I can think of worse things, Mo."

She threw off his arm and sat up. "Oh, really? Are you certain you're not schizophrenic?"

Nate also sat up. "Of course not."

"Well, you could've fooled me. You told me emphatically that you'll never marry again. Why the change of heart?"

"That's before I got to know you."

It didn't matter how much she loved Nate. Morgan didn't want to conceive a child or get married without love. "We had an in-depth conversation for the first time six weeks ago, and then I asked you about it last night, so why the change of heart? What more do you know about me now?"

"I know all I need to know."

"And that is?" she asked.

"I watched you tonight with that little girl. You didn't hesitate when she asked for your monkey. Then there was Queenie and her kids. I'd heard that her husband walked out on her and that she's been struggling financially. Her folks are elderly and on fixed incomes, so there's not much they can do for her and their grandchildren. You didn't have to do what you did."

"Throwing away food is sinful. And because you witnessed a couple acts of kindness you talk about wanting to marry me?"

"Given time, I'm certain we can fall in love with each other. You can't deny we're not good together in and out of bed."

Morgan wanted to scream. "Why do you make it sound so clinical?" His arms went around her shoulders, pulling her close.

"I'm trying to be reasonable and considerate. You were the one who said you wanted to wait a few years before you would consider marriage and motherhood. If we do this thing, take things to the next level, I want it to be sooner rather than later. I don't want to become a father for the first time at forty. By the time our kids reach school age I'll probably be completely gray and other kids will start teasing them, saying I'm their grandfather."

Morgan laughed despite the seriousness of their conversation. Somehow this wasn't how she'd envisioned Nate proposing to her. He made it seem like a business deal. Even though Morgan loved Nate, one thing she wasn't was desperate. She refused to accept a marriage proposal without love. The two were indivisible.

"Marriage is not a business deal," she flung at him. "It's not a joke or something to play around about."

"Remember, I'm the one with more experience when it comes to marriage and business deals, and I'm sorry, baby, I didn't mean to insult you."

She buried her face between his neck and shoulder. "Apology accepted. I should've realized you were speaking hypothetically," she said, inhaling the lingering scent of his aftershave. Morgan knew her namesake would be proud of her. She was thinking with her head instead of her heart.

Nate buried his face in her short hair. "The only thing I'm going to ask is that you give me a chance to love you the way you deserved to be loved."

Morgan swallowed hard in an attempt not to cry. Pressing her fist against Nate's back she bit her lip. She nodded, because the lump in her throat wouldn't permit her to speak. She wasn't certain how long they held each other before Nate eased her back onto the mattress, cradling her to his chest until she fell into a deep, dreamless slumber.

Chapter Twenty

Nate adjusted the pillows under his shoulders as he supported his back against the headboard. Ribbons of sunlight filtered through the shutters, threading their way over the bed.

He woke early and lay motionless, watching Morgan as she slept.

Sleep hadn't been as kind to him. He still had to come to grips with the realization that he'd indirectly proposed to Morgan. He hadn't gone on one knee to ask if she would marry him. He'd just thrown it out there as if discussing which restaurant they would go to for dinner. She'd accused him of being clinical and he'd denied it. *I can think of worse things.* Why did he say that to her? He shook his head in disbelief. She deserved a lot better than a backhanded marriage proposal.

Nate hadn't lied when he told Morgan that, given time, he was certain they would fall in love with each other. It had taken six weeks for him to come out of his shell, and he had Morgan to thank for that. If she hadn't solicited his involvement in the Angels Landing Plantation restoration, there was no doubt he would've continued as a loner.

Knowing he was going to see Morgan brightened his workdays, and their sleeping together had become an added bonus. When he'd suggested becoming her love slave, Nate never imagined she would take him up on his offer. He'd done it as a challenge, to see if she was willing to shed her inhibitions. And she had, shocking him when she'd given him the most exquisite blow job he'd ever had.

He knew that sharing incredible sex wasn't enough to form the basis of a marriage, or to salvage a shaky one. It went beyond that. There had to be love, mutual respect, and trust. And for him, trust superseded love, because people fell in and out of love every day.

Bryce telling Nate that he was going to become an uncle again, and Morgan calling to inform him that Rachel had given birth to identical twin boys, had renewed his desire to become a father. It'd taken him about six hours to carve, sand, and prime matching bookends for the twins. And when he'd visited the Parlor Bookstore to look for children's books, he'd wanted the gift to be for his own children. Watching Morgan interact with the little girl struck a chord in him that was shocking. If or when he fathered a child, he wanted a woman like Morgan to be the mother.

Nate smiled when Morgan let out a soft sigh. He knew she liked him. Morgan had been forthcoming with that, but he wondered if she would ever love him. When she confessed to loving him when he gave her the gift, he knew she meant platonically, but what about romantic love? His feelings for her were different from what he'd experienced with any other woman. Whenever he was with her, he experienced a sense of peace.

Without warning, Morgan opened her eyes. A momentary expression of confusion crossed her features before she smiled. "Good morning," she mumbled, covering her mouth and hiding a yawn.

Nate nuzzled the side of her neck. "Good morning. Did you sleep well?"

She moaned. "I slept great. What time is it?"

"I don't know. I don't own a watch."

Rolling over on her back, Morgan met his eyes. "How can you go around without a watch?"

Sliding off the mound of pillows cradling his shoulders, Nate rested his chin on the top of Morgan's head. "I don't have to punch a clock, so I don't concern myself with the time. I wake up before the sun comes up and I go to bed when I'm tired."

"No rules, no stress," Morgan mumbled against his bare chest.

"There you go," he drawled.

"If you weren't here with me, then you'd probably be working."

Nate wiggled his nose when wisps of Morgan's hair brushed it. "No, I wouldn't. Shaw and Sons is closed for the duration of the fair."

"What would you be if you weren't a carpenter?" Morgan asked, continuing her questioning.

"A carpenter."

"You never wanted to be anything else?" Morgan asked.

"Nope. Are you hungry?" he asked, smoothly changing the subject.

"A little, but I'd like to go for a walk along the beach first."

Whipping back the sheet, Nate dipped his head and fastened his mouth to Morgan's buttock, causing her to gasp. "Do you think I could have a little snack before we leave?" He inhaled her silken skin, recognizing the aroma of vanilla and white musk along with other unrecognizable notes in her perfume.

"Please don't," she pleaded.

"Don't what, baby?"

"I have to go to the bathroom."

Nate slid off the bed, scooped Morgan up into his arms as if she were a child, then carried her to the bathroom. He placed her in front of the commode and took a step backward, staring at the bloodred polish on her toenails. "Nice color." His gaze moved up, lingering on a pair of firm breasts that reminded him of large chocolate muffins topped with Hershey's Kisses. "You have beautiful, perky breasts."

Morgan crossed her arms over her chest. "Do you mind?"

His eyebrows lifted. "Mind what?"

"Giving me some privacy."

"I thought you gave inhibition time off so you could be a naughty girl," he said teasingly.

"Naughty has nothing to do with this." Morgan was still smiling when Nate left her in the bathroom. She returned to the bedroom minutes later, smothering another yawn with her hand. "I need a shower so I can wake up."

"We'll shower together." He stared deeply into her

eyes. They were dark, unfathomable, and he wondered what she was thinking at that moment. "This is the first time in a very long time I don't feel alone."

Morgan traced the letters of the tattoo on his chest with her forefinger. "You shouldn't," she said in a feathery whisper. "Not when you carry her over your heart."

He placed his hand over hers. "I'm not talking about my mother, Morgan. I'm talking about you." Nate increased the pressure on her fingers when she went still. "I'm not perfect. I've made mistakes, but there is one thing I know. I will never hurt you."

Morgan lowered her gaze, shielding her innermost thoughts. "Call me crazy, but I believe you."

He pressed his mouth to her forehead, astounded at the sense of peace he always found whenever he shared the same space with her. She was right. Although they weren't able to change their pasts, they did have the power to determine their futures. And he wanted this woman in his arms for a very long time.

Reaching for a condom and picking her up, Nate walked back into the bathroom. He placed the condom on a shelf in the shower stall. Turning on the faucet, he adjusted the temperature as water flowed over their bodies. Cradling her face between his hands, he kissed Morgan with all the emotion he could summon for the woman who had affected him as no other had. His hands came down, moving over her throat, shoulders, breasts, and belly. He'd become a sculptor, his fingertips caressing every dip and curve of her body.

His hand moved up her inner thigh, finding her moist and pulsing. Nate was loath to remove his hand when he reached for the packet. Seconds later, fully sheathed, he wrapped one arm around her waist, lifting Morgan while easing his erection into her hot, tight body. They moaned in unison when flesh joined flesh.

Her arms curved around his head, her legs around his waist, and together they established a slow, deliberate rhythm in which they ceased to exist as separate entities.

Nothing mattered to Morgan except the unbridled passion escaping beyond the boundaries of common sense. She felt pleasure swirling between her thighs like a vortex, and she gasped in sweet agony with each thrust of Nate's hips. Her nipples swelled against the hardness of his chest, and she wanted to get even closer as their bodies moved in perfect rhythm, in exquisite harmony with each other.

"Nate!" She screamed out his name when he touched her so deeply she felt him in her stomach. She closed her eyes. Then her love and passion eddied through her like hot butter. The explosions continued as she melted all over him. Seconds later, he groaned deeply in erotic pleasure, moaning her name over and over until it became a litany. He eased her down to the floor of the shower, where they lay, limbs entwined, waiting for their breathing to resume a normal rate.

Smiling, Morgan opened her eyes. "Sharing a shower with you is fun."

Nate buried his face between her neck and shoulder. "It was beyond fun, baby. It was spectacular."

Somehow they found the strength to stand up. Reaching for the bath sponge, she squeezed a generous dollop of gel on it and handed it to Nate. He became a sculptor once again as he soaped every inch of her body. She repeated the favor, and when they emerged from the bathroom wrapped in thick white towels, Morgan knew the unbridled act of love had changed her forever.

Nate sucked in his breath as he descended the steps of the jet that had touched down at Las Vegas's McCarran International Airport. The desert heat seemed to swallow him whole. He pulled his shirt from the waistband of his slacks. It was two o'clock in the afternoon local time, and the mercury registered 113 degrees.

He would've looked forward to returning to the city where he'd spent so much time if it hadn't been for Morgan. They'd spent the three nights of the fair on Sullivan's Island. After the first night she brought Rasputin with her, the cat opting to spend most of his time sleeping in a patch of sun in the guesthouse. They returned to Cavanaugh Island midafternoon on the Fourth.

As promised, Nate had become Morgan's sous-chef, chopping and dicing ingredients for her gumbo. She'd won second prize in the one-pot contest, losing to Kara's cousin Virginia Patton-Smith, who entered a red rice and sausage dish. Gussie garnered a first prize ribbon for her sweet potato pie, and the Danes went wild. It was the first time in four decades that not one but two Dane women took home ribbons in the cooking contests.

The fair came to an end Sunday morning at the stroke of midnight with a spectacular display of fireworks, accompanied by synchronized prerecorded patriotic music. Those who hadn't gathered on the beach watched from their porches or backyards. The nighttime sky was ablaze with color. Morgan had invited Francine and David to an impromptu backyard barbecue, where they'd lounged on recliners to watch the fireworks. Nate told David he was unable to join them for Morgan's birthday celebration, but urged them not to change their plans.

A dark luxury sedan maneuvered onto the tarmac at the same time Nate stepped off the last stair. One of two flight attendants followed, carrying his bag. A wide smile split Nate's face when he saw a very different-looking Dwight alight from the rear of the car. Missing was the long hair, beard, tie-dyed shirt, and sandals. They were replaced with a crisp white shirt, dark tailored slacks, and slip-ons. The two men embraced as the chauffeur took Nate's bag from the flight attendant.

Nate studied his former business partner, marveling at his conservative appearance. "You look great, DW."

Dwight ran a hand over the stubble on his head. "I'm getting used to the new look. I've lost my belly and started working out. I'm still seeing a neurologist because I have cognition issues. Enough about me." He patted Nate's shoulder. "Let's get out of this inferno."

Ducking his head, Nate slipped into the air-cooled Mercedes-Benz sedan. Dwight got in and sat beside him. "I can't believe I used to work outside in this heat."

"That's when you were young and stupid," Dwight said, laughing.

"I wasn't that stupid," Nate countered. "I made a lot of money in those days."

Large gray eyes met his. "Do you miss those days, Nate?"

Nate's gaze shifted to the back of the driver's head. "Not at all. My life is very different now."

"Talk to me, buddy."

He told Dwight everything about his return to Cavanaugh Island.

"What's up with you and this girl?" Dwight asked. "Are you in love with her?"

"Why would you ask me that?"

"Because I know you better than you know yourself. Your voice changes whenever you mention her name. Now, what's up?"

Stretching out his legs, Nate glanced out the side window at the passing landscape. "I've told her that I like her."

Dwight cocked his head. "You like her?"

"I like her a lot."

"Do you love her, Nate?"

"I don't know," he said after a noticeable pause. "She's different, unlike any other woman I've ever known."

"Including Kim?"

Nate exhaled an audible breath. "They're like night and day."

Dwight smiled. "I guess you're saying she's a winner."

"What makes it so crazy is that I indirectly proposed to her." He repeated to Dwight what he'd said to Morgan.

Crossing his arms over his chest, Dwight shook his head. "I've never known you to be so indecisive. You can't mention marriage without telling her you love her. I learned that the hard way when I asked Nicole to marry me. I'd showed her the ring, but she refused to take it because I hadn't told her that I loved her. I paid more than three hundred thousand dollars for a mother of a rock, and she gave me the stink eye because I didn't say those three little words. It was only after I called her mother and she told me why Nicole had an attitude that I swallowed my pride and told her what she needed to hear, what I knew to be true in my heart."

"Do you love her?"

"Hell, yeah, I love Nicole. If I didn't, I never would've asked her to spend the rest of her life with me in the first place. Now, when am I going to return the favor and stand in as your best man for the second and, hopefully, the last time?"

Nate massaged his forehead with his fingertips. "I don't know. She's giving me mixed signals. One minute she claims she's not able to balance marriage, motherhood, and a career at this time in her life. And then the next she says that's exactly what she wants."

"How old is she?"

"She'll turn thirty-three on Saturday."

"You're talking about the day after tomorrow? Why the hell didn't you say something, Nate?"

"Remember I'd asked you whether you could the change the date, and—"

"I know what I said," Dwight interrupted. "If I'd known Saturday was your girlfriend's birthday I would've changed your flight reservation."

"Don't worry about it," Nate said. "We're going to celebrate when I get back. I've already sent her something, but I suppose I should buy her something else to make up for not being with her on her special day."

"Come on, man. You're in Vegas. Buying something for your lady shouldn't be a problem."

Morgan stood up when Samara ushered Virginia Patton-Smith into her office. No one was more surprised than Morgan when Virgie called, asking for a consultation.

She extended her hand to the attractive attorney with flawless sable-brown skin. "Please come in and sit down, Virgie."

Virgie hesitated, her gaze taking in the furnishings in the office. "Your office is exquisite." She stared at Morgan. Frosty gray eyes identified her as a direct descendant of Shipley Patton, the original owner of Angels Landing Plantation. There had been a time when the Pattons had regarded themselves as Cavanaugh Island royalty, refusing to mix outside their privileged social circle, but that changed dramatically once Kara inherited the bulk of Taylor Patton's estate. They'd rejected her claim as Taylor's secret love child, but Kara stood her ground, refusing to be intimidated. In the end it was the Pattons who'd finally accepted her as their own.

"Thank you, Virgie. Would you like something to drink?"

Virgie shook her softly coiffed head of black hair. "Nothing, please. I hope you don't think I came by to gloat about taking first place in the one-pot competition."

Morgan laced her fingers together, staring at her manicured hands. "The thought never crossed my mind." Her head popped up as she met Virgie's eyes. "I entered my gumbo recipe on a dare, never believing I would win anything."

"Well, you did. Congratulations."

"Same to you, Virgie. Now, how can I help you?"

"I read your interview in the *Chronicle,* where you mentioned something about starting up open house tours once the restoration is completed. I'm familiar with similar tours in Savannah, and after my cousins and I held a family meeting, we all agreed we'd like to add our homes to the list."

Morgan pressed her palms together. "I don't have a list, but I'm willing to begin with you and your relatives."

"There's a problem."

"What kind of problem?"

"Our homes need serious makeovers," she said. "We want to hire your firm to decorate them."

Morgan felt her pulse quicken. "How many homes are you talking about?"

"It'll be about five, maybe six, for both interior and the gardens."

"So you want an interior decorator and a landscape architect?"

Virgie flashed a smile, showing her even white teeth. "Exactly. Do you think your firm can handle it?"

"May I be honest with you, Virgie?" The other woman nodded. "Right now I am the firm, and I have to assess what you want to know if I can take on your project."

Morgan would have to hire an assistant. There was no way she would be able to decorate the interiors of half a dozen homes by herself within the given time frame of the restoration.

"Kara told me it would be at least a couple of years before the restoration is completed, but we would like to start now. We're willing to pay whatever you want."

The Pattons lived in homes that were exact replicas of the mansion, but built to a smaller scale. It wasn't about money as much as it was about having the time to devote to redesigning and decorating six houses with an average of four bedrooms each. "I'll let you know after I see what I have to work with. You may have to go to Ellison and Murphy."

Virgie rose to her feet. "We're split on whether to hire Ellison and Murphy. I would appreciate it if you'd let me know before the end of the month, so we know how to proceed."

Morgan also stood up. She knew it was impossible for her to accept Virgie's offer without an assistant. The fact that the Pattons came to her instead of her former employer served to boost her confidence; however, this wasn't about being self-satisfied, and Morgan knew when she needed help. She would call a former classmate to see if he'd be willing to relocate to Cavanaugh Island for the duration of the restoration.

"That shouldn't be a problem," she said to Virgie. Morgan escorted her to the reception area, waiting until she walked out.

"This was delivered while you were talking to Virgie." Samara reached down and handed her a box marked FRAGILE.

"Thank you." Morgan took the box, staring at the shipping label. Someone had sent her something from Waterford Crystal.

She would open the box after she called Abram Daniels. Returning to her office, she closed the door, set the box on a chair, and then scrolled through her cell phone directory for Abram's number. The last time she contacted Abram he'd e-mailed her with the news that he was now living and working in Philadelphia. It took less than ten minutes to outline her proposal to the incredibly talented interior designer.

"It sounds exciting, Morgan. Right now I'm freelancing, but if I can get a few days off, I'll come down to see you."

"Do you have an idea of when you'll be able to come?" she asked him.

"I know it can't be next week. I may be able to take some time off the following week, but I'll have to talk to my boss first."

"Thank you, Abram. As long as you can get here before the end of the month."

"Not a problem."

Morgan ended the call. She sat staring at the box. Someone had probably sent her something for her birthday. She'd followed through with her plan to celebrate with David and Francine, even though Nate wasn't scheduled to return home until Sunday afternoon. This week there wouldn't be a Dane Sunday dinner. Irene and Anthony were taking their sons and Amanda to Orlando for a week of baseball camp.

She glanced at the clock on her desk when it chimed the hour. It was eleven, and that meant it was eight o'clock in Vegas. Nate had called to say his friend's wedding was scheduled for eleven, followed by a sit-down luncheon for the guests, and then later that night there would be a buffet dinner with dancing and live entertainment.

He said he missed her and wished her happy birthday. Morgan's heart felt like a stone in her chest when he ended the call. There was no declaration of love, and again she wondered if she wanted more from Nate than he was able to give. He'd talked about marriage and children, but that meant nothing without love. Now she knew how David's girlfriend felt. Petra had given David five years of her life without even a hint that he wanted her to share his future.

Was that what she had to look forward to from Nate?

Chapter Twenty-One

Morgan found an empty parking space a few doors away from David's three-story home in historic downtown Charleston. Those with residences along the Battery had magnificent views of the harbor and Cooper River. She would've shared a ride to the mainland with Francine, but her friend said David had asked her to help him host the celebration. She rang the doorbell, and when the door opened she thought she was seeing an apparition.

"Aren't you going to say hello?" asked the familiar deep voice.

"Hel...lo," she croaked. "What are you doing here? I...I thought you were still in Vegas." Morgan couldn't understand why she was stuttering.

She had to admit Nate looked absolutely yummy in an exquisite tailored dark gray single-button suit, a matching silk tie, and a stark white shirt. Seconds later, she found herself crushed against his chest, his mouth covering hers in an explosive kiss. "Happy birthday, baby."

Morgan couldn't stop shaking. It was apparent Francine knew he was coming back earlier than planned but had decided not to tell her. "Thank you."

"You look gorgeous tonight."

She thanked Nate again. It had taken her a while to decide what to wear. Most of her evening wear was black, but she felt the color appeared too somber for the occasion. Eventually she chose a red sleeveless silk sheath with an asymmetrical neckline and black patent leather stilettos.

Taking her hand, Nate pulled her into the expansive entryway and into the living room. A chorus of happy birthdays greeted her when she stared numbly at those who'd gathered to celebrate the occasion. Her parents had come, along with Rachel and James, who was in uniform. It was obvious he was scheduled to work the night shift. She smiled at Kara and Jeff, and then at David and Francine.

Morgan shook her head. "I don't believe you guys. I thought it was just going to be me, David, and Francine."

Francine came over and kissed her. "Fooled you, didn't we?"

"I'm going to get you back for this," she whispered. "Now I know why you didn't want to cancel it."

Francine waved to Nate. "Please get your girlfriend something to drink to steady her nerves. Miss Usually Calm and Collected is shaking like a leaf."

Nate gave Morgan a flute of Champagne, and she took furtive sips until she was able to relax enough to greet everyone individually, thanking them for sharing the momentous occasion with her. David had decided on a catered sit-down dinner, and the caterer's efficient wait-

staff served course after course of delicious Lowcountry
and French cuisine. Nate was seated opposite her at the
table in the formal dining room, and she stared at him
through lowered lashes every chance she could get. She
still didn't want to believe he'd changed his travel schedule so that he could be back in time to celebrate her
birthday with her.

The conversation was lively, as Kara kept everyone
laughing about how quickly her cravings changed from
one month to the next. First it was watermelon, and now
it was salmon patties.

Morgan met her father's eyes, he mouthing that he
loved her. Nodding, she blew him a kiss. She knew her
parents were concerned that she would never settle down
long enough to marry and give them more grandchildren.
She wanted to tell them the man sitting across from her
was the one she wanted to marry, but she was uncertain
whether that would ever become a reality.

After coffee and slices of red velvet cake from the
Muffin Corner, Morgan opened her gifts. There were gift
cards from her parents, David, Kara and Jeff, and Rachel
and James. There was a homemade card from her nephews, along with a gift card from the Snells. Francine had
also given her a gift card to her favorite boutique and a
gift certificate to the Beauty Box for a full day of spa services. Everyone stared at Nate when he handed Morgan a
gaily wrapped flat box.

"I bet it's a piece of jewelry," Francine announced.

David glared at her. "Fran! You'll spoil his surprise."

Morgan tried to steady her fingers when she removed
the bow and paper, and then opened the box. A tennis
bracelet of princess-cut rubies and diamonds lay on

a bed of white satin. Judging from the weight of the bracelet and the size of the stones, she knew that the piece, set in platinum, had set Nate back several thousand dollars. Her birthstone was a ruby. She held it up to stunned silence.

Francine recovered first. "Put it on."

Morgan extended her arm. Nate placed it on her left wrist, securing it with the double safety catch. "Thank you," she whispered. "It's beautiful."

"As beautiful as you are." Those close enough to overhear Nate exchanged glances.

Morgan paused, composing her thoughts. "I'm a little tipsy from the Champagne, full as a tick from eating so much, and deliriously happy that I was able to share this very special day with the people I love. Thank you so much." She turned to David. "You are truly special."

He nodded. "So are you, Morgan. And I promise not to bill you for the hours it took to put this together." A groan went up from the assembly. "It's a lawyer joke, folks," David called out.

Gussie came over and kissed her daughter. "Are you sure you're going to be all right driving back to the Creek?"

"I'll take her home," Nate volunteered.

Morgan looked at him. "How did you get here?"

"My flight got into Charleston around six thirty, and I took a cab directly here."

"Please take care of my daughter, Nate," Gussie said in a quiet voice.

He smiled at her. "I will."

One by one the guests took their leave, hugging and kissing Morgan and wishing her well. She knew her thirty-third birthday would be one she would remember for a very long time.

Morgan settled back in the passenger seat and closed her eyes. "You're just full of surprises, aren't you?"

Nate adjusted the driver's seat and mirrors on the Escalade, then pulled away from the curb. "How so?"

"I had no idea you'd be back tonight, and I didn't expect you to give me two gifts—which, by the way, are exquisite."

"So you like the decanter?"

She opened her eyes, staring at his distinctive profile. "'Like' doesn't begin to describe it." Nate had ordered a cobalt-blue ship's decanter in Waterford's signature diamond-and-wedge Lismore pattern. "I put it on the credenza in the dining room."

"I didn't know what to get you, but when I described your home to Sharon, she suggested crystal."

"I must remember to thank her," Morgan said. "Did she have anything to do with the bracelet?" Light from the streetlights they passed came through the windows and reflected off the precious stones in the bracelet around her wrist.

"No. When I was talking to Dwight about not being with you for your birthday, it hit me that I should get something for you instead of your house. When I saw the bracelet in a jewelry store at the hotel, I took a chance and bought it. A sign in the store window said that rubies are July's birthstone."

"You have excellent taste. Thank you for thinking of me."

"Do you think of me when we're not together?"

Her expression changed, revealing her uneasiness. "Of course. Why would you ask me that?"

"Just checking."

"I told you before that if I'm dating you, then I'm totally committed to whatever relationship we have."

The remainder of the ride to Haven Creek passed in complete silence. Nate parked under the carport at Morgan's house. "Bryce and Stacy set a date."

"When is it?"

Nate flashed a wide grin. "I know I'm not giving you much notice, but it's next Saturday."

"You're kidding."

"I said the same thing to my brother, and he said Stacy doesn't want to wait, because the school year starts next month and she wants all her legal papers to read 'Stacy Shaw.'"

"Will the wedding be on the island?"

"No. The Butlers are members of a small Charleston church. The reception dinner will be held at Magnolias."

Morgan was more than familiar with the upscale Charleston restaurant. The food and service were impeccable. "Very nice. You're going to have to help me with ideas for a wedding gift."

"Don't worry about that, Mo. I'm going to give them a check from both of us."

"You don't have to do that."

Unbuckling his seat belt, he leaned over and kissed her. "Yes, I do. And please don't argue with me because I'm bigger than you."

"Bully."

"I'll never bully you, baby."

She gave him a long, penetrating stare. "You look tired."

"I took a couple of naps on the return flight, but I'm still a little wiped out."

"Did Dwight have strippers at his bachelor party?" she asked.

"No comment."

"Nathaniel!" Throwing back her head, she laughed. "Now I know he did, because you don't want to talk about it."

He opened his door, came around the truck, and opened hers. He assisted her off the seat. Retrieving his luggage from the second row of seats, Nate closed the door. "Let's go inside."

Reaching into her small handbag, Morgan took out her house keys. No wonder he was exhausted. She'd thought it was jet lag, not strippers, that had left him with a slight puffiness under his luminous eyes. Rasputin was there to meet her when she opened the door, winding himself around her legs. He rubbed his head against Nate's trousers, and then trotted off to the cat playhouse. The big shoe had become her pet's favorite spot to hide.

Turning, she smiled at Nate. "Why don't you go and turn in? I have a few things to do before I come to bed."

She had some reading to do and e-mails to respond to. Going into her home office, she turned on the computer. There was the message she'd been waiting for. Abram had confirmed a date for his trip to Cavanaugh Island. She quickly replied that she would make his travel arrangements. She would also put him up in her home, because the No VACANCY sign at the Cove Inn remained permanently in view during the summer season. There were a few other messages, but she decided not to reply to them until the following day.

Going into the half bath off the pantry, she cleansed her face of makeup, brushed her teeth, and then walked on bare feet to her bedroom. Nate was in bed, asleep. She noticed his suit was thrown carelessly over a chair. Picking up the jacket, she read the label: H. HUNTSMAN & SONS. He owned a handmade suit from the world-renowned tailors on London's Savile Row. Smiling, she hung up his suit and tie.

Morgan turned over, encountering empty space. She raised her head, sniffed the air, and smelled bacon. Throwing back the sheet, she scrambled out of bed, brushed her teeth, showered, and was dressed in under fifteen minutes. She walked into the kitchen to find Nate in a white T-shirt, ripped jeans, and bare feet, putting out place settings at the cooking island.

"Something smells wonderful." Nate's head popped up and she felt her stomach muscles contract when she stared at his stubble.

He pulled out a chair. "Come sit down. You're just in time. I was going to bring you breakfast in bed."

Morgan raised her head, moaning softly when Nate kissed her. "I've never had breakfast in bed."

"We'll try it another time." He kissed her forehead. "Thanks for hanging up my suit."

She met his eyes. "It's a very nice suit."

Nate smiled. "It wears nicely."

"It costs enough to wear nicely."

"So you recognize the cut?"

Resting her elbows on the countertop, Morgan shook her head. "No. I recognize the label." She watched as Nate cracked eggs, then added distilled white vinegar to milk, causing it to curdle. She realized he was making buttermilk pancakes.

"I was in London for an extended period of time, and one day when I was window-shopping on Savile Row I saw H. Huntsman & Sons. They usually don't accept blokes who walk in off the street, but after I dropped a few names, they told me to come back later that day. I did, and the rest is history."

"You only have the one suit?"

"No. I have a tuxedo, a white dinner jacket and dress trousers, and a blue pinstripe."

Morgan pointed to his jeans. "Yet you prefer wearing ripped jeans."

"They're comfortable. Do you want juice and coffee?"

"Yes, please."

"Sit," he ordered when she made the motion to slip off the stool. "I'm waiting on you this morning, birthday girl."

She flashed a dimpled smile. "And I'll do the same for you when it's your birthday. By the way, when is your birthday?"

"I'm not telling."

"Hey! That's not fair."

"Haven't you heard that all's fair in love and war?"

"That doesn't apply to us, Nate. We're not in love and we're not at war with each other."

"Have you ever read Eric Hoffer?"

"No."

"He wrote in *Working and Thinking on the Waterfront* that fair play is not blaming others for our problems. Therefore, don't tell me I'm not fair."

Morgan sat up straight. "Are you saying I'm wrong because you won't tell me your birth date?"

"I'm not saying that. At least not directly."

"Then what are you saying, Nate? That it's wrong for us to be together? That we'll never love each other?"

"You're twisting my words, Morgan."

She shook her head. "No, I'm not. What's the big deal about asking when your birthday is?"

Resting his palms on the countertop, he stared at her. "This is about more than my birthday, Morgan. What is it you want from me?"

She took a deep breath. "I want to know where I stand with you." She waved her hand. "We act like a couple and you refer to me as your girlfriend, but when I ask where things are going you don't see a future for us."

He leaned closer. "Do you want me to tell you that I love you?"

"No! I don't want you to say things you don't mean. And no more talk about marriage and babies." *Because it's never going to happen*, she added silently.

Nate stood up straight. "Okay."

Morgan knew her frustration had come from loving Nate so much that her heart hurt. She loved him, but he didn't love her. And she wondered how long she would be able to stay in a one-sided relationship.

"I'll drive you home when you're ready to leave."

"Are you putting me out?"

Morgan blew out her breath in exasperation. "I'm not putting you out, Nate."

"So I can stay?"

Slipping off the stool, she curtsied. "Yes, Your Highness. You can stay as long as you'd like."

"You shouldn't say that, princess."

"I don't..." Her words trailed off when the telephone

rang. "Excuse me," she said, walking over to the wall phone. Rachel's number came up on the display. "Good morning, Sis."

"They're coming home today."

"What are you talking about?"

"I just got a call from the hospital and we can bring the twins home today. They're both five pounds."

Morgan pressed a hand to her throat. Her nephews were medically cleared to leave the hospital. "Do you want me to come with you?"

"No. I called Mama and she's coming with me and James. Come over later this afternoon. By that time I'll need a break."

"You can't continue to breast-feed two babies, Rach, if you're not eating or resting as much as you should."

"We'll talk about that when I see you. Mama just walked in. I'll see you later."

Morgan hung up the phone to find Nate staring at her. "Stephen and Dennis are coming home. Would you like to go with me to meet them?"

"Maybe another time, baby. I have to get back and work on the armoire. The Island Fair and going to Vegas kind of screwed up my schedule. And I still want to show you the drawings I made for the slave village."

"That can wait, Nate."

He beckoned her. "Come sit down. How do you like your pancakes? Regular or silver-dollar?"

"Silver-dollar, please."

Nate moved about the kitchen with ease. He'd broiled the bacon to perfection, the pancakes were light and flavorful, and he'd even made freshly squeezed orange juice. They ate while listening to music, and it seemed like the most natural thing in the world for them to be sharing Sunday morning breakfast.

"Leave it," she told Nate when he picked up a plate. "You cooked, so I'll clean."

He set down the plate. "I'd better go and get my things."

Morgan filled one side of the sink with warm soapy water for the dishes and flatware and the other side with water for the pots and pans. She'd reached for her purse and car keys when Nate returned, carrying his luggage and a garment bag.

She drove the short distance to the barn, staring through the windshield as he got out. He came around to the driver's side. "What time is the wedding?" she asked.

Nate looked at her mouth. "I'll pick you up at two. The ceremony is scheduled for three."

Leaning out the open window, she touched his jaw. "Thank you again for everything."

Brushing his mouth over hers, Nate whispered, "I'm not letting you go."

He didn't give Morgan time to react before he turned on his heels and walked away. She was staring at the space where he'd been after he'd gotten out of the car. His words haunted her until she walked into Rachel's house so that she could hold her new nephews for the first time.

Chapter Twenty-Two

~⌒⌐

Morgan watched Stacy Butler gaze into the eyes of her groom. Her voice was clear as she repeated her vows, promising to love Bryce through good and bad times. She wore a simple white strapless A-line gown with a sweetheart neckline. Her ash-blond hair was pulled off her face in an elegant chignon, which was festooned with a jeweled comb and white feathers.

Bryce and Nate wore white dinner jackets, black dress trousers, and deep rose-pink silk bow ties and boutonnieres. Stacy's sister stood in as her maid of honor, and her deep pink halter-style gown flattered her golden tan and sun-bleached hair. Stacy wanted a small, intimate gathering, and she'd gotten her wish. The wedding party and invited guests numbered an even three dozen.

Her gaze shifted to Bryce's parents. Odessa dabbed at her eyes while Lucas patted her back in an attempt to comfort her. It was a happy occasion, so Morgan didn't know why people cried at weddings. She zoned out for a minute, wondering how long it would be before her big day. Would she laugh, smile, or cry when walking down the aisle? What was ironic was that despite how many weddings she'd attended, she hadn't thought about what she wanted for her own wedding until she became involved with Nate.

Morgan returned her attention to the ceremony as the bride and groom exchanged rings, and then a passionate kiss. The young couple's smiles were as bright as incandescent bulbs. She laughed with the others in the church when Stacy did a happy dance while Bryce turned to hug Nate.

The bride and groom walked down the white carpet and out of the church, followed by the wedding party and the parents of the couple. Nate had reserved a car to take Morgan to Magnolias while he lingered behind with the wedding party for photographs.

They hadn't seen each other all week, but managed to communicate by texting. She'd spent every day in Angels Landing, consulting with the Pattons. Virgie had made the right decision by bringing her in as designer, because Morgan would've never recommended that the Pattons put their residences on the list of house tours in their current condition.

It'd taken her a while to convince the Pattons that less was more when it came to furnishing the rooms. They only came around to her point of view when she showed them the before-and-after digital photos she'd uploaded to her iPad.

A man in a black suit approached her. "Miss Dane?"

She nodded. "Yes."

"I'll drive you to the restaurant."

He escorted her to a Lincoln Town Car, held the door while she got in, and then closed it behind her. Relaxing against the leather seat, Morgan thought about her relationship with Nate. He was mature, considerate, and giving. She just wondered where their relationship was headed. She'd accused Nate of sending her mixed signals, but Morgan realized that she, too, was equally guilty. *I wouldn't be able to balance marriage, motherhood, and a career at this time in my life.* Her words to Nate had come back to haunt her, because she loved him enough to want to become his wife and the mother of his children. Staring out the window as the Town Car motored through the Charleston neighborhoods, Morgan took in the sights: barefoot children playing on manicured lawns; sprawling homes set several hundred feet back from the road; streets void of litter or debris. The familiar landmarks of downtown Charleston came into view, and the ride ended as the driver maneuvered up to the popular restaurant overlooking Charleston's historic district.

The chauffeur came around to assist her. She walked to the Magnolias entrance, where she was greeted by the maître d'. He gave her a too-bright grin. "Welcome to Magnolias."

She returned his smile. "Thank you. I'm here for the Butler-Shaw reception dinner."

The impeccably dressed man signaled a young woman. "Please escort her to the Wine Room."

The young woman flashed a practiced smile. She took a listing of names from her blouse pocket. "Please follow me, Miss..."

"Dane," Morgan said.

"Miss Dane, you'll be seated at table three."

She followed the hostess into a room that had a beautiful bay window overlooking the historic district. Countless bottles of wine were stored in built-in mahogany shelves. Six round tables, each with seating for six, were set with pristine tablecloths, silver, damask napkins, and bouquets of white and deep pink roses as centerpieces.

"Please help yourself to our cocktail buffet, Miss Dane."

Morgan went over to the bar. "I'd like a ginger ale."

"Are you certain you don't want something stronger?" asked a sonorous male voice.

She turned to find a man staring boldly at her. His deeply tanned skin, straight salt-and-pepper hair, which he had brushed off his forehead, and refined features were mesmerizing. His eyes were a mixture of brown and green. She towered over him by several inches in her heels, but that didn't seem to bother him as he continued to leer at her.

She smiled and heard him suck in his breath. "I'm very sure."

He extended his hand. "Ian Rush."

Morgan took his hand. His palm was smooth, just the opposite of Nate's. "Morgan Dane." Ian smiled, exhibiting a mouth filled with a set of natural white teeth that would've pleased both of her dentist parents.

"A beautiful name for a very exotic and exquisite woman."

She avoided rolling her eyes. If Ian was flirting with her, then it was all for naught. Morgan wasn't looking for a man, because she already had one. "Thank you. But as to something stronger, ginger ale will do." She accepted the glass of pop from the bartender.

"Is it because you're driving?" Ian asked.

Morgan took a sip of the cold beverage, staring at him over the rim. "No, I'm not driving."

He cocked his head. "Are you here with someone?"

She gave him a mischievous grin. "I will be when the best man arrives."

Ian's expression did not change. "So you're dating Bryce's brother." The query was a statement. Morgan nodded. "I'm the principal at Stacy's school. She's a dynamic teacher, and all the children love her."

Nate had mentioned Stacy's plans to have her baby, take a six-week maternity leave, and then return to the classroom for the remainder of the school year. Odessa had offered to babysit her grandson or granddaughter, obviating the need for the young couple to pay for child care.

Morgan was introduced to Bryce's fiancée the second night of the Island Fair, and found her warm and bubbly. She had the perfect personality for interacting with young children. "After meeting her, I know why they would."

Ian glanced over Morgan's shoulder. "Please excuse me. I see another one of my teachers."

She breathed a sigh of relief when Ian walked away. For all his attractiveness, she still wasn't interested, and he was trying too hard.

As more people filled the Wine Room, the noise level escalated. More than half the guests were on staff at the school where Stacy taught. A few had come with their husbands, wives, and partners, and Morgan found herself at the singles table seated between Ian and his assistant principal, who had indulged too much during the cocktail hour. The wedding party and their parents finally arrived amid applause and cheers.

Sommeliers circulated with bottles of wine, and Morgan opted for rosé. Waiters hovered over guests, jotting down their dining selections. Meanwhile, the appetizers—fried green tomatoes; salt-and-pepper fried shrimp; southern-style egg rolls filled with collard greens, chicken, tasso ham, and red pepper purée and served with spicy mustard and peach chutney dipping sauces; and pickled shrimp served on house-made benne-seed crackers—were set out on each table.

She ordered the maple-glazed salmon. The entrée came with a warm spinach salad, which included goat cheese, tomatoes, artichoke hearts, and mushrooms, all dressed with a dill-shallot vinaigrette. Ian ordered a New York strip steak, and his assistant principal ordered the bourbon-glazed porterhouse pork chop. Conversations floating around the table were lively as waiters efficiently refilled cocktail orders.

Morgan's eyes met Nate's when she glanced in his direction. Stacy's sister, Amber, leaned against him as if her spine wouldn't allow her to sit upright. She wondered if the woman had had too much to drink or was desperately seeking Nate's attention. From his expression he appeared to be totally immune to her overt attempt at seduction. Amber, like Ian, was trying too hard.

Nate narrowed his eyes when he saw his sister-in-law's boss taking furtive glances at Morgan's décolletage. She'd worn a black tank dress with a scooped neckline, and the pervert couldn't take his eyes off her.

"What on earth did that napkin do to you?" Odessa asked sotto voce. "You're strangling it to death."

He stared at the cloth and at the veins protruding in the back of his hand. "I'm okay."

"Are you really?"

He looked at Odessa, who was sitting on his right. She was stunning. She'd positioned a small pillbox hat covered with pale pink silk rose petals on the back of her head. It matched her silk suit and high-heeled shoes. He met her dark eyes, which glistened like polished coal.

"Yes, I'm fine."

"I don't think you are," Odessa said accusingly. "If looks could kill, Stacy's boss would be facedown in his plate as we speak."

Nate gritted his teeth. "You don't know what you're talking about."

"You think not? I saw you with Morgan at the fair, and it's as plain as the nose on your face that you're in love with the girl." She paused when Nate refused to confirm or deny her claim. "Have you told her?" Odessa continued.

"What goes on between Morgan and me doesn't concern you, Odessa."

"Why shouldn't it? I'm married to your father, and that makes us family." She leaned closer. "You think I don't know that you resent me for marrying him." She had lowered her voice to a whisper. "I love your father and he loves me. What you think or believe will never change that. What I can't understand is how you can hate me yet love Bryce."

Nate stared at his plate. "I don't hate you, Odessa."

"But you do resent me."

He shook his head. "Not as much as I used to."

"What's changed?"

A hint of a smile touched the corners of his mouth. "I've matured enough to accept things as they are. You're my father's wife and my brother's mother. And you're right about Bryce. I do love him, and I'd do anything to help him."

"You...you've done so much for him already..." Her words stopped with the flow of tears flowing down her face.

Nate sat, stunned, and then pushed back his chair, cupping a hand under her elbow. "Come with me."

Lucas half rose from his chair. "What's going on?"

Nate patted his father on the back. "Don't worry, Dad. I've got this."

"Why is Odessa crying?"

"I'll take care of her," Nate told Lucas.

Wrapping an arm around her waist, he led Odessa out of the private room and to a waiting area in the restaurant. Easing her to a padded bench, he reached into his jacket's breast pocket and withdrew a handkerchief. Nate hunkered down in front of his stepmother and held her chin, gently blotting her tears.

"Hey, mother of the groom," he crooned. "You're ruining your makeup."

Odessa took the handkerchief, pressing it to the corners of her eyes. "I'm sorry, Nate. I have recurring nightmares of Bryce going to jail."

"He's not going to jail. He's a married man with a baby on the way. There's no way he's going to jeopardize that."

She sniffled. "I took up for him even when he was wrong. Lucas would tell me that I was too soft on Bryce, but he's my only child and I wanted him to love me."

Nate sat next to Odessa, stretching out his legs and crossing his feet at the ankles. "You can't make someone love you if they don't."

Odessa held the handkerchief against her nose. She closed her eyes, exhaling an audible breath. "I promised your mother I'd never repeat this, but you have a right to know."

Nate went still. "What are you talking about?"

"You were still so young when Manda had been diagnosed with cervical cancer. She was pregnant with Sharon. A month after she delivered, she was admitted to the hospital for a total hysterectomy. She underwent chemo and radiation, and for years she was in remission. Then the cancer came back, but in her pancreas.

"We talked at least twice a month, and not once did she tell me she was sick. We grew up a block from each other. Manda told me I was the sister she never had. I used to hang out at her house so I didn't have to hear Mama and Daddy fighting about his gambling, drinking, and whoring. I wanted what Manda had. Two parents who loved her and each other. And it was no different when she grew up. She married a man who adored her and their children."

"You wanted to be my mother so much that you took her husband?"

"It's not like that, Nate."

He glared at her. "Please tell me how it was."

"I'm not going to deny I wanted a man like your father, but it was never my intention to marry him."

"But you did."

"Because Manda knew I had feelings for Lucas."

"Do you expect me to believe you?" Nate forced himself not to raise his voice. Not only was Odessa deceptive, she was also a liar.

"What I'd like is for you to hear me out. I had no idea that Manda was sick again until I spoke to her and she broke down crying because of the pain. I left my job and gave up my apartment to come to Cavanaugh Island to take care of her. One look at Manda and I knew the cancer had ravished her body.

"One day she asked me to get Lucas because she wanted to talk to both of us. She made me promise to not only take care of her children but also to take care of her husband."

Nate looked at Odessa as if she'd taken leave of her senses. "You're telling me that my mother told you to sleep with her husband?"

"No. She didn't tell me directly. She knew I loved her and respected her relationship with your father, but she also knew that I wanted what my best friend had, and that included her husband. I'd fallen in love with Lucas, but wallowed in guilt because Manda saw what I'd tried so hard to hide. She said it was okay to act on my feelings. She was dying and wanted her husband to have someone who would love him and her children as much as she did." Odessa's voice broke with emotion. "Manda was admitted to hospice care. Lucas was lonely and I was there to comfort him. One thing led to another, and one day we wound up sleeping together. You can't imagine the guilt I felt, but I loved him too much to stop.

"Once I realized I was pregnant, Lucas and I went to see Manda to let her know, but she had slipped into a coma. I sat with her around the clock until she came out of it long enough for me to tell her that Lucas would get his third child. She couldn't talk, but managed to smile and nod her head. Then she slipped away."

Nate buried his face in his hands. He did not want to believe what Odessa had said, because it was too bizarre. "I can't believe my father went along with this," he said through his fingers.

"We granted a dying woman her wish. She wanted me to take care of her husband and children, and I did. You and Sharon aren't just Lucas's children—you're *our* children. You're as much my son as Bryce is. The only difference is that I didn't give birth to you. It's the same with Sharon. She's my daughter, and Gabby and Greg are my grandchildren."

Lowering his hands, Nate felt as if he'd gone a few rounds with a professional boxer. His head and chest hurt. He couldn't believe he'd spent nearly twenty years harboring distrust and resentment, when it'd been his mother's wishes for Odessa and Lucas to get together.

The words he'd carved on the plaque came to mind: *The day the child realizes that all adults are imperfect, he becomes an adolescent; the day he forgives them, he becomes an adult; the day he forgives himself, he becomes wise.*

He felt the gentle touch of Odessa's hand on his. His fingers closed around hers. "I know it sounds incredible, but if you don't believe me, then ask your father."

Nate reversed their hands, kissing her fingers. "No. What we talked about should stay between us."

"Like what goes on in Vegas?"

He smiled. "Exactly."

Odessa sobered. "We've talked about everything and everyone but Morgan. Do you love her, Nate?"

Lines fanned out around Nate's eyes when he smiled. It was the second time within a week someone had asked him if he loved Morgan. "I don't know."

Pulling her hand from his grip, Odessa stood up. "Don't be no fool, Nathaniel Shaw. Every single man sitting in that room would like to have what you're about to lose if you don't put a ring on her finger."

Nate also stood. "Why you put the mout on me?" he asked, slipping into dialect.

Odessa sucked her teeth. "I'm not. You married that hungry-looking whore when you should've never given her a second look. But with Morgan, you tell me you don't know. I bet you'll get it together after she's gone. A girl like Morgan won't stay single forever."

Odessa was wrong. He wasn't going to lose Morgan. Suddenly, Nate saw movement out of the corner of his eye. "Mrs. Shaw, your husband is looking for you," he said in a singsong voice.

"Hi, honey," she said sweetly, as Lucas approached.

"Are you all right?" Lucas asked.

Nate rested a hand on Odessa's back. "She's better now," he answered for Odessa.

Odessa gave Nate his handkerchief. "Thanks for lending me your shoulder. If I get this emotional over my son's wedding, what am I going to do when I become a grandmother?"

Cradling his wife's face, Lucas kissed her forehead. "We'll probably have to sedate you." He nodded to Nate. "Thanks."

"No problem."

Waiting until Lucas and Odessa had disappeared from his line of vision, Nate pounded his fist into his other hand. He was still attempting to process what Odessa had disclosed about the secret agreement.

Odessa's disclosure and her warning about losing Morgan made him feel as if he'd entered an emotional vortex, that he was spinning out of control and had no chance of slowing down.

Nate knew he couldn't just shake off the distrust that had festered within him for half his life. It would take time, and he knew his reluctance to open himself to loving Morgan was a result of that distrust. However, he'd been given a chance to start over.

Adjusting his bow tie, he returned to the private room. He froze when he saw Morgan laughing as Ian whispered something in her ear. *I saw you with Morgan at the fair, and it's as plain as the nose on your face that you're in love with the girl. Every single man sitting in that room would like to have what you're about to lose if you don't put a ring on her finger.*

Could Odessa see what he couldn't? There were times when he felt he was in love with Morgan and suppressed the feeling as it came up. There was no denying the intense physical attraction, but their relationship went beyond sleeping together. And how long could he refuse to acknowledge what was obvious to everyone but himself?

Walking over to her, he rested a hand on her shoulder. She turned to smile up at him. "Let's go." Pulling back her chair, he helped her to stand.

"Uh, okay. Is something wrong?"

"I need to talk to you."

"What do you want to talk about?" Morgan asked.

"We'll talk outside." Nate escorted her out of the room

and over to an area across from the lobby. "What's with all the flirting?"

Morgan's jaw dropped. "What?"

"Do you enjoy disrespecting me in front of my family?"

Her eyes narrowed. "I don't know what the hell you're talking about. But if it's because I'm laughing and talking with a man—"

"Not a man, Morgan," he said, interrupting her. "It's been a few men."

Going on tiptoe, Morgan leaned into him. "Don't you dare go there! If you're that concerned about me talking to other men, then you should put up or shut up. I'm sick and tired of you giving me mixed signals. I'm also not your ex-wife! I'm going to ask you one question and I'd like an honest answer. Do you love me?" The seconds ticked by as tension swelled between them. "Wow. Your not saying anything tells me everything I need to know." Turning on her heels, she walked back into the room, leaving Nate staring at her back.

Nate waited to return to the dining room. He was reeling from the realization he may have lost Morgan. When he saw her laughing and talking with the other male guests, all he could think of was his ex bragging about the number of men she'd slept with. He ran a hand over his face. How could he be so stupid? He knew Morgan was nothing like Kim. He must have still been affected by the conversation he had with Odessa.

He walked back into the room to find Morgan talking to his father. Lucas had nodded to whatever it was she said to him. She avoided Nate's eyes when she returned to her table.

"What's going on between you and Morgan?" Lucas asked as Nate reclaimed his chair.

"Nothing."

The older man's eyebrows lifted a fraction. "Don't tell me it's nothing. She just asked me to drive her back to the Creek." He rested a hand on Nate's sleeve. "Listen, you don't have to tell me what went down between the two of you, but from experience, son, you need to give her time to cool off."

He flashed a brittle smile. "Everything's cool, Dad."

"Why don't I believe you?"

Nate gave his father a direct stare. "You don't have to. As I said, everything's all good."

He'd said it not only to reassure his father but also to reassure himself. He had to move past his trust issues or he would lose Morgan forever.

Chapter Twenty-Three

Nate realized his mistake when he didn't hear from or see Morgan for a week. Lucas had mentioned not crowding her and giving her time to cool off. Well, a week had come and gone, and she still hadn't contacted him.

He did what he'd done when he first returned to Cavanaugh Island—he threw himself into his projects. With Bryce helping him, he finished the armoire doors in record time. Even when his brother and sister-in-law closed the door to their bedroom, Nate continued working. There were some nights when he managed to get by on three hours of sleep, even though he would pay for it the next day. It was the first time that working hadn't been therapeutic, and he knew why.

Nate missed Morgan. It wasn't just her passion; it was her smile, the sound of her voice, the lingering scent of her perfume in his truck or on his skin after they'd made love. Oh, how he loved making love to her.

Taking off his protective eyeglasses, he placed them

on the worktable. "I'm going out for a while," he said to Bryce.

Bryce's head popped up. He was sanding a newel post for a new staircase. "Okay." He removed his own glasses. "I'm going to take lunch now. I told Mom and Dad I'd eat with them today."

"Tell them I'll see them for dinner."

Nate washed up in the bathroom, then headed outside to his truck. He started up the vehicle and stared through the windshield. He'd thought about driving to the Cove to see Morgan, but quickly changed his mind. He would drive into Charleston, stop to eat something, and then do some sightseeing before returning to the island. Maybe getting away for a few hours would help him clear his head.

Morgan picked up the receiver and replaced it just as quickly. She'd found herself unconsciously reaching for the phone to call Nate, but each time she stopped herself because she was waiting for him to call her and apologize for believing that she was no better than his ex, who'd admitted to sleeping with the world! She was miserable, and it wasn't nice to think bad thoughts, but she hoped Nate was miserable as well.

Yet something told her she had to be mature about the situation. All she had to do was extend the olive branch, and if he rejected it then she would know how to proceed. After all, she had lived without Nate in her life before he returned to Haven Creek, and she could continue to go on with her life even if they were no longer together.

Picking up the receiver again, she tapped the number for Shaw & Sons Woodworking instead of Nate's cell phone. It rang four times before switching over to voice mail. Morgan cleared her throat. "Good afternoon, Nate. This is Morgan. I'd like for you to call me back when you get this message. It's not an emergency." She ended the call. Her voice was normal and businesslike. Now she would wait.

Business had picked up, even if her personal life was going downhill fast. That was a good thing. She'd contacted Abram Daniels, her former classmate and interior designer extraordinaire, to ask if he would be willing to work for her, and much to her shock he'd agreed. He'd worked freelance for a Philadelphia-based design company, and his fiancée was an office manager with a Bucks County design firm. Now Morgan could concentrate on the restoration project while Abram dealt with the firm's interior design clients. His fiancée would become the receptionist. The fact she was knowledgeable about interior design was definitely a plus, especially since Samara would return to her teaching position in another week. Morgan had offered to let Abram and his girlfriend stay with her until they could find a place of their own. As soon as the summer season ended, those vacationing on the island would leave, and rooms at the Cove Inn would once again become available.

Nate drove around aimlessly. He stopped long enough to eat lunch alfresco. It gave him an opportunity to do a little people watching. Street musicians on Charleston's downtown Market Street changed from a bluesy number to a military tune when four Citadel cadets came along, marching in formation. His cell phone rang. Reaching into the pocket of his jeans, Nate looked at the display.

"What's up, Bryce?"

"Morgan called the shop a little while ago. She wants you to call her."

"Did she leave a message?"

"She said it wasn't an emergency."

"Thanks."

"Don't hang up, Nate. Mom wants to know if you'll eat with us."

"Tell her yes."

Nate ended the call. Morgan had called the shop. If she'd wanted to speak directly to him, she would've called his cell. The fact that she said it wasn't an emergency meant that it probably had something to do with the restoration. He would call her back later.

He drove back to Haven Creek in time to shower, change his clothes, and make it to his father's house for dinner. Bryce talked a mile a minute. His probation officer had approved his leaving the island to attend classes on the mainland. Stacy's request to transfer from a mainland public school to the one on the Landing was approved. She was assigned to teach kindergarten for the first time, and Bryce went with her to clean and decorate her classroom. Nate smiled. It appeared as if his brother and sister-in-law were working to make a go of their marriage.

Odessa touched a napkin to the corners of her mouth. "Nate, when are you and Lucas going up to North Carolina to deliver the armoire?"

He lifted a shoulder. "Anytime Dad is ready." They'd completed the piece two weeks earlier than projected.

Lucas took a sip of water. "We can go tomorrow."

Odessa smiled at her husband. "That means you have to go to bed early."

"No, I don't," Lucas countered. "Nate's going to do the driving."

Nate stared across the table at his father. "Are we going to do everything in one day?"

"No, son. It's two hundred miles between here and Charlotte, then it's going to take at least three hours to put the thing together. We'll stay overnight and start back the following morning."

"You better get some sleep, bro," Bryce suggested.

"You're not sleeping, Nate?" Odessa asked.

He managed to look sheepish. It wasn't that he wasn't sleeping, but he had forced himself to work to the point of exhaustion, so that when he did go to bed he would fall asleep immediately and not think about Morgan. "I've been up working."

Lucas pushed back his chair. "If I'm going to share the driving, then I'd better turn in early."

Nate also stood. "Don't worry, Dad. I'll be all right for tomorrow."

Coming around the table, Lucas rested a hand on Nate's shoulder. "Come sit on the back porch with me for a few minutes."

Nate walked with his father to the porch, waiting until the older man sat in his favorite recliner before settling down in a comfortable armchair. "What's up, Dad?"

Tenting his fingers, Lucas peered at his firstborn. "That's what I should be asking you. Are you still seeing Morgan?"

There was a noticeable pause, then Nate said, "No."

"Why not?"

"Because it's over, Dad."

"What did you do to her?"

A frown creased Nate's forehead. "What makes you think I did something?"

"She was quiet as a church mouse when I drove her home after Bryce and Stacy's wedding. I told you to try and make things right between the two of you, and here it is now one week later and you tell me it's over."

"Stay out of it, please, Dad."

Lucas's hand came down heavily on the arm of the recliner. "Don't tell me to stay out of it when I see you moping around like you lost your best friend. You get up before the chickens and go to bed at an ungodly hour every night. I'm going to ask you one question, and I'd like an honest answer. Do you love that girl?"

It was a question Nate had asked himself over and over during his involvement with Morgan, and the answer was always yes. "Yes, I do."

Lucas smiled. "Thank you for being truthful…finally." He sobered. "It's not easy figuring out women. I should know, because I've been married twice. Your mother and I had our ups and downs, but thankfully we had more ups than downs. It's different with Odessa, because by the time I married her I knew what was expected of me as a husband. I know folks were talking when I took up with Odessa, and it got worse when Bryce came along."

Nate listened intently as his father corroborated what Odessa had revealed. The word he repeated over and over was *guilt*. He'd felt guilty sleeping with his wife's best friend when Manda was still alive. Guilty because he'd gotten Odessa pregnant while he was still married. Guilty because he'd slept with a woman in his marriage bed as his wife lay dying.

"Guilt ate me up from the inside out, but when Bryce was born, I felt as if I'd been forgiven, because Manda and I always talked about having another child. If you ask whether I would've done things differently if I had a do over, I probably would say yes, because I would've waited for a respectable period of mourning before marrying Odessa. I'm not perfect, Nate. I've made mistakes, but at least I'm man enough to admit my mistakes, unlike you, with your stiff-neck pride."

"You like Morgan, don't you?"

Lucas smiled. "What's there not to like? What I don't understand is why you were willing to marry that emaciated tramp, but…" His words drifted off when he saw Nate grinning. "What's so funny?"

"You, Dad. You missed your calling. You should've been a preacher."

"The next thing that's going to come out my mouth will definitely not be reverential."

Nate chuckled. "Is that really a word?"

"Damn right. If you don't believe me, then look it up." Lucas leaned forward, sandwiching his hand between his knees. "When I lay in that hospital bed hooked up to tubes, I promised myself that if I didn't die I would make it my life's mission to protect my children." He waved his other hand. "It doesn't matter that you're an adult. You, Sharon, and Bryce are still my children. If I had to close my eyes tonight I would die happy knowing my kids are happy. You've heard the expression 'I feel your pain.' Well, I feel your pain. Promise me you'll talk to Morgan and try to work things out with her."

"What's in it for you?" Nate asked.

Lucas flashed a Cheshire cat smile. "Another daughter-in-law and, hopefully, a few more grandchildren." His smile faded. "You deserve a second chance at happiness."

"Like you, Dad?"

"Yes, like me. The difference is I was blessed enough to have had two incredible wives. Now it's your turn to have at least one."

"I've made mistakes with Morgan."

"Are they mistakes that can be corrected?"

"Yes...I promise I'll talk to her."

"Don't tell me what you think I want to hear. I'm going to say one more thing, then I'm going to bed. I've only cried twice in my adult life. Once at Manda's funeral, and once when your strumpet of an ex-wife went on national television to talk about the number of men she'd slept with. Please, son, don't make me cry for you again."

Nate sat motionless, watching his father push off the chair and walk away. He was still sitting in the same position when Odessa appeared with a mug of coffee and a small dish of homemade shortbread cookies.

"I know you like my shortbread cookies. I filled a small tin of them so you can take some home with you."

He took the plate and mug from her. "Thank you."

"I hope things work out between you and that pretty girl." Nate stared at her. "Lucas told me," Odessa added.

"I hope they work out, too."

Waiting until he was alone, Nate closed his eyes. He'd admitted to his father that he loved Morgan, but that wasn't doing him much good. What he had to do was tell *her*. He had to admit he was scared to death of what might happen. But Morgan was worth it.

* * *

Nate parked his truck behind Morgan's shop, then strolled through Moss Alley to the entrance. He opened the door. There was no one sitting at the reception desk. Seconds later Morgan appeared from the back. She looked like a deer caught in the headlights. She looked gorgeous in a white silk blouse, black pencil skirt, and black patent leather pumps.

"Good afternoon, Morgan." He held up a plastic bag stamped with the Jack's Fish House logo. "I brought lunch. Have you eaten?"

Her dimples winked at him when she smiled. "No."

"You don't have a receptionist?"

"I'm expecting a new one in a couple of weeks." Morgan brushed past him, locked the door, and then turned over the sign. "Is there something wrong with your voice mail? I left you a message three days ago."

Nate wanted to laugh. This was how it started with them two months ago. "I got the message, but I had to go to North Carolina to deliver the armoire."

"So you finished it?" He nodded. "Come on back."

Nate bit his lip as he stared at the sway of her hips in the fitted skirt. He missed Morgan in and out of bed. His father was right when he mentioned his stiff-neck pride, and it was pride that wouldn't permit him to go to Morgan and beg for forgiveness.

"What did you bring?" she asked, smiling at him over her shoulder.

"Smothered chicken, black-eyed peas, and cabbage."

"Yum."

Morgan stared at Nate as they sat at the table in the lounge, eating the scrumptious meal. He reached for the last biscuit while she put a glass of ice-cold sweet tea to her mouth. It was as if nothing had changed, as if no time had passed during their separation.

"How is your family?" she asked.

"They're good. And yours?"

"They're wonderful. The twins are getting big."

Nate set down his fork. "I came here to tell you that I made a mistake, and I want you to marry me."

Morgan's impassive expression did not change. "No."

"No?"

"What part of 'no' don't you understand, Nate? The *n* or the *o*?"

"I . . . I thought you wanted marriage."

She blinked. "I do, but not with someone as clueless as you are. You come in here and say you made a mistake, but offer no explanation for the way you acted at your brother's reception dinner. So my answer is no."

The pain Nate felt far exceeded any he'd experienced, including that of Kim's infidelity. "Morgan . . . I love you."

"And I love you. I've loved you for so long that I can't remember when I didn't love you, but I'm not going to marry you when you're still holding on to your past. You saw me talking to a group of men and in your eyes I'd become your ex. Marriage is based on love and *trust*. There can't be one without the other."

Nate ran both hands over his head. "Trusting people is something I've had difficulty with since I was fifteen." Reaching across the table, he held Morgan's hands as he revealed the circumstances behind his mother's illness—how he'd witnessed Odessa with his father before his mother passed away, and Odessa's relationship with his mother and father.

"It's not easy for me to tell a woman that I love her, but

I love you, Morgan Dane, and if I have to spend every day for the rest of my life proving that to you, then I will."

A smile trembled over her lips. "Every day?"

He nodded. "Yes."

"I'm willing to settle for Sundays."

Nate felt his heart stop, then start up again. "What are you telling me?"

"Ask me again, Nate."

Rising to his feet, Nate rounded the table and went down on one knee. "Will you, Morgan Dane, do me the honor of becoming my wife?"

Throwing both arms around his head, Morgan pulled him close. "Yes, Nathaniel Shaw, I will marry you."

Epilogue

~

Morgan emerged from the bathroom in a tantalizing lace-and-silk gown that concealed and revealed in just the right places. She and Nate had selected the second Saturday in October for their wedding, and it'd rained the day before and the day of the celebration. A tropical depression had stalled over the island, preventing them from holding the ceremony on the beach. The venue was changed to the Haven Creek Baptist Church, where family and friends crowded into the small sanctuary to witness the ceremony that bound together two families with roots going back at least seven generations.

Nate had selected DW as his best man, and Morgan had chosen Francine as her maid of honor. Morgan insisted on simplicity—from her pearl-colored bias-cut silk crepe gown, tulle veil, and silk-covered stilettos to her South Sea pearl necklace and studs. Francine's aquamarine A-line silk gown was the perfect shade for her hair and complexion. Nate's nephew Gregory was the ring bearer, and Morgan's niece, Amanda, did the honors as the flower girl.

The white-and-aqua color scheme was repeated in the tablecloths, the cake decorations, and the flower arrangements in her bouquet, Francine's bouquet, and on each of the tables in the ballroom at the Market Pavilion Hotel, located in downtown Charleston just minutes from the waterfront.

She and Nate couldn't decide whether they wanted a DJ or live band, so they contracted for both. It was the same with a photographer and videographer. They would have stills and videos to remind them of their very special day. Morgan didn't cry as her father led her down the aisle of the church. Instead, she couldn't stop smiling, especially when Nate ran his tongue over his lips as if he were sampling a delicious concoction. When it came time for him to kiss his wife, Nate picked her up, dipped her low, and kissed her for a full thirty seconds. The assembly burst into laughter, adding to her embarrassment.

A caravan of cars motored along the causeway to the mainland for the reception for 250 guests, which included a cocktail hour with carving stations, an open bar, a five-course dinner, and a Viennese dessert table and cordials. There was nonstop dancing and eating. The partying continued as Morgan and Nate slipped away to begin their honeymoon.

They'd mutually agreed to spend their week on Sullivan's Island, in the cottage where Nate had made the most exquisite love to her. They'd also contacted a real estate agent to help them buy a property that would suit their needs on a permanent basis. It would be their hideaway, a place where they could eventually take their children on vacation. They'd narrowed the choices down to two. Both properties were close to the beach and far enough from the restaurants and public tennis courts to give them a modicum of privacy.

Nate sat up in bed, pulling back the sheet so she could get in. "You look so beautiful."

Morgan pressed her body along the length of his. "I feel beautiful. Being in love will do that to a woman."

He combed his fingers through the hair that curled over her forehead, ears, and along the nape of her neck. "You know, I almost lost it when I turned to see you on your father's arm as he led you down the aisle. Dwight kept telling me to be cool, but how could I when the woman I love, the woman who makes me feel complete, is willing to share my dreams, my life, and my future?"

"I like Dwight." Morgan had invited Nate's former business partner and his wife to stay with her and Nate before and after the wedding.

"And he likes you, Mo."

She nuzzled his neck. "I'm glad you decided to come back to Haven Creek."

Turning to face Morgan, he said, "And I'm glad you decided to stay."

His hand burned her thigh through the delicate fabric of her nightgown, but his touch was light. Her core grew warm, then moist.

Morgan didn't remember her husband removing her nightgown, but hours later she did remember sharing with him the sweetest ecstasy she'd ever felt, an ecstasy that transported her to a place she'd never been. She never imagined on the day she'd walked into Perry's and sat in the same booth with Nate that she would one day become Mrs. Nathaniel Phillip Shaw.

It was only after she and Nate were husband and wife that her maid of honor had whispered in her ear that she'd seen her married to Nate in one of her visions. Francine claimed she didn't tell her because that would've ruined the surprise. She also promised not to tell Morgan how many children she and Nate would have.

The tall, skinny girl who had been the high school wallflower had had the last laugh. And, like Cinderella, she had found her prince and together they would have their happily ever after.

Deborah Robinson desperately
needs a fresh start.

When she returns to her grandmother's home
on Cavanaugh Island, will handsome Dr. Asa
Monroe have the remedy she needs?

Please turn this page for an excerpt from

Sanctuary Cove.

Chapter One

❧

"Barbara, are you sure you don't mind looking after Whitney and Crystal for the week? You know I can always take them with me."

"Deborah Robinson! Do you realize how many times you've asked the same question and I've given you the same answer? No, I don't mind at all. Now go before you miss your ferry. And no cell phone calls from the car."

"Thanks for everything," Deborah whispered, hugging her friend. "I'll call you from the island."

Deborah ran across the front lawn, jumped into her car, fastened the seat belt, and pulled away from the curb. Smiling at years of happy memories as she drove through the back streets of Charleston, Deborah made it to the pier before sailing time. She drove onto the ferry, turned off the car, and got out to stand at the rail, instantly refreshed by the cool breeze. This time her return to the small community of Sanctuary Cove wouldn't be for a weekend or minivacation, but to air out the house she'd inherited from her grandparents in order to make it her home and to look at a vacant store she'd rented where she'd open her bookstore.

Two blasts from the ferry's horn echoed it was time to sail; a man on the pier tossed the thick coil of hemp to another worker on the ferry, freeing it; below deck engines belched, coughed, and rumbled. There came another horn blast, and the ferryman deftly steered the boat through the narrow inlet until he reached open water.

Resting her elbows on the rail, Deborah watched as steeples and spires of the many churches rising above the landscape disappeared from view. As the boat headed in a southeast direction she stared at the island shorelines of Kiawah, Seabrook, and Edisto Islands before the ferryboat slowed, chugging slowly and docking at Cavanaugh Island. She was the last one off the boat and waved to the captain as he tipped his hat.

Driving off the ferry, she felt herself blinking back tears, remembering the last time she'd come here. It had been Thanksgiving and she, Louis, and their kids had decided to celebrate the holiday at the Cove rather than in Charleston. Louis never could have imagined as he'd carved turkey that a week later he would become embroiled in a scandal. That he would be seen in a compromising position with one of his female students.

Despite declaring that he was simply comforting her and that there was nothing improper going on between him and the student, Louis Robinson was suspended pending a school board hearing. Tensions and emotions were fever-pitched as Charlestonians formed opposing factions while Louis awaited his fate. Deborah blamed those who were quick to judge her husband for his death, and all of their condolences fell on deaf ears when the truth was finally revealed. The truth had come too late. She'd lost her husband of eighteen years and Whitney and Crystal their father.

Slowing and coming to a complete stop, she reached for a tissue and blotted the tears, praying for a time when the tears wouldn't come without warning, or so easily. It took several minutes, but after taking a few deep breaths, she was back in control.

Stepping on the accelerator, Deborah drove slowly along the paved road, bordered on both sides by palmetto trees and ancient oaks draped with Spanish moss.

She maneuvered onto the quaint Main Street and suddenly felt another rush of sadness, but this one was not personal. Like so many small towns across the United States she realized the Cove was slowly dying. She noticed more boarded-up storefronts; the sidewalks were cracked and even the Cove Inn, a boardinghouse and one of the grandest houses on the island, needed a new coat of white paint.

Deborah drove into the small parking lot behind Jack's Fish House. After only a cup of coffee earlier that morning, she needed to eat before throwing herself into the chore of cleaning the house. There were more than a dozen cars in the lot; some she recognized as belonging to local fishermen.

The winter temperature on Cavanaugh was at least ten degrees warmer than in Charleston, so she left her wool jacket in the car. Reaching for her purse she walked up from the lot to the entrance of the restaurant, an establishment that was known for serving some of the best seafood in the Lowcountry.

The familiar interior of Jack's Fish House hadn't changed in decades. Tables hewn from tree trunks bore the names and initials of countless lovers, ex-lovers, and those who wanted to achieve immortality by carving their names into a piece of wood. Only the light fixtures had changed from bulbs covered by frosted globes to hanging lamps with Tiffany-style shades. A trio of ceiling fans turned at the lowest speed to offset the buildup of heat coming from the kitchen each time the café doors swung open. The year before the Jacksons had added a quartet of flat-screen televisions, primarily for the fishermen who went out at dawn and returned midday with their nets laden with crabs, oysters, and shrimp.

Deborah walked past restaurant regulars and a few strange faces to sit at a round table for two in a far corner. The mouthwatering aromas coming from dishes carried by the waitstaff triggered a hunger she hadn't felt in weeks. She knew she'd lost too much weight, and although she had cooked for Whitney and Crystal, she would take only a few forkfuls of food before feeling full.

Suddenly, a shadow fell over the table and her head popped up. Luvina Jackson, wearing a pair of overalls and a bibbed apron, arms crossed under her ample bosom, gave Deborah a sad smile. Her gray hair was covered with a hairnet. "Stand up, baby, and let Vina hold you. I'm so sorry about Louis."

Deborah couldn't hold back tears as she sank into the comforting softness of Luvina's well-rounded figure. The smell of yeast and lily of the valley wafted in her nostrils, a fragrance Luvina had worn for as long as Deborah remembered.

"Thank you, Miss Vina."

Luvina rocked her back and forth. "You know the Cove would have turned out for you if you hadn't had a private service."

"I know that, Miss Vina. But I would've lost it if the hypocrites who were so quick to judge Louis would've shown up to pay their so-called respects."

"All you had to do was say the word and we would've been there for you with bells on. Ain't no way we gonna let dem two-face, egg-suckin' vultures hurt one of our own. We would have turned it out."

"Then we all would've been on the front page of *The State* or *The Post and Courier*, not to mention footage on the local television news," Deborah murmured.

"I just want you to know we would have been there for you, baby. How are your kids doing?"

Easing out of her embrace, Deborah met Luvina's eyes. "They're coping as well as they can. But kids are kids and they are much more resilient than grown folks. They're spending the week with friends until school begins again."

"Thank goodness for that. Enough talk. I know you came in here to git somethin' to eat. Whatcha want?"

Deborah smiled. Even though she'd been born and raised in Charleston, coming back to the Cove and listening to the different inflections interspersed with the Gullah dialect made her feel as if she had come home. "Do you have any okra gumbo?"

Luvina's broad dark face, with features that bore her Gullah ancestry, softened as she smiled. "I jest put up a long pot earlier dis mornin'."

Deborah returned Luvina's smile. She liked Jack's

okra gumbo because they fried the okra with oil to reduce the slime and added corn to the savory dish. "I'll have a bowl with a couple of buttered biscuits."

"Do you want rice?"

"No, thank you. But I'm going to order something to take home for dinner."

"Whatcha want fo' dinner?"

"Anything that's good, Miss Vina."

Eyes wide, Luvina stared at Deborah. "Now you got to know that everything we makes at Jack's is good. Have you been gone so long that you forgot that?"

"No, ma'am."

"Let me put somethin' together for you. You like ox-tails?"

"I love them."

"Good. Then I'll fix you some oxtails with ham hocks. I'll also give you some rice, because you need some meat on your bones. Collards and a slice of my coconut cake should fill you right up."

"That sounds good, Miss Vina."

"Rest yourself and I'll be right back."

When Deborah sat down, closed her eyes, and pressed the back of her head to the wall behind her, she realized she was hungry and unbelievably tired. Tired from stress that had worn her down like a steady rush of water over a pile of rocks.

Her parents had come up from Florida for the funeral and had all but begged her to move down there, but Deborah told them she couldn't uproot Whitney and Crystal. Whitney was in his last year of high school, and fifteen-year-old Crystal would have problems adjusting and making friends at a new school. Crystal had taken her father's death much harder than Whitney, who'd grieved in private.

Her musings were interrupted when Luvina's granddaughter walked over to the table with a large glass of sweet tea and a plate with two biscuits. "Sorry about Mr. Robinson, Miss Deborah. All the kids cried for days when we heard he'd drowned. He was the best math teacher in the whole high school."

Deborah smiled at the girl, who lived on the island but went to high school with her children. "Thank you, Johnetta. How are you?"

"I'm good, Miss Deborah. Right now I'm applying to nursing schools up north, but my mama and daddy don't want me to leave the state, so I have to apply to one here."

"Charleston Southern University has a school of nursing. You can live here while you're taking classes. That would save you a lot of money."

Johnetta smiled, displaying the braces on her teeth. "You're right. I could take the ferry or get my father to drop me off when he goes to work."

"That sounds like a plan."

"Thank you, Miss Deborah. I'm going to go and bring out your food."

Deborah stared at the tall girl, who'd at one time admitted she liked Whitney, but he'd acted as if she didn't exist. She'd wanted to tell Johnetta that Whitney was more interested in sports than he was in a relationship with a girl. It wasn't as if he didn't like girls, but sports and academics were his priority.

Johnetta returned with a bowl of okra gumbo and after the first spoonful Deborah felt as if she'd been revived.

The soup was delicious, the biscuits light and buttery, and the sweet tea brewed to perfection. She'd tried over and over, but whenever she brewed tea it was either too strong or too weak. Too strong meant adding copious amounts of sugar and too weak made it taste like sugar water.

She finished her lunch and paid the check, reminding Johnetta she'd come back to pick up her takeout order. Leaving Jack's, Deborah strolled along Main Street, stopping to stare through the windows of stores and shops. Grass had sprouted up through the cracks in the sidewalk. There had been a time when there were no cracks and the only thing that had littered the sidewalks or curbs was sand and palmetto leaves. The sand-littered streets added to the charm of the town, but the dead leaves and debris were swept away by shopkeepers every morning.

She continued her stroll, turning onto Moss Alley, and then came to a complete stop. Moss Alley was appropriately named because of the large oak draped in Spanish moss on the corner. Shading her eyes, Deborah peered through the glass window of a store that had once been a gift shop. The space wasn't particularly wide, but deep enough for her bookstore. And what made it even more attractive was it had a second floor—space where she could store her inventory.

A flutter of excitement raced through her. It was perfect for The Parlor. It was off the main street, but on the corner where anyone walking or driving by would notice it. With hand-painted letters on the plate glass, a colorful awning, and furniture resembling a parlor, it would generate enough curiosity to draw in customers.

She walked down the street, stopping at the opposite end of the block. Smiling, she waved through the window of the Muffin Corner at the woman behind the counter, who beckoned her.

She opened the screen door and was met with tantalizing aromas of fruit and freshly made cakes, pies, and doughnuts. Lester and Mabel Kelly had opened the shop the year before. Both had worked as pastry chefs for a hotel chain, but had tired of the frantic pace of baking for catered parties and returned to the Cove to open the Muffin Corner.

Mabel Kelly flashed a gap-tooth smile when Deborah walked in. Coming from behind the counter, she hugged her. "How's it going, girl?"

Deborah returned the hug. "I'm good."

Pulling back, Mabel narrowed her eyes. She and Deborah were the same age, thirty-eight, but there was sadness in Deborah's eyes that made her appear older. "I'm sorry about Louis, Debs. It's a damn shame folks accused him of something he didn't do, and would never think of doing. I can tell you that folks here were ready to get in their cars and start some mess Charleston hasn't seen in a while."

"I know that, Mabel."

"Is that why you decided to have a private funeral?"

"It was one of the reasons."

"You know I called your house but some woman named Barbara answered. Damn, you thought I was trying to set up a lunch date with President Obama the way she interrogated me. In the end, I told her to let you know I'd called."

"She did, Mabel. And, I do appreciate you calling."

"Can I get you something?"

"No thanks. I just came from Jack's."

Physically Deborah and Mabel were complete opposites. Mabel was barely five foot and had what people call birthing hips, yet she'd never had any children. She said she didn't want any because she'd helped her father raise six younger siblings after her mother got hooked on drugs. The year she'd turned fourteen her mother had taken the ferry to Charleston to score and never came back. There were reports that someone had seen her in Savannah, strung out, but it was never confirmed.

The wind chime over the door tinkled musically. "Excuse me, Debs," Mabel whispered. "Let me take care of this customer, then we'll sit and talk." Her smile grew wider. "Afternoon, Asa. Can I get you to sample today's special along with your black coffee with a shot of espresso?"

"No thank you, Mabel. I'll just have coffee," she heard the man reply.

Deborah sat, enjoying the aromas of the shop before her gaze lingered on Mabel's customer. He was a tall, slender, middle-aged black man. Though he was dressed casually in khakis, long-sleeved light blue button-down shirt, and black leather slip-ons, Deborah couldn't take her eyes off the handsome stranger. He didn't look familiar, so either he was a newcomer, visitor, or tourist. Cavanaugh Island didn't get many tourists during the winter months, but the balmy seventy-degree temperatures attracted a few snowbirds from the Northeast and Midwest.

Without warning, he turned and caught her staring. Their gazes met and fused, and they shared a smile. He continued to stare and Deborah couldn't control the rush of heat in her face; she lowered her eyes and didn't glance up again until the wind chime tinkled when the door closed behind the very attractive man.

"I like what you've done with the shop," Deborah said to Mabel when she joined her at the table.

"We don't have a Starbucks here in the Cove, so Lester and I decided to offer something other than regular coffee to go along with the muffins. Business has really picked up since we put in the tables. We mostly get retirees who order their favorite muffin, coffee, and read the newspaper whenever it gets too hot to sit in the square or during rainy weather. It's a big hit, especially with the snowbirds." Mabel bit her lip. "If it wasn't for the snowbirds, businesses in the Cove would really have a hard time staying open."

"It's that bad?" Deborah asked.

"Just say it could be better. Most of us are hanging on by the skin of our teeth, waiting for the summer season. Take Asa Monroe, the man who just left."

"What about him?" she asked. For a reason she couldn't fathom, Deborah wanted to know more about the stranger who unknowingly intrigued her.

"He rents a suite at the Cove Inn, been here about six weeks. He eats lunch at Jack's, sends his laundry out, and comes in every day for his black coffee with a shot of espresso. Multiply that by twenty or thirty snowbirds and it's enough revenue to keep small shopkeepers afloat until the summer season."

Deborah nodded. "I noticed a few more vacant stores since the last time I was here."

"The gift shop closed up last month."

"I just rented it."

A beat passed before Mabel said, "You're kidding?"

"No I'm not. I'm moving to the Cove and—"

"Permanently?"

Deborah nodded again. "Yes. I'm also moving my bookstore. I called the chamber and they gave me a listing of the vacant stores. Once I found out the gift shop had closed, I realized it would be perfect. It has more square footage than my Charleston store and having a second floor is a bonus."

Mabel leaned closer. "What about your kids?"

"Nothing's going to change, Mabel, except that they'll live here instead of in Charleston. They'll still go to the same high school and hang out with their same friends."

"What are you going to do with your house on the mainland?"

"I'm putting it up for sale. I know the real estate market is soft," Deborah said quickly when Mabel opened her mouth, "but I'm willing to accept a reasonable offer because I don't want to rent it." She glanced at her watch, then stood up, Mabel rising with her. "I have to get back to the house. I'll drop by again in a couple of days."

"How long are you staying?"

"I'm leaving New Year's Eve. I promised the kids I'd be back in time to bring in the new year with them." Extending her arms, Deborah hugged Mabel.

She left the Muffin Corner, stopping again at the vacant store on Moss Alley that was soon to be the new home of The Parlor bookstore.

Kara Newell has been named the sole proprietor to a gorgeous estate in South Carolina.

But the sudden change in her fortune has made her a target.

Will the charming sheriff sent to protect her keep her safe?

Please turn this page for an excerpt from

Angels Landing.

Chapter One

⁓

"Good morning, ma'am. May I help you?"

Kara returned the receptionist's friendly smile with a bright one of her own. She'd recently celebrated her thirty-third birthday, and it was the first time she'd ever been called "ma'am"; but then she had to remind herself that she wasn't in New York but in the South. Here it was customary to greet people with "yes, ma'am" and "sir," rather than "missy" or "yo, my man."

"I'm Kara Newell, and I have a ten o'clock appointment with Mr. Sullivan," she said, introducing herself.

The receptionist's smile was still in place when she replied, "Please have a seat, Miss Newell. Mr. Sullivan will be with you shortly."

Kara sat down in a plush armchair in the law firm's waiting area. The walls were covered with a wheatlike fabric and artwork depicting fox hunting scenes. She'd planned to take a break from her social worker position at a New York City agency by visiting her family in Little

Rock, Arkansas. She never anticipated having to travel to Charleston, South Carolina, instead.

The certified letter from Sullivan, Webster, Matthews and Sullivan requesting her attendance at the reading of a will had come as a complete shock. When she'd spoken to Mr. David Sullivan Jr. to inform him that she didn't know a Taylor Patton, the attorney reassured her that his client had been more than familiar with her.

Kara had called her parents to let them know she wouldn't be coming to Little Rock as scheduled because she had to take care of some business. She didn't tell her mother what that business was because it was still a mystery to her as to why she'd been summoned to the reading of a stranger's will. It was only when the attorney mentioned it had something to do with a relative she wasn't familiar with that she'd decided to make the trip.

She unbuttoned the jacket to her wool pantsuit. Although the temperatures had been below freezing when she'd boarded the flight in New York City, it was at least fifty degrees warmer in Charleston. One of the things she'd missed most about living in the South was the mild winters. By the time the jet touched down, Kara barely had time to hail a taxi, check into her downtown Charleston hotel room, shower, and grab a quick bite to eat before it was time to leave. She sat up straight when a tall, slender black man approached her.

"Miss Newell?"

Pushing off the chair, Kara smiled. "Yes."

"Good morning, Miss Newell. David Sullivan," he said in introduction, extending his hand.

His hand was soft, his grip firm, which took her by surprise. As she took in the sight of him, she realized he didn't quite fit the description she'd had. The one time she'd spoken to Mr. Sullivan, there was something in his tone that made her think he was much older than he looked. Now she realized they were about the same age. Conservatively dressed in a navy blue pin-striped suit, white shirt, blue-and-white dotted tie, and black wing tips, he released her hand.

"It's nice meeting you, Mr. Sullivan."

David inclined his head. "Same here, Miss Newell. It's nice having a face to go along with the voice." Taking her elbow, he led her out of the waiting room and down a carpeted hallway to a set of double ornately carved oak doors at the end of the hallway. "I'd like to caution you before we go in. I don't want you to reply or react to anything directed toward you. Taylor Patton was my client, and that means indirectly you are also my client."

A shiver of uneasiness swept over Kara like a blast of frigid air. What, she mused, was she about to walk into? For the first time since she'd read the letter, she chided herself for not revealing its contents to her mother.

"What do you mean?" Kara asked.

"I can't explain it now, Miss Newell. But I want you to trust me enough to know that I'm going to make certain to protect your interests."

When the doors opened, Kara suddenly felt as if she were about to go on trial. The room was filled with people sitting around a massive rosewood conference table. She heard a slight gasp from the man sitting nearest the door, but he recovered quickly when she stared at him. The hazel eyes glaring at her—so much like her own—were cold, angry. The resemblance between her and the man was remarkable. So much so that they could have been brother and sister. But Kara didn't have a brother—at least not one she was aware of. She was an only child.

David directed her to a chair at the opposite end of the room, seating her on his left while he took his place at the head of the table. He still hadn't revealed to Kara why he'd wanted her to attend the reading of the will of Taylor Patton, but his cautioning was enough to let her know she was involved in something that was about to change her life. The fact that she resembled several of those in the conference room led Kara to believe there was a possibility she just might be related to the deceased.

Resting her hands in her lap, Kara listened as David informed everyone that a stenographer would record the proceedings, asking those present to introduce themselves for the record. Kara glanced at the stenographer sitting in a corner, fingers poised on the keys of the steno-type machine resting on a tripod.

David touched her hand, nodding. "Kara Elise Newell," she said, beginning the introductions. One by one the eleven others gave their names.

The men were Pattons, while the women were hyphenated Pattons, with one exception. Kara glanced at Analeigh Patton's hands. Unlike the others, her fingers were bare. A hint of a smile inched up the corners of Analeigh's mouth, and a slow smile found its way to Kara's eyes.

Everyone's attention was directed toward David when he cleared his voice, slipped on a pair of black horn-rimmed glasses, and opened the folder in front of him. " 'I, Taylor Scott Patton of Palmetto Lane, Cavanaugh Island, South Carolina, do hereby make, publish, and declare this to be my Last Will and Testament, hereby expressly revoking all wills and codicils, heretofore made by me.' "

Kara felt her mind wandering when David mentioned that as the executor he would judicially pay the deceased's enforceable debts and administrative expenses of Taylor's estate as soon as possible. Taylor hadn't married; therefore, there was no spouse to whom he would have bequeathed his belongings. All of the Pattons leaned forward as if the motion had been choreographed in advance when David paused briefly. Then he continued to read.

" 'I do give and bequeath to my daughter, Kara Elise Newell, all my personal effects and all my tangible personal property, including automobiles owned by me and held for my personal use at the time of my death, cash on hand in bank accounts in my own name, securities, or other intangibles.' "

Kara went completely still, unable to utter a sound as pandemonium followed. The room was full of screams, tears, shouts of fraud, and threats to her person. Another two minutes passed before David was able to restore a modicum of civility. "Ladies, gentlemen, please restrain yourselves. Remember, this proceeding is being recorded, so please refrain from threatening my client. By the way, there is more."

The man who'd glared at Kara stood up. "What's left? My uncle has given this *impostor* everything."

"Please sit down, Harlan. I can assure you that Miss Newell is not an impostor," David said.

Kara wanted to agree with the Pattons. Austin Newell, not Taylor Patton, was her father. She closed her eyes, her heart pounding a runaway rhythm, as David outlined the conditions of what she'd inherited: She must restore Angels Landing to its original condition; make Angels Landing her legal residence for the next five years; and allow the groundskeeper and his wife, who would receive a lump sum of fifty thousand dollars, to continue to live out their natural lives in one of the two guesthouses. In addition, she could not sell any parcel of land to a nonfamily member without unanimous approval of all Cavanaugh Island Pattons, and the house and its contents could only be deeded to a Patton.

She opened her eyes and let out an inaudible sigh when David enumerated names and monies set aside in trust for three grandnephews and two grandnieces for their college education. This pronouncement satisfied some, but not all. There were yet more threats and promises to contest the will.

Forty-five minutes after she'd entered the conference room, Kara found herself alone with Taylor Patton's attorney. Holding her head in her hands, she tried to grasp what had just happened. She hadn't risen with the others because she wasn't certain whether her legs would've supported her body. David had warned her not to say anything, and she hadn't, but only because she couldn't. Reaching for the glass of water that had been placed before each chair, she took a sip.

David removed his glasses and laced his fingers together. "So, Miss Newell, you are now the owner of a house listed on the National Register of Historic Places and two thousand acres of prime land on Cavanaugh Island."

Kara's eyelids fluttered as if she'd just surfaced from a trance. "I'm sorry to inform you, but Taylor Patton is not my father."

David's eyes narrowed. "Did your mother ever mention Taylor Patton's name?"

She shook her head. "No. The only father I know is Austin Newell."

"Well, I can assure you that you *are* Taylor's biological daughter. In fact, you are his only child."

Kara closed her eyes. When she opened them, they were filled with fear and confusion. "How is that possible?" The query was a whisper.

"That is something you'll have to discuss with your mother."

She would talk to her mother, but not over the phone. What she and Jeannette Newell needed to discuss had to be done face-to-face. Combing her fingers through her hair, Kara held it off her forehead. "Please tell me this is a dream."

David sat on the edge of the table, staring at Kara's bowed head, a look of compassion across his features. "Even if I did, it still wouldn't change anything." Reaching into the breast pocket of his suit jacket, he took out a small kraft envelope, spilling its contents on the table in front of her. "These are keys to the house in Angels Landing, Taylor's car, and his safe-deposit box in a bank in Sanctuary Cove."

Kara released her hair, the chin-length, chemically straightened strands falling into place. "Where's Sanctuary Cove?"

"It's on Cavanaugh Island, southeast of Angels Landing. You only have ten days to transfer the accounts from Taylor's to your name. By the way, do you have a rental?"

"No. I took a taxi from the airport to the hotel."

"Good."

"Good?" Kara repeated.

David smiled. "Yes. It means I don't have to get some-one to drop it off for you. I'm going to have our driver take you back to the hotel so you can pick up your lug-gage, and then he'll take you to Angels Landing."

"I'm sorry, but I'm planning to leave for Little Rock tomorrow."

"Can you hold off leaving for a few days?"

"David. May I call you David?" He nodded. "When you wrote and asked me to come here, I never could've imagined that the man I've believed was my father all these years is not my father. Not to mention that I now have a bunch of cousins who can't wait to put out a hit on me so they can inherit my unforeseen assets, assets I don't need or want."

"Are you saying you're going to walk away from your birthright?"

"A birthright I knew nothing about."

David leaned in closer. "A birthright you need to pro-tect, Kara. If you walk away from this, then you'll be playing right into the hands of the developers who've preyed on the folks who've lived on the Sea Island and who'll turn their inhabitants' birthright into a playground for millionaires."

Kara felt as if her emotions were under attack. "But . . . but the will states I can only sell the land to a Pat-ton."

"Pattons who want to sell more than half of Angels Landing."

"Why would they want to do that?" A pregnant silence filled the room as she and David stared at each other.

"Greed, Kara. If they can get you to go along with their

way of thinking and you sell your two thousand acres, the monies they'll receive for the sale will be divided among them evenly."

An expression of confusion crossed her face. "How many acres do they hold collectively?"

"Probably about four hundred," David said.

"Hypothetically, if I decide to hand over my shares and we sell twenty-four hundred acres at let's say a thousand dollars per acre. Are you telling me two-point-four million will be divided among twelve of us?"

He didn't respond. Instead, she did the calculations in her head. Instead of $2 million she would get $200,000. "The split seems a little inequitable, especially if I hold the majority shares."

David's dark eyebrows lifted a fraction. "They see you as an outsider, someone who will take the money and run. Please don't prove them right."

"What do you expect me to do?"

"I'd like you to give yourself a week to think about it. Stay at the house, tour the island. If you decide you prefer the Big Apple to the Lowcountry, then you walk away and..."

"I walk away and what?" Kara asked when David didn't finish his statement.

"The surviving heirs will contest the will, it will go into probate, and after the state of South Carolina gets its share, the family will get what's left."

She gave the dapper attorney a long, penetrating stare. He was asking for a week while her supposed biological father had asked her for five years. Right now Kara had three weeks of vacation time: one she could spend in Angels Landing and the other two in Arkansas before returning to New York. She hadn't told her parents when to expect her, so Kara decided to change her travel plans yet again.

"Okay. I'll try it for a week."

David blew out an audible breath. "Thank you." He stood, walked over to the wall phone, and pushed the speaker feature. "Please tell Linc I need him to drive a client to her hotel. He's to wait for her to check out, and then I want him to take her to Taylor Patton's house." He ended the call and came over to cup Kara's elbow when she stood up. "I'm going to call my cousin, Jeffrey Hamilton, who's the island's sheriff and have him stop in to check on you. I'll be in court for the next two days, but as soon as there is a recess, I'll come out to see you. Meanwhile, Jeff or one of his deputies will help you if you need anything."

Kara nodded her head in agreement, trying to keep her emotions in check. Taylor Patton was her biological father?

Jeffrey Hamilton leaned back in his chair, booted feet propped up on the corner of the scarred desk. He'd submitted his department's budget to the mayor and town council at the January meeting, yet it was mid-March and he was still awaiting delivery of new office furniture. Ever since he'd been appointed sheriff of Cavanaugh Island, Jeff had attempted to refurbish his office and expand the force from three deputies to four. Sadly, things seemed to be taking a lot longer than he'd first thought.

The cell phone on his desk rang. Glancing at the display, Jeff answered it on the second ring. "What's up, David?"

"Is there anyone in your jail that needs legal counsel?"

He laughed softly. "Sorry, Cuz, but I haven't locked up anyone in more than three weeks. Are you calling to let me know that you're ready to pop the question to that gorgeous oral surgeon you've been seeing?"

"We're not even close to that. I'd like you to go out to Angels Landing and check on the new owner. Her name is Kara Newell."

"Is there anything I should know about her?" Jeff asked.

"I may as well tell you now because gossip about her is going to spread across the island faster than a cat can lick its whiskers. She's Taylor Patton's daughter."

"I was under the impression that Taylor didn't have any children."

"Most of us thought the same thing."

Jeff shifted, and his chair groaned like someone in pain. "How are the others taking the news?"

"Let's just say they're not too happy that she exists. That's why I'm calling you."

"Don't worry, David. I'll keep an eye on her." He knew his cousin couldn't divulge how he'd come by the proof because he was still bound by attorney-client privilege, even in death.

"Thanks, Jeff. By the way, how is Aunt Corrine?"

"Grandmomma's good. Have you made plans for Easter?"

"Yep. Petra and I are going down to St. Thomas for a few days. You're welcome to join us."

Jeff stared at his spit-shined boots. After spending twenty years in the Marine Corps, he still enjoyed the age-old tradition of shining his shoes and boots. "I'd love to, but I gave my deputies time off to spend with their families."

"Speaking of families, Jeff, when are you going to settle down and have a couple of kids?"

He sat up and lowered his feet. "After you get married and have one."

David's chuckle came through the earpiece. "You've got a few years on me, Cuz, so you're first. I have to hang up because I have a meeting with a new client. Call me if Kara is having trouble with her new family."

"No problem," Jeff promised.

He ended the call, then slipped the cell phone into the case attached to his gun belt. He was walking out of his office when his clerk, Winnie Powell, entered the police station through the back door.

Winnie smiled, her bright blue eyes sparkling like blue topaz. She fluffed up her short, curly hair. "It looks like rain."

He returned her smile. "We could use a little of that." The winter had been unusually dry. "I'm going over to Angels Landing."

Winnie nodded as Jeff headed out of the station. Once in the parking lot that served the town hall, courthouse, and police station, the humidity wrapped around him like a wet blanket. He got into the Jeep and started the engine. The vehicle had been emblazoned with a sheriff logo on the passenger-side doors and refitted with a partition separating the front seats from the rear ones. Within minutes of driving, the rain had begun as Winnie predicted, the sound of the wipers breaking the silence.

Slowing to ten miles an hour, Jeff drove through downtown Sanctuary Cove, passing Jack's Fish House, the town square with its fountain and marble statue of patriot militia General Francis Marion atop a stallion, and the

Cove Inn, the town's boardinghouse. Once he'd taken over as sheriff, he'd convinced the town council to lower the town's speed limit to fifteen miles an hour because there were no traffic lights in the Cove and to discourage teenagers from drag racing. Amazingly, there hadn't been posted speed limits for years.

Maneuvering onto an unpaved road, he shifted into four-wheel drive. A marker pointing the way to Angels Landing came into view, and Jeff turned onto Palmetto Lane and headed to the house that had given this section of Cavanaugh Island its name. The few times he'd come to Angels Landing, Jeff felt as if he'd stepped back in time. The antebellum mansion at the end of a live oak allée was breathtaking with its columned, wraparound porch. The rose-colored limestone Greek Revival home, with its pale pink marble columns and black-shuttered tall windows, had been one of the finest homes on the island.

Jeff parked next to the vintage Mercedes-Benz sedan that had belonged to Taylor Patton. Reaching for his cap on the passenger seat, he pulled it on. The rain was now a steady drizzle as he sprinted to the front door, which opened as he wiped his boots on the thick rush mat.

"Why, if it isn't Corrine Hamilton's grandbaby boy. What brings you out this way?"

Jeff took off his cap and curbed the urge to roll his eyes upward. The petite woman and her groundskeeper husband had worked for the Pattons for longer than he could remember. He also wanted to remind Mrs. Todd that at forty he had left boyhood behind many years before.

"Good afternoon, Miss Iris. I'm here to see Ms. Kara Newell. Is she in?"

Mrs. Todd's dark eyes narrowed suspiciously behind her rimless glasses. "Did she do something, son?"

Jeff tightened his grip on his cap. It was apparent that the housekeeper had transferred her loyalty from Taylor to his daughter within weeks of his death. Those who lived on Cavanaugh Island joked that it was easier to gain access to the Oval Office than to cross the threshold to this historic house.

"No, she didn't, Miss Iris. David Sullivan asked me to look in on her."

Mrs. Todd opened the door wider. "Why didn't you say that in the first place?" She smiled. "Follow me. She's in the garden room."

Jeff shook his head in amazement as he followed the elderly woman, who was dressed in a crisp gray uniform that matched the coronet of braids atop her head. It had been years since he'd stepped foot into the house, but like the exterior, nothing had changed. It had the same vases, lamps, tables, and chairs. Mrs. Todd directed him down a narrow carpeted hallway to a doorway on the south side of the property.

He stopped at the entrance to a room filled with potted plants, trees, and flowers. The sound of soft music flowed from somewhere in the indoor oasis. His gaze shifted to the housekeeper when she approached the woman reclining in a cushioned chaise and spoke quietly to her.

Jeff felt his heart stop when Kara Newell swung her long, slender, bare legs over the chaise and stood up to face him.

She was absolutely stunning. Anyone familiar with the Pattons would recognize the startling resemblance between Kara and her paternal grandmother Theodora—or

Teddy as she had been affectionately called by her husband. His gaze went from her tousled hair, pulled up in a short ponytail, to the tawny face with large hazel eyes, cute button nose, and lushly curved full lips, then lower to a white tank top and olive-green shorts. Each time she took a breath, the swell of her breasts were visible above the top's neckline. Scolding himself, he focused his attention on her face rather than staring at her chest. She was slim but had curves in all the right places.

He inclined his head. "Ms. Newell."

Kara smiled and offered her hand. "Please call me Kara."

Taking three long strides, Jeff grasped her hand, holding it gently within his much larger one. "Jeff Hamilton."

"David told me you would stop by. Would you like to sit down?"

"Thank you." He waited until Kara sat on a pull-up chair at a small round table covered with a floral tablecloth before sitting on the matching one.

A pair of eyes with glints of gold and green met his. "May I offer you something to eat or drink?" Kara asked Jeff.

"No, thank you." He crossed one jean-covered knee over the other. "Have you settled in?"

Kara assumed a similar pose, staring at the polish on her bare toes. "There's not going to be much settling in. I'll only be here a week."

Leaning forward, Jeff lowered his leg, planting both feet on the worn rug. "Are you telling me that you don't plan to live here?"

"No, I'm not telling you that."

"Then what is it you're *not* saying?"

"Why do I get the impression that you're interrogating me, Sheriff Hamilton?"

Jeff's impassive expression did not change with her accusation. "If I were interrogating you, Kara, you wouldn't have to ask. All I want is a yes or no as to whether you plan to live on Cavanaugh Island."

"I can't give you a yes or no, Sheriff Hamilton."

"It's Jeff."

"Okay, Jeff. As I said, I can't answer that question right now. I promised David I would spend a week on the island before making a decision. Only two hours ago I was told the man I believed to be my father isn't." She looked away from him, trying to hold back the tears forming in her eyes. "When I walked into that conference room earlier this morning and saw people staring at me who look like me...to say it was a shock is putting it mildly. Then I was told that I've inherited a house, two thousand acres of land that my so-called relatives want me to sell to a group of greedy developers, and I must live here for five years. If I do so, it means I have to resign from my job, give up my Manhattan apartment, which has an incredible view of the East River, and lose contact with a group of friends I've become extremely close to."

"Yes, I can understand how difficult that may be. Not only will you have to uproot your entire life, but you'll also have to deal with the family issue." Jeff lifted his broad shoulders under a long-sleeved chambray shirt. "The upside is you can always get another job and make new friends. And instead of views of the river, you'll have views of the ocean."

Kara folded her arms across her chest. "You make it sound so easy."

A hint of a smile tilted the corners of Jeff's mouth. "Because it is. I gave up a military career to come back here to take care of my grandmother."

"That's different."

"You think so, Kara?"

"Of course it is. There is no discussion when it comes to family. You do what you have to do," Kara said.

"Like you have to accept your birthright and honor your father's last wishes."

"What's with this birthright thing?" she asked.

Jeff stood up. "I'll tell you sometime soon. Right now, I have to get back."

Kara also rose to her feet. "When will I see you again?"

"Tomorrow. I'm off, and if you don't have anything planned, I'll come by and take you to Jack's for lunch and give you a crash course in Lowcountry culture."

"I'd like you to answer one question for me, Jeff."

"What's that?"

"Do you have something against the Pattons?"

"Nothing personal. I just don't like it when people threaten others."

Her eyes grew wider. "Did David tell you what happened?"

"He didn't have to. You can say I read between the lines. As sheriff of Cavanaugh, I have zero tolerance for those who break the law. And to me threats are a serious offense. I'll pick you up at twelve."

Jeff didn't give Kara a chance to accept or reject his offer when he turned on his heels and walked out of the room. He'd been back for almost a year, and it was the first time that a woman had captured his attention for more than a few minutes.

There was something about Kara, other than her natural beauty, that had him enthralled. He didn't know whether it was her big-city attitude, but whatever it was, he intended to discover it before the week ended and Kara was out of his life for good.

THE DISH

Where Authors Give You the Inside Scoop

♥ ♥ ♥ ♥ ♥ ♥ ♥ ♥ ♥ ♥ ♥ ♥ ♥ ♥ ♥

From the desk of Vicky Dreiling

Dear Reader,

Some characters demand center stage. Like Andrew Carrington, the Earl of Bellingham, known as Bell to his friends. Bellingham first walked on stage as a minor character in my third historical romance *How to Ravish a Rake*. I had not planned him, but from the moment he spoke, I knew he would have his own book because of his incredible charisma. He also had the starring role in the e-novella *A Season for Sin*. As I began to write the e-novella, I realized that it was almost effortless. Frankly, I was and still am infatuated with him. That makes me laugh, because he is a figment of my imagination, but from the beginning, I could not ignore his strong presence.

After *A Season for Sin* was published, I started writing the full-length book WHAT A WICKED EARL WANTS so that Bell could have the happily ever after he richly deserved. A chance encounter brings Bellingham and the heroine, Laura, together. Bellingham is a rake who hopes to make a conquest of her, but despite their attraction, there are major obstacles. Laura is a respectable widow, mother, and daughter of a vicar. Bellingham only wants a temporary liaison, but he finds himself rescuing the lovely lady. His offer of help leads him down a path he never could have imagined.

I've dreamed about my characters previously, but my dreams about Bell and Laura were so vivid that I woke up repeatedly during the writing of WHAT A WICKED EARL WANTS. Usually when I dream about my books in progress, I only see the characters momentarily. But when I dreamed about Bell and Laura, entire scenes played themselves in my head, DVD style, and sometimes a few of them in a night. While I didn't get up in the middle of the night to write those scenes down, thankfully I remembered them the next morning and some of those dreams have made their way into the book. I'll give you a hint of one dream I used in a scene. It involves some funny "rules."

This couple surprised me repeatedly when I was awake and writing, too. I was enthralled with Bellingham and Laura. Yes, I know the ideas come from me, but sometimes, it almost feels as if the characters really do leap off the page. That was certainly the case for Bell and Laura.

As the writing progressed, I often felt as if I were peeling off another layer of Bellingham's character. He is a man with deep wounds and very determined not to stir up the past. Yet I realized that subconsciously his actions were informed by all that had happened to him as a young man. I knew it would take a very special heroine to help him reconcile his past. Laura knows what he needs, and though he doesn't make it easy for her, she never gives up.

I confess I still have a bit of a crush on Bellingham. ☺
I hope you will, too.

Enjoy!

[signature: Vicky Dreiling]

VickyDreiling.com
Facebook.com
Twitter @vickydreiling

♥ ♥ ♥ ♥ ♥ ♥ ♥ ♥ ♥ ♥ ♥ ♥ ♥ ♥ ♥

From the desk of Stella Cameron

Frog Crossing
Out West

Dear Reader,

My dog, Millie, doesn't like salt water, or bath water, or
rain—but it is the sight of all seven pounds of her trying
to drink Puget Sound that stays with me. Urged to walk
into about half an inch of ripples bubbling over pebbles
on a beach, she slurped madly as if she could get rid of
anything wet that might touch her feet.

That picture just popped into my head once more,
just as I thought about what I might write to you about

the Chimney Rock books and how stories shape up for me.

We were standing at the water's edge on Whidbey Island, looking across Saratoga Passage toward Camano Island. *Darkness Bound*, the first book in the series, was finished and now it was time for DARKNESS BRED, on sale now.

Elin and Sean were already my heroine and hero. I knew that much before I finished the previous story, but there were so many other questions hanging around. And so many unfinished and important parts of lives I had already shown you. When we write books there's a balancing act between telling/showing too much, and the opposite. Every character clamors to climb in but only those important to the current story can have a ticket to enter. The trick is to weed out the loudest and least interesting from the ones we *have* to know about.

The hidden world on Whidbey Island is busy, and gets busier. Once you are inside it's not just colorful and varied, sometimes endearing and often scary, it is also addictive. Magic and mystery rub shoulders with what sometimes seems…just simply irresistible. How can I not want to explore every character's tale?

That's what makes me feel a bit like Millie draining Puget Sound of water—I have to clear away what I don't want until I find the best stuff. Only I'm more fortunate than my dog because I do get to make all the difference.

Now you have your ticket to ride along with me again—enjoy every inch!

All the best,

Stella Cameron

From the desk of Rochelle Alers

Dear Reader,

How many of us had high school crushes, then years later come face-to-face with the boy who will always hold a special place in our hearts? This is what happens with Morgan Dane in HAVEN CREEK. At thirteen she'd believed herself in love with high school hunk, Nathaniel Shaw, but as a tall, skinny girl constantly teased for her prepubescent body, she can only worship him from afar.

I wanted HAVEN CREEK to become a modern-day fairy tale complete with a beautiful princess and a handsome prince, and, as in every fairy tale, there is something that will keep them apart before they're able to live happily ever after. The princess in HAVEN CREEK lives her life by a set of inflexible rules, while it is a family secret that makes it nearly impossible for the prince to trust anyone.

You will reunite with architect Morgan Dane, who has been commissioned to oversee the restoration of Angels Landing Plantation. As she begins the task of hiring local artisans for the project, she knows the perfect candidate to supervise the reconstruction of the slave village. He is master carpenter and prodigal son Nathaniel Shaw.

Although Nate has returned to his boyhood home, he has become a recluse while he concentrates on running his family's furniture-making business and keeping his younger brother out of trouble. But everything changes when Morgan asks him to become involved in her restoration project. It isn't what she's offering that presents a challenge to Nate, but it is Morgan herself. When he left the Creek she was a shy teenage girl. Now she is a confident, thirtysomething woman holding him completely enthralled with her brains *and* her beauty.

In HAVEN CREEK you will travel back to the Lowcountry with its magnificent sunsets; slow, meandering creeks and streams; primordial swamps teeming with indigenous wildlife; a pristine beach serving as a year-round recreational area; and the residents of the island with whom you've become familiar.

Church, community, and family—and not necessarily in that order—are an integral part of Lowcountry life, and never is that more apparent than on Cavanaugh Island. As soon as you read the first page of HAVEN CREEK you will be given an up-close and personal look into the Gullah culture with its island-wide celebrations, interactions at family Sunday dinners, and a quixotic young woman who has the gift of sight.

The gossipmongers are back along with the region's famous mouth-watering cuisine and a supporting cast of characters—young *and* old—who will keep you laughing throughout the novel.

Read, enjoy, and do let me hear from you!!!

Rochelle Alers

ralersbooks@aol.com
www.rochellealers.org

From the desk of Laura Drake

Dear Readers,

Who can resist a cowboy?

Not me. Especially a bull rider, who has the courage to get on two thousand pounds of attitude that wants to throw him in the dirt and dance on his dangling parts. But you don't need to be familiar with rodeo to enjoy THE SWEET SPOT. It's an emotional story first, about two people dealing with real-life problems, and rediscovering love at the end of a long dirt road.

To introduce you to Charla Rae Denny, the heroine of THE SWEET SPOT, I thought I'd share with you her list of life lessons:

1. Before you throw your ex off your ranch, be sure you know how to run it.
2. A Goth-Dolly Parton lookalike *can* make a great friend. And Dumpster monkeys are helpful, too.
3. Next time, start a hardware store instead of a bucking bull business—the stock doesn't try to commit suicide every few minutes.
4. "Never trust a husband too far, nor a bachelor too near." —Helen Rowland
5. If you're the subject of the latest gossip-fest, stay away from the Clip-n-Curl.
6. Life is full of second chances, if you can get over yourself enough to grab them.

7. "To forgive is to set a prisoner free, and discover that
   the prisoner is you." —Louis B. Smede

I hope you'll enjoy THE SWEET SPOT, and look for
JB and Charla in the next two books in the series!